ALSO BY ROBERT MASELLO

The
Romanov Cross

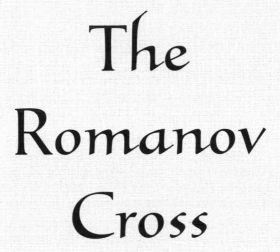

The Romanov Cross

A Novel

ROBERT MASELLO

BANTAM BOOKS
NEW YORK

The Romanov Cross is a work of fiction. Names, places, and incidents are the products of the author's imagination or are used fictitiously. Any resemblance to actual persons, living or dead, events, or locales is entirely coincidental.

Published in the United States by Bantam Books, an imprint of the Random House Publishing Group, a division of Random House, Inc., New York.

BANTAM BOOKS and the rooster colophon are registered trademarks of Random House, Inc.

Library of Congress Cataloging-in-Publication Data

Masello, Robert.
The Romanov cross : a novel / Robert Masello.
p.   cm.
ISBN 978-0-553-80780-6 (acid-free paper) — ISBN 978-0-345-53359-3 (ebook)
1. Antiquities—Collection and preservation—Fiction.   I. Title.
PS3613.A81925R66 2013
813'.6—dc23
2012015943

Printed in the United States of America on acid-free paper

www.bantamdell.com

2 4 6 8 9 7 5 3 1

Book design by Caroline Cunningham

For my cousin Chuck—

who can talk me through pretty much

any problem.

With deepest gratitude.

The
Romanov
Cross

Prologue

"Sergei, do not die," the girl said, turning around in the open boat. "I forbid you to die." She had hoped, in vain, that her voice would not falter.

When she tried to reach out to him, he pulled away, still holding on to the tiller with dead-white fingers.

"No, no," he said, drawing back in horror. "Don't touch me." His eyes were wild, the stubble on his pale young cheeks flecked with blood and foam. "You have to sail there," he said, as he pointed with one trembling finger over the prow of the boat. "There!" he said, demanding that Ana—a willful teenager, who had never been responsible for anything more than picking a frock—turn, and do what he, a farm boy no more than a few years her senior, was ordering.

Reluctantly she looked back, the ragged sail crackling above her head, and saw in the distance, beyond a cloud of fog, the indistinct outline of an island, dark and forbidding, rising from the sea. From the boat, it looked like a clenched fist, encircled by a misty-gray bracelet. Ana had never seen a more unwelcoming sight.

"Look for the fires," he croaked. "They will light fires."

"But I can't sail the boat alone. You have to do it."

Sergei shook his head and coughed so hard the blood ran between his fingers. He glanced down at his soiled hand, his eyes glazed, and whispered, "May God protect you, *malenkaya*." And then, as calmly as if he were turning in bed, he rolled over the side of the boat and into the icy waters of the strait.

"Sergei!" she screamed, plunging toward the stern so abruptly she threatened to capsize the boat.

But he was already gone, floating off with his sealskin coat billowing out around him like the spread wings of a bat. For a few more seconds, he bobbed on the surface, riding the waves until the weight of his body and his boots and his clothes dragged him down. All that remained was a single wilted and frozen blue cornflower floating on the water.

The sight of it made her want to weep.

She was alone in the boat—alone in the world—and the tiller was already lurching wildly from one side to the other, screeching louder than the gulls swooping in and out of the fog. The hollow place in her heart, the place where she had already stored so many deaths, would now have to find room for Sergei's, too.

How many more could she possibly be expected to hold there?

Clambering over the icy thwart, her fur coat as wet and heavy as armor, she perched on the little wooden seat in the stern. Even with her hood pulled low, the wind blew sleet and spray into her face. But at least the gusts were driving her toward the island. Her gloves were as stiff as icicles, and it was a struggle to loop the rope to the sail around one wrist, as she had seen Sergei do, and grasp the tiller with the other. The open boat cut through the waves, rising and falling, rising and falling. The fog surrounded her like a shroud, and she was so exhausted, so cold and so hungry, that she fell into a kind of stupor.

Her thoughts wandered to her garden in Tsarskoe Selo, the private enclave outside St. Petersburg, where she had grown her own roses, and to the fifteenth birthday party her parents had thrown for her there. It was only two years ago, a time before her life had gone from a dream to a nightmare. Now it seemed like something she must have imagined out of whole cloth. She thought of her sister, giving her a book of poems by her favorite writer—Pushkin—and her little brother sitting on his pony, as Nagorny, the rough sailor who had become his constant attendant, held the reins.

Her father, in his military uniform, had been standing stiffly on the verandah, holding her mother's hand.

A wave dashed her full in the face, the frigid water running down her neck and under the collar of her coat. She shivered as the tiller threatened to slip out of her hand, and the rope attached to the sail cut into her wrist like a tourniquet. Her boots were slick with ice, and her bad foot had no feeling left in it at all.

But she also remembered, towering right behind her mother, the monk with the black eyes and the long, tangled beard. The bejeweled cross that he wore on his cassock, she was wearing now, under her corsets and coat; it had protected her from much, just as the monk had promised, but she doubted that even the cross would be enough to save her now.

As the boat came closer to the shore, it bucked like a horse trying to throw its rider, and she had to brace herself firmly against the stern. The slush in the hull was several inches deep and washed back and forth over whatever was left of her frozen provisions.

If she did not reach land tonight, she would surely follow poor Sergei into the freezing sea. Gulls and ospreys circled in the pewter sky, taunting her with their cries.

She pulled in on the sail, and the boat keeled, slicing through the waters. She was close enough now that she could see a jumble of boulders littering the beach and a dense wall of snow-covered forest just beyond them. But where were the fires that Sergei had promised? With the back of her sleeve, she wiped the seawater from her eyes— she had always been nearsighted but too vain to wear glasses. Dr. Botkin had once offered her a pair, at the house with the whitewashed windows, the house where . . .

No, she could not think about that. She had to keep her thoughts from straying there . . . especially now, when her life once again hung in the balance.

An osprey shot across the bow of the boat, then doubled back past the creaking mast, and as her eyes followed it, she saw a flickering glow—a torch as tall as a tree—burning on the cliffs ahead.

And then, squinting hard, she saw another.

Her heart rose in her chest.

There was a scraping sound as the surf dragged the bottom of the boat across a bed of sharp rocks and shells. She loosened her grip on the rope, and the sail swung wide, snapping as loud as a gunshot. She clung to the tiller with her frozen hands as the boat bumped and spun onto the wet sand and gravel, lodging there as the tide surged back out again.

She could barely move, but she knew that if she hesitated, the next wave could come in and pull her back out to sea again. Now, before her last ounce of strength abandoned her, she had to force herself to clamber to the front of the boat and step onto the island.

She got up unsteadily—her left foot as numb as a post—and struggled over the thwarts, the boat pitching and groaning beneath her. She thought she heard a bell clanging, a deep booming sound that reverberated off the rocks and trees. Touching the place on her breast where the cross rested, she murmured a prayer of thanks to St. Peter for delivering her from evil.

And then, nearly toppling over, she stepped into the water—which quickly rose above the tops of her boots—and staggered onto the beach. Her feet slipped and stumbled on the wet stones, but she crawled a few yards up the sand before allowing herself to fall to her knees. Her head was bowed, as if awaiting the blow of an axe, and her breath came only in ragged gasps. All she could hear was the ice crackling in her hair. But she was alive, and that was what mattered. She had survived the trek over the frozen tundra, the journey across the open sea . . . and the horrors of the house with the whitewashed windows. She had made it to a new continent, and as she peered down the beach, she could see dark shapes in the twilight, running toward her.

Yes, they were coming, to rescue her. Sergei had spoken the truth.

If she'd had the strength, she'd have called out to them, or waved an arm.

But her limbs had no feeling left in them, and her teeth were chattering in her skull.

The figures were coming so fast, and running so low, she could hardly believe her eyes.

And then she felt an even greater chill clutch at her heart, as she realized what the running shapes really were.

She whipped around toward the boat again, but it had already been dislodged and was disappearing into the fog.

Had she come so far . . . for this?

But she was too exhausted, too paralyzed with cold and despair, even to try to save herself.

She stared in terror down the beach as, shoulders heaving and eyes blazing orange in the dusk, the pack of ravening black wolves galloped toward her across the rocks and sand.

Part One

Chapter 1

"You okay, Major?"

Slater knew what he looked like, and he knew why Sergeant Groves was asking. He had taken a fistful of pills that morning, but the fever was back. He put out a hand to steady himself, then yanked it back off the hood of the jeep. The metal was as hot as a stove.

"I'll survive," he said, rubbing the tips of his fingers against his camo pants. That morning, he had visited the Marine barracks and watched as two more men had been airlifted out, both of them at death's door; he wasn't sure they'd make it. Despite all the normal precautions, the malaria, which he'd contracted himself a year before on a mission to Darfur, had decimated this camp. As a U.S. Army doctor and field epidemiologist, Major Frank Slater had been dispatched to figure out what else could be done—and fast.

The rice paddies he was looking at now were a prime breeding ground for the deadly mosquitoes, and the base had been built not only too close by, but directly downwind. At night, when they liked to feed, swarms of insects lifted off the paddies and descended en masse on the barracks and the canteen and the guard towers. Once, in the Euphrates Valley, Slater had seen a cloud of bugs rising so thick and high in the sky that he'd mistaken it for an oncoming storm.

"So, which way do you want to go with this?" Sergeant Groves asked. An African-American as tough and uncompromising as the Cleveland streets that he hailed from—"by the time I left, all we were making there was icicles," he'd once told Slater—he always spoke with purpose and brevity. "Spray the swamp or move the base?"

Slater was debating that very thing when he was distracted by a pair of travelers—a young girl, maybe nine or ten, and her father—slogging through the paddy with an overburdened mule. Nearly everyone in Afghanistan had been exposed to malaria—it was as common as the flu in the rest of the world—and over the generations they had either died or developed a rudimentary immunity. They often got sick, but they had learned to live with it.

The young Americans, on the other hand, fresh from farms in Wisconsin and mountain towns in Colorado, didn't fare as well.

The girl was leading the mule, while her father steadied the huge baskets of grain thrown across its scrawny back.

"I'm on it," Private Diaz said, stepping out from the driver's seat of the jeep. His M4 was already cradled in his hands. One thing the soldiers learned fast in the Middle East was that even the most innocuous sight could be their last. Baskets could carry explosives. Mules could be time bombs. Even kids could be used as decoys, or sacrificed altogether by the jihadis. On a previous mission, Slater had had to sort through the rubble of a girls' school in Kandahar province after a Taliban, working undercover as a school custodian, had driven a motorcycle festooned with explosives straight into the classroom.

"Allahu Akbar!" the janitor had shouted with jubilation, "God is great!" just before blowing them all to kingdom come.

For the past ten years, Slater had seen death, in one form or another, nearly every day, but he still wasn't sure which was worse—the fact that it could still shock him or the fact that on most days it didn't. Just how hard, he often wondered, could a man let his heart become? How hard did it need to be?

The girl was looking back at him now with big dark eyes under her headscarf as she led the mule out of the paddy and up onto the embankment. The father switched at its rump with a hollow reed. The private, his rifle slung forward, ordered them to stop where they were. His Arabic was pretty basic, but the hand gesture and the loaded gun were universally understood.

Slater and Groves—his right-hand man on every mission he had undertaken from Iraq to Somalia—watched as Private Diaz approached them.

"Open the baskets," he said, making a motion with one hand to indicate what he wanted. The father issued an order to his daughter, who flipped the lid off one basket, then waited as the soldier peered inside.

"The other one, too," Diaz said, stepping around the mule's lowered head.

The girl did as he ordered, standing beside the basket as Diaz poked the muzzle of his gun into the grain.

And just as Slater was about to order him to let them move along—was this any way to win hearts and minds?—a bright ribbon of iridescent green shot up out of the basket, fast as a lightning bolt, and struck the girl on the face. She went down as if hit by a mallet, writhing on the ground, and the private jumped back in surprise.

"Jesus," he was saying over and over as he pointed the rifle futilely at the thrashing body of the girl. "It's a viper!"

But Slater already knew that, and even as her father was wailing in terror, he was racing to her side. The snake still had its fangs buried in her cheek, secreting its venom, its tail shaking ferociously. Slater pulled his field knife from its scabbard—a knife he normally used to cut tissue samples from diseased cadavers—and with the other hand grabbed for the viper's tail. Twice he felt its rough mottled surface, strong as a steel pipe, slip through his fingers, but on the third try he held it taut and was able to slice through the vertebrae. Half of the snake came away with a spill of blood, but the head was still fixed in its mortal bite.

The girl's eyes were shut and her limbs were flailing, and it was only after Groves used his own broad hands to hold her down that Slater was able to pinch the back of the dying viper's head and pull the fangs loose. The snake's tongue flicked like a whip, but the light in its yellow eyes was fading. Slater pinched harder until the tongue slowed and the eyes lost their luster altogether. He tossed the carcass down the embankment, and Diaz, for good measure, unleashed a burst of shots from his rifle that rolled the coils down into the murky water.

"Get me my kit!" Slater hollered, and Diaz ran to the jeep.

Groves—as burly as a fullback but tender as a nurse—was crouched over the girl, examining the wound. There were two long gashes in her cheek, bloody smears on her tawny skin. The venom, some of the most powerful in the animal kingdom, was already coursing through her veins.

Her father, wailing and praying aloud, rocked on his sandaled feet. Even the mule brayed in dumb alarm.

Diaz handed Slater the kit, already open, and Slater, his hands moving on automatic pilot, went about administering the anticoagulant and doing his best to stabilize her, but he knew that only the antivenin, in short supply these days, could save the girl's life.

And even then, only if it was used in the next hour.

"Round up the nearest chopper," he said to Diaz. "We need to get this girl to the med center."

But the soldier hesitated. "No offense, sir, but orders are that the med runs are only for military casualties. They won't come for a civilian."

Groves looked over at Slater with mournful eyes and said, "He's right. Ever since that chopper was shot down three days ago, the orders have been ironclad. EMS duties are out."

Slater heard them, but wondered if they were really prepared to stand by and let the girl die. Her father was screaming the few words of English he knew, "Help! U.S.A! Please, help!" He was on his knees in the dust, wringing his woven cap in his hands.

Her little heart was beating like a trip-hammer and her limbs were convulsing, and Slater knew that any further delay would seal the girl's fate forever. Someone this size and weight, injected with a full dose of a pit viper's poison—and he had seen enough of these snakes to know that this one had been fully mature—could not last long before her blood cells began to disintegrate.

"Keep her as still as you can," he said to Groves and Diaz, then ran back to the jeep, grabbed the radio mike, and called it in to the main base.

"Marine down!" Slater said, "viper bite. Immediate—I say, immediate—evac needed!"

He saw Groves and the private exchange a glance.

"Your coordinates?" a voice on the radio crackled.

The coordinates? Slater, the blood pounding in his head from his own fever, fumbled to muster them. "We're about two klicks from the Khan Neshin outpost," he said, focusing as hard as he could, "just southwest of the rice paddies."

Groves suddenly appeared at his side and grabbed the mike out of his hands, but instead of countermanding the major's order, he gave the exact coordinates.

"Tell 'em they can finish the rations dump later," Groves barked. "We need that chopper over here now! And tell the med center to get as much of the antivenin ready as they've got!"

Slater, his legs unsteady, crouched down in the shade of the jeep.

"You didn't need to get mixed up in this," Slater said after Groves signed off. "I'll take the heat."

"Don't worry," Groves said. "There'll be plenty to go around."

For the next half hour, Slater kept the girl as tranquilized as he could—the more she thrashed, the faster the poison circulated in her system—while the sergeant and the private kept a close watch on the neighboring fields. Taliban fighters were drawn to trouble like sharks to blood, and if they suspected a chopper was going to be flying in, they'd be scrambling through their stockpiles for one last Stinger missile. Nor did Slater want to go back to the outpost and ask for backup; somebody might see what was really going on and cancel the mission.

"I hear it!" Groves said, turning toward a low rise of scrubby hills.

So could Slater. The thrumming of its rotors preceded by only seconds the sight of the Black Hawk itself, soaring over the ridgeline. After doing a quick reconnaissance loop, the pilot put the chopper down a dozen yards from the jeep, its blades still spinning, its engine churning. The side hatch slid open, and two grunts with a stretcher leapt out into the cloud of dust.

"Where?" one shouted, wiping the whirling dirt from his goggles.

Diaz pointed to the girl lying low on the embankment between Slater and the sergeant.

The two soldiers stopped in their tracks, and over the loud rumble of the idling helicopter, one shouted, "A civilian?"

The other said, "Combat casualties only! Strict orders."

"That's right," Slater said, tapping the major's oak leaf cluster on his shirt, "and I'm giving them here! This girl is going to the med center, and she's going now!"

The first soldier hesitated, still unsure, but the second one laid his end of the stretcher on the ground at her feet. "I've got a daughter back home," he mumbled, as he wrapped the girl in a poncho liner, then helped Groves to lift her onto the canvas.

"I'm taking full responsibility," Slater said. "Let's move!"

But when the girl's father tried to climb into the chopper, the pilot shook his head violently and waved his hand. "No can do!" he shouted. "We're carrying too much weight already."

Slater had to push the man away; there wasn't time to explain. "Tell him what's going on!" he shouted to the sergeant.

The father was screaming and crying—Diaz was trying to restrain him—as Slater slid the hatch shut and banged on the back of the pilot's seat. "Okay, go, go, go!"

To evade possible fire, the chopper banked steeply to one side on takeoff, then zigzagged away from the rice paddies; these irrigated areas, called the green zone, were some of the deadliest terrain in Afghanistan, havens for snipers and insurgents. Slater heard a quick clattering on the bottom of the Black Hawk, a sound like typewriter keys clicking, and knew that at least one Taliban fighter had managed to get off a few rounds. The helicopter flew higher, soaring up and over the barren red hills, where the rusted carcasses of Soviet troop carriers could be seen half-buried in the dirt and sand. Now it would just be a race against time. The girl's face was swollen up like she had the mumps, and Slater slipped the oxygen mask onto her as gently as he could. Her ears were like perfect little shells, he thought, as he looped the straps around the back of her head. She took no notice of what was being done, or where she was. She was delirious with the pain and the shock and the natural adrenaline that her body was instinctively pumping through her veins nonstop.

The soldiers stayed clear, strapped into their seats beside the ration pallets they'd been delivering and watching silently as Major Slater treated her. The one with the daughter looked like he was saying a prayer under his breath. But this little Afghan girl was Slater's problem now, and they all knew it.

By the time the chopper cleared the med center perimeter and touched down, her eyes had shut, and when Slater lifted the lids, all he could see was the whites. Her limbs were pretty still, only occasionally rocked by sudden paroxysms as if jolts of electricity were shooting through her. Slater knew the signs weren't good. It would have been different if he'd had the antivenin with him in the field, but it was costly stuff, in short supply, and it deteriorated rapidly if it wasn't kept refrigerated.

Some of the staff at the med center looked surprised at the new admission—a local girl, when they'd been expecting a Marine—but Slater issued his orders with such conviction that not a second was lost. Covered with dirt and sweat, his fingers stained with snake blood, he was still clutching her limp hand as she was wheeled into the O.R., where the trauma team was ready with the IV lines.

"Careful when you insert those," Slater warned. "The entry points are going to seep from the venom."

"Major," the surgeon said, calmly, "we know what we're doing. We can take it from here."

But when he tried to let go, the girl's fingers feebly squeezed his own. Maybe she thought it was her dad.

"Hang in there, honey," Slater said softly, though he doubted she could hear, or understand, him. "Don't give up." He extricated his fingers, and a nurse quickly brushed him aside so that she could get at the wound and sterilize the site. The surgeon took a syringe filled with the antivenin, held it up to the light, and expressed the air from the plunger.

Slater, knowing that he was simply in the way now, stepped outside and watched through the porthole in the swinging doors. The doctor and two nurses went through their paces with methodical precision and speed. But Slater was afraid that too much time had passed since the attack.

A shiver hit him, and he slumped into a crouch by the doors. This was the worst recurrence of the malaria he'd had in months, and the sudden blast of air-conditioning made him long for a blanket. But if he let on how bad it was, he could find himself restricted to desk duty in Washington—a fate he feared worse than death. He just needed to get back to his bunk, swallow some meds, and sweat it out for a day or two. The blood was beating in his temples like a drum.

And it got no better when he heard the voice of his commanding officer, Colonel Keener, bellowing from down the hall. "Did you call in this mission, Major Slater?"

"I did."

"You did, *sir.*" Keener corrected him, glancing at a printout in his hand. "And you claimed this was a Marine? A Marine casualty?"

"I did," he replied, "sir."

"And you're aware that we're not an ambulance service? That you diverted a Black Hawk from its scheduled, combat-related run, to address a strictly civilian matter?" His frustration became more evident with every word he spoke. "Maybe you didn't read the advisory—the one that was issued to all base personnel just two days ago?"

"Every word."

Slater knew his attitude wasn't helping his case, but he didn't care. Truth be told, he hadn't cared about protocols and orders and commands for years. He'd become a doctor so that he could save lives, pure and simple; he'd become an epidemiologist so that he could save thousands of lives, in some of the world's worst places. But today, he was back to trying to save just one.

Just one little girl, with perfect little ears. And a father, off somewhere in Khan Neshin, no doubt begging Allah for a miracle . . . a miracle that wasn't likely to be granted.

"You know, of course, that I will have to report this incident, and the AFIP is going to have to send out another staffer now to decide what to do about our malaria problem," the colonel was saying. "That could take days, and cost us American lives." He said the word "American" in such a way as to make it plain that they were all that counted in this world. "You may consider yourself off duty and restricted to the base, Doctor, until further notice. In case you don't know it, you're in some very deep shit."

Slater had hardly needed to be told. While Keener stood there fuming, wondering what other threat he could issue, the major fished in his pocket for the Chloriquine tablets he was taking every few hours. He tried to swallow them dry, but his mouth was too parched. Brushing past the colonel, he staggered to the water fountain, got the pills down, then held his head under the arc of cool water. His scalp felt like a forest fire that was finally getting hosed down.

The surgeon came out of the O.R., looked at each one of them, then went to the colonel's side and said something softly in his ear. The colonel nodded solemnly, and the surgeon ducked back inside the swinging doors.

"What?" Slater said, pressing his fingertips into his wet scalp. The water was running down the back of his neck.

"It looks like you blew your career for nothing," Keener replied. "The girl just died."

All that Slater remembered, later on, was the look on the colonel's face—the look he'd seen on a hundred other official faces intent only on following orders—before he threw the punch that knocked the colonel off his feet. He also had a vague recollection of wobbling above him, as Keener lay there, stunned and speechless, on the grimy green linoleum.

But the actual punch, which must have been a haymaker, was a mystery.

Then he returned to the fountain and put his head back down under the spray. If there were tears still in him, he thought, he'd be shedding them now. But there weren't any. They had dried up years ago.

From the far end of the hall, he could hear the sound of raised voices and running boots as the MPs rushed to arrest him.

Chapter 2

The waters off the northern coast of Alaska were bad enough in summer, when the sun was shining around the clock and you could at least see the ice floes coming at you, but now—in late November, with a squall blowing in—they were about the worst place on earth to be.

Especially in a crab-catching tub like the *Neptune II*.

Harley Vane, the skipper, knew he'd be lucky just to keep the ship in one piece. He'd been fishing in the Bering Sea for almost twenty years, and both the crabbing and the storms had gotten worse the whole time. The crabbing he could figure out; his boat, and a dozen others, kept returning to the same spots, depleting the population and never giving it enough time to replenish itself. All the skippers knew they were committing a slow form of suicide, but nobody was going to be the first to stop.

And then there was the weather. The currents were getting stronger and more unpredictable all the time, the winds higher, the ice more broken up and difficult to avoid. He knew that all that global warming stuff was a load of crap—hadn't the snowfall last year been the highest in five years? But judging from the sea-lanes, which were less frozen and more wide open than he had ever seen them, something was definitely afoot. As he sat in the wheelhouse, steering the boat through a turbulent ocean of fifteen-foot swells and hunks of glacier the size of cars, he had to buckle himself into his raised seat to keep from falling over. The rolling and pitching of the boat was so bad he considered reaching for the hand mike and calling the deckhands inside, but the *Neptune*'s catch so far had been bad—the last string of pots had averaged less than a hundred crabs each—and until their tanks were full, the boat would have to stay at sea. Back onshore, there were bills to pay, so he had to keep slinging the pots, no matter what.

"You want some coffee?" Lucas said, coming up from below with an extra mug in his hand. He was still wearing his yellow anorak, streaming with icy water.

"Christ Almighty," Harley said, taking the coffee, "you're soaking the place."

"Yeah, well, it's wet out there," Lucas said. "You oughta try it sometime."

"I tried it plenty," Harley said. He'd worked the decks since he was eleven years old, back when his dad had owned the first *Neptune* and his older brother had been able to throw the hook and snag the buoys. And he remembered his father sitting on a stool just like this, ruling the wheelhouse and looking out through the row of rectangular windows at the main deck of the boat. The view hadn't changed much, with its ice-coated mast, its iron crane, its big gray buckets for sorting the catch. Once that boat had gone down, Harley and his brother Charlie had invested in this one. But unlike the original, the *Neptune II* featured a double bank of white spotlights above the bridge. At this time of year, when the sun came out for no more than a few hours at midday, the lights threw a steady but white and ghostly glow over the deck. Sometimes, to Harley, it was like watching a black-and-white movie down there.

Now, from his perch, where he was surrounded by his video and computer screens—another innovation that his dad had resisted—he could see the four crewmen on deck throwing the lines, hauling in the pots with the crabs still clinging to the steel mesh, then emptying the catch into the buckets and onto the conveyor belt to the hold. An enormous wave—at least a twenty-five-footer—suddenly rose up, like a balloon inflating, and broke over the bow of the boat. The icy spray splashed all the way up to the windows of the wheelhouse.

"It's getting too dangerous out there," Lucas said, clinging to the back of the other stool. "We're gonna get hit by a rogue wave bigger than that one, and somebody's going overboard."

"I just hope it's Farrell, that lazy son of a bitch."

Lucas took a sip of his own coffee and kept his own counsel.

Harley checked the screens. On one, he had a sonar reading that showed him what lay beneath his own rolling hull; right now, it was thirty fathoms of frigid black water, with an underwater sea mount rising half that high. On the others, he had his navigation and radar data, giving him his position and speed and direction. Glancing at the screens now, he knew what Lucas was about to say.

"You do know, don't you, that you're going to run right into the rock pile off St. Peter's Island if you don't change course soon?"

"You think I'm blind?"

"I think you're like your brother. You'll risk the whole damn boat to catch a full pot of crab."

Although Harley didn't say anything, he knew Lucas was right—at least about his brother. And about his dad, too, for that matter, may the old bastard rest in peace. There was a streak of crazy in those two—a streak that Harley liked to think he had avoided. That was why he was skipper now. But it didn't mean he liked to be told what to do, much less by some college-boy deckhand who'd done maybe two or three seasons, max, on a crab boat. Harley stayed the course and waited for Lucas to dare to say another thing.

But he didn't.

Down on the deck, Harley could see Kubelik and Farrell pulling up another pot—a steel cage ten feet square—this one brimming with crabs, hundreds of them scrabbling all over each other, their claws flailing, grasping at the mesh, struggling to escape. This was the first full pot Harley had seen in days, packed with keepers. When the bottom was dropped open, the crabs poured out onto the sorting counter, and the crewmen quickly went about throwing them into buckets, down the hole, or—in the case of those too mutilated or small to use—whipping them back into the ocean like Frisbees.

Harley didn't care how close to St. Peter's he got. If this was where the damn crabs were, this was where he was going.

For the next half hour, the *Neptune II* steamed ahead, throwing strings of pots and bucking the increasingly heavy seas. A chunk of ice broke off the crane and plummeted onto the deck, nearly killing the Samoan guy he'd hired in that waterfront bar. But every time Harley heard one of the deckhands shout into the intercom, "290 pounds!" or "300!" he resolved to keep on going. If this could just keep up, he could return to Port Orlov in a couple of days and not hear a word of bitching from his brother.

And then, if things really went his way, maybe he'd be able to convince Angie Dobbs to go someplace warm with him. L.A., or Miami Beach. He knew that he wasn't enough of a draw all by himself—ten years ago, Angie had been runner-up for Miss Teen Alaska—but if he could promise her a free trip out of this hellhole, he figured she'd take it. And maybe even give him some action just to be polite. It wasn't like she hadn't been around—Christ, half the town claimed to have had her, and Harley had long felt unfairly overlooked.

"Skipper!" he heard over the intercom. Sounded like Farrell, probably about to complain about the length of the shift.

"What?" Harley said, unhappy at the break in his reverie.

"We got something!" he shouted over the howling wind.

"Yeah, I've been watching. You got the best damn catch of the season."

"No," Farrell said, "no, take a look!"

And now, lifting himself up from his seat to get a better view of the deck, Harley could see what Farrell, the hood thrown back on his yellow slicker, was wildly pointing at.

A box—big and black, with icy water cascading down its sides—was tangled in the hooks and lines, and with the help of a couple of the other crew members, it was being hauled over the railing. What the hell . . .

"I'll be right down!" Harley called before turning to Lucas and telling him to hold the boat in position. "And do not fuck with the course."

Harley grabbed his anorak off a hook on the wall. As he barreled down the narrow creaking stairs, he pulled a pair of thermal, waterproof gloves out of the pocket and wrestled them on. Just a few minutes out on deck unprotected and your fingers could freeze like fish sticks. Yanking the hood up over his head, he pulled the sliding door open, and was almost blown back into the cabin by the driving wind.

Forcing his way outside, the door slamming back into its groove behind him, he plowed up the deck with one hand clinging to the inside rail. Even in the gathering dusk, he could see, maybe three miles to starboard, the ragged silhouette of St. Peter's Island sticking up out of the rolling sea. That one island, with its steep cliffs and rocky shoals, had claimed more lives than any other off the coast of Alaska, and he could see why even the native Inuit had always given it a wide berth. For as long as he could remember, they had considered it an unholy place, a place where unhappy and evil spirits, the ones who could not ride the highways of the Aurora Borealis up into the sky, were condemned to linger on earth. Some said that these doomed souls were the spirits of the mad Russians who had once colonized the island, and that they were now trapped in the bodies of the black wolves that roamed the cliffs. Harley could almost believe it.

"What do we do with it?" Farrell shouted as the great black box swung in the lines and netting overhead.

It was about six feet long, three feet wide, and its lid was carved with some design Harley couldn't make out yet. The other crewmen were staring at it dumbfounded, and Harley directed the Samoan and a couple of others to get it down and onto the conveyor belt. Whatever it was, he didn't want to lose it, and whatever might be inside it, he didn't want the deckhands to find out before he did.

Farrell used a gaffing hook to pull the box clear of the railing, while the Samoan guided it onto the deck. It landed on one end with a loud thump, and a crack opened down the center of the lid. "Quick!" Harley said, lending a hand and pushing the box toward the belt. Harley guessed its weight at maybe two hundred waterlogged pounds, and once they had securely positioned it on the belt, Harley threw the switch and watched as it was carried the length of the deck, then down into the hold below.

"Okay, show's over," he shouted over the wind and crashing waves. "Haul in those pots! Now!"

Then, as the men cast one more look over their shoulders and returned to their labors, he went back toward the bridge. But instead of going up to the pilot's cabin, he stumbled down the swaying steps to the hold, where he found the engineer, Richter, studying the box.

"What the hell is this?" Richter said. "You know you could have busted the belt with this damned thing?" Richter was usually just called the Old Man, and he'd worked on crab and cod and swordfish boats for nearly fifty years.

"I don't know what it is," Harley said. "It just came up in the lines."

Richter, pulling at his bushy white eyebrows, stood back and surveyed the box, which had come to rest at the end of the now-stationary belt. Mutilated crabs, most of them dead but some of them still twitching, lay all over the wet floor. The overhead lights cast a sickly yellow glow around the huge holding tanks and roaring turbines. The air reeked of gasoline and brine.

"I'll tell you what I think it is," Richter said. "This damn thing is a coffin."

Harley had reluctantly come to the same conclusion. It wasn't built in the customary shape of a coffin, but the general dimensions were right.

"And you don't want to bring coffins aboard," Richter grumbled over the engine noise. "Didn't your father teach you a goddamned thing?"

Harley was sick to death of hearing about his father. Everybody from Nome to Prudhoe Bay always had a story. He ran a hand over the lid of the box, brushing off some of the icy water, and bent closer to observe the carvings. Most of them had been worn away, but it looked like there was some writing here. Not in English, but in those characters he'd seen on the old Russian buildings that still remained here and there in Alaska. In school, they'd taught him about how the Russians had settled the area first, way back in the 1700s, and then, in one of the colossal blunders of all time, had sold it to the United States after the Civil War. This looked like that kind of writing, and in the dim light of the hold he could also make out a chiseled figure. Bending closer, he saw that it was sort of like a saint, but a really fierce-looking one, with a long robe, a short beard, and a key ring in one hand. He felt a sudden shudder descend his spine.

"Get me a flashlight," he told the old man.

"What for?"

"Just get me one."

Moving his head this way and that, trying to avoid throwing a shadow onto the box, Harley peered through the crack in the lid, and when Richter slapped a flashlight into his hand, he pointed the beam into the box and put his nose to the wood.

"God will punish you for what you're doing."

But Harley wasn't listening. Although the crack was very narrow, he caught again a glimpse of something glistening inside the box. Something that glinted like a bright green eye.

Like an emerald.

"The dead oughta be left in peace," Richter solemnly intoned.

On general grounds, Harley agreed. Still, it didn't mean they got to hang on to their jewelry.

"What did you see in there?" the Old Man asked, finally overcome by his own curiosity. "Was it a native or a white man?"

"Can't tell," Harley replied, snapping off the flashlight and leaning back. "Too dark." Nobody needed to know about this. Not yet. "Get me a tarp," he said, and when the old man didn't budge, he went and got one himself. He threw it over the box, then lashed it in place with heavy ropes. "Nobody touches this until we get back to port," he said, and Richter conspicuously crossed himself.

Harley climbed the slippery stairs to the deck level, then up to the wheelhouse, where Lucas was still holding the course as ordered. But with Harley back, he couldn't hold his tongue any longer.

"St. Peter's Island," he warned. "It's less than a mile off the starboard prow. If we don't steer clear of the rocks right now, they're gonna rip the shit out of the boat."

Harley took off his soaking gear and resumed his chair. In the pale moonlight, the island loomed like a gigantic black skull rising up out of the sea. A belt of fog clung to its shores like a shroud.

"Take us ten degrees west," Harley said, and Lucas spun the wheel as fast as he could.

"What was that thing in the nets?" he asked, as the ship was buffeted by another crest of freezing water.

"You worry about the course," Harley said, staring out at the dark sea. "Leave the rest to me."

"I was just thinking, if it's salvage of some kind, then it has to be reported to—"

The ship suddenly juddered from bow to stern, shaking like a dog throwing off water, and from deep below there was the sound of metal groaning. Lucas nearly slipped off his feet, as Harley clung to the control panel in front of him.

"Ice?" Harley said, though he already knew better. Lucas, wide-eyed and white with fear, said, "Rocks."

A second jolt hit the ship, knocking it to one side, as waves swept the deck and the crab pots swung wildly in the air. One of them hit the Samoan, who, windmilling his arms in an attempt to regain his balance, was carried by the next surge over the side. Farrell and Kubelik were clinging desperately to the mast, the crane, and the icy ropes.

"Jesus Christ," Harley said, groping for the hand mike.

Lucas was draped across the wheel as if it were a life preserver.

"Mayday!" Harley shouted into the microphone. "This is the *Neptune II,* northwest of St. Peter's Island. Man overboard! Do you read me? Mayday!"

From belowdecks, there was another grinding sound, like sheet metal being crumpled in an auto yard, and the engineer, Richter, was bleating over the intercom. "The bulkhead's breached! You hear me up there? The pumps won't handle it!"

"We read you, *Neptune,*" a Coast Guard voice crackled over the mike. "You have a man overboard?"

"Yes," Harley said, "and we're taking on water!" He rattled off their position, then tossed the mike to Lucas, as he slipped off his stool.

"Don't leave me here!" Lucas said, his voice strained and trembling.

"Handle it!" Harley shouted.

"Where the hell are you going?"

"Down below!" Harley answered, as he lurched toward the gangway. "To check the damage!" And something else.

As Lucas clung to the wheel, Harley scrambled down the steps. But he could tell already, just from the tilt of the deck and the terrible racket in the hold, that the ship was lost. He'd be lucky to escape this night alive. They all would.

Maybe Old Man Richter had been right about that damned box, after all.

Chapter 3

For a court-martial so hastily convened, Major Frank Slater thought things were moving along pretty smoothly.

Seated beside his Army-appointed lawyer—a kid with a blond crew cut and the look of someone who had seen more action in a Hooters than he had on any battlefield—Slater had nothing much to do besides sit there in his nice clean uniform and listen to the damning testimony that he neither denied nor apologized for.

Colonel Keener, whose duties in Afghanistan had been deemed too important to send him back to D.C. for the court-martial, testified against Slater by Skype. The computer monitor had been set up on a trolley in front of the panel of five military judges, and Slater and his attorney, Lieutenant Bonham, listened closely as the colonel related the various crimes and infractions that the major—"an epidemiologist," Keener explained, as if he were labeling him a child molester, "who has no more business being in the Army than my dog does"—had committed in Khan Neshin.

Assaulting a superior officer—which fell under Article 128 of the

Uniform Code of Military Justice, Slater learned—was a slam-dunk for the prosecution. After Colonel Keener had made his initial statement, he was asked to stand by while corroborating evidence was supplied. That, too, was easy. A nurse had happened to be down the hall in the med center, and although she had been too far away to hear what the colonel had said to Slater just before the altercation, she had been flown back to the States to testify that she had indeed seen the major throw the punch that had decked the colonel.

"Just one punch?" the head judge, a retired general, asked.

"That's all it took," the nurse said.

Slater thought he saw a tiny smile crease the general's lips.

"And then I called the MPs," the nurse went on.

"And you have no knowledge of what transpired just before?" the judge asked.

"I found out later on," she replied. "The little girl had died in the O.R., and the doctor—I mean, Major Slater—just lost it." Hazarding a sympathetic glance at the defendant, she added, "It seemed like a really momentary thing . . . like he'd tried so hard to save her, and then, finding out that it was all for nothing, it just sort of tipped him over the edge."

The general made a note, and the four other judges, all officers, followed his lead and did the same. Because it was a general court-martial—more serious in nature than either a summary or special trial—all told there were five officers deliberating, including three other old men and a woman who looked as if she'd swapped her spine for a ramrod. The prosecutor offered into evidence an X-ray, taken at the med center, of a fracture to Colonel Keener's jawline. When it was shown to Slater for confirmation, he said, "It's a good likeness."

"What was that?" the general asked, cupping his ear.

"My client," Lieutenant Bonham cut in, before handing the X-ray back to the bailiff, "says that he does not contest this exhibit." Then he shot Slater a murderous look.

But once the assault and battery charge had been duly noted and the evidence entered into the records, the court moved on to what was considered—from the Army's point of view—the even more serious charges. While punches got thrown all the time, especially in war zones, it wasn't often that a commissioned officer issued an order that he knew to be a lie, and in so doing jeopardized a helicopter and its crew. When Slater had called in the mission from the rice paddies, he had not only made a False Official Statement (Article 107 of the code)—punishable with a dishonorable discharge, forfeiture of all pay and allowances, and confinement for a period of five years—but he had put military property and personnel at risk. (Article 108, among others.)

For Slater, the worst part of the proceeding wasn't hearing all the charges leveled at him. That much he expected. No, the worst part was having to watch as his friend and right-hand man, Sergeant Jerome Groves, was forced to take the stand. Slater had already ordered Groves to tell the truth and let the blame fall entirely on his commanding officer, where it belonged, but he knew it would be tough. He and Groves had a long history together.

When the prosecutor leaned in and said, "Sergeant Groves, it was you who called in your exact coordinates to the air rescue—is that correct?" Groves hesitated, and Slater nodded at him to go on. No point in denying facts that were indisputable.

"Yes. But Major Slater was simply trying to save the—"

"And you knew," the prosecutor went on, twirling his eyeglasses in one hand, "that the purpose of the mission was to airlift a civilian, not a member of the armed forces, to a medical facility?"

"All due respect, sir, but it was a kid," Groves said. "What would you have done? She'd been bitten by a viper and she'd have—"

"I repeat," the prosecutor interrupted again, "you knew it was not U.S. Army personnel?"

"I did."

"And yet you remained a party to the deception?"

"On my orders!" Slater barked, lifting himself out of his chair. He was afraid that Groves was not going to muster enough of a defense. "The sergeant only did what I told him to do as his commanding officer. What I *ordered* him to do."

Predictably, Slater was ordered to sit down and shut up, in pretty much those words, or he would be removed from his own trial. After he sat back down, Lieutenant Bonham rose from his chair and conducted his own interrogation of the witness, advancing more or less the same argument, but in a legally reasoned, and more dispassionate, manner. Slater had given him explicit instructions to see to it that Groves was exonerated on all charges.

When the sergeant had been dismissed from the witness stand, he slunk by Slater's chair and muttered, "Sorry, Frank," as he passed.

"No reason to be," Slater said.

The general in charge of the tribunal demanded again that there be no communication between the witnesses, and after shuffling his stack of papers, asked the lawyers to proceed to the summation.

The prosecutor, who looked confident that he had a winning hand, went through the litany of charges and all the articles of the military code that Slater had managed to break—even Slater was surprised that he'd managed to commit so many infractions in such a short space of time—before sitting down again with his hands folded over his abdomen like a guy waiting for the soufflé to be served.

Lieutenant Bonham stood up with a lot less confidence and proceeded to make his own arguments in defense of Major Slater. A lot of it was legal jargon, but Slater also had to sit still for a long recapitulation of his own military and medical accomplishments.

"May it be entered into the record that Major Slater enlisted in the United States Army thirteen years ago, with a medical degree from Johns Hopkins, a specialty in tropical and infectious diseases, and an advanced degree in statistics and epidemiology from the Georgetown University Program in Public Health. Those credentials have served him—and this country—exceptionally well in some of the most dangerous and hotly disputed scenes of engagement, ranging from Somalia to Sarajevo. He has earned three special commendations, a Purple Heart, and attained the rank of major, which he holds at the time of this hearing. He is also a victim of an especially chronic strain of malaria, to which he was exposed in the line of duty but which he has never allowed to interfere with the assignments given him by the

United States Armed Forces Institute of Pathology, here in Washington, D.C., where he is based. This disease, I would argue, should be considered a mitigating factor for any possible misconduct. Among its symptoms are fevers, hallucinatory episodes, and insomnia—which in and of themselves can contribute to acts of an irrational and impulsive nature. Acts which Major Slater, if he had been wholly in control of his behavior, would never have countenanced, much less committed."

Slater had to hand it to the kid. It was a very persuasive and well-put summation . . . even if he hated the part about the malaria. It wasn't the malaria that made him throw that punch or call in the chopper. Right now, sitting comfortably in the courtroom, his illness at bay and his thoughts as clear as the blue November sky outside, he would have done exactly the same things all over again. And it wasn't just the little Afghan girl that had done it—she was just the proverbial straw that had broken the camel's back. This explosion had been building for years. He had seen too much horror, he had witnessed too many deaths, too many barbarities. He had flown to too many desolate corners of the earth, armed with too little to offer in the way of aid or relief. Under a mosquito net in Darfur, by the light of a bright moon, he had finally gotten around to reading Joseph Conrad's *Heart of Darkness,* and he had quickly understood why that volunteer from Oxfam had so urgently pressed the book on him. Maybe, without his noticing it, he had been turning into the mysterious character, Kurtz, a man who saw so much of the cruelty that man can inflict that it had finally driven him mad.

When Lieutenant Bonham had finished his appeal to the court, the general in charge of the tribunal ordered the room to be cleared so that the judges could deliberate, and Slater was taken back to a holding cell, where he was given a Coke, a bag of chips, and an egg salad sandwich wrapped in plastic.

"You hungry?" he said, sliding the sandwich toward his lawyer.

"Yes, but not that hungry."

"What do you think our chances are?" he said, popping open the Coke.

"Guilty on all counts—that goes without saying."

Slater knew he was right, but it still wasn't exactly pleasant to hear.

"But there's a lot of mitigating factors in your favor, so the sentencing could be light. And I think Colonel Keener has a certain reputation as a prick. That could help, too." Gesturing at the bag of chips, Bonham said, "But if you're not going to eat those . . ."

"Help yourself."

Slater pushed his chair back and stared out the narrow window placed high in the wall and covered with chicken wire. It was about a foot and a half square. Nothing bigger than a beagle could have ever made it through.

Bonham checked his BlackBerry for messages, sent a few texts, then put it away. He polished off the potato chips and brushed his fingers clean with a hankie.

"There's no reason to stick around in here on my account," Slater said.

The lieutenant said, "Not much I can do anywhere else."

"How long do you think it'll be?"

"No telling." Bonham drummed his fingers on the tabletop. "But maybe I could try to pry some news out of the bailiff."

"You do that," Slater said. But before the young lawyer closed the door behind him, he added, "You did a good job."

Unexpectedly, Bonham glowed. "You think so, Major?"

"Yeah," Slater said. "You just had a lousy case."

Alone in the cell, Slater sipped the Coke and waited. A couple of rooms away, his fate was being decided by five judges who'd never even laid eyes on him before. It was a hard thought to hold in his head—that in a matter of minutes, maybe hours, he would learn, from the lips of a retired general, what the dire consequences of his actions might be. Reflecting on it all now, a month later and a world away, Slater couldn't fault himself for what he did in trying to save the girl's life. What else could he have done and still been able to face himself in the mirror? As for the punch . . . well, that was ill-advised, to say the least. And it wasn't the first time his temper had gotten him into trouble. But whenever he remembered the look on the colonel's face, the smug tone in which he'd announced the girl's death . . . well, his fist went right back into a ball and he wanted to slug him again. Only this time he wanted to stay completely awake and aware the whole time.

The question was, would he still feel that way after serving five years in a military prison?

There was no clock in the holding cell. There was no phone, or TV, or magazine rack. The walls were cinder block, the door was steel. There was nothing for a prisoner to look at, nothing to do, except sit there and contemplate his destiny, which was something Slater had been doing everything he could to avoid.

He slumped forward and put his head down on the table—the wood was worn and scarred and the smell reminded him of his grammar-school classrooms—and closed his eyes. At night he could never sleep, but during the day his weariness often overwhelmed him. A few nights before, he had called his ex-wife, Martha, in Silver Spring. She hadn't sounded all that happy to hear from him—and that was before he told her why he was stateside again. Once he had, he could hear her sigh, mostly in sympathy, but there was also a note of relief in it—relief that she had severed their relationship when she had, and that this latest act of self-immolation was not her problem anymore.

"Where are they keeping you?" she asked, and he had explained that he was free on his own recognizance until the trial began—though without a passport, he wasn't going to go very far.

"Do you want me to come and see you?" she said. "Would that help?"

But he really didn't see how it would. He had only called to let her know what was up, in case she ever got curious about his where-abouts . . . or the Army notified her that her portion of his Army pension would be severely diminished.

Not that she needed the money.

Her new husband was a partner in a lobbying firm on K Street, and her own dermatology practice was going strong. He had seen ads for it in local magazines, and once or twice he had seen her interviewed on the local news about Botox and collagen. She had gotten what she wanted out of life . . . and he had got what he deserved. Or so he figured most people would see it.

When his lawyer came back to get him, he didn't know how much time had passed. He had nodded off, and his cheek bore the impression of the cracks in the wood. At the front of the courtroom, all the judges were sitting stiffly in their chairs, but there was one thing different. In the back, on a plastic chair, was Dr. Lena Levinson, chief of the pathology institute, with a thick folder in her lap and a stern expression on her face. When he nodded in her direction, she glared back at him reproachfully, then answered a call on her cell phone.

"Will the defendant please stand?" the general said, and Slater stood up beside Lieutenant Bonham. He was surprised to find his knees a little weaker than he'd planned.

Clearing his throat, the general continued. "On the several charges brought by this court-martial against Dr. Frank James Slater, Major in the United States Army, the verdict of the court is as follows." Slater braced himself, as did Bonham, who looked so pale it was all Slater could do not to put an arm around his shoulders.

"Guilty" was the one word Slater distinctly heard, over and over again. But then he had expected that.

It was the sentencing he dreaded.

And that, too, was going as badly as possible. He was stripped of his rank, then dismissed—dishonorably—from the Army. All pay, all allowances, and all benefits were forfeited, now and in perpetuity. It was only when the question of imprisonment came up that the general paused, while Slater waited with bated breath for the hammer to come down.

"On the subject of incarceration, which these charges normally carry, the court has heard outside counsel, and read an amicus curia brief submitted only hours ago." His eyes flitted toward Dr. Levinson. "In view of Dr. Slater's long and valuable service to this country, and in the national interest, the court has unanimously elected to forgo all such punishment at this time."

No prison time? And in the national interest? Slater was stunned, and even Bonham looked confused.

The general read some summary remarks into the record—names, dates, articles of the military code adjudicated—then looked around the room, as if leaving time for any objections before saying, "This court-martial is hereby concluded."

Slater—suddenly a civilian, even if a disgraced one, after thirteen years—could hardly believe his ears. Bonham was clapping him on the back, and even the general threw him a glance that was less condemnatory than rueful. On his way out, Slater found Dr. Levinson standing beside the door.

"I can only assume," he said, "that your testimony here today had something to do with my reprieve?"

"It did."

"Thank you," he said, from the bottom of his heart. She was a tough old buzzard, but he knew that they had always understood, and appreciated, each other.

"And now we have to talk, Dr. Slater."

"About the national interest?"

"As a matter of fact," she said, "yes."

Chapter 4

Harley Vane had become what you'd call a local celebrity. All the papers in Alaska, Oregon, and Washington State had carried his miraculous story of courage and survival, and he'd even received some national attention from an assortment of radio shows and a couple of TV stations.

At the hospital, where he'd recuperated for the first three days after his rescue, the nurses had treated him like a rock star, and Angie Dobbs had even come by to visit him. She said his drinks would be free at the Yardarm, and the way she said it made him think something else might be coming his way, too. At last.

This morning, the docs had promised him he'd be allowed to go if his numbers all checked out. Harley knew they would; he felt fine again, and he needed to see his brother Charlie. According to the nurses, Charlie had already come by, just a few hours after the Coast Guard cutter had picked him up, but Harley had been too disoriented to remember anything about it. There was a big blank spot in his memory, and there were plenty of times when he wished it were even bigger.

He remembered all too well barreling down the stairs to the hold. On the way down, he had pulled on a life vest, stuffed a flare in its pocket, then grabbed the emergency fire axe off the wall and stuck its handle in his belt. Water was gushing in from some unseen hole that had been ripped in the hull, somewhere beneath the holding tanks for the crabs. Thousands of them were suddenly loose again, scuttling up the walls, clinging to the ceiling, or paddling around on the rising tide. Old Man Richter was up to his knees in freezing water, trying to get the pumps working again.

"They won't start!" he shouted. "They won't start!"

"Get out!" Harley said. "Get out now!"

But Richter turned around and went back to work; he was the kind of guy, Harley knew, who would plan to go down with the ship.

Harley didn't need that right now. He waded through the icy water, crabs nipping at his boots and thighs, and grabbed Richter by his bony shoulder. "I'm telling you to go on deck—now!"

"You shoulda let me get these serviced before we left port," Richter said. "I told you they needed work!"

Another wave hit the ship broadside, and Richter tumbled into the water. His hand shot up, and Harley snatched it. He dragged the Old Man onto his feet again, but there were crabs all over him already, their pincers grasping at his wet clothes, or snapping furiously in the air. A big one, pink as bubblegum, was crawling up his chest, and Harley batted it off.

"Get out," he screamed at the Old Man, "or I'll drown you myself!" With a hard shove, he sent him toward the stairs. And then he sloshed through the debris to the coffin, still lashed to the conveyor belt. With fingers so cold they were almost numb, he fumbled at the ropes, but then gave up and chopped at them with the axe. The ropes and tarp fell away, and Harley took aim at the rusty hasps holding the lid closed. It took him several swings to knock each one loose, but when the last one went, he stuck the blade of the axe sideways into the groove and pried the lid up. It came up slowly, with a groan, and Harley had to push hard before it opened all the way and fell of its own momentum into the water. There was a splash, then the lid was bobbing like a surfboard around the hold.

The water was up to Harley's thighs, and he was beginning to freeze. The lights flickered, but they stayed on. Inside the box he saw what looked like a mummy—a petrified face, all teeth and hair, grimacing with empty eye sockets, the hands folded to touch its own shoulders. Still, it was recognizably the corpse of a young man, maybe nineteen or twenty, and dressed in what looked like the frozen remains of a woolen tunic, with a rounded, Cossack-style collar, and black sealskin coat. But around the young man's neck he saw what he had come for. It was one of those old Russian crosses, the ones with three sideways beams of different lengths, but embedded in it there were several old stones, glinting green in the dim light. He tried to pull it loose, but it was still on its chain. Much as he loathed the idea, there was nothing to do but reach down and lift the corpse's head. Touching it felt like touching a bag of old shells and crumpled paper; the skin rustled and the skull weighed on his hand like an empty, fragile egg.

But the cross still wouldn't come loose.

The chain was entangled in the boy's long brown hair, and it was only after he had yanked at it several times, hard enough that the head was nearly severed from the spine, that it came up and over the crown.

He stuffed it deep into the inner compartment of his anorak, then zipped the pocket firmly closed. A couple of crabs had already clambered over the end of the coffin and spilled onto the corpse. Their claws were shredding the remains of the fabric and probing the hard flesh. One was worrying a toe and would have it loose in no time.

Let 'em have it, Harley thought, *and the sooner the better.* The water was still rising. It was up to his waist now, and the ship was so canted over that he could barely keep his balance as he reached for the stair railing. He hauled himself up, hand over hand, as the water surged behind him, and as something—hard and persistent—batted at his calves. Glancing back, he saw that the coffin lid, carved with the saint or angel or whatever it was, was floating up the stairs with him, like a faithful hound nipping at his heels.

On deck, everything was chaos. The howling wind was ripping at the lines and the pots, and the lifeboat had already been launched. *Fuck you, too,* Harley thought, *looks like it's every man for himself tonight.*

He wondered who had made it on board and who hadn't. A flare went up from the water, and in its dead-white glow he saw the lifeboat, cradled between two mighty waves off the starboard side. The deckhands were trying to put some distance between themselves and the *Neptune,* lest they be sucked under when it sank. Harley thought he could make out Farrell at the tiller and Lucas clinging to the oarlocks, but over the wind blasting in his ears he heard a voice—Richter's—shouting from somewhere down the deck.

The Old Man, in an orange life vest, was clinging to the mast.

Harley couldn't hear a word he was saying—what could it matter?—but he saw him lift one arm and point out to sea, toward the looming black mass of St. Peter's Island. It was big as a mountain now, and through the spray and the waves Harley could see the jutting rocks sticking up like spikes and barricades all around its shoreline.

Another flare rocketed into the sky, this one leaving a phosphorescent green trail, and in its light Harley saw the lifeboat spinning around and around in a whirlpool, before it suddenly broke free and was dashed against the rocks. The crew spilled out like jelly beans from a jar, and the splintered timbers of the boat flew in every direction. Before the green light had dissipated, Harley saw the bobbing vests of his deckhands caught in the eddies and the swirls, each one of them being sucked under and lost beneath the angry black tide.

As he looked up at the wheelhouse, a blue computer screen came crashing through a window, and the lights went black. The deck lurched under his feet, and he was sent sprawling into the crab pots. The cages were still full; when the boat went down with the cages still sealed, the captured crabs would have to eat each other until they died.

Harley's mind was racing, wondering whether to stick with the wreckage of the boat or try making it to the crew cabin to retrieve a raft, when a wave crashed over the bulwarks on the port side and carried him, head over heels, into the ocean. He plunged in an instant into the icy water, the breath nearly knocked from his lungs, the salt stinging his blinded eyes. He was struggling to regain the surface, but the water was churning so hard, he couldn't tell which way was up.

He tried to stay calm enough to let the oxygen in his chest, and the air in his life vest, right him and send him upward again, but it didn't seem to be working. He panicked and kicked out, pumping his arms. He collided with something, a rocky outcropping, and used it to push himself away. Gasping, he broke the surface of the water, and reaching out in the darkness, clutched something floating nearby. It was wood, and as he grappled it more tightly in his arms, he could feel its rough carvings. And he knew it was the coffin lid.

He managed to pull himself halfway on top of it, then wrapped his arms around its sides. The waves lifted him up and threw him down, over and over again, eventually pushing him through a narrow passageway between the jagged rocks, with the sea boiling all around him. He could barely see where he was going, and his arms were so numb he wondered how much longer he could hang on. But when he felt his knees scraping on the rocks and shells of the shoreline, he somehow managed to stagger to his feet, then struggle through the pounding surf until he reached the beach. There, he collapsed in a shivering heap, with the cross, still lodged in his pocket, poking him in the ribs.

The coffin lid, gleaming in the moonlight, skimmed to a stop on the pebbles and sand.

How long he lay there he didn't know. Cold and hard as the ground was, it felt like a warm blanket compared to the icy sea. He took deep breaths, coughing out the salt water and the gravel that now clung to his lips, but he knew that if he lay there much longer, he'd die of exposure. Rolling onto his back, he gazed up at the night sky, where even behind the banks of angry, scudding clouds, he could see the dazzling pinpricks of the distant stars. Shaking himself from head to foot like a dog throwing off water, he sat up and stared out at the sea. There was no sign of the *Neptune II,* or any of the other crewmen. Even their flares had long since disappeared from the sky. Harley prayed that the Coast Guard was on its way.

Fumbling at the straps of the life vest, he yanked its straps off, then groped for the flare he'd stuck in its pocket. He didn't want to use it too soon, but he didn't know how long he could survive in the state he was in, either. He searched the length of the beach for any kind of shelter, but there was nothing. Not even a rock large enough to huddle behind.

The only alternative was to scale the cliff somehow, and that would have been impossible even in broad daylight, with all the proper ropes and gear. Harley had always harbored nothing but scorn for climbers. It was bad enough to risk your ass crabbing, but at least there was money in it. Why do it for the glory of getting to the top of a pile of rocks?

The wind tore at the sleeves of his anorak, and the ocean spray forced him to shield his eyes and squint. He strained to hear anything besides the roaring of the wind, to see any sign of rescue.

But there was nothing. He was going to freeze to death on this island—all those fucking legends were true, and he was going to wind up as one more of the miserable souls that haunted the place—and to make it even worse, he was going to die with the first piece of good luck he'd had in ages jammed into the pocket of his anorak. He could feel the Russian cross, with the emeralds embedded in it, prodding his ribs.

Hunching down to get out of the wind and placing the flare between his soaking boots, he reached inside the coat, fumbling at the zipper, and took the cross out. It was a heavy thing, silver, with emeralds on one side, and, when he turned it over, some sort of inscription on the back. Even without knowing anything more about it, Harley knew it would be worth a fortune. Charlie would know, or Voynovich in Nome.

If they ever found his body, that is.

Once more, he scanned the night sky, and this time, far in the distance, he thought he saw a flashing light.

Just for a second.

A flashing red light.

But then he saw it again.

He rammed the cross back in his pocket and leapt to his feet with the flare in hand. He ripped the safety cap off, held it high, and yanked the cord.

The flare rocketed up into the sky, leaving a trail of white sparks, before blossoming—high, high above him—in a shower of green phosphorescent light that bathed the beach in its glow.

"Here!" Harley shouted, jumping up and down and waving his arms. "Here!" He knew he couldn't be seen, he knew he couldn't be heard, but it was enough to get the blood pumping again. "I'm here!"

There was no way they could have missed the flare, he told himself, no way in the world.

And even as the green streamers began to break up and scatter in the wind, Harley saw the red lights turning toward the island, and heard—or was he just imagining it?—the roar of the helicopter's propellers.

Good Christ, he was going to make it. Maybe that cross was his good-luck charm, after all.

Or not.

No sooner had his heart lifted than he caught, out of the corner of his eye, a movement at the far end of the beach.

Just a shadow, prowling onto the sand and gravel.

The green glow in the sky was nearly gone, but in its fading light he saw the shadow joined by another. They were moving low, and slowly, as if drawn by the flare, but beginning to find something of even greater interest.

Harley stared out to sea again and saw the chopper's lights coming closer.

Then looked back down the crescent of the beach, and saw that the two shadows had become three.

Then four.

His impulse was to shout and make himself plain to the Coast Guard pilot, but at the same time he dreaded attracting the attention of the beasts only a few hundred yards away. He knew what they must be—the black wolves indigenous to the island.

Or, if you believed the stories, the lost souls of the long-dead Russians.

He didn't know what to do, but instinctively ran toward the pounding surf line. If he had to, he'd wade back into the sea and try to cling to one of the nearest rocks. Wolves weren't swimmers.

But they were trackers, and as he watched in horror, they appeared to pick up his scent and raise their snouts to the wind. Harley searched for a weapon. The coffin lid lay nearby, but he could barely lift it, much less wield it in a fight. He pried a stone loose from the beach, and then another, and gripped them tightly in his hands.

The helicopter was hovering closer, but clearly feared getting its blades too close to the cliff, especially in such a driving wind.

A blazing white searchlight suddenly swiveled in his direction, sweeping first the rocks and shoals, then arcing toward the beach and centering on the coffin lid. Harley ran into its beam, waving and screaming, and a booming voice, distorted by the wind, said, "We see you!"

They were the best three words Harley had ever heard.

But glancing down the beach, he could see that the wolves had seen him, too.

"Move as far from the cliffs as you can!"

The spotlight still trained on him, Harley splashed into the water up to his ankles.

A wire basket was being lowered from the chopper, swinging on the end of a long, thick, nylon cord. The cord was unspooling rapidly, dropping the basket like a spider skittering down its own web.

But not as fast as Harley wanted it to. The wolves were picking up speed, scrabbling across the slick rocks and wet sand.

"Come on, for Christ's sake!" Harley shouted. "Come on!"

The basket was swinging wildly, caught in the crosscurrents whirling around the beach.

The lead wolf was running headlong now—how could it have missed him framed in the spotlight like he was?—and Harley was racing back and forth trying to figure out where the basket would come down.

"Drop it!" he screamed. "Drop it!"

The basket swung like a pendulum just above his head, but when Harley jumped, his heavy boots stuck in the mud and sand.

The basket moved away, and the wolf pack got closer. The leader was splashing along the shoreline.

Harley kicked his feet free of the sand, and when the basket swung back, he leapt again, and this time he was able to grab the mesh of the basket.

"Strap yourself in!" he heard from above. "And hold on tight!"

Harley didn't need to be told to hold on tight. He slammed his butt into the basket, threw the strap around his waist and fastened its buckle to the clamp, then clutched the rope for dear life.

The leader of the pack lunged at him just as Harley felt the winch tighten and the basket lift. He kicked a boot out and caught the wolf on its snarling muzzle. The basket swung out over the surf as the chopper maneuvered away from the cliffs.

Harley saw the rocky beach fall away beneath him, the wolf pack, denied their prey, milling around the coffin lid now. *Close, but no cigar,* he thought with jubilation.

Up, up he went, swinging in the frigid air, the wolves and the beach itself disappearing in the darkness. But just before he was gathered into the belly of the helicopter, he thought he glimpsed, on the top of the island's highest cliff, a yellow light, like a lantern, hovering in the gloom.

Chapter 5

"Glad you could make it," Dr. Levinson said, as Slater slunk into the conference room twenty minutes late.

Considering everything he owed her, the last thing he wanted to do was to be late to the first meeting she'd requested since the trial. "Sorry, but I had some trouble at the gate."

Trouble he should have seen coming. Monday-morning traffic in D.C. was always bad, but today was the first time since his court-martial that he'd tried to enter the Walter Reed Army Medical Center through the STAFF ONLY gate on Aspen Street. His officer status, he learned, had already been revoked—the Army could be efficient as hell when they wanted to be—and though the guards knew him well, they had been obliged to hold him for clearance before letting him pass. Especially as he was attached to the AFIP—the Armed Forces Institute of Pathology—where some of the country's most highly classified work on deadly contagions and biological warfare was done. Dr. Slater, as he was now simply known, was given a day pass, a new decal for his windshield, and instructions to enter the grounds through the Civilian Employee Gate on 16th Street from now on.

The soldier at the gate said, "Sorry, sir," as he finally raised the crossbar.

And Slater said, "No reason to be—and no reason to call me sir anymore, either."

"No . . . Doctor."

Slater drove his government-issue Ford Taurus onto the huge campus, wondering when the car would be repossessed, then looped past several of the other buildings, including the old Army Medical Museum (now the National Museum of Health and Medicine), before parking in his reserved spot on the A level of the institute's garage. They couldn't take that away from him—he did still have a job as a senior epidemiologist for the Division of Infectious and Tropical Disease Pathology. And according to Dr. Levinson, his expertise was now required on a subject of national interest.

At the moment, however, all he saw was a conference table, with Dr. Levinson squinting hard at an open laptop in front of her.

"How are you feeling?" she said, but it was more than just a courtesy question. "Have you had any recurrences of the malaria?"

"I'm fine," he said, working to keep his voice even and his gaze level. Shrugging off his overcoat—he'd rushed straight upstairs without stopping at his office—he took a seat at the table. The blue suit he was wearing hung loose on his frame; he'd lost weight in Afghanistan.

"Don't lie to me, Dr. Slater. It's important."

"Whatever you need," he said, trying to dodge the question, "I am available."

Whether or not she believed him, or was just too intent on gaining his services to push it any further, he did not know. But leaning back in her chair and surveying him carefully, she said, "We all have a certain number of chips we can call in, and frankly, I used up most of mine at your trial."

"I understand that," he said, "and I appreciate it."

"Good, I'm happy to hear that. Because now I'm going to tell you how you can pay me back."

"Shoot."

"We have a problem."

So far no surprise. Slater's job was nothing but dealing with problems.

"In Alaska."

Now that *was* a surprise. Slater had been dispatched to some far-flung spots, but seldom anywhere in the United States.

"First, I want you to see some things." She tapped a few keys on her laptop, and a slide appeared on a screen that had lowered behind her. It was a shot of a snowy road, with a long line of telephone poles running along one side, but all of them were teetering at odd angles.

"This shot was taken a few days ago, outside a town called Port Orlov."

"I've never heard of it."

"No one has. It's a tiny fishing village, on the northwest tip of the Seward Peninsula. This shot was taken there, too," she said, tapping again, and bringing up a picture of an A-frame house that had slipped off its foundation.

"And here's the Inuit totem pole that has stood in the center of town since 1867, to commemorate the Russian sale of the Alaska territory." Miraculously, the old wooden column, with faded paint on the faces of eagles and otters, was still standing, but at an angle that reminded Slater of the Leaning Tower of Pisa. Plainly, the ground was shifting, but that was a problem for the geologists, was it not?

"Earthquake activity?" he asked, and Dr. Levinson shook her head.

"We've checked all the seismological data, and no, that's not it."

She tapped again, and a series of shots came up, of mailboxes that had fallen over, of concrete steps that had cracked, of wharves that had buckled.

"It's climate change," she said. "The average air temperature's rising, the offshore currents are getting warmer . . . and the permafrost is starting to thaw."

Okay, that sounded like a perfectly reasonable conclusion. But he still didn't see how any of it fell into his bailiwick.

As if she could guess what he was thinking, Dr. Levinson clicked on the next slide. "And then this turned up," she said.

At first he thought it was just an old dark door, or maybe an antique dining table, but then he looked more closely and saw that its surface was elaborately carved and depicted a classical figure, maybe a saint, in a flowing robe, and holding a set of keys on a ring. A long crack ran down one side of the wood.

"I assume it's the top of a coffin," Slater said, and when she didn't correct him, he added, "but who's that on top?"

"St. Peter, holding the keys to Heaven and Hell."

"Where did it come from?"

"The Coast Guard retrieved it. A fishing boat had pulled it up in the nets, and when the boat hit some rocks and went under, one of the crew was able to hang on to it long enough to get to shore."

"He sounds like Ishmael."

"His name's Harley Vane, and from what I've read in the initial reports, he's a piece of work. He's claimed the lid as salvage, and he still has it."

That seemed a bit strange to Slater, but maybe if he'd had occasion to hitch a ride on a coffin lid, he'd feel attached to it, too. "Where's it from?"

"Our best guess is that it came from the cemetery on a place called St. Peter's Island, a few miles west of Port Orlov."

Another slide came up. An aerial shot of a hulking black island, with a bank of fog clinging to its shores.

"The island is nearly impregnable, but a sect of religious zealots, most of them from Siberia, did manage to settle there around 1912."

"Don't tell me anyone's still there," Slater said, though one look at the forbidding island was enough to make him wonder how anyone could ever have chosen to call it home in the first place.

"No one alive," Levinson said, and now she leaned forward on the table, her arms folded and her expression grave. She looked at him over the top of her bifocals. "They all died, in the space of a week or two. In 1918."

The date was a dead giveaway, and now he could see where this had all been going. "The Spanish flu?"

Levinson nodded.

It was all coming together. "So the same disturbances to the ground in Port Orlov are showing up on the island, too."

She remained silent while he worked it out.

"And as the permafrost thaws, things that were buried are coming to the surface. Things like old caskets."

"The graveyard was built on a cliff, away from the settlement itself," she said, filling in another piece. "But now the cliff is giving way."

And shedding coffins . . . coffins filled with victims of the flu. "Is the concern," he said, thinking aloud, "that the Spanish flu virus might still be viable in the frozen corpses?"

"It's a remote possibility," she conceded, "but it's a possibility that we have to deal with, nonetheless."

As an epidemiologist, Slater did not need to be told what could happen if the Spanish flu was ever released again into the world. In a few short years, the Spanish flu pandemic had swept the globe, and although there were still disputes about the final death toll, the figure of 50 million was well accepted. In his own view, Slater had always thought that the casualty count on the Indian subcontinent had been vastly understated. What was not in dispute was that the Spanish flu had been the most devastating plague ever to hit the human race, and that to this day no one had ever completely figured it out, or discovered a way to combat it. Its victims died the most excruciating of deaths, literally drowning in a froth of their own blood and secretions, and although some of the most thorough research into mapping its genetic structure had been done right here, at the Armed Forces Institute of Pathology, the scientific community was still no closer to a cure.

"And this man Harley Vane," Slater said, continuing his train of thought. "Was he ever exposed to a body from that coffin?"

"He says no," Dr. Levinson replied. "He says the lid alone came up in the nets." She said it as if she wasn't sure if she believed it. "And all the other crew members died at sea."

A slab of wood, even one that had been part of a coffin a hundred years ago, was not going to carry any contagion; Slater was certain of that. But he was also certain of what Dr. Levinson uttered for the both of them next.

"We need to secure the cemetery," she declared, "before any more caskets pop up, and we need to do it as expeditiously, and with as little hoopla, as possible. That kind of quick and thorough work is your specialty, Dr. Slater."

He accepted the compliment without comment. It was a fact.

"And then we will need to exhume one or more of the bodies, take all the usual core samples, and have them meticulously examined and analyzed, under Biohazard 3 protocols." She pursed her lips, and waited. The only sound was the low hum of the air-filtration system that serviced every inch of the institute's offices and laboratories. Her words hung in the air, awaiting a response, but there was only one that Slater could give.

"When do I leave?" he asked.

"Yesterday."

Chapter 6

Her brother's cries split the night, echoing down the long marble corridors and sweeping staircases of the palace. Anastasia—or Ana, for short—sat up in her bed. Her sister Olga was already awake under her own pile of blankets. This had happened so many times before.

"Poor Alexei," Ana said. "It's getting worse again."

"There's nothing you can do," Olga said. "There's nothing any of us can do."

"Dr. Botkin is here."

"There's nothing Dr. Botkin can do, either," Olga said, wearily. "Go back to sleep."

Olga lifted one of her plump pillows and stuck her head under it, but Ana could not fall asleep again. Alexei screamed, there were slippered footsteps running in the hall outside, and Ana had to go and see for herself. She got out of bed, put on a padded robe of Chinese silk—a gift from the always generous Emir of Bokhara—and crept out into the hall. When her little brown spaniel, Jemmy, tried to follow, she nudged her back into the bedroom with her foot.

Several doors down, she could see light spilling from the Tsarevitch's suite of rooms, and she could hear voices in urgent consultation. As the heir to the throne of Russia, Alexei—or Alexis, as he was known outside the family—was the most precious thing in the whole empire, more valuable than Anastasia and her three sisters combined (a point that none of them disputed; it was just a fact of life). But he was also the only one of the five children afflicted with a mortal disease. Hemophilia.

The family had all come to the royal compound only a week before, hoping for some relief from the pressures and public demands of life in the Winter Palace of St. Petersburg. Just fifteen miles from the capital, and reached by a private railway line, Tsarskoe Selo—or, "the tsar's village"—was comprised of eight hundred immaculately groomed and guarded acres, where peacocks strutted with their brilliant tail feathers fanning out and a pack of tame deer roamed free. Cossacks on horseback, with sabers at their sides, rode the iron-fenced perimeters at all hours, and from every window of the two hundred rooms in the palace a strutting sentry could be seen. An additional garrison of five thousand troops was stationed in the nearest village.

Inside the palace, commissioned by Catherine the Great in the eighteenth century, every room was adorned with crystal chandeliers and richly colored Oriental carpets, huge, porcelain stoves warmed the chambers and scented the air. Fresh flowers, from as close as the greenhouses on the grounds, or as far away as the imperial gardens in the Crimea, bloomed in vases everywhere. Scores of liveried footmen, in dozens of different uniforms, silently performed every function from opening doors to carrying bowls of smoking incense from one chamber to another; it was the duty of four in particular—Ethiopians whose skin, Ana thought, glowed as hard and bright as ebony—to precede the Emperor Nicholas, or the Empress Alexandra, into any room. The mere sight of one of these fearsome black servants, in his bejeweled turban, brocade vest, and shining scimitar, alerted everyone within that one of Russia's imperial majesties was about to enter.

Two of these guards were standing now on either side of Alexei's door, but gave no notice of the fourteen-year-old Grand Duchess Anastasia as she scurried into the anteroom. A couple of the young Tsarevitch's consulting physicians were huddled in thought by the fireplace, stroking their chins nervously, while the inner chamber was dimly lighted by electric lamps with heavy, hooded shades. The Empress sat on the bed, her reddish-gold hair piled in a hasty knot atop her head, her long fingers smoothing her son's brow; Dr. Botkin, a stout man who had never once been seen in anything but his black frock coat (he had even worn it on the beach at Livadia, to everyone's amusement), stood beside her, holding a thermometer to the light. He did not look pleased, and when he spoke, Alexandra simply nodded.

Inching into the room, Ana finally could see her younger brother nestled down deep in the bed, with pillows piled up under his head and others raising his swollen leg. The day before, he had taken a spill off a swing—the kind of fall Ana and her sisters would have walked away from with no more than a scraped knee—but for Alexei any such accident could prove fatal. Growing up, Ana and her sisters had been warned a thousand times not to so much as jostle their frail brother. A cut or scratch that looked harmless on the surface could be causing deep and irreparable damage beneath the skin, as the blood—unable to clot—relentlessly hemorrhaged into the joints or muscles. His left leg was swollen now to twice its size, tightly swaddled in gauze that was changed every hour or two as the pooling blood seeped through the pores of his skin. His eyes, normally so bright and mischievous, were sunk deep in his head, surrounded by circles as black as soot.

Their father was in Poland on a diplomatic call, but Ana assumed that, as always, he had received a telegram by now and was hurrying back as fast as the trains and carriages could take him.

The question, each time something like this occurred, was, *Would the young heir survive this latest attack?*

Ana could not imagine such a terrible day. It would be as if the sky itself had fallen. She did not know how her parents—her mother, in particular—would be able to endure such an event. It was unthinkable . . . and so she tried, very hard, never to think about it.

"What are you doing up?" her mother said, suddenly taking note of her. "You should be asleep."

"Will Alexei be all right?"

"Alexei will be all right," Dr. Botkin put in. "We will see him through. You should go back to bed. There's nothing for you to worry about."

Her mother smiled faintly, but unconvincingly, and Ana took a step closer to the bed. Her brother saw her and tried to smile, but a sudden paroxysm of pain arched his back, set his eyes back even farther in his head, and caused him to scream in agony. The Empress clapped her hands over her ears, and then, as if ashamed at her reaction, quickly drew them away and reached for her son's sweaty hands.

The gong on the grandfather clock rang twelve times, and as the last peal faded away there was the sound of sentries' voices, then the clatter of hooves in the courtyard outside. Ana ran to the window and yanked back the heavy drapes, expecting to see her father the Tsar leaping from his carriage, but instead she saw a burly man in a black cassock, dismounting from a swaybacked mare.

It was Grigori Rasputin, the *starets,* or holy man, from Siberia.

Her mother, standing beside her and gripping the curtain with white knuckles, said, "Thanks be to God."

And even Ana offered up a prayer. If anyone could save her brother, it was this monk with the long black beard and the broad hands and the pockmarked face. She had seen him do it before.

Minutes later, he strode into the room, and everyone else in it, even the Tsaritsa, seemed to recede into the shadows. Although his name alone—which meant "dissolute"—should have served as a warning, he was instead treated with civility, and even deference (which was common, as long as Alexandra, his most ardent supporter and friend, was present). His robes were secured by a frayed leather belt, his boots were covered with mud, and he gave off the aroma of a barnyard stall, but it was his eyes that commanded attention. Ana had never seen such eyes as Rasputin possessed—as blue as the Baltic and as penetrating as a dagger. When he presided over the evening prayers of herself and her sisters, she felt that there was nothing he did not know, nothing in her heart he could not see, nothing in her soul he could not forgive. And though he was roughly affectionate with all of the siblings, Ana had always felt that there was a unique bond between the two of them.

"You are the youngest sister," he had once confided to her, "but it is you to whom a special destiny is granted. Even your name— Anastasia—means 'the breaker of chains.' Did you know that, my child?"

So she had heard; in her honor, her father had freed some youthful political prisoners on the day of her birth.

But as for what chains she herself would ever break, the monk had never said, and she had never had the courage to ask.

Her mother was drawing the *starets* toward the bed, and Dr. Botkin diplomatically stepped away. Ana knew that there was no love lost between the doctor and Rasputin, but she also knew that her mother had placed her ultimate faith in the holy man and not the physician. Everyone else knew it, too.

Most of all, Rasputin.

The monk stood at the foot of the bed, towering over the ailing Tsarevitch, and with his eyes raised to heaven, began to murmur a prayer. In one hand, he clutched a heavy pectoral cross— emerald-encrusted and hanging from his neck on a silver chain. Ana had once seen it in the cabinets of her mother's mauve boudoir, along with the rest of the renowned Romanov jewels.

His beard jutted out like a stiff black beehive, and his words rumbled like the echo of a distant train. Low, and constant, and though Ana could barely make out what he was saying, the sound alone was strangely comforting. She could see her brother's tortured eyes turning toward Rasputin, and after a minute or two, his moaning ceased, and his breathing appeared to become more regular. It was a transformation she had seen before though neither she, nor anyone else, seemed to know what caused it. Her mother ascribed it to the power of God—"the Lord speaks through Father Grigori"—but the court physicians remained baffled.

Rasputin came around to the side of the bed and clasped the boy's hands between his own rough paws. "The bleeding will stop," he said, "the pain will go away." He stroked the Tsarevitch's hands, as the Tsaritsa looked on through a flood of her own tears. He repeated these words, again and again, before saying, "You will rest, Alexei. You will rest. And when you wake, you will be better. Your leg will not be so swollen, you will not feel the pain." He leaned forward, his beard covering the boy's face and the emerald cross dangling into the bedclothes, to kiss him lightly on his forehead. "And you will sing out for your oatmeal with honey and jam." He smiled, a smile as crooked as the part that ran down the center of his matted hair, and uttered another prayer under his breath. As he stepped back from the bed, his muddy boots left a puddle on the carpet.

But Alexei wasn't writhing in pain. He was, miraculously, asleep, and with a silent wave of his arms, Rasputin—as if he were the Tsar himself—ushered them all into the next room.

"You, too, little Ana," he whispered, draping a hand on the shoulder of her blue silk robe, before closing the doors to the bedchamber behind him. The emerald cross, swinging against his cassock, winked in the glow from the hearth, and on a sudden impulse, she kissed it.

Rasputin said, "Ah, Christ speaks to you, doesn't he, little one?"

Ana did not know the answer to that, any more than she knew why she had just done what she just did.

But Father Grigori smiled through his broken teeth as if he knew full well.

Chapter 7

Although Dr. Levinson had spoken with a touch of hyperbole, Slater soon discovered that she'd meant what she said. He was instructed to draw up a game plan and risk assessment, a preliminary budget (though Dr. Levinson had made it clear on his way out that cost was to be no object), put together a team of whatever specialists he would require, and have it all on her desk in seventy-two hours. Normally, it was the kind of thing that would have taken weeks, if not months— not only to be put together but to be vetted by everyone else in the chain of command. But again, Dr. Levinson had made it plain that this project would have the highest-priority clearance not only from AFIP, but from the Army, the Air Force, and the Coast Guard, all of which would have to be involved at one stage or another. The Centers for Disease Control in Atlanta had also offered their full cooperation and support. "But I don't want them meddling," Levinson had said. "They take a month to make a cup of coffee."

Dr. Slater had returned to his offices, rolled up his sleeves, and started making out the ideal roster to assist him. He would need a team of people who were as dedicated as they were skilled, and as competent as they were fearless. They would be performing some of the most sensitive and dangerous work imaginable, and under what were sure to be very tricky and adverse conditions. It was one thing to do an autopsy in a state-of-the-art lab; it was altogether another to take organ core samples in an open graveyard, on a freezing island, where the ground beneath your feet could give way at any time. He would have to choose his people very carefully.

First of all, the logistics would be crucial. There would be tons of gear—quite literally—that would have to be brought to the island site. Everything from decontamination tents to jackhammers, generators to refrigerators (even in Alaska). For a job this big and complicated, there was only one man he trusted—Sergeant Jerome Groves, who was due to be redeployed to some hot zone in the Middle East at the end of the week. All things considered, he might be glad to get the call.

Slater put his name at the top of the list.

The next thing he'd need would be that geologist he'd been think-ing about earlier. Before Slater and his team put even one shovel into the earth, they would need to use ground-penetrating radar to assess what lay beneath the soil, and to make sure—before doing irreversible damage—that the coffins, and the bodies inside, had not shifted or become separated from each other over the past century. During a typhoid outbreak in Croatia, he had once worked with a Russian who had read the underground water tables as easily as if he were reading a menu in a restaurant. He was attached at the time to the Trofimuk United Institute of Geology, Geophysics and Mineralogy, the Siberian branch of the Russian Academy of Sciences, but Slater had no idea what he was doing now. Still, Professor Vassily Kozak was the man he wanted, and he added his name to the list.

As for the virology and autopsy work, Slater could take care of most of that himself. But he would still need another pair of hands, and another set of eyes, to assist him in the cemetery, and to help him run the lab. It took him only a few seconds to come up with Dr. Eva Lantos, a virologist with a Ph.D. from M.I.T. and a mind like a steel trap. The last time he'd heard from her, she'd been living in Boston with her latest girlfriend, and working on the mole-rat genome, but if anybody was up for an adventure, it would be Eva.

Slater made a few calls, left a few messages that were, because of the top secret nature of the mission, a lot more cryptic than he'd have liked, and started burrowing through the accompanying paperwork the AFIP had gathered for him. By the time he had written a preliminary request list and sent the memo back to Dr. Levinson's office, he glanced out the window and saw that it was already dark out; he'd forgotten to have lunch and had somehow powered himself through the day with nothing but black coffee and a packet of trail mix he'd found in his desk. As a doctor—particularly one who suffered from recurring bouts of malaria—he knew perfectly well that he needed to keep to a healthy and well-regulated diet, and do whatever he could to lower his stress levels. But that was a laugh, of course. He had no sooner escaped spending five years in the brig than he'd been posted to an Arctic island on a Level-3 mission. Fishing his pill case out of his pocket, he swallowed a couple of Chloriquine tablets, flicked off the desk lamp, and went down to get something to eat.

Because of the erratic schedules of scientists and researchers, the cafeteria was kept open around the clock, so he grabbed a quick sandwich and a Snapple. A couple of people said hi, and "Weren't you overseas somewhere?" and he realized, with relief, that the news of his assault on a commanding officer and his subsequent court-martial hadn't received much play here. The civilians on staff had no idea of its gravity—all they knew about military discipline was what they'd seen on episodes of *JAG*—and the army personnel were so involved in their own projects and plans, they weren't concerned with anyone else's.

He ate alone, and after tossing the sandwich wrapper and the empty bottle into the trash, he considered heading home, but then he thought, to what? An empty apartment? He could always go to the gym and work out, but there was something so forlorn about the gym at night. The fluorescent lights, the acrid odor of sweat that had been building up all day, the weary attendant mopping the locker-room floor. Not to mention all the other guys who, like him, had nowhere better to go.

And even if his body was flagging, his mind was still percolating

just fine right now. That was both his blessing and his curse. It always
had been. If his brain were equipped with an on/off switch, he had yet
to find it. Nights were the worst. His thoughts could take him anywhere and everywhere; it was like a wild ride at an amusement park
that never stopped. And right now the roller-coaster car was hurtling
him along toward one destination in particular—the AFIP Tissue Repository, housed next door in the archives of the old Army Medical
Museum. It had been founded, with his typical foresight and wisdom,
by Abraham Lincoln himself—and it hadn't changed all that much
ever since.

The most comprehensive collection of tissue samples in the world,
the Repository contained over 3 million specimens—among them
pieces of lung tissue from a private at Camp Jackson, South Carolina,
the first American soldier who had succumbed to the 1918 flu. Before
setting out for the wilds of Alaska, Dr. Slater wanted to see the slides
himself and get a look at this ancient enemy he was about to confront.

But when he tried his security card on the main concourse leading
to the museum, he found there was a glitch in his clearance—no
doubt another problem arising from his military discharge. And
though he knew he could get it fixed the next day, that didn't help him
now. He passed the laminated card, which he wore on a chain around
his neck, under the scanner one more time, just for luck, and watched
as the lights stayed red. A third try he suspected would set off an internal alarm. He waited around in the corridor for a minute or two, hoping to piggyback on someone else going his way, but at this time of
night the offices were largely deserted and no one else was around,
much less heading over to the gloomy confines of the old museum.

Still, there was another route, and though it was a lot more circu-
itous, it would allow him to circumvent the particular security system
obstructing him now. Going back toward his office, he took a sharp
right through the environmental and toxicology wing, descended the
fire stairs to the garage level, then walked briskly across the unheated,
and nearly empty, garage. Not briskly enough, he thought, as he felt a
sudden chill. He picked up the pace, scurrying down a flight of crumbling stairs that opened into a subbasement corridor, originally de-

signed for the discreet unloading of cadavers by horse-drawn carriages in the years following the Civil War.

The hallways here were made of red brick, faded with age, and the lights in the ceiling, each one in a little wire nest, were incandescent bulbs, and low-wattage at that. The doors he passed bore frosted-glass panes, with gold hand lettering and labels that read HISTOLOGY, WAR WOUND RECORDS, or DEPARTMENT OF PALEOPATHOLOGY. It was hard to believe that this warren was still occupied, but Slater knew that the whole Walter Reed complex had long since outgrown its campus, and no nook or cranny was allowed to lie fallow for long.

As he turned the corner toward the Tissue Repository, he came upon the old display cases that had once been part of the public exhibitions. Although they were no longer part of any organized tours, the cabinets exhibited, on dusty shelves behind thick glass, a collection of formaldehyde-filled jars. Some of them dated back to the midnineteenth century, and held specimens of gross physical anomalies— twins conjoined at the torso, or fetuses born with the fused legs and feet of *sirenomella* victims. Because of their fishlike tails and amphibious eyes, they were named after the mythical sirens, or mermaids, and had seldom survived their birth by more than a day. Now, many decades later, they still floated, silently, intact, and unchanged, in the limbo of their murky jars.

Just inside the doors to the Repository, a night clerk in a crisply pressed tan uniform, his head down and earbuds in place, was typing away on his computer keyboard. He looked up in surprise when Slater entered, quickly yanked the buds, straightened in his chair, and slid a clipboard across the desk for Slater to sign in.

"I'll need your ID, too," he said. Slater held out his security card, while the clerk jotted down the number, then checked it online against the name on the register. Slater prayed that a problem wouldn't crop up, but the clerk nodded, and said, "What can I do for you, sir?"

Slater explained what he was after, but as the clerk started to get up from his chair, he said, "You can stay put. I know my way around in here, and I can get it myself."

"You sure?" the clerk said, sounding like he'd love to get back to what he'd been doing. Slater caught a glimpse on the computer of some video war game.

"Yes. It won't take me long."

And then, inexplicably, the clerk pulled some Kleenex from a box and handed a wad to Slater.

"What's this for?"

"Pardon my saying so, sir, but you're sweating." He gestured at his forehead, and when Slater dabbed at his skin, the tissues did indeed come away damp.

"Thanks," Slater said, "I guess I was in too big a hurry to get here."

The clerk shrugged and, surveying the spooky vault, said, "That'll be a first, sir."

The Repository was huge, with several chambers interconnecting under brick archways, all of them retrofitted with rows of bright track lights mounted above microscope-equipped workstations. Long aisles were lined with endless rows of metal cabinets, each of them divided into drawers, no deeper than a deck of cards, containing the tissue and bone samples. Organized first by the pathology, then by the organic or anatomical origin, and then again by era, the samples had been gathered and sent to the archives from barracks and battlefields all over the world, and unless size was an issue, the oldest ones in any category were usually deposited in the bottom drawers of each section. It took Slater, who hadn't been down in these archives for several years, a half hour just to find his way into the right corner of the right room. It was the last chamber in the chain, and like all the others he had passed through, no one else was in it.

Crouching down, he pulled out one drawer, checked the samples, closed it, and opened another. Here, he found what he was looking for. The last remains of Private Roscoe Vaughan, an artillery trainee at Camp Jackson, South Carolina, in 1918 . . . and the first known Army casualty of what had been dubbed, however inaccurately, the Spanish flu. Forty-three thousand others would follow him to the grave. Though it was little known, during the Great War, more of the doughboys had died from the flu than in combat.

All that was left of the private now was a block of paraffin, no bigger than a crouton, in which the Army surgeon, Captain K. P. Hedge-forth, had embedded slices of lung tissue he had taken from the dead soldier. Preserved in formaldehyde, the block had been dispatched to Washington and kept there in a little brown box on a shelf for nearly eighty years before its deadly secrets had been explored by AFIP scientists.

Slater took the cube, now in a glassine envelope, and several of the slides that had been prepared from its contents back at Camp Jackson, to the examining table at the far end of the room. All of this material had been declared utterly inert, and was used now solely for teaching and historical research purposes. But samples taken from it in 1996, then put through the polymerase chain reaction, had yielded enough information to enable the institute's pathologists to reconstruct the entire genetic structure of the virus. Unlike this dead source material, the results of those molecular tests were now lodged, under the strictest security precautions, in little vials in a deep freeze in an undisclosed location nearly impossible to access, especially for someone with Dr. Slater's compromised credentials. For him to get in touch with the origins of the epidemic whose victims' graves he was about to desecrate, this musty archival material would be the closest he could come.

But something in his gut had told him that he needed to do it. Although epidemiology was often thought to be a cold-blooded discipline, one where its practitioners exercised objectivity and disinterested judgment in the face of appalling realities, Slater had never approached the job that way. He was a fighter, and in order to fully engage in battle, he needed some visceral sense of his enemy.

Though the electricians had done their best, the lighting at this spot was dicey; the brick ceiling was curved like a barrel, and the illumination from the lights mounted overhead was too bright in some spots and too weak in others. Slater found that he had to pull his stool first this way then that in order to keep the shadows from impinging on his work surface. Behind the walls, he could hear the muffled clanging of old pipes.

Private Vaughan had been a "well-nourished" young man, according to one of the documents he'd read that afternoon; another had called him "chubby." He stood about five feet ten inches, and was, like most of the other infantrymen, eager to get to France before the fighting stopped. He had been trained, in the scrubby dunes around the camp, to maintain and deploy field artillery. But on the morning of September 19, 1918, instead of joining his platoon, he reported to sick bay, complaining of chills and fever. He was suffering from a dry cough, a dull headache, and his face was flushed. Although his heartbeat was regular, his throat was congested, and he said he was having trouble catching his breath. The doctor, who'd seen the flu before, consigned him to a cot.

But this was not like any flu the world had ever encountered.

Over the next few days, Private Vaughan got progressively worse. His fever rose, leaving him delirious much of the time and shivering under a pile of blankets that could never get high enough. His face took on a purplish tinge and his feet turned black. A secondary infection, pneumonia, set in, and his lungs began to fill with mucus. When he tried to speak, bubbles of blood broke on his lips, and while the doctors and nurses looked on in helpless horror, Private Vaughan slowly drowned in his own fluids. At 6:30 A.M. on September 26, he was declared dead.

Private Vaughan was the proverbial canary in the coal mine.

The Spanish flu, so named because it had cut a devastating path through Spain on its way to the New World, would eventually claim the lives of 675,000 American civilians. The body counts in other countries would be immensely higher. And before it had burned itself out, the fate of nations—and the planet itself—would be drastically altered. For those who thought the carnage of the First World War was the worst calamity humanity could endure, the Spanish flu proved them hopelessly mistaken.

Slater looked at the little cube of tissue-impregnated paraffin— once a chunk cut from a candle—and marveled at the devastation that it represented. Powering up the microscope, he slid one of the original slides, prepared by Dr. Hedgeforth, into view; the glass was so much thicker than current slides that he had to lift the eyepiece and do a bit of juggling to make it feasible.

He bent his head, made a few adjustments to the magnification, and observed a pale yellow background—a thin sliver of the paraffin— and in its center a dark smudge, like a crumb of burned toast on a pat of butter.

That smudge was a tiny piece of the private's left lung, which had been so sodden and engorged with blood that Dr. Hedgeforth had said it looked like a slab of liver.

Even after all these years, the slides and candle wax gave off a whiff of formaldehyde, and the scent took Slater back to dissection labs and all-nighters in med school. As he studied the slides, and adjusted the magnification, he was able to bring out, in one of the last, a clearer view not only of the amorphous cells, faintly lavender and forever fixed in their positions, but fragments of the deadly virus that resembled bits of barbed wire. It was, he thought, like looking at an ancient battlefield—a place of death and destruction. You were looking back in time to something that had ended long ago but whose impression was even now unaltered. It was news from a world that had ceased to exist . . . news conveyed, in this instance, by a young soldier whose very essence had returned to the stars.

How long Slater stayed at it, he hardly knew. He lost himself in his research and his thoughts, the silence around him broken only by the occasional, distant clang of the heating pipes behind the old brick walls. In his own way, he was girding himself for combat. The enemy was right here, safely vanquished and preserved beneath the glass slide, but it was the same foe he would soon confront in the Arctic . . . though there, all bets would be off.

His thoughts had become cloudy—and he might even have dozed off on his stool for a few seconds—when he became aware that there was someone in the archway behind him. He slowly turned his head. One of the track lights hit him square in the eyes, and he had to raise one hand to shield his gaze from the glare.

For a split second, it was as if he was looking at the dead doughboy whose tissues he had been studying . . . but then the young man in the uniform spoke.

"We're closing up, sir," the night clerk said. "The archives open again at eight A.M."

Slater nodded, then removed the last slide from the microscope, put the paraffin cube back into its glassine envelope, and slipped off his stool. He wobbled for a moment, but he ascribed that to having sat in one position for too long, and a precarious position to boot. He just needed to get the sample and the slides back in the drawer, go home, and get a good night's rest.

Even the empty apartment seemed beckoning now.

Making his way under the archways, he felt an unexpected draft at his back and had to control the impulse to shiver as he passed the clerk, standing at the door with a set of keys dangling in one hand. It was only when he had rounded the corner and was safely out of the clerk's sight that Slater dared to take his pill case from his pocket and, while leaning up against the redbrick wall of the corridor outside, quickly down a couple of the antimalarial pills dry.

Physician, he thought, with his eyes closed and his head spinning, *heal thyself.*

But when he opened his eyes again, his gaze was met by the silent stare of the siren baby, forever swimming in its formaldehyde jar. Would the Russian corpses, he wondered, be so well and safely preserved?

Chapter 8

Harley Vane had been telling his story for days, but he was fast running out of new people to tell it to. By now, everyone had heard about how he had been out on deck overseeing the retrieval of the old casket, while Lucas Muller, that college boy, had altered the course of the boat to carry it too close to the rocks off St. Peter's Island.

"I never should have left him alone at the wheel," Harley had mused aloud to a reporter for the *Barrow Gazette,* "but I always liked to give a kid a chance."

He'd also recounted how, after the boat had hit the rocks, he had single-handedly carted Richter the engineer up from the hold—"the old man was drowning in a sea of crabs"—and tried to get him into the lifeboat, only to find that the crew had already launched it. Shaking his head, he had told the local reporter, "If they'd just waited, I could have gotten them all out of there alive."

It was only when he had assured himself that no one else was still aboard, and the *Neptune II* was lost, that he had reluctantly plunged into the churning sea and taken his miraculous trip to shore atop the carved coffin lid. "Sometimes, I wish I'd just let myself go down with the ship and my crew," he'd mused, while the *Gazette*'s photographer had taken a shot of him gazing soulfully out to sea.

Not that many of the locals believed it, however. Port Orlov was a tiny town, and the Vane boys had lived there their whole lives. Their mother had absconded back when they were kids—"bewitched," their father had said, "by a local shaman"—and the boys had grown up wild and, as they got older, downright dangerous. Charlie, the older one, had led the way, breaking and entering other folks' cabins when they were off on hunting trips, fouling another boat's halibut with gasoline to raise the price of his own, and finally wrecking the first *Neptune* by falling asleep, drunk and stoned, at the wheel. The boat had run out of fuel at sea, gotten caught up in some ice, and crumpled like a tin can. After that, nobody would sail with Charlie Vane at the helm. Now, with the *Neptune II* at the bottom of the sea, it looked like nobody was likely to join a crew if Harley was in command, either.

"Hail the conquering hero," Charlie said, dryly, when Harley showed up at the family homestead. It was a rambling old structure with a lighted cross mounted on the roof like an antenna. The whole house was raised a few feet off the ground on cement pylons, and so ill conceived and built that every room felt like it had been an add-on. The floors sloped, the ceilings were either too low or too high, and ramps had been placed anywhere that Charlie's wheelchair would have trouble going. After sinking the boat, Charlie had tried to operate a nautical sales franchise, but a couple of months in, he'd tried to run the rapids at Heron River Gorge, at the full height of the spring runoff, and when his canoe cratered on the rocks, he'd emerged a paraplegic. The burglary rate around town had dropped precipitously in the immediate aftermath of the accident. "Come on into the meeting room," he said, turning the chair down a wooden ramp.

What Charlie called the meeting room was a big raw space with a timbered ceiling and a dozen old rugs thrown on the floor to keep the cold from coming through. A stack of folding chairs leaned against one wall, in case he ever got more than a few people to attend one of his Sunday prayer meetings. In the two years since his accident, he'd claimed to have found God, and to spread the word he'd started an online ministry called Vane's Holy Writ, which was a strange brew of evangelism, antigovernment polemics, and conspiracy theory. Harley, who had glanced at the site once or twice and even attended a couple of the prayer meetings, was never entirely sure if his brother actually believed the crazy shit he was saying or was just pulling another con. Once he'd even asked him, point-blank, if he was serious, and Charlie had indignantly ordered him out of the house.

But that could have been part of the con, too.

"You want some tea?" he asked, and Harley, who was frozen stiff from the long walk to the house, said okay, even though the tea in Charlie's house was all but undrinkable.

"Tea!" Charlie shouted, propelling his chair over a knotty patch where the rugs overlapped. On the trestle table he used as a desk, he had two computers—one for what he called his research, and the other permanently displaying his website and its logo: a timber wolf, fangs bared, defending a wooden cross.

Harley flopped down on a dilapidated armchair that smelled like a wet dog.

"So," Charlie said, rubbing his stubbly chin with one hand, "I've been reading about your adventures. You're a hero. What's it feel like?"

"It's all right," Harley said.

"Just all right?" Charlie scoffed. "I'd have thought you'd be on top of the world by now—or at least on top of Angie Dobbs."

That was just the kind of remark that got Harley so confused. On the one hand, his brother went around claiming to be a man of God, all pure and everything, and on the other he was exactly the same mocking asshole he'd always been—at least when nobody else was around to hear him.

"You make any money off of it yet?" Charlie asked. "I saw that article in the *Barrow Gazette*, and I bet you gave 'em the interview for free. You did, didn't you?"

"You don't *charge* to be in the paper."

"That's what they tell you, but you think movie stars and singers and baseball players don't get paid every time they open their mouths?"

"I'm not a movie star."

"No," Charlie said, "that's for damn sure."

Rebekah, Charlie's wife, came in with a tray of tea and some muffins that would probably taste just as bad. Harley had never been asked to any wedding, and he strongly doubted there'd been one, but then his brother had probably claimed to have channeled the Holy Spirit directly. Rebekah was a scrawny woman, and his brother had found her on the Internet, when she responded to his online ad for a "helpmeet." She'd brought her younger sister Bathsheba along, too. She poured out the tea, made from tree bark or anything else that contained no caffeine—all stimulants were against his brother's religion now—and served up the muffins that were sure to contain no sugar or spice of any kind. Harley figured she made them from sawdust left lying around the wood chipper out back.

Harley said hi, but Rebekah, in her usual long dress with its buttoned-up collar, just nodded. On her way out, she said to Charlie, "We're almost out of fuel oil." She had a thick New England accent—she was from some hick town not much bigger than Port Orlov—where she'd been living in a so-called Christian commune that had been broken up by the state. Still, Harley often wondered what had made her, and her sister, do something so stupid as to come all this way to Alaska.

Charlie grunted and, once she was gone, picked up where he'd left off. "Maybe you oughta let me handle the press from now on."

"There's not much left of it. Nobody's called me today, except the Coast Guard. They want to know more about that coffin top that came up in the nets."

"What'd they say, exactly?"

Harley knew that his brother would be intrigued by that. "They want to be sure that's all that came up."

"That's what you told 'em, right?"

"What do you think?" Harley said, looking steadily into his brother's dark eyes. "Of course I did." He sipped the hot tea, which tasted like it was made from boiled leather.

Charlie met his gaze and didn't blink.

Screw it, Harley thought; *it was now or never.* "You came to the hospital," he said, pointedly, "and you left with my anorak."

"What about it? You want your coat back, it's in the hall closet."

Harley put the cup down on a stack of old newspapers, went out into the hall, and came back with his coat. He sat down and began rummaging through the various zipped pockets, and apart from a packet of throat lozenges, came up empty-handed. "Okay," he said, "where is it?"

"Where's what?" Charlie answered, but with that malicious glint in his eye that told Harley he knew perfectly well what he was talking about. It was like they were kids again, and Charlie was holding out on him.

"You know what. The cross that was in the inside pocket."

Charlie's face slowly creased into a grin, revealing a row of crooked gray teeth. "What cross?"

Harley put out his hand and said, "Give it to me, Charlie."

"Or what? Are you gonna beat up your own brother—your own crippled brother?"

Nobody ever milked a wheelchair the way his brother did. "If I have to, I'll turn this whole goddamned house upside down."

"Oh, I don't think Rebekah and Bathsheba would let that happen," Charlie said, and Harley knew he was right. The two sisters might be bony as skeletons, but they were tough and, though he hated to admit it, scary as hell. Their eyes were black as little pebbles, set in dead-white, pockmarked faces, and he'd once seen Rebekah wring a fox's neck without even looking down at it. Even scarier, he had the impression Bathsheba kind of had a crush on him. It was one more reason he'd had to move out.

Before the stalemate went on much longer, Charlie seemed to have tired of the joke, and gesturing at the gun rack below the window, he said, "It's in the ammo drawer."

For a split second, Harley wondered if the ammo drawer was booby-trapped, but then opened it and found the cross, wrapped in a clean rag. It looked like Charlie had shined it up a bit, and the stones—emeralds, for sure—glistened in the light from the computer screens.

"Lucky you didn't shoot your mouth off about that," Charlie said.

Harley turned it over in his hands, marveling at the weight of it, wondering if the silver sheen was real, wondering what the gems would be worth, wondering what the Russian words inscribed on the back meant. There was a fence named Gus Voynovich in Nome—he and Charlie had used him now and then in the past—and if anybody knew what it was really worth, he'd be the one. The guy was a crook, of course, but he knew his business.

"So I figure it's a fifty-fifty deal," Charlie said.

"What are you talking about?"

"You're going to fence it at the Gold Mine, right?" The Gold Mine was Voynovich's pawnshop in Nome. "Well, you owe me half of whatever Voynovich gives us for it."

"That's bullshit. I found it. I nearly *died* getting it."

"And if I hadn't picked up your coat, the Coast Guard, or some fucking orderly, would have it by now. And then how much of a share do you think you'd have gotten?"

"I'll give you ten percent."

"I'm not arguing about this with you, Harley. I could just as soon have taken a gun out of that rack and told you to get the hell off of church property." Vane's Holy Writ was headquartered in the old house, and as a result, Charlie paid no property taxes. He also drew a tidy disability benefits check every month. "Now, there's really only one question left for us to discuss."

"What the hell is that?"

"How much else is there?"

"How much of what else? The coffin's gone, it sank, same as the boat. Don't you read the papers?"

"The coffin came from somewhere. And that somewhere would be St. Peter's Island. It's one of those old Russians who lived there. Who knows what else is buried in the other graves?"

Harley sat very still, the cross growing heavier in his hand by the second. "What are you saying?"

"I'm saying, we've got to go back out there, before somebody else does, and do some digging."

"You want me to dig up graves?" Harley said, feeling exactly the same way he did when Charlie had told him to climb through the skylight of the liquor store on Front Street.

"Listen to me," Charlie said, leaning forward in his wheelchair. "Don't you remember the stories?"

"Sure I do. The damn place is haunted." He didn't add anything about the black wolves . . . or that yellow light he thought he'd seen on the cliffs.

"Now you don't really believe that stuff, do you? If you ask me, the Russians made up all that crap years ago, just to keep everybody off the island."

"There was never any reason to go *on* the island."

"No, there wasn't," Charlie agreed. "Back then." Everyone knew there was nothing on St. Peter's but the remains of the old Russian village, its wooden cabins no doubt fallen to pieces by now, and guarded, supposedly, by an old lady with a lantern, who walked the cliffs at night, luring mariners to their death. "But there is a reason now."

Harley didn't know what to say, or how to counter what his brother was saying. That's how it had always been. Charlie had always won the arguments—sometimes all at once, and sometimes just by waiting Harley out.

"What other options have you got?" Charlie taunted him. "You think you're ever gonna get another boat? Or a crew? Your fishing days are over, bro, in case you didn't know it already." He smiled broadly and smoothed his hands on the front of his flannel shirt. "This cross is what I'd call heaven-sent . . . and one thing I do know is that God doesn't knock twice."

Harley wasn't so sure it was God knocking at the door at all.

But nodding at the Russian artifact, Charlie added, "And you might want to leave that here for safekeeping. That tin-can trailer you live in isn't exactly burglarproof, now is it?"

Chapter 9

Slater wasn't proud of what he was doing—sitting in his car, in the dark, parked outside his ex-wife's house—but he hadn't really intended to find himself here.

At most, he'd intended to cruise slowly past the house and take a look on his way home from the AFIP, but then a wave of exhaustion suddenly overcame him, and he'd had to pull over under the umbrella of a big elm tree. In preparation for the exhumation work in Alaska, he'd put himself on an antiviral regimen that he knew could have some debilitating effects, and the coffee he'd picked up at Starbucks apparently wasn't doing much to counteract it.

Once he'd parked, he'd turned off his lights, reclined his seat, and looked out his window at the stately Tudor house, with its white walls and its neat brown trim, its gabled roof and trim hedges. Even the driveway didn't have a leaf on it. It was like a picture from a magazine. The first floor was dark, except for the porch light, but the windows upstairs were lighted, and once in a while he could see someone moving behind the mullioned glass. Martha and her husband had two kids, a boy and a girl.

The whole thing, he thought, couldn't be more perfect. And it could have been his . . . if he'd wanted it.

He'd met Martha when they were both in medical school at Johns Hopkins. She was paying her own way, while his was being bankrolled by the Army. When he went off to Georgetown to pursue his studies in epidemiology, she had followed him there, working on her specialty in dermatology. After they got married, he knew what she was hoping for—she wanted him to hold down a nice safe Army post on the grounds of the Walter Reed Army Medical Center while she built up her private practice in the Washington suburbs. And for a time, he tried. He did the whole office and administrative thing, shuffling paper, attending meetings, giving lectures, but over time he felt more and more restless. It got especially bad when he received reports from the field, detailed accounts of what was being done on the front lines to save lives and eradicate disease. That was what he had trained for, that was what he wanted to be doing—not sitting in an air-conditioned office, evaluating programs and rubber-stamping reports. He had put in for overseas duty, and Martha had reluctantly agreed to let him try it.

But if she hoped he would get it out of his system, she was wrong. The more he did it, the more he wanted to do. After a year or two, he no longer felt out of place in some godforsaken jungle; he felt out of place at a cocktail party in Chevy Chase. And much as he and Martha loved each other, they both recognized that they were going in separate directions. The night she dropped him off at the base for his morning flight to an Army camp in the Dominican Republic, where there'd been an outbreak of dengue fever, she said good-bye and take good care of yourself, but they'd both known it was more than that. When he came back nine weeks later, he opened the door to their condo with a sense of foreboding in his heart; the letter he found waiting for him on the kitchen counter said everything he'd expected, but he'd still had to read it several times just to absorb every word. To this day, if he'd had to, he could recite it line for line.

Slater took a sip of his coffee, cold now, and watched as an upstairs window was cranked open a few inches and a curtain drawn. He thought he caught a snatch of conversation on the wind, a boy's voice saying something about homework, and a woman's laugh. Martha's laugh. A few seconds later, the light went out.

Slater put his seat back even farther and closed his eyes. God, he was tired. It was cold out, but he still had his coat on, and it wasn't bad inside the car. And it had been such a long day. Long, but productive. At least the mission was chugging along, and his dream team was coming together nicely. Dr. Eva Lantos had jumped at the chance to get out of her lab in Boston—"I will be so glad to give the mole-rat genome a rest!"—and Vassily Kozak had been tracked down to an industrial waste dump on the outskirts of Irkutsk, where he was completing a study of the chemical pollutants in the soil.

"I have recommended," he said in his heavily accented English, "they should shut the city of Irkutsk, but they do not like this idea."

"I'm not surprised."

"Not me either."

Slater had told him, in strictest confidence, what he wanted him for in Alaska. Vassily had listened carefully as Slater continued to outline the task ahead, finally interrupting only to ask, "This Spanish flu—it killed many Russians?"

"Ten or twelve million, by the best estimates," Slater replied.

"Do you think that it is still infectious?"

Slater knew that Vassily was asking him an honest question, and all he could do was give him the straightest answer he could. "No, I don't believe it is," he said, "but I can't guarantee anything."

Russians, even now, knew something about death—the twentieth-century toll, from warfare and disease, had been extraordinary by any measure. Other nationalities sometimes forgot their own past disasters, but for Russians a dreadful knowledge was bred in their bones, and Slater respected the caution it inspired to this day. "If you come, I'll want you to start on an antiviral regimen right now, the same one everyone else on the team will be on—myself included."

"And you will send me the names of these drugs?"

"I'll do better. I'll have them hand-delivered to you in Irkutsk."

Vassily grunted, still thinking things over, as Slater explained some of the clearances that Vassily would have to get both from the Academy of Sciences on the Russian end, and the National Security Council, the AFIP, and maybe even the FBI on the other. And when he was done, he said, "I rest my case," and waited for the verdict.

"I think maybe," the professor said, "I have done enough in Irkutsk."

Slater smiled and clenched his fist in triumph.

"And it would be a good thing, yes, to work with you again. Maybe we can make some history."

Although history was the one thing Slater hoped they would *not* be making—his most fervent wish was that the mission would prove in the end to have been utterly unnecessary—he would take his victories any way he got them.

Now, only one big piece of the team was still lacking, and that afternoon Slater had driven over to the base at Fort McNair. The adjutant told him where to find Sergeant Groves, and he'd entered the gym as inconspicuously as possible. He hung out by the back, watching the bout, and even though Groves and his opponent were wearing padded gloves and helmets, every blow echoed with a thud.

The other soldiers had abruptly curtailed their workouts, dropping their jump ropes, giving the punching bags a rest, holding the dumbbells down by their sides. This was simply too good a match to ignore.

For somebody built like a bulldog, Groves was surprisingly nimble on his feet, bobbing and weaving his way around the ring. The other fighter was a white guy with a longer reach, though, and a couple of inches on him. A few times he let loose with a long, looping punch that caught the sergeant on his shoulder or the side of his head. Once, Groves was even rocked back on his heels by a powerful shot to the ribs.

But each time he was hit, he put his head down lower and came in again, like Mike Tyson minus the Maori tattoos.

A bell went off, and the two fighters immediately let their arms fall and retired to their respective stools. Groves had his head down, and was sipping water through a straw.

"The sergeant can really kick ass," a soldier in a West Point T-shirt observed.

"You better believe it," Slater replied.

"I hear he's done three tours over there."

"Four."

The soldier glanced at Slater, who was unfamiliar and looked out of place in his civilian clothes—jeans and a white shirt, under an overcoat—and no doubt wondered how he knew. There was the staccato rattle of a punching bag being put back to use.

The bell rang again, and the two fighters got up and started circling the center of the ring. Groves was gleaming with sweat, but otherwise looked like he was raring to go. The other guy, however, was holding his hands a little lower, his shoulders were sagging, and halfway through the round he was throwing wild punches that failed to connect with anything.

"Oh yeah, Groves is gonna take him out," the West Pointer said.

And true to the prediction, Groves waited no more than thirty seconds before moving in like a locomotive and unleashing a sudden volley of blows that sent his opponent not only against the ropes, but unexpectedly through them. The guy landed on the mat, spitting out his mouth guard and huffing for breath, while a pal helped him off with his helmet.

"Jesus, Groves," the guy said, "take it easy." He took another breath. "It's not like there's a purse."

Groves spat out his own mouthpiece, and said, "Gotta fight like there is, Lieutenant. You always gotta fight like there is."

Groves separated the ropes and stepped down from the ring. He was sitting on the bench, putting his gear back in his bag, when Slater left the corner of the gym and said, "So, is this your idea of downtime?"

The sergeant didn't have to look up. "Hey, Frank—I've been expecting you."

"That was a nice fight."

Groves snorted and vigorously rubbed a towel over the top of his sweaty, shaved head.

Slater sat down on the bench. "When are you supposed to deploy?"

"Next Friday, with the Eighth Battalion."

"Where?"

"Does it matter?" Groves said. "It'll be 110 in the shade, with all the sand you can eat."

Slater nodded as a couple of other guys clambered into the ring. "I don't see how I can compete with that," he joked. "Sounds like a regular resort."

Groves zipped up his bag, then turned toward Slater, who saw now that his lip was split.

"I got your messages," Groves said, "but I still don't get it."

"Get what?"

"Why you're going out on another job—and in Alaska, of all places—when you've just been busted from the corps."

"I'm going strictly as an epidemiologist. No Army this time, just civilian AFIP."

"And do they know that you still get the shakes from the malaria? Since you're the one who brought up the idea of taking time off, don't you think you need to take a nice long furlough yourself?"

"I never know what to do with it," Slater said, in what even he considered the understatement of the year. "And at least it won't be the Middle East this time. Nobody's shooting at anybody. It's strictly medical research."

"Then why do you need me?" the sergeant asked.

"Because I need someone I can trust to help me run the operation. In one week, we're going to be off-loading roughly three tons of equipment on an island that I'm told is nearly inaccessible. There's no place for a plane to land, no safe harbor for a ship of any size. We're going to have to bring in the supplies by chopper, a lot like we did in Afghanistan, and we've got to hit the ground running."

Groves blew out a breath and looked up as two new fighters feinted and jabbed.

"Why now? Why this time of year?"

"Why not?" Slater said, "It's the holiday season—where would you rather be than the Arctic?"

"It's dark there. Almost all the time. Anybody think of that?"

"Yes, of course we have," Slater replied. Indeed, artificial illumination was one of the first things he had entered into the budget proposal—klieg lamps, ramp lights, and backup generators to make sure they never went down. When dealing with viral material, inert or not, a lighting malfunction could be as dangerous as a refrigeration failure. "But the job can't wait."

One of the fighters in the ring landed a low blow, and the other one complained loudly.

"Walk it off!" Groves shouted.

The match resumed, and Slater waited. In spite of all the sergeant's objections, Slater knew his man. The call to duty in Afghanistan would be strong, but the plea from his old major would be stronger. Groves's sense of loyalty wouldn't allow him to let Slater go off on his own, much less after such a personal appeal.

"I've already got my orders," Groves finally said without taking his eyes from the ring. The two fighters were in a clinch, heads butting like rams. "Who's gonna get my deployment changed?"

"Don't sweat it. Everything will be taken care of." Slater put out his hand and said, "Don't forget to pack warm."

"Yeah," the sergeant replied, taking his hand resignedly, "I'll do that."

All in all, Slater thought, it had been a successful day. What he needed now was a good, solid night's rest. Looking down the suburban street, he saw a door open, a dog come out and lift its leg on a tree, then scamper back inside. Still feeling drowsy from the drugs, he heated up the car, then closed his eyes, for what he planned would be a ten-minute nap before driving the rest of the way home. But when he awoke, stiff and sore in his seat, he heard a light tapping on his window. When he opened his eyes, Martha was standing there in a jogging suit, a key in her hand.

Slater, suitably mortified, touched the button and the window rolled down.

"Please don't tell me you've been here all night," she said.

Slater glanced at his watch. It was five thirty in the morning. A

gray dawn was breaking. Christ, he wondered, was he becoming nar-
coleptic from all the drug interactions?

"Don't tell me you jog at this hour," he said, hoping to strike a tone
that would mask his embarrassment.

Martha shook her head ruefully. "You want to come in and
warm up?"

"I don't think that would be such a good idea."

"No," she said, "it wouldn't."

There was an awkward moment before Martha said, "I'm glad the
court-martial went as well as it did."

"All things considered," he said, "I got lucky."

"So, are you posted here in the States again?"

"Not for long."

"Where are you going next?"

"It's classified," he said, and they both smiled. They had had almost this identical conversation so many times in the past that to be
having it again now—on a chilly suburban street, with Martha in her
jogging suit and Slater slumped in his car—struck them both as ab-
surd.

For a moment, they held each other's gaze, with a thousand things
to say but all of them said before. For Slater, it was like looking at a
vision of what might have been, the life he could have led—and right
now, with his back feeling like a plank and his legs half-asleep and his
brain in a muddle—it didn't look so bad. He had to keep himself from
lifting one cold hand through the window simply to caress her cheek
for a moment. As part of the annual exam for field epidemiologists
deployed on high-stress missions, an Army psychiatrist had recently
told him there was a notable lack of intimacy in his life. "You can't run
from it forever," he'd said. "Given what you face on the job, you're
going to need some human anchor, some safe harbor, in your life."
After a pause, the shrink had added, "Or else you can find yourself
drifting off the emotional map and into uncharted waters."

Slater knew he was right, because look where he had just washed
up. "Well, okay then," he said, as if he and his ex had just concluded

the most casual confab. Turning the key in the ignition, he said, "It's been great catching up."

"Yeah," she said, playfully batting at his window as he raised it, "don't be a stranger." She had a bittersweet smile on her face, and for a second or two he wondered if she, too, had been running through that same little might-have-been scenario.

He lifted a hand in farewell as he pulled the car away from the curb, and then he slowed down to watch in his rearview mirror as she set off down the street, an ever-diminishing figure in a blue jogging suit. She turned the corner without looking back and, like so much in his life, was gone.

Chapter 10

Port Orlov wasn't always called that. Originally, it was a little Inuit village, built to take advantage of a natural harbor. For hundreds of years, the natives had lived in rough but sturdy dwellings made of caribou hides and sealskins, each family's totem pole raised beside the door. Their slender kayaks, in which they had chased down bowhead whales migrating through the Bering Strait, had lined the shore.

But in the late 1700s, one of the many Russian trading vessels that ventured into these waters in search of furs, skins, and walrus tusks had discovered the village, and there the Russians had enacted the same play—the same grim tragedy—as they had all over the Aleutian islands and along the coast of what the natives themselves called Al-ak-shak, or "Great Land." First, the visitors came in peace, offering to buy all the sea-otter pelts and ivory and bearskins that the Inuits had on hand. Then they traded rum and guns for as much as the native hunters could go out and capture. Then, when the Inuits began to offer some resistance—arguing that to kill so many of the creatures, and in such a wanton manner, was not only wrong, but ultimately threatening to the natives' way of life—the Russians savagely beat them into submission, enslaving and slaughtering them by the thousands. By the time Captain Orlov and his like were done, less than a hundred years later, the Inuits, who had numbered over eighteen thousand on their arrival, had been winnowed down to a precious few, and the otters, cormorants, and sea lions that they had once relied upon for their own survival had been hunted to the brink of extinction.

The old totem pole in town had the faces of some of these creatures carved into it—the otters and wolves playing an especially prominent role—but nowadays the pole was leaning at a crazy angle, and nobody had gotten around to righting it. A fresh coat of paint wouldn't have been amiss, either.

Harley Vane, the hood of his coat pulled up over his head and his hands stuffed deep into the pockets of his parka, kicked some gravel at it as he passed—he wasn't into any of that native shit. He was headed for the town bar, the Yardarm, to do a little business. It was only four thirty in the afternoon, but the daily ration of sunlight was already long gone. From now on, the days would only get shorter and shorter—comprising at best an hour or two of light at midday—before the hazy sun sank below the horizon again and the stars filled the sky. The street, inordinately wide to allow for the occasional, sixteen-wheel big rig, was rutted and cracked. And, apart from the snowplow rumbling past, deserted.

In front of the Yardarm, Harley saw the usual array of rusty pickups and dented vans, including—just as he expected—Eddie Pavlik's plumbing truck. Eddie did more business selling grass out of the back of that truck than he ever did rooting out clogged pipes.

Harley stepped into the noisy bar and threw his hood back. The sudden rush of the warm air made his hair frizz out, and he quickly smoothed it down before Angie Dobbs could catch sight of him. He spotted her now, in her waitress apron, delivering a pizza to some clowns sitting near the pool tables. Eddie was racking up the balls for Russell Wright.

Harley must have walked through this room, crammed with wooden tables and chairs, sawdust on the floor, maybe a thousand times, but ever since the night of the accident at sea he felt like things were different, like people were looking at him. At first, he was convinced they were all impressed—his picture had been in the papers, and the story he'd told was pretty amazing. Nobody else had made it out alive. But now, he got a different vibe.

Sometimes he felt like they were snickering at him behind his back.

"Hey," he said as Russell squinted down the length of his pool cue. Eddie was leaning against the wall nursing a beer. Harley wondered if Angie had noticed him yet.

"Hey," they both replied, but Russell, the quiet one, started methodically putting away the balls, while Eddie went off on one of his typical tears. "You see that California is going to legalize pot? You see where it's going to be on the ballot and everything? Shit, I don't know whether to go down there and plant a hundred acres of the shit, or get one of those medical dispensary licenses—they've got those in a lot of states now—where you're allowed to sell the stuff and use it with no hassles. I mean, you tell me why the government gets to tell me what I can, and cannot, put in my own body. Where is *that* in the Constitution?"

With Eddie, most things eventually came back to the Constitution, which Harley was one hundred percent certain he had never read. Neither had Harley, of course, so for all he knew, it really did include a whole long list of things you could and could not put in your body. But right now, it seemed like a very good idea to put a beer in.

Angie was still handing out bottles and glasses. Her blond hair was all frizzed out, too, but it just made her look hot. She had a silver ring through her lower lip and a tattoo on her shoulder that said MICK— the name of a guy she'd had a baby with when she was sixteen. Sometimes Harley would see the kid around town with his grandmother, who was raising him.

"You get in any more newspapers?" Eddie asked. "I swear, you should call up some of those TV shows, like *Deadliest Catch*."

"Yeah," Russell said, having just scratched on the cue ball, "you could reenact the shipwreck—"

"And maybe you could even get somebody to make a movie of it. You could buy yourself a new boat with the money."

"And a new crew," Russell said, "while you're at it."

Eddie laughed and clapped his hands together. "Yeah, man, and good luck with that!" He bent over double, laughing, and that's when Harley realized how drunk he was. "They'll be fighting for that gig." Then he tried to line up his own shot and missed it altogether.

But this was exactly what Harley meant about the weird new vibe he got in town. At first it was all like, thank God the sea had spared even one, but then it started to be something else. People who knew him—and who didn't in a town the size of Port Orlov?—looked at him sideways. Harley started to think that they didn't believe him— at least not entirely. And when Lucas Muller's dad had bumped into him at the lumberyard, he'd stared him down. Harley figured it was because he'd laid the blame on Lucas for the shipwreck. Harley had tried to stare back just as hard, but he lost. Then Muller handed him a leaflet that said there would be a memorial service for all the lost crewmen on the coming Sunday, at the town church.

"I expect they'll want you to say a few words," Muller said. "You think you can do that?"

He sounded like he didn't think so, which was why Harley said, "Sure. No problem."

The only reason the service had been put off so long was they were waiting to see how many bodies they could recover first. They'd found three—Lucas, Farrell, and that Samoan. Two others, Kubelik and Old Man Richter, were still missing.

Harley spotted Angie coming their way. She had a bowl of un-shelled peanuts and three beers on the tray.

"Bring 'em *on*!" Eddie said, snaring two bottles and putting one of them aside for Russell, who was now back to shooting.

Angie handed the last one to Harley and said, "I hear you're talk-ing at the church next Sunday."

"Yeah," Harley said, "everybody's been asking me to." He threw ten bucks onto her tray.

"I'm getting off tonight at nine."

"That right?" he stammered.

"Uh-huh. And my mom's got little Mick."

Why she'd named the baby after that creep, who hadn't even stuck around long enough to see it get born, never failed to baffle Harley.

"I could come over," she said.

"Sure," Harley said, trying not to sound too eager. "I think I'll be around."

"Hey, Angie!" one of her customers called, waving an empty bottle. "We're dry over here!" It was Geordie Ayakuk, who worked at the Inuit Community Affairs Center. Harley had never liked him, and liked him even less for breaking up his moment.

But once Angie was gone, and Eddie and Russell had tired of playing pool—with no money left to wager, they got bored fast—Harley was able to work his way around to what he'd come to talk to them about. At a table jammed between the jukebox and the men's room door, they huddled over their beers and a bowl of unshelled peanuts while Harley did his best to pitch them his—or, more accurately, his brother Charlie's—idea.

"I saw it myself, with my own eyes," Harley said, as the two men listened closely. Eddie's work shirt smelled like he hadn't changed it since his last plumbing job, and Russell's sleeves were rolled up to show the tattoo he'd given himself when he was in solitary at the Spring Creek Correctional Facility. It was supposed to be an eagle, but it had come out looking more like a bat.

"If you saw jewels, why didn't you take them right then?" Russell said. "Before the ship went down?"

"Because I didn't know that the ship was going to go down," Harley explained, for the second time. "Obviously, if I'd known that, I'd have taken the damn thing then and there." He did not consider it wise to let on that he'd actually snagged the cross; if he did, he'd have Eddie and Russell trying to rob him next.

"And you say it was what?" Eddie asked. "A necklace with emeralds in it?"

"Maybe. But like I said, it was hard to get a good look 'cause the crack in the lid wasn't very big."

"Maybe that was all that there is," Russell said, cracking open another peanut. "What makes you think there's more out there?"

"I don't know," Harley said. "I'm not making any promises. But if there's other coffins popping out of the ground like this one did, then who knows what they've got inside?"

While Russell remained dubious, Eddie, Harley could see, was starting to get excited. "Didn't you guys ever hear the stories?" Eddie said. "My uncle used to tell me about how there were these crazy Russians, a long time ago, who'd escaped from Siberia and settled out on the island because nobody could ever get to them there. They had a secret religion and lived there without any contact with the mainland."

"How'd they get away with that?" Russell said. "That's American territory."

"Actually, it belonged by treaty to the fuckin' natives around here," Harley explained, "who saw enough wampum and said you can have it. And nobody's gone there since because it's got such a bad rep."

"You mean because they all died out there?"

"Yeah," Harley said. "And those black wolves don't help any, either." He could still see that alpha wolf, leaping up at his foot as the Coast Guard chopper hauled his frozen ass up off the beach. "Even the Inuit don't go there because they say the place is haunted."

"What a load of shit," Russell said.

"Exactly," Harley said, as convincingly as he could. "Exactly." That yellow light could have been a total illusion. "It's all bullshit. The real reason nobody goes out there is because it's a bitch and a half just to find any way onto the island. Those rocks have fucked me up once already, and I do not mean to get fucked again."

"You guys need another round?" Angie said, stopping at their table with a fresh bowl of peanuts. "I'm going off duty in an hour," she added, throwing a significant look at Harley.

"Yeah, sure," Harley said, "I'm buying."

"Be right back."

"I hear she's got a ring through her nipple, too," Eddie observed, "just like the one through her lip." Harley could hardly wait to find out.

"How much do we get again?" Russell asked.

"Because it's my idea, I'm taking seventy-five percent of whatever we find," Harley said. Half of that, he knew, he would have to give to Charlie. "The rest of it you two can split."

Russell was plainly mulling it over while Eddie was already counting his money. "I bet we can use the *Kodiak,*" he said, referring to his uncle's runty old trawler. "Half the time he's too drunk to go out fishing anyway."

"And we'll need some shovels, maybe a hacksaw and a blowtorch, too," Harley said. "Even if the coffins are only a foot or two down, it's going to be a nightmare getting through the permafrost."

Angie plunked the beers down, and Harley paid again. He had half a mind to take the bar bill out of their cut.

They fell silent until Geordie Ayakuk had finished lumbering past their table to the men's room, then Harley said in a low voice, "So, do you want to do this thing or not?"

"Definitely," Eddie said, slapping his palm on the table and scattering peanut shells everywhere.

Russell still looked dubious.

"What's bothering you?" Harley asked.

Russell stirred in his seat and rubbed the tat on his forearm. "We're diggin' people up. Dead people, in their graves. That's not right."

"We're not going to take them out, for Christ's sake," Eddie expostulated. "Two minutes and they're all covered up again, just like always."

Geordie came out of the men's room, and as he passed Harley he chortled, "You been on *Dancing with the Stars* yet?"

"Stay tuned," Harley snarled. Then, to Russell, he said, "So?"

"Come on," Eddie wheedled. "It'll be a blast. Think of how many propane deliveries you'd have to make to get this kind of money."

"If you don't come in on it," Harley said, "you have got to keep your mouth shut."

"You think I don't know that?" Russell said. "I just don't want to wind up back in Spring Creek."

"You won't," Harley said. "All we're doing is . . . prospecting. It's an old Alaskan tradition. The gold mine just happens to be a graveyard this time."

Eddie liked that, and laughed so hard it made Russell start to smile. That's when Harley knew he had him. He put out his hand, fist clenched, and Eddie bumped his knuckles against it. Then, a few seconds later, Russell slowly lifted his hand and bumped him, too.

When Harley left the Yardarm a few minutes later, in time to go home and throw a fresh sheet on the bed, there was a powerful wind blowing from the northwest—the direction of St. Peter's Island. For a second, he thought he could hear the baying of the wolves. He put up his hood, drew it tight, and looked up and down the deserted street. This was going to be his lucky night. Angie Dobbs, at last. And, to get the good times rolling, he stepped to the curb, took out the hunting knife he always carried in the back of his belt, and jabbed it into the front tire of Geordie Ayakuk's jeep.

Chapter 11

The wind around St. Peter's Island was even stronger than usual, but instead of dissipating the fog that clung to the rocky shores, it had whipped it into a milky stew. It howled around the old wooden buildings of the Russian colony like a pack of wolves, and whistled through the breaks in the stockade wall.

Old Man Richter could hear the gusts tearing at the roof timbers, but the ramshackle church, with its onion dome, had stood for many decades, and he doubted it would collapse tonight. And tonight was all he needed.

He would be dead by morning.

He wasn't terribly afraid of that anymore. He'd had plenty of time to get used to the idea. Ever since he was swept off the *Neptune II*, he had been cheating death at one turn or another . . . first by clinging to a piece of the shattered lifeboat, then by crawling ashore and climbing a flight of stony steps, no more than a foot wide, that led him to higher ground . . . and into the ruins of the old colony.

He had collapsed in this church, under a pile of petrified furs, for a day, maybe even two. In his dreams, he'd heard what sounded like helicopters and foghorns, but he'd been unable to awaken, unable to move. And who would believe that anyone, much less Old Man Richter, could ever have survived a shipwreck like that? He was sure that no one else had.

He prayed that that idiot Harley Vane was the first to drown.

He had hoped to restore his strength with sleep, and maybe some food, but all he found in his pockets were a couple of waterlogged candy bars that he'd been rationing out to himself. There was nothing in the church but some old straw that he'd chewed on like a horse, and a pool of rainwater that had dripped through a hole in the dome. Even to get to that puddle, he'd had to drag himself along on his elbows. His feet were frostbitten, and they'd gone from blue to purple to black, the discoloration inexorably rising up his legs. For days, he had drifted in and out of consciousness, astonished each time that he'd managed to awake at all.

And, truth be told, disappointed, too.

He wanted it to be over. He'd lived long enough, and he wasn't much interested in being rescued now, when they'd only have to cut off his legs—and a few of his fingers, too, now that he couldn't feel them either—and leave him to wither away in the corner of some nursing home. He was only sorry to be so alone. He would have liked to see one more human face before he died. He'd have liked to have someone there to say good-bye to. Someone who might even have held on to his frozen old paw while he went.

It was dark, so dark he wasn't sure he was actually seeing anything at all, or just pictures made up in his mind. He kept seeing his wife, and she'd been dead for twenty years now. And a horse he had when he was a kid. Brown, with a white nose. Named Queenie. Why couldn't he remember what had happened to her? He took a train once, when he was a thirteen-year-old boy, from Tacoma to St. Paul, and it was the best time he'd ever had in his life. The porter took him up and down the train cars, showing him how everything worked. He'd always liked to know how things worked.

There was a window in the church, with half a shutter still covering it. That half a shutter had been banging all night. Richter wondered how it could have stayed on at all, and for so long, loose like that. It banged again now, and a blast of wind swept into the church, stirring up the dirt and straw.

Another picture crossed his mind . . . of a lantern, burning bright.

It was as if it had just gone by the window outside.

His thoughts returned to the train car. He remembered how entranced he was by all the gauges and switches in the engineer's compartment, and how he had asked what each one did. It was like entering Aladdin's cave.

There was a creaking sound over by the door, the door that Richter had wedged shut days ago. It was opening now, and a light—a yellow light—was coming inside. Richter turned his head on the stiff old furs, and just past the corner of a pew he saw what looked like one of those old kerosene lanterns floating through the air.

He heard a shuffling sound—like a bad foot being dragged along the boards—and coming closer down the nave.

"I'm over here," he croaked. "On the floor." *Was he going to get his wish? Was he going to be spared a solitary death?*

The lantern came even closer, and as he squinted up into the darkness, he could start to make out who was holding it.

He saw a face, a woman's face, gaunt the way his wife's had been when the cancer had done its worst. Long gray hair, and a toothless smile . . . a smile that made him feel colder than ever before.

The lamp came down farther, and a hand slipped under the fur and took hold of his own. Now he wished to Christ that he had never prayed for company. Her fingers felt like twigs.

She said something—it sounded as if it was meant to be a comfort—in a language he could not understand.

He wanted to cry out, but he didn't have any breath left in him. His blood felt like it had stopped in his veins. He gasped once or twice. Her hand gripped him tighter, and he died with his eyes wide open, staring into the lanternlight, and with his mouth frozen in a silent scream.

The woman repeated her words, then let go of his hand and hobbled away.

She drew the shawl around her shoulders, even though she did not feel the cold, and left the church. She did not know the old man's name, but she knew where he had come from. She had seen the ship go down.

She had seen many ships go down . . . for many years.

Following the path she had long trodden, she drifted through the colony, remembering the sound of voices raised in prayer, the aroma of fresh fish roasting in the pan, the warmth of a blazing fire.

How long had it been since she had heard anything but the baying of the wolves—her kindred spirits—or felt anything warmer than the touch of that old man's dying hand?

But what more did she deserve? She was the harbinger of death, and the terrible mercy that had spared her own life—not once, but twice—was less forgiving to others.

"You are a special child," the monk had told her. "God has a special destiny in mind for you."

The night he told her that, he had given her the silver cross on a gilded chain. It was encrusted with emeralds, green as a cat's eyes, and he had had its back inscribed with a message meant only for her. "Let this be our secret," he had said, as he put one of his broad hands, the hands that had healed her younger brother, atop her head. It was as if a healing balm were pouring over her; her eyes had closed, and her breathing had slowed, and even her left foot, the one that was misshapen and gave her such constant trouble, stopped hurting.

"I give you this blessing," he said, "to protect you from all evil." And then he had chanted some words in a low voice. Not for the first time, she could smell the alcohol on his breath, and she knew there were people who said vile things about him. "Nothing may harm you now," he said, and she had not doubted it. "If you believe in my power—"

"I do, Father, I do."

"—then you must believe, too, in the power of this cross."

Holding the lantern aloft, she passed beyond the stockade walls, down the hillside, and into the trees. Although she did not see them, she knew that the black wolves—spirits of the unquiet dead—were keeping company with her, moving stealthily through the woods. How long had it been before she learned that they did not grow in number, nor did they die? How long before she had realized that each mysterious creature harbored a soul, a soul as lost as her own, stranded somewhere between this world and the next? Or that their fate and hers were inextricably bound?

As she approached the graveyard, her companions held back, keeping to the trees and the shadows. Her fingertips grazed the wooden gateposts, tracing and retracing the words that she had once carved there. *Forgive me,* they said, over and over again, but who was there to do so?

A strong wind was blowing a scrim of snow across the ground. She walked among the toppled headstones and petrified crosses but stopped when she came to the edge of the cemetery overlooking the sea. A piece of the earth had fallen away, like a rotted tooth pulled from a gum. Even now, if she could have burrowed into the ravaged ground and found her own place there, she would have done so. But as Rasputin had told her, a special destiny awaited her.

Nearly a century had passed, and in all that time she had never been entirely sure if those words had been his blessing, meant to give her strength against adversity, or a curse upon her own head, and the heads of all her family.

But whatever their intent, his words had served admirably as both.

Part Two

Chapter 12

"We'll be coming up on St. Peter's Island in about ten minutes," the pilot said, his voice crackling over Slater's headphones; even with the phones on, the rattling of the propellers and the thrumming of the twin engines on the Sikorsky S-64 Skycrane made it hard to hear. "I just wanted to make sure you guys got a good look at the place before the light goes." On the horizon, the sun was a copper dollar sinking below the hazy outline of eastern Siberia. "We don't get much daylight at this time of year."

"In Irkutsk, I had sunlamps," Professor Kozak said into his own microphone. "Three," he said, holding up three gloved fingers for Slater to see. "One in every room."

Slater nodded amicably, balancing a sealed envelope on his lap. The two men were packed in shoulder to shoulder behind the pilot and copilot, and flying over the icy, teal-blue waters of the Bering Strait; below them, the Pacific and Arctic Oceans converged, and the International Date Line cut an invisible line between Little Diomede Island, which belonged to the United States, and Big Diomede, which was Russian territory. While Sergeant Groves was back in Nome, organizing the rest of the cargo and waiting to shepherd Dr. Eva Lantos on the last leg of her journey from Boston, Slater had decided to go on ahead in the first chopper, along with his borrowed Russian geologist. There was no time to lose, and he wanted them both to get a good look at the lay of the land on St. Peter's. Many decisions, he knew, had to be made, and they had to be made fast.

It had been an arduous and complicated trip already. Slater had flown from D.C. to L.A. to Seattle before catching a flight to Anchorage, and from there hopping on a supply plane to Nome, where the two helicopters were being loaded with the mountain of equipment and provisions the expedition would require. When the first one's cargo bay had been filled, with everything from inflatable labs to hard rubber ground mats, then securely locked down, Slater and the burly professor, who hadn't seen each other since picking their way across a minefield in Croatia, climbed aboard.

Unlike most helicopters, the Sikorsky was designed chiefly for the transportation of heavy cargo loads—up to twenty thousand pounds—and as a result it looked a lot like a gigantic praying mantis, with a bulbous cabin dangling up front for the pilots and passengers (no more than five people at a time) and a long, slim cargo bay with an extendable crane for lowering, or lifting, supplies from great heights. Two rotors—one with six long blades mounted above the chassis, and the other propping up the tail—kept it airborne. To Slater, it felt a lot like traveling in a construction vehicle.

For many miles, they had traveled along the rugged coastline of Alaska and over vast stretches of overgrown taiga, where aspens and grasses and dense brush thrived, and barren tundra where the soil was more unforgiving. Now and then he could make out polar bears lumbering across the ice floes, or caribou herds pawing for lichen buried beneath the frost. As they passed over a swath of land extending out into the sea, Slater tapped the copilot on the shoulder and pointed down at the gabled rooflines and crooked fences of a small town.

"Cape Prince of Wales," the copilot said. "Founded in 1778."

"By Captain Cook," Professor Kozak said, proud to pitch in.

There wasn't much to see, and at the rate they were going— roughly 120 miles per hour—the tiny town, cradled by a rocky ridge, was already disappearing from view. But Slater knew its sad history well. It wasn't so different from that of its neighbor, Port Orlov.

Called Kingigin, or "high bluff" by its native inhabitants, it had once been a thriving Eskimo village and a lively trading post for deer-skins, ivory, jade, flint, beads, and baleen. On the westernmost point of the North American continent, lying just south of the polar circle and with nothing but a dogsled trail leading to it from the mainland, the town should have been as safe from the Spanish flu epidemic of 1918 as any place on earth. There wasn't even a telegraph connection. But through a series of calamitous events, Wales, like a handful of other Alaskan hamlets, wound up suffering the highest mortality rates in America.

In October of that year, the steamship *Victoria* sailed into Nome, and the city's doctor, aware of the danger, met the ship at the dock, where he insisted on examining the passengers and crew; he even went so far as to quarantine several dozen at Holy Cross Hospital. But when only one of them got sick after five days there (and even that illness was chalked up to tonsillitis), the doctor permitted the patients to be released. A hospital worker died of the flu four days later, and within forty-eight hours the whole city of Nome was placed under quarantine.

But by then the damage had been done. Mail had been unloaded from the ship, and even though every shred of it had been fumigated, the sailors who handed the bags to the local mail carriers had been unwitting bearers of the virus. Now, the mailmen, too, riding their dogsleds to every far-flung outpost in the territory, acted as the plague's deadly agents. Wherever they went, they brought with them the contagion, and by the time rescuers reached the village of Wales, three weeks after the mail had been delivered, they found scenes of utter devastation—decaying corpses piled in snowdrifts, packs of wild dogs tearing at the remains. In one hut, a man was found with his arms wrapped around his stove, frozen solid, and he had had to be buried, still kneeling, in a square box. The survivors were found starv-ing, drinking nothing but reindeer broth, in the one-room school-house.

"Look at that!" the professor exclaimed, pointing to Cape Mountain now passing below them. "That, my friend, is the end of the Continental Divide." His breath reeked of spearmint gum, which he was chewing assiduously to keep his ears from getting plugged.

A jagged brown peak, slick with snow and ice, Cape Mountain sat atop a gigantic slab of granite, shaped like an axe. The natives liked to say that the slab was the spot where Paul Bunyan had put his hatchet down, after he'd chopped down every tree in the Arctic. Slater could see how the legend got started.

"When we get to St. Peter's," the pilot said, "I'll come in from the east, do a complete three-sixty, then we can hover wherever you want." He consulted the fuel gauges, then added, "But not for long."

At the thought of finally seeing the island, Slater felt his heart race, and he straightened up in his seat, which wasn't easy given the bulk of the parka he was wearing and the over-the-shoulder restraints. The professor didn't leave him much room, either, but he was enthusiastic company, and for that reason alone, Slater knew he'd picked the right man for what could prove to be the very bleak job ahead.

As the chopper approached, Slater could see—straight ahead and framed between the pilots' shoulders—a gnarled hunk of black stone, surrounded by jutting rocks that broke the surface of the roiling waters. Its foundation was largely obscured by ice and mist. Slater could see snatches of beach, though they looked too steep and small for a helicopter, much less this one, to land on. Chiseled into the stone cliff, there appeared to be a winding set of steps.

"That whole island, it is from a volcano," the professor observed over the headphones, admiringly. "Basaltic lava, two million years old." He took off his spectacles, blew some dust from the lenses—filling the cabin with the scent of spearmint again—then hastily put them back on.

The chopper banked to the right, and now Slater got a better view out his own side window. Steep cliffs, dotted with nesting terns, rose to an uneven plateau, raggedly forested with deep green spruce and alders.

"Can you get closer?" Slater asked.

"Will do," the pilot replied, "but the winds get tricky around the cliffs."

The chopper descended and made a closer pass. But that was when Slater suddenly saw something, camouflaged by the patchy forest, which made him grab Kozak's sleeve and point down.

An onion-shaped dome, made of rough timber and pocked with holes, poked its head up through the trees.

"The Russian colony," the pilot said, circling.

Although the helicopter was buffeted by nasty crosswinds, the pilot was able to hold it steady enough that Slater could get the lay of the land. The old church was surrounded by several other ramshackle structures—old cabins teetering on their raised foundations, empty livestock pens, a well with a rusted bucket. A stockade wall, partly dismantled, enclosed what was left of the village.

But where was the cemetery?

The same thing must have occurred to the professor, who plucked at Slater's sleeve and pointed off toward a trail leading away from what was once the main gate. It disappeared into a dense grove of evergreens.

"Could you move west?" Slater requested, and the pilot said, "Roger. But we've only got a few more minutes before we have to head into Port Orlov for refueling."

The Sikorsky turned, its propellers churning even more loudly in hover mode than they did when flying, and followed the trail over the tops of the trees, until a rocky promontory appeared below. It jutted out from the plateau like an ironing board, its windswept ground dotted with old wooden crosses, toppling over, and gray-stone slabs.

It made sense, Slater thought. The graveyard had been sited as far from the colony as possible.

And in the gathering gloom, he saw a ragged spot at the very end of the promontory, where the earth and stone hung precariously above the cliffs, as if a limb had been ripped away from the body of the island . . . and now he knew precisely where the coffin found floating at sea had originated.

"Lights out," the pilot said, and the last rays of the sun vanished as abruptly as a candle's flame being snuffed. Darkness descended over the island, and the helicopter swiftly banked away from the steep, unforgiving cliffs.

But one question remained in Slater's head. This had been possibly the most isolated colony on the planet, surrounded by ice floes and rocky coastlines, with no mail, and no intercourse with the locals. It should have been the safest place on earth during the 1918 pandemic. But even here, the Spanish flu had managed to insinuate its deadly tentacles, and he wondered if he would ever find out how. Not for the first time, he felt a flicker of grudging admiration for his terrible foe. Damn, it was wily.

"Those are crabbing boats below," the pilot observed, as Slater looked down to see their running lights bucking in the choppy seas. "Worst job in the whole world."

Funny, Slater thought. He had often heard his own job described that way.

Chapter 13

The Winter Palace was never more beautiful than when it was done up for the Christmas Ball. Anastasia looked forward to it every year—particularly in a year as tragic and bloody as this one had been. Although millions of ill-equipped Russian soldiers were still desperately fighting the Germans along the far-flung borders of the empire, here, tonight, you would never know it. As she gazed down at the vast, snowy forecourt, hundreds of sleek carriages and gleaming motorcars, jingling sleighs and bright red troikas, drew to a halt in front of the massive entry hall of the palace, and the Tsar and Tsaritsa's guests, decked out in all their finery, disembarked, laughing and chattering among themselves. Even from the window seat in her room, the young grand duchess could catch some of their exchanges—most of them spoken in French as it was so much more fashionable than Russian—and spot some of the more familiar faces; just then, in fact, stepping out of one of the most ornately gilded carriages, drawn by four splendid white horses with golden tassels in their manes and tails, she saw the young Grand Duke Dmitri, her father's cousin, and his fast friend, Prince Felix Yussoupov, scion of the richest family in Russia.

Rumor had it that the Yussoupovs were even richer than the imperial family, something that Anastasia found impossible to believe. Who could possibly have more than the Tsar? The very thought struck her as rude, even if Felix himself was among the most charming and sought-after young men in all of St. Petersburg.

For well over an hour, the guests assembled in the grand ballroom until, at eight thirty sharp, the Master of Ceremonies banged an ebony staff three times on the marble floor and announced the presence of their imperial majesties. The mahogany doors, trimmed in gold, were thrown open, and Anastasia and her three sisters followed their father and mother into the immense ballroom, lighted by crystal chandeliers. All around them, men in medal-bedecked uniforms and black tailcoats bowed, while the women in billowing silk gowns curtsied with a fluttering sound that reminded Anastasia of flocks of geese taking flight above a field. Gems of every color and size sparkled at the ladies' necks and ears and adorned their wrists and fingers. A prima ballerina from the St. Petersburg Ballet wore white shoes with heels and buckles made of pavé diamonds.

The orchestra broke into a polonaise, and while her parents went about greeting the guests—her mother wearing that telltale air of distraction that fell over her whenever her son Alexei was suffering from one of his agonizing bouts—Anastasia blushed fiercely and simply did her best not to trip over the hem of her long white dress. Because of the deformity to her left foot, her shoes were specially made for her by the court cobbler in Moscow, but the polished parquet floor was extremely difficult to navigate, and she dreaded taking a spill with every aristocrat in the land on hand to watch. The Grand Marshal of the Court, Count Paul Benckendorff, took her by the arm and proffered a glass of champagne.

Anastasia quickly looked around and said, "What if Mama were to see?"

"What if she does?" the count said with a laugh. The ends of his gray moustache stuck out from his face as straight as a pencil. "It's New Year's Eve, and you're fifteen!"

When she still hesitated, he said, "Drink up!" and, laughing along with him now, she did. (In all honesty, she had sipped champagne several times before, but she knew that her mother still did not approve.) "And reserve the chaconne for me," he added with a wink before moving off to welcome a party from the British Embassy.

While her older sisters danced, Anastasia looked on, making mental notes of everything she saw, the better to tell her brother Alexei the next morning. The Heir Apparent was sequestered in the royal family's private apartments, recovering from a nosebleed that had begun with nothing more than a sneeze the day before. But because of his disease, the bleeding would not stop, and Dr. Botkin, in consultation with the best surgeons in St. Petersburg, was still debating whether or not to risk cauterizing the burst blood vessel that had caused it. Every doctor, Anastasia knew well, dreaded being the one who might do the Tsarevitch greater, or grave, harm. As a result, they generally chose to do nothing but wait and watch and pray that each crisis would pass.

Rasputin had, of course, been summoned—indeed, he was due at the ball—but, as often occurred, no one had been able to find him yet. Famous as he was, he also led a secretive private life. Anastasia had heard tales about that, too—some of them quite scandalous—but her mother adamantly insisted that the stories were all a pack of lies, made up by political and personal enemies of the man she called, with reverence and affection, Father Grigori.

By now, there must have been close to a thousand people in the ballroom, and scores of servants were circulating on the perimeter of the dance floor with silver trays of caviar and sliced sturgeon, flutes of champagne and glasses of claret. Massive buffet tables, laden with everything from lobster salad to whipped cream and pastry tarts, were set up in the adjoining chambers. But Anastasia was so enraptured by the beauty of the ball that she longed to sweep around the room to the strains of the mazurka or the waltz. She only trusted herself, however, in the arms of a few, among them the count. When he returned for the chaconne, and wrapped a strong arm around her waist, she knew that he would support her and guide her steps; as they danced she was able to tilt her head back and feel herself briefly transported. The champagne, she thought, was a great help; she should drink it more often. She saw her sisters—Olga and Tatiana and Marie—moving around her, and to her they looked as graceful as swans. Was she forever to feel like the ugly duckling, she wondered— which made it all the more surprising when she saw a hand in a white-leather glove descend upon the count's shoulder and heard a voice say, "May I intrude?"

The count put his head back, and said, "But I was just hitting my stride, Prince!"

Yussoupov smiled and as the count relinquished his hold, boldly stepped in. Anastasia could hardly believe what was happening. Prince Felix Yussoupov could dance with anyone he liked, anytime he liked. He had dark, wavy hair, and a long, almost feminine face, with dark, soulful eyes. His lashes were longer than any of her own sisters', and as she looked at them now, closer than she had ever seen them before, she could swear that they had been tinted and curled, and she remembered the gossip she had overheard—that the young prince liked to be seen around town masquerading as a woman, in furs and jewels and silken gowns. She had never known what to make of such tales, especially as he had recently married a celebrated beauty named Irina— who was nowhere in sight at the ball.

As if intuiting her thought, he said, "The Princess Irina's in the Crimea, at Kokoz."

No matter how splendid the Yussoupovs' palace there was—and the accounts of its magnificence were many—Anastasia could not imagine missing the Tsar's Christmas Ball.

"But I see another guest is missing, too," he said, as she sailed in his arms across the dance floor. The prince was an even more adept dancer than the count.

"Alexei is asleep," she said. "He was out hunting all day." Like the others in the royal family, she had been tutored to conceal the gravity of her brother's condition.

The prince nodded and smiled, but she understood now that it wasn't her brother he had been referring to.

"Oh, do you mean Father Grigori?" she said.

For some reason, Yussoupov seemed to find that funny, and laughed. Even his teeth were perfect—small and even and brilliantly white.

"Yes, of course, *Father Grigori*," he said, and now she knew he was making fun of her for calling him that. "Our friend Rasputin must be on quite a bender if he's late to the Winter Palace ball."

Anastasia was perplexed.

"He's coming tonight, isn't he?"

"I should think so," she replied. But did he think that she oversaw the guest list?

"I ask because you two seem to have a special rapport, *n'est-ce pas*? Whenever we go out drinking together, the good Father Grigori speaks of your family often—but he talks about you more often than all the others combined."

That he spoke of them at all was shocking to Anastasia, but she couldn't help but wonder what it was he said about her. She was secretly flattered. Without her having to ask, Yussoupov obliged.

"He seems to think that you carry what he calls a 'spark of holy fire.' And if anyone should know about such stuff as that, it's Rasputin."

Anastasia was growing dizzy, though she couldn't tell if it was from the twirling of the dance, the champagne, or the confusion she felt at the strange turns of the conversation. What did Felix Yussoupov want from her?

"Does he ever speak of me?" he asked.

"Not that I can think of. Why would he?"

"We are the best of friends," he said, with feigned indignation, "that's why. But he can have a wicked tongue on him, and I've just been curious to know if my name ever came up behind the closed doors of the imperial apartments." His eyes, deep and dark and penetrating, were staring into hers, and she felt as if a wolf were sizing her up for dinner.

"I think I need to sit down," she said, suddenly feeling unsteady on her feet.

The prince, without missing a beat, swept her from the floor and onto a gilded divan framed between a pair of floor-length mirrors. Two other ladies quickly moved to make room for their royal addition.

"Forgive me," the prince said, bowing at the waist with one hand folded behind his back. "I fear my conversation has proved tiresome to Your Royal Highness." Anastasia still had the sense that he was somehow mocking her. Mocking a grand duchess! "I'm sure our mutual friend will turn up any minute. Wherever the champagne is flowing, Father Grigori cannot be far behind."

As he retired, the other ladies fluttered their eyes and tried to catch his attention, but to no avail. He was already hailing Grand Duke Dmitri Pavlovich and gesturing toward one of the buffet chambers. And so the ladies set their sights on Anastasia, instead.

"You look very lovely tonight, Your Highness," one of them gushed, and the other said, "But where has your mother gone to? Her dress was quite beautiful and I was eager to study it more closely." She leaned closer with a smile and said, "That way I can get a better copy made when I leave for Paris."

Flattery was something Anastasia, like any member of the royal family, was inured to. Her mother and father had brought her up, as best they could, to ignore it. For an honest opinion, there were family members one could turn to, and certain confidantes and retainers, such as Dr. Botkin, the French tutor Pierre Gilliard, or Anna Demidova, her mother's maid who had served the Tsaritsa forever and whose loyalty and love were undoubted. And even though Jemmy was just a cocker spaniel, Anastasia knew that the little dog would love her just the same whether she was a grand duchess or a peasant girl. She wished that people could be more like dogs.

A servant offered her another glass of champagne, and with her mother nowhere in sight, she saw no reason not to take it. She was done dancing for the night—her left foot already ached a bit—and she chatted amiably with the two ladies, both of whom turned out to be the wives of ministers of something or other (ministers came and went so routinely that Anastasia never bothered to get their names straight) and began to wonder at her mother's absence. The Tsar himself was holding court at one end of the ballroom, but it was beginning to dawn on Anastasia that if her mother had already disappeared—and Father Grigori had not shown up at all—there could only be one reason.

Alexei must have taken a turn for the worse.

Excusing herself, she skirted the dance floor, waved good night to Count Benckendorff, and lifting her long skirt a few inches, scurried down one of the vast galleries lined with towering columns of jasper, marble, and malachite. Some late-arriving guests swiftly stopped to bow and curtsy as she passed, then she was hurrying up the main staircase and down several more corridors, decorated with rich tapestries and gloomy oil portraits, until she reached the family's private quarters in the East Wing. Comprised of only twenty or thirty rooms, most of them overlooking an enclosed park, this was the Romanovs' sanctuary, the place where they could live a relatively normal, uninhibited, and unobserved life. The Ethiopian guards silently opened the doors as she approached, and just as silently closed them behind her a moment later.

She was running toward her brother's rooms when she happened to notice that the door to her mother's private chapel was ajar. Candlelight flickered from within, and when she peered around the open door, she saw Rasputin standing before the altar, surrounded by votive candles and dozens of holy icons—portraits of the Virgin Mary, or various saints, daubed in gold and silver, on resin wood or bronze. He did not hear her as she entered, so absorbed was he in his prayers, and though she did not wish to startle him, she needed to know if her brother was in danger.

"Father Grigori," she murmured, and as if he had known she was there all along, he said, without turning, "I have comforted the Tsarevitch, and he will live."

She waited, relieved—what kind of Christmas would this have been if he had not?—and wondering if she should leave the *starets* to his prayers.

"But my own time is fast approaching," he said, the candlelight glinting off the pectoral cross.

He turned his head without turning his body, and despite her reverence for the holy man, Anastasia was reminded of a snake sinuously twisting its neck around. His eyes were smoldering in their sockets.

"I shall not live to see the New Year," he said. "I have written it all down in a letter I have given to Simanovich."

Simanovich, Anastasia knew, was his personal secretary, a slovenly man who reeked of tobacco juice and sweat.

"But it is for your father to read one day. If I am killed by common assassins, by my brothers the peasants, then you and your family have nothing to fear; the Romanovs shall rule for hundreds of years." Then he raised a finger in warning, his beard bristling as if with electricity. "But if I am murdered by the boyars—if it is the nobles who take my life—then their hands will be soiled with my blood for twenty-five years. Brothers will kill brothers. If any relation to your family brings about my death, then woe to the dynasty. The Russian people will rise against you with murder in their hearts."

The blood froze in Anastasia's veins. She had never heard him speak in such apocalyptic tones, and for the first time she drew back from him in fear.

"That is why you must take this," he said, grasping the emerald cross on its chain. "You must wear it always."

He lifted the cross over his head, then draped it over hers, turning it so she could see the back. Their heads were so close she could smell the liquor on his breath and see the dead-white skin beneath the zigzag part in his long black hair. "It was to be my Christmas present to you. Look, my child, look."

There was an inscription now, but in the flickering light of the votive candles, it was too hard to read.

"See? See what it says?" he implored. "'To my little one.'" *Malenkaya.* "'No one can break the chains of love that bind us.'"

It was signed, she could see now, "Your loving father, Grigori."

"It is time you knew," he said. "Although I will not be here in body, I shall always be watching over you in spirit. This cross shall be your shield."

"But why me?" Anastasia said, her voice quavering to her own surprise, "and not the others?" She wished that her mother—or anyone, for that matter—would intrude on the private chapel and break this awful spell she felt being cast. "Why not my sisters? They're older and"—she hesitated, ashamed, then blurted out what she was thinking—"more beautiful than I'll ever be."

Rasputin scoffed and reared back. "You are the one most beautiful in the sight of God," he said, raising his own gaze toward the stained-glass ceiling.

"But what about Alexei? He's the one who will rule Russia one day."

"Hear me," Rasputin said, before lowering his own voice and eyes. "The blood of your family is poisoned; the Tsarevitch is poisoned. It was *matushka* who carried the taint."

He often called the Tsar and Tsaritsa by the traditional endearments *matushka* and *batushka,* terms that suggested they were the loving mother and father of their people. And though Anastasia had indeed learned about the curse of hemophilia being hereditary—she had heard her own mother one night wailing in her boudoir that it was she who had brought this suffering upon her son—she had never heard the monk utter anything so blunt and damning.

"This curse you carry in your veins will be your own salvation one day. A plague shall overwhelm the world, but you shall be proof against it."

Anastasia thought he was babbling now, caught in the throes of some holy trance, and all she wanted was to break away. She deeply regretted ever leaving the ballroom.

"Thank you, Father, for the gift," she mumbled, touching the cross—it was heavier than she might ever have imagined, and beautiful as it was, she wished that she did not have it. "I should go and look in on my brother now." She drew back slowly, like a rabbit keeping a stoat in its view.

Rasputin's gaze did not waver, nor did he move, as she edged toward the door. In his black cassock, framed by the dull glint of the holy icons in the candlelight, he looked like a pillar of smoke.

Not knowing what to say, she murmured, "The blessings of Christmas upon you, Father."

"Pray for me," he said.

And then, just as she put her good foot out behind her and stepped from the confines of the chapel, she heard him mutter, "For I am no longer among the living."

Chapter 14

Perched atop the hard seat of the Zamboni, Nika Tincook wrestled with the sticky gears. The machine was probably thirty years old by now, so a little trouble was only to be expected. Besides, the city budget of Port Orlov did not allow for any new expenditures. No one knew that better than she did.

Wrapped in the beaver-skin coat her grandmother had made for her, topped off with a Seattle Seahawks stocking cap, Nika shoved the gearshift again, and this time it caught. Under the lights of the hockey rink, she steered the old Zamboni in wide, slow sweeps, cleaning and resurfacing the ice. She always found the job relaxing, almost like skating with her hands folded behind her back. No one else was out there—everybody was home making dinner—and she could be completely alone with her thoughts.

Which was all the more reason why she was annoyed at the increasing noise she began to hear. At first, she thought something had gone wrong with the Zamboni again, and she actually bent forward in her seat to hear the motor better, but then she realized the commotion was coming from somewhere farther off. And it was coming fast.

Looking up at the sky, she saw lights approaching—red and white ones—but not spread apart the way they would be on a bush plane.

They were concentrated, and two bright beams were searching the ground as the craft got closer. It was a chopper—a long and weirdly articulated one—and as it clattered into view above the town's community center, she realized with horror that the beams were now moving in her direction and fixing on the rink. She was bathed in a blinding white glow, and a bullhorn started issuing orders from on high.

"Please move the Zamboni off the ice," the voice announced.

"What the—" But she was already turning the wheel and gunning the engine up to its full ten miles per hour. The racket from the chopper was deafening, and bits of snow and ice skittered every which way across the rink.

As soon as she'd driven down the ramp and into the municipal garage, where the city kept everything from its snowplows to its ambulance, she switched off the engine and raced back outside.

The helicopter, its wheels extended like an insect's legs, was lowering itself onto the ice that she had just finished polishing. What could this possibly be about? Please God, not another news crew dispatched to recap the *Neptune* disaster and interview the sole survivor, Harley Vane. Like a lot of people, she didn't even believe Harley's account, but the truth, unfortunately, lay somewhere at the bottom of the Bering Sea.

The rotors were turned off, and as they wheezed into silence, the hatchway opened, and a burly man with glasses stepped out. He slipped on the ice and landed with a smack on his rump. Laughing, he was helped up by another man, lean and tall, who guided him toward the steel bleachers. Nika crunched across the hard-packed snow and hollered, "Who are you?"

The two men noticed her for the first time. The tall one had dark eyes, dark hair, and reminded her of long-distance runners she had known—and dated—in college. He moved across the slippery ice with a becoming assurance and agility, but he didn't reply.

"And who told you," she went on, "that you could land on our hockey rink?"

Pulling off a glove, he extended his hand. "Frank Slater," he said, "and sorry about the rink. But we were low on fuel when we saw your lights."

"Lucky there wasn't a game on."

"And I am Vassily Kozak," the professor said, bowing his head, "of the Trofimuk United Institute of Geology, Geophysics and Mineralogy. It is a part of the Russian Academy of Sciences."

Now Nika was more puzzled than ever.

"We're here on some important business," Slater said, and though she ought to be used to it by now, her back went up at the slight hint of condescension in his voice. Because she was a woman, and young, and, to be fair, had been caught driving the Zamboni, he was just assuming she was some underling.

"I need to talk to the mayor of Port Orlov," he said, showing her a bulky sealed envelope addressed to the city hall. "Could you show me where to find him?"

"Is the mayor expecting you?" she said, as sweetly as she could muster.

"I'm afraid not."

"You came all this way, in the biggest chopper I've ever seen, without making an appointment?"

"There wasn't time."

"Right," she said, skeptically. "Email is so slow these days."

The professor was looking around with interest, and he said to them both, "Would you forgive me if I went for a short walk? I would like to stretch my legs."

"No problem," Nika said. "It's hard to get lost in Port Orlov. The street's that way," she said, pointing off to one side of the big clumsy buildings, raised on cinder blocks, that comprised the community center. To Slater, she said, "You can follow me."

They picked their way across the hard, uneven ground and entered the center. Geordie, her nephew, was sitting at a computer console, plowing his way through a bag of potato chips.

"Why don't you bring us some coffee?" she said. "And knock off the chips."

She led Slater down the hall, past the community bulletin board covered with ads for craft workshops and used ski gear, and into an office with battered metal furniture and a ceiling made of white acoustical tiles, several of which were sagging.

"Have a seat, Mr. Slater," she said, shrugging off her coat and hat.

"Actually, it's Dr. Slater," he said, in an offhand tone that carried a welcome touch of humility. "I'm here from the Armed Forces Institute of Pathology, in Washington."

If she hadn't guessed already, now she knew that this was a serious matter.

Geordie waddled in with the cups of coffee and a couple of non-dairy creamers.

"You can just leave those there," she said, clearing a space on the desk by shoving stacks of papers around. Slater took off his own coat and put the envelope down on a free corner.

"I should warn you," he said, "another chopper will be arriving tomorrow morning, so if there's anyplace in particular you'd like it to land, just let me know."

At least he was being accommodating, she thought, despite all the mystery. But two helicopters?

"So what's all this about?" she said.

"It's best, I think, if any information was disseminated from your own mayor's office."

"In that case," she said, picking up the envelope, and using a whale-bone letter opener, "let's see what we've got."

He started to protest, even raising one hand to take the envelope back, but the smile on her lips must have given her away.

"Don't tell me," he said. "You're N. J. Tincook—the mayor?"

She pulled out the folder inside. "Nikaluk Jane Tincook, but most folks just call me Nika. Nice to meet you," she said, though her eyes were fixed on the official warnings, and top secret clearance stamps, on the cover of the report. The title alone was enough to knock her out of her chair. "AFIP Project Plan, St. Peter's Island, Alaska (17th District): Geological Survey, Exhumation, Core Sampling, and Viral Analysis Procedures." And the report attached, she saw from a quick riffle through the pages, must have been sixty or seventy pages long, all of it in dense, single-spaced prose, with elaborate footnotes, indices, charts, and diagrams. The last time she'd had to wade through something like this was in grad school at Berkeley. "You expect me to read this now?" she said. "And make sense of it?"

"No, I don't," he said.

"Then why didn't you send it on in advance?"

"Because, as you've seen from the cover clearances, we're trying to stay under the radar as much as possible."

"Why?" She was starting to feel exasperated again, and it looked like Dr. Slater could see it. He sipped his coffee, and then, in a very calm and deliberate tone, said, "Let me explain." She had the sense that he had done this kind of thing many times before, that he was used to talking to people who had been, for reasons he was not at liberty to explain, kept in the dark.

As he laid out the case before her, her suspicions were confirmed. The stuff about the coffin lid and Harley Vane she already knew, just as she knew most of what he told her about the old Russian colony. She had grown up in Port Orlov; everyone there knew that a sect of crazy Russians had once inhabited the island and that they'd been wiped out in 1918 by the Spanish flu. She even knew that the sect had been followers of the mad monk Rasputin, who was said to have bewitched the royal family of Russia, the Romanovs, in the years before the Revolution. But out of politeness, and curiosity about where all this was going, she let him run on. As the grandma who raised her had always said, God gave us only one mouth, but two ears. So listen.

Truth be told, she also liked the sound of his voice, now that he was talking to her like an equal.

"Rasputin's patron saint was St. Peter," Slater explained.

And see, she thought, *that was something she hadn't known.*

"The coffin lid bore an impression of the saint, holding the keys to Heaven and Hell. That's one way we knew where it came from."

"But apart from Harley Vane's washing up there, nobody's set foot on that island for years. It's got a very bad reputation among the locals. How do you know for sure?"

"We did a flyover an hour ago. We could see where the graveyard had given way. The permafrost has thawed, and the cliff is eroding."

Nika's phone rang, and she hollered, "Pick it up, Geordie! No calls."

"That's why we have to set up an inspection site there, exhume the bodies, take samples, and make sure that there is no viable virus present."

And it suddenly dawned on her, with full clarity, why this had all been kept so secret. My God, they were talking about doing something that was, first of all, a serious desecration of old graves—the sort of thing her own Inuit people would take a very dim view of—but even worse, they were talking about the potential release of a plague that had wiped out untold millions. That was one lesson that no native Alaskan escaped.

"But why here? Those bodies have been buried for almost a hundred years. Why would you think that they would contain a live virus when there are graveyards all over the globe filled with people who died from the flu?"

"But the bodies there weren't flash frozen and kept in that state ever since."

In her mind's eye, she pictured the woolly-mammoth carcass that had been unearthed, nearly perfectly preserved, when they built the oil and gas refinery just outside town. She was just six years old then, but she remembered staring at it, feeling so sad, and wondering if it had been killed by a dinosaur.

"What about the risk to this town? If there's a threat a few miles offshore, that's a lot too close for comfort in my book. Are we going to have to evacuate? And if so, for how long? Who's going to pay for that, and where are we supposed to go?"

She had a dozen other questions, too, but he held up his hand and said, "Hold on, hold on. It's all in that report."

"Thanks very much," she said, acidly, "but as we've already discussed, it'll take me all night to read that thing."

"The risk," Dr. Slater said, "has been calculated to be well within reasonable limits, and just to be on the safe side, we will be proceeding under Biohazard 3 conditions at all times. Any specimens will be taken on and off the island by Coast Guard helicopter. They won't even pass through Port Orlov. We will only need this town as a temporary staging area. We'll have assembled, and be gone, by the day after tomorrow. Nobody needs to go anywhere."

For the moment, she was pacified, but she still wasn't happy. She had come back to this town in the middle of nowhere because she felt a responsibility to it, and to her native people. She knew the history of their suffering, and she knew the toll those terrible misdeeds continued to take, down to the present day. There wasn't an Inuit family that didn't still feel the pain from the loss of their way of life, not a family that wasn't fractured by depression or alcoholism or drugs. She had made it out, with a scholarship first to the University of Alaska in Fairbanks, and then the graduate program in anthropology at Berkeley. But she had come back, to be their voice and their defender. Only right now, she wasn't sure how best to go about it.

The phone rang again, cut short by Geordie picking up down the hall.

"I know I've given you a lot to digest," Slater said, but before she could answer, Geordie hollered, "When you said no calls, did you mean the sanitation plant, too?"

"Yes!" she called back, exasperated.

"But I'd be happy to answer any other questions you have. I know you'll have plenty more."

A gust of cold air blew down the corridor, followed by the sound of stamping feet. Professor Kozak leaned in the doorway, his glasses fogged and his face ruddy. "Is anyone hungry? I am hungry enough to eat the bear!"

It was just the note of comic relief that Nika needed. She smiled, and Dr. Slater smiled, too. His face took on a wry, but appealing, expression. She found herself wondering where else he had been before winding up in this remote corner of Alaska. From the weariness that she also saw in his face, she guessed it had been a lot of the world's hot spots. "I'm not sure they're serving bear," she said, slipping the report into her desk drawer, then locking it, "but I know a place that does the best mooseburger north of Nome."

Chapter 15

Charlie had been in the middle of a webcast, sending out the word from the Vane's Holy Writ headquarters—and of course soliciting funds so that the church could continue its "community outreach programs in the most removed and spiritually deprived regions of America's great northwest"—when his whole damn house started to shake.

His wife Rebekah had come running into the room with her hands over her head and her half-wit sister Bathsheba right behind her shouting, "It's the Rapture! Prepare yourself for the Lord!"

Charlie almost might have believed it himself, except that the sound from on high reminded him so much of a helicopter. Out the window, he could see spotlights whisking back and forth across the backyard and the garage, where he kept his specially equipped and modified minivan.

Whipping around from the Skype camera on his computer, he'd wheeled his chair out of the meeting room and onto the back deck, just in time to see this huge friggin' chopper moving like a giant dragonfly over his land. It was no more than fifty feet off the ground and looked to him like it was on some kind of close-surveillance mission. For a moment, he wondered if the federal government was sending a black-ops team to take him out; he'd certainly been known to say some inflammatory things about those bastards in Washington. The lighted cross on top of his roof, it suddenly occurred to him, might as well have been a bull's-eye.

But the chopper moved on, skimming the treetops, then disappearing over the ridge and heading in the general direction of the community center. He listened as its roar gradually decreased, then grabbed his cell phone out of the pocket of his cardigan and called Harley. First he got the automated message, but he called back immediately, and this time Harley, sounding groggy, picked up.

"How the hell did you sleep through that?" Charlie demanded.

"Sleep through what?"

"That helicopter that just about knocked my chimney off."

"What are you talking about?"

"I'm talking about the military chopper that's scoping out the town. I bet it's got something to do with you and that coffin."

"Charlie, next time you decide to flip out, call somebody else."

"Don't you dare hang up," he warned. "Now get up and get your ass down to the Yardarm and find out what's going on." The Yardarm Bar and Grill was the local equivalent of a switchboard.

"Why don't you go?"

"'Cause I'm in the middle of my broadcast."

Harley laughed. "To who? You really think anybody's listening out there?"

Charlie did sometimes wonder how many there were, but envelopes containing small checks and five-dollar bills did occasionally show up in his mailbox, so there had to be some. Not to mention the fact that he had two women in his house who had found him over the Web.

"I'm not gonna argue about this," Charlie said, with the authority that always carried the day. "Get going."

When he hung up and turned around on the cold deck, Rebekah was standing in the doorway with her hands in the pockets of one of her long dresses. Bathsheba was lurking right behind her, apparently persuaded that the Rapture had been postponed. Their white faces and beaked noses put him in mind of seagulls.

"We lost the connection online," Rebekah said. "I told you we don't have enough bandwidth."

Harley dropped the phone on the mattress and lay there for a while. Why did Charlie always get to call the shots? It couldn't be because he was in a wheelchair; it had been like this his whole life. Angie had told Harley he should just leave Port Orlov and start over someplace where his brother couldn't boss him around. And he was starting to think that, dumb as she was, she was right about that much. If this grave-yard gig worked out, and the coffins did contain valuable stuff, then that just might be his ticket to the good life in the Lower 48.

He wouldn't even give his brother his phone number.

Getting up, he stumbled around the trailer, looking for some clean clothes—or clothes that would pass for clean—and ran his fingers through his hair in lieu of a proper brush. The floor was ankle deep in detritus—beer cans, cereal boxes, martial-arts magazines—and all of it was bathed in a faint violet glow from the snake cage on the counter next to the microwave. Glancing in, he saw Fergie curled on the rock, and he said, "You hungry?" He couldn't remember when he had last fed her, so he opened the freezer and took out a frozen mouse—it was curled up like a question mark in a plastic baggie—and nuked it for about a minute. Once he had left one in too long and the stench had made the trailer unlivable for a week. He'd had to move back home with Charlie and the witches, and that was so creepy he couldn't wait to get out of there. Bathsheba, in particular, kept turning up outside his door on one dumb pretext or another.

The trailer was parked about a hundred yards off Front Street, be-tween the lumberyard and a place called the Arctic Circle Gun Shoppe. Harley had never asked anybody if he could park it there, and nobody had ever told him he couldn't. That was one thing that you *could* say for Alaska—the place was still wide open.

But freezing. Even though the Yardarm was only a few minutes' walk away, by the time he got there his ears were burning from the cold, and he had to stand in the doorway soaking up the heat. The usual crowd was around, Angie was carrying out a tray of burgers and fries, but some things were different: there were two guys at the bar he had never seen before—real straight-arrow types, still in their Coast Guard uniforms—and over in the far corner, Nika Tincook was at a table with two other men he'd never laid eyes on. Four strangers in one night, in a bar in Port Orlov—that was positively breaking news.

On her way back to the kitchen, Harley snagged Angie by the arm and said, "What's up?"

"Harley, don't do that here—the boss is watching."

But he couldn't fail to notice that her eyes had flitted in the direction of the two Coast Guard dudes, one of whom had glanced back.

"Who are they?"

"Pilots."

"I can see that."

"Were you just handling those dead mice again?" she said, wrinkling her nose. She brushed at the place on her arm where he'd been holding her.

"What are they doing here?"

"You got me. Why don't you ask them?"

She pulled away and went back through the swinging doors into the kitchen.

Harley, hoping nobody had noticed how she shrugged him off all of a sudden, sauntered over toward the bar and eased himself onto a stool near the Coast Guardsmen. Engrossed in their own conversation, they didn't acknowledge him in any way.

He ordered a beer and then, leaning toward them, said, "Never seen you guys around town."

"Just passing through," the one with the blond crew cut said, but without turning around.

"On that chopper that flew in?"

The red-haired one—who'd been checking out Angie—nodded warily.

"Oh yeah? If you don't mind my asking, what's the job?"

"Routine," the redhead said, and when Harley looked over at the crew-cut guy, he, too, just stared down into his nearly empty mug and said, "Training mission."

Then they kind of closed up like a clamshell, talking to each other in low tones, and Harley felt like a horse's ass sitting there on the stool next to them. But he wasn't about to get up and leave right away because that would make it look even worse. Instead, he sat there and finished his beer, trying to draw the bartender into conversation about the latest Seahawks game. But even Al was too busy to talk.

There was a boisterous laugh from the rear, back near the pool tables, and Harley saw it was from the husky guy in glasses, the one sitting between the tall, thin guy and Port Orlov's illustrious mayor, Nika. Harley had never had a thing for native chicks—he liked leggy blondes, even if they were fake blondes like Angie—but for Nika, he had often told his pals Eddie and Russell, he would make an exception. She couldn't have been more than five-three, five-four, with big, dark eyes and hair as black as a seal. But he loved the way she was built—trim and hard, and when the weather was good and she went around town in just a fleece jacket, with her long hair loose and whipping in the wind, he had to admit she got him going.

After putting away one more beer and hanging out by the jukebox like he cared what played next, he meandered back toward the pool tables. Selecting a cue from the rack, he pretended to be checking its tip and its straightness, and then, as if offhandedly, noticed Nika sitting a few feet away. "Hey, Your Honor," he said, facetiously.

"Harley."

"Want to run a few balls with me?"

"Another time."

He was debating what his next move should be when the tall guy, with the remains of a burger and fries on the plate in front of him, saved him the trouble. "Is that Harley as in Vane?" he asked.

"The one and only. Accept no substitutes."

"Frank Slater," he said, rising enough to extend a hand. "I'm pleased to meet you. I heard about your ordeal."

"Yeah, that's what it was, all right."

"Do you mind if I ask you a few questions?" he said, pushing out an extra chair. "I'm a doctor—it's in our nature." This was too good to be true, Harley thought, even if Nika did look like she was going to shit a brick. Harley turned the chair around so that he could lean his arms on the back as he sat down.

"This is Professor Kozak," Slater said.

"Prof." When they shook, the guy's grip was like a vise—not like any professor's that Harley'd ever heard of. Had to be a Russkie.

"I'm glad to see you look completely recovered," the doctor observed. "No residual effects then?"

"Nah, I'm okay," Harley said, though if the guy had asked about any mental effects, he could have told him a different story. Every time he closed his eyes, he had a nightmare about being chased by a pack of black wolves, only they all had human faces.

"You know, there's something called PTSD—post-traumatic stress disorder—and it can hit you days, weeks, or even months, after something like what happened to you."

Harley had seen enough TV shows to know all about it. "Yeah, yeah, I've heard."

"I just wanted you to keep it in mind," he said, "and let you know that you should see someone if you start having some problems dealing with the fallout. It would be completely normal if you did."

Harley snickered. "Yeah, okay. If I start freaking out, I'll just go and see one of the shrinks we don't have, at the hospital that doesn't exist."

The doc nodded, like he knew he'd just made an ass of himself, but at the same time Harley felt this weird urge to take him up on the offer and get some of this crap off his chest—to tell him about the dreams of the wolves and the sight of somebody with a yellow lantern. It wasn't like he could confess any of it to Russell or Eddie—they'd just tell him to have another beer—and even Angie would think he was acting like a pussy.

"You mind if I ask you a question now?" Harley said.

"Shoot."

"What are you doing out here in the armpit of Alaska?" Glancing at Nika, he added, "No offense, Your Honor."

"None taken. And you can knock off the 'Your Honor' stuff."

He liked that it had gotten to her.

Slater bobbed his head, wiped up some ketchup with the last of his fries, and said, "Just some preparedness drills with the Coast Guard. Better safe than sorry."

But his eyes didn't meet Harley's, and now Harley knew that something pretty big must be up, after all. Charlie's suspicions were right; he might be an asshole, but he was smart. Harley would give him that.

"By the way," Slater said, "what ever happened to that coffin lid that you rode to shore like a surfboard? I saw a photo of it in the paper."

"Why?"

"Just curious."

"As a doctor?"

Slater's expression gave away nothing—and everything.

"I was thinking about putting it up on eBay," Harley taunted. "But if you want to make me a cash offer . . ."

"Actually," Slater said, "I was thinking along rather different lines. I was thinking that it doesn't belong to you, and it ought to go back where it came from."

"Oh yeah? Where's that?"

"To the graveyard, on St. Peter's Island."

Then Slater looked straight at Harley, no bullshit anymore, and Harley could see he was dealing with more than some doc on a training run. So it was high time that the doc knew who *he* was dealing with, too.

"Law of the sea," Harley said. "I found it, it's salvage, and it's mine. And no one better fuck with me." He stood up, pushing off from the chair. "See you around," he said, before glancing at Nika and adding, "Your Honor."

"I do not think I would trust that man," Kozak said, as Harley stalked off. Finishing off his mug of beer, he plunked the glass down on the table and burped softly.

"I think you would be right not to," Nika said. "Harley and his brother Charlie are both bad news."

Kozak excused himself to head for the men's room, and Slater asked her for the full rundown.

"We'd be here all night," Nika said, "just going through the police blotter." But she gave him the capsule description of the Vane family and its long history in the town of Port Orlov. He seemed particularly intrigued when she mentioned that Charlie ran an evangelical mission over the Web.

"So that explains the lighted cross above that house in the woods," he said. "I couldn't help but notice it from the chopper."

"X marks the spot."

"And you think he's for real?"

That was a tough one, and even Nika was of two minds. "I think he thinks so. But can a leopard really change its spots? Underneath, I've got to believe that Charlie Vane is still the same petty crook he's always been. You can judge for yourself tomorrow."

"How come?"

"He's sure to be at the funeral service for the crew of the *Neptune II*. The whole town will turn out."

"I'm not sure the professor and I should attend."

Nika laughed. "You might as well. I mean, if you think your being here is some kind of secret, you've never been to a town like Port Orlov. Harley's probably bragging already about how he told you to stuff it. If he's lucky, it'll be a good enough story to get Angie Dobbs back into bed with him."

"Who's Angie Dobbs?"

"The town's most eligible bachelorette," Nika replied. "The blond waitress over by the jukebox."

Indeed, Harley was loudly regaling her, and a couple of others, with some tale or other. Slater wryly shook his head.

"It sounds like you've got your hands full running this town."

Nika shrugged; she didn't want him to think she felt that way. But it was the truth, nevertheless. Port Orlov, like so many Inuit villages in Alaska, was a wreck. With far too few social services and way too many problems, there were times when she felt marooned in the wilderness. Even if the town could just manage to get a decent, full-time medical clinic, it would be a huge step forward, but try finding the money for it, much less a doctor to staff it. For all of her noble intentions, Nika only had two hands and there were only so many hours in the day.

"We make do with what we've got," she finally said.

"Sometimes," he sympathized, "the satisfaction has to come from knowing you've done all that you can. No matter what the odds."

She had the feeling that he was talking about his own work, too, and she wondered what terrible scenarios he might be revisiting in his mind. He had the look of a man who'd seen things no one should see, done things no one should ever have to have done. And despite their differences—not to mention that fact that they'd gotten off to a bumpy start at the hockey rink—she was starting to feel as if Slater might prove to be a kindred spirit.

In a backwater like this, they weren't easy to come by.

Chapter 16

"Who do you trust?" Charlie asked, staring into the Skype lens attached to his computer.

"You mean which doctor?" the woman asked, confused. "I don't know, they're all so confusing, talking about carcinomas and—"

"Who do you *trust*?" Charlie broke in, his powerful hands gripping the wheels of his chair.

The woman on the screen visibly drew into herself, shoulders hunched, head down. Her straggly hair looked plastered to her skull.

"Who gives it to you straight?"

"You do?" she ventured, like a student hoping she'd found the right answer.

"Wrong!" he exploded.

She shrank further.

"I'm just the vessel, I'm just the messenger. *Jesus* gives it to you straight. 'Whosoever liveth and believeth in me shall never die.' Jesus is saying, put your faith in me—all your faith, not just a little bit, not just whatever you think you can spare—but the whole enchilada."

"I do," she pleaded, "I do believe in the whole thing, in God, but—"

"No 'buts' allowed! God says give it all, and I will return it all, one hundred fold. What's holding you back?"

She paused. Children's voices could be heard from another room. "I'm afraid," she said in a furtive voice. "I'm so afraid."

Charlie realized he was losing her; he was coming on too strong. This woman was still in the grip of worldly concerns, she was afraid of dying, and she was putting her faith in all the wrong places. He deliberately lowered his voice and adopted a more consoling tone. "I was once like you," he said, "before God took away the use of my legs. I lived in fear, every day, fear of losing whatever I had—my health, my family, the love of my friends." Even Charlie had to admit that the love of his friends was a bit of a stretch, but he was on a roll and could be forgiven. "And then, God gave me a good hard slap, he wrapped my canoe around a rock in the Heron River Gorge and stuck me in this wheelchair like he was planting a turnip in the ground." In the time before the Forestry Service had gotten there to rescue him, Charlie had seen Jesus, as plain as he saw this woman on his computer screen now. He was wearing a long white robe, just like in the pictures, only his hair was long and black and the crown of thorns sparkled, kind of like it was made of tinsel. "And I have been growing ever since. My body has shriveled, but my spirit is as tall as a sequoia." He had never seen Jesus again, but he knew that that day would come—either in this world, or the next.

Just out of range of the lens, and in a low voice not meant to be picked up by the computer, Rebekah said, "We're going to be late." She was standing in the doorway to the meeting room, her coat and gloves already on.

He waved one hand behind him, again too low to be seen, to signal that he had heard her. The woman on the screen was crying.

"I'm not as strong as you," she murmured. "Between the biopsies and the scans and all the tests, I'm just . . . exhausted."

"I hear you, Sister." He called all of his online parishioners either Sister or Brother. "But God never gives us more than He thinks we can handle."

"Bathsheba's waiting in the car," Rebekah hissed.

"I have to go now. There's a prayer service in town; they're waiting for me." Although he might have given her the impression that he was presiding at the prayer service, which wasn't exactly true, he hadn't lied, either. There *was* a service—the memorial for the crewmen who had drowned on the *Neptune II*—but the only reason they'd be waiting for him was because he was planning to pick up his brother, Harley, who was supposed to offer some remarks. Charlie had already written them out for him.

"God be with you, Sister," he concluded. "If you don't abandon Him, He won't abandon you. Never forget that."

"I try not to."

"PayPal," Rebekah urged in a low voice from the doorway.

"Right," Charlie said, so wrapped up in his divine mission that he had almost forgotten the Lord's instructions to find the means to spread the word. "And don't forget to send in your tithe via PayPal."

The woman nodded, blowing her nose into a wadded-up ball of Kleenex.

"Bless you, Sister."

"Bless you," she said, before signing off.

Rebekah, sighing in exasperation—"You must think this place runs on prayers instead of money!"—wheeled him down the ramp to the garage, then helped as he hoisted himself into the driver's seat of the blue minivan. His upper-body strength was still good. While Rebekah stowed the chair in the back, Bathsheba huddled over a book. If Charlie asked her what she was reading, she would claim it was Scripture, but more than once, it had turned out to be one of those *Twilight* books about vampires and such. Charlie had had to chastise her severely.

The service was scheduled for noon, and Charlie knew that Harley would barely be up in time. He backed the car out of the garage, using the array of rotary cable hand controls that allowed him to drive without having to use his feet on the gas or brake pedals; it was all done by twisting the specially installed shift on the steering wheel. The driveway was long and bumpy, and the main road wasn't much better.

"I don't like you talking to that woman so much," Rebekah said.

It took a second for Charlie even to figure out who she was talking about.

"She's just calling for sympathy," Rebekah went on.

"She's dying, for Christ's sake."

"That's no excuse. We all die."

"She's part of my flock."

"Then shear her and be done with it."

Bathsheba tittered in the backseat, and Charlie glanced in the rear-view mirror.

"What's so funny?"

"Nothing."

After they'd moved in with him, it had taken Charlie a few days before he realized that Bathsheba wasn't just shy—she was actually a bit slow. Her older sister looked after her.

Still, he needed help around the house, and even more help running the Vane's Holy Writ website and church. Rebekah had a lot of business sense, and Bathsheba could be entrusted with the simple housekeeping chores and such. Beyond that, however, she could be a problem. "We're not going to have any trouble today, are we?" he asked over his shoulder.

Bathsheba pretended not to know what he was referring to.

"No fits? No antics?" The last time they'd set foot in the Lutheran Church, which served as the all-purpose house of worship for Port Orlov, Bathsheba had claimed to be assailed by devils. Raised in a tiny fundamentalist, Northeastern sect that had splintered off the mainstream a hundred years ago, the two women had arrived in Port Orlov with some pretty well-established, if unorthodox, ideas. But Charlie chalked up incidents like that last one to those damn books Bathsheba read. Thank God the town library, housed in the community center, consisted of about three shelves of tattered *Reader's Digest* books.

"Don't you worry about my sister," Rebekah said sharply. "You take care of that brother of yours." Indeed, he was planning to do just that; he had a very full agenda for both Harley and those two screw-loose friends of his, Eddie and Russell.

They drove in silence until they reached the outskirts of the town, then turned onto Front Street, pulling in between the lumberyard and the gun shop. The trailer still rested on the rusty steel hitch, a foot off the ground.

"Go get him," Charlie said to Rebekah, and she said, "It's cold out. Just honk the horn."

Obedience, Charlie thought, would be the theme for his next video sermon.

He honked, and watched as the window blind was raised. He could see the outline of Harley's head, framed by the pale violet glow of the snake tank. Charlie had never actually been inside the trailer, but Rebekah had been, and she'd filled him in on the gory details.

The door opened and Harley stumbled down the steps, still zipping his coat. His hair looked wet from the shower. He climbed into the backseat next to Bathsheba, who stashed her book out of sight. Charlie looked back and said, "Show me the speech you're going to make."

"What speech? I'm just gonna say a couple of things and sit down as fast as I can."

"I thought you'd say that." Charlie fished some typewritten notes out of his coat pocket. "Read these over on the way. It's what you're going to say."

Harley grudgingly took the paper and studied it as Charlie drove. Charlie rather fancied his own way with words—over the years he had been able to talk his way out of more than one rap, including armed burglary and assault—and even if he couldn't be the one declaiming them, it would be his words spoken from the pulpit of the town church.

With his handicapped sticker, Charlie was able to park the van right beside the front stairs. Rebekah pushed his chair up the ramp. Just inside, not far from the plaque that listed all the fishermen who had been lost at sea in the past hundred years, there were bulletin boards covered with the names and photos of the newly dead. Lucas Muller. Freddie Farrell. Jonah Tasi, the Samoan. Buddy Kubelik. Old

Man Richter. It said here that the old man's first name was Aloysius. No wonder he never used it. The photos showed the men holding up fish they'd caught, or crouching over dead elk, or hoisting beer mugs at the Yardarm. Some people had tacked on little notes and cards saying good-bye.

As Charlie's wheelchair was maneuvered down the aisle, the other people seemed to take quick notice of him, then turn away. Charlie knew that his entourage made something of a spectacle, and he liked that. This town had always been too small for him and his ambitions, but it wasn't until the accident—and his being saved—that he'd found the message, and the means, to make himself heard around the world. Vane's Holy Writ wasn't a powerful force yet, but he had every confidence that one day it would be. In His own good time, the Lord would show him how.

Rebekah stopped the chair beside the very front pew, and Charlie was pleased to see that the mayor and a couple of men beside her— one of whom looked like a Russkie—had to scoot down to make room for them. These must be the guys from the chopper, and Charlie was happy to catch a glimpse of them. Know your enemy, that's what he'd always said. And the Lord, he felt sure, would have no quarrel with common sense. That was where a lot of people went wrong, in his view; they thought the Lord wanted you to act like some Simple Simon, to go around expecting the best of everybody and trusting them like some dumb dog. What a load. The Lord wanted you to use your God-given wits to aid Him in His cause—and Charlie had never come up short in that department.

But speaking of which . . . the Right Reverend Wallach, a worthless milquetoast who couldn't stir a bowl of Cheerios much less a congregation, ascended to the pulpit with a Bible in one hand and in the other a white life preserver from the *Neptune II,* which he hung from a hook attached to the lectern. It was not the first time the hook had been used for that purpose, nor would it be the last. The Bering Sea wasn't getting any kinder.

"We are gathered here today," the reverend said, "in remembrance of the good men who lost their lives doing what they did so well, and with such joy."

Ten seconds in, and Charlie had already nearly guffawed. Anybody who thought crabbers did it for the fun of it was out of his mind. It was just about the worst work in the world. He'd done it for years, before the first *Neptune* went down, and hadn't missed it for a single minute since. Extending his ministry was what he lived for now, and to that end he would do whatever he had to. Or, more to the point, whatever Harley, and his pals Eddie and Russell, had to do. Before the service, he'd spotted those other two losers smoking a joint outside.

Harley had already broached the subject of the job to them, so Charlie wasn't going to have to waste a lot of time on persuasion. Getting onto St. Peter's Island, and digging up graves that might still be sealed in the permafrost, was going to require a lot of hard work. What bothered Charlie was that he'd let this potential gold mine sit there, right under his nose, his whole life. Was it Providence that had finally opened his eyes? If there was more treasure where that emerald-embossed cross had come from, he was finally going to have the resources to do whatever he wanted. He'd be able to flood the whole planet with the holy word. Jesus might have put the stash in his way for that very reason.

And who knew how much of it there might be?

Ever since he'd found the cross in Harley's anorak, he'd been digging through Internet sites, ordering books and downloading monographs, even posing as a professor at the University of Alaska in order to call up a couple of experts on Russian history and grill them. And everything he'd learned—like the fact that the colony was founded by a batch of fanatical Siberians who had settled on the island between 1910 and 1918—only whetted his appetite more.

"We are going to hear today from members of the lost men's families," the reverend was droning on. "And also from the captain of the unfortunate vessel capsized on that fateful night, for he alone lived to tell the tale."

And a tale it would be, Charlie thought.

"Let us begin," the reverend said, "with Mr. Muller, the father of the youngest crewman, Lucas."

As Muller, who ran a hardware supply store, stepped solemnly to the pulpit, Charlie tapped his fingers impatiently on his knees. He was still pondering his latest findings. Turns out, these Siberians had been followers of the mad monk, Rasputin, the one who had bewitched the last Tsar and Tsaritsa of Russia. The Romanovs. Some of this stuff had come back to him from school—you couldn't grow up in Alaska and know nothing about the Russians who lived right across the strait—but what he hadn't known about was the Romanov jewels. He hadn't known that the Tsar and his family had owned one of the most astonishing collections of jewelry the world had ever seen.

And that a lot of it was still missing to this day.

"My boy never failed at anything he put his mind to," Mr. Muller was saying. "He was smart as a whip and worked as hard as any man I ever knew."

Charlie knew that the blame for the shipwreck had been attributed to Lucas's piloting of the boat, and he guessed that this was the father's way of redeeming his son's reputation. He hoped that Harley wouldn't decide to ad-lib and rub any salt in that wound.

As Muller yielded the pulpit to the Samoan sailor's mother, Charlie went over the list in his mind again—the endless array of tiaras and necklaces, earrings and bracelets, gilded crosses and enameled eggs— eggs, made by some jeweler named Fabergé—that had comprised the royal collection. The Tsaritsa, infatuated with her holy man from the steppes, had given him lavish presents, and there were even rumors that she had become his mistress. But who would ever know, or give a damn, about that now? All that mattered to Charlie was the obvious value of the cross—and the fact that it had been found on the island. If the cross was there, the rest of the missing Romanov jewels might be there, too.

The Samoan's mother had given way to Farrell's sister, and then to an engineering buddy of Old Man Richter, and it was finally time for

Harley, who slouched to the pulpit like a man about to be hanged. Charlie wanted to holler at him to straighten up, but he was relieved to see him take out the comments Charlie had written for him and start reading.

Rebekah nodded approvingly, and glanced over at Charlie with her beady, hard eyes. Bathsheba had put down whatever trashy book she'd brought and was actually paying some attention.

"Mankind is forever caught in the crosshairs of God's grace," Harley was saying—a line Charlie was particularly fond of. "Belief is the path that we all must take. That path will lead us through the trials and tribulations of life, and protect us from the many evils and the countless plagues that assail us. Even as I clung to the lid of that coffin, I trusted in God to deliver me to shore."

Charlie knew that God was probably the last thing on Harley's mind that night, but it sure sounded good. Harley then read Charlie's account of all the other deeply religious revelations he'd had as he fought his way through the freezing sea—full of doubts and fears— before landing on the shore, where his faith had finally deposited him.

"I only wish that I had been able to save my fellow crew members who had shared in that awful voyage with me," he concluded. "But I do know now that they are all resting, safe and dry, in God's loving hands."

When he wrapped up, Charlie wanted to applaud, or maybe even proclaim in some way that those were his words, but he just didn't see how to do it gracefully. The mayor got up next—big surprise—and made some remarks that she probably thought would help get her elected again (as if anybody in his right mind would want the job, anyway) before the Reverend Wallach recited the Lord's Prayer, and announced that hot drinks and refreshments were now being served in the annex.

"I do okay?" Harley shuffled over to ask his brother. He stuffed the paper into the back pocket of his jeans.

"You mumbled some of the lines, but yeah, it was fine."

"You're supposed to make eye contact," Rebekah put in.

"I didn't ask you."

"Well, if you'd been smart, you would have."

There was no love lost, Charlie knew, between his brother and Rebekah. Until the sisters had shown up, Harley had lived in the old family homestead, too, but once the women had taken over, Harley, and his pet snake, had been none too subtly eased out the door.

"I thought you did good," Bathsheba said shyly.

"Where are the idiots?" Charlie asked, and Harley, knowing exactly who he was referring to, looked around the emptying church. "Over in the annex, I guess."

"Get them and meet me out at the van."

Rebekah wheeled him back outside, then went to join her sister at the refreshment tables. Charlie knew the two sisters would be about as welcome there as ants at a picnic.

A few minutes later, Harley showed up with Eddie and Russell. Their hands were so filled with donuts and bagels and cardboard cups of coffee they didn't know how to get the van's doors opened. Finally, Harley put his own cup on the hood of the car and slid open the side door. Charlie wondered to himself how these three would ever be able to accomplish anything more complicated.

But it was his job to make sure they did.

"What's the word?" he asked as they settled into the backseats. "Have you got a boat?"

The three of them exchanged baffled looks before Eddie volunteered that he could probably make off with his uncle's boat for a few days. "But I might have to throw him a few bucks if he finds out."

"Throw him a six-pack and he'll never find out anything," Russell said.

"You boys have got to get onto that island by tomorrow," Charlie said.

"And do what?" Russell asked, crumbs spilling from his mouth. He had the look, Charlie thought, of a cow chewing its cud.

"Get the jewels before these government guys get there."

"Who says they're even going there?" Eddie asked.

Charlie took a second to calm himself, then said, "They don't do surveillance runs over places they don't plan to go. And they don't give my brother, Harley, here grief about that coffin lid if they're not planning to look for the rest of it themselves."

"But they're gonna have all this equipment and shit," Eddie said.

"That's why you're going to get there first, and land on the leeward side of the island," Charlie explained. "As far from the beach as you can get."

"There's nowhere else to put in," Eddie replied.

"A big boat, no, but your uncle's trawler draws under six feet. You can get it into a cove. And of course you'll have to wait until dark." These days, darkness was falling sooner and sooner in the afternoon. "You can't light any fires, either. When the feds do come, you don't want them smelling your smoke or spotting the campsite. A cave would be good. Find a cave."

"For how long?" Eddie whined.

"As long as it takes," Charlie replied. "And bring some guns."

"Guns?" Russell said, finding his voice again. "I'm not shooting it out with a bunch of Coast Guardsmen. Two years at Spring Creek was plenty for me."

"Wolves," Charlie said. "The island's got wolves, in case you haven't heard."

"Oh."

Some of the townspeople were filtering out of the annex now, pulling on hats and gloves. Geordie Ayakuk, eating a hot dog, had on neither. These natives had natural blubber, Charlie thought—another sign of God's mysterious handiwork.

The two sisters appeared in the throng, coming toward the van, and it was as if Harley and his cronies had seen a ghost.

"Okay then," Eddie said, hastily unlatching the side door and sliding it open. "I better get going."

"Me, too," Russell said, spilling out after him.

Harley remained in the front passenger seat. With a dubious expression, he said, "How long do you really think this is going to take?"

"It all depends."

"On what?"

"On how fast you can dig."

Rebekah was now standing by the car door, plainly waiting for Harley to give up the front seat to her.

"I'll drop you off at your trailer," Charlie said, "and you can get started on the packing."

But Harley took one look at Bathsheba—eager to share a ride in the backseat with him—and said, "Forget it—I'll walk."

Chapter 17

As the van pulled away, Harley put up the collar on his parka and trudged down Front Street in a biting wind. It was only midday, but the clouds were thick and the light was already fading from the sky. Everything around him—the smattering of storefronts, the crooked totem pole, the rusted-out trucks with the monster tires—was bathed in a dull pewter-colored glow, like it was all contained under some overturned bowl. What would it be like, he wondered, to see hot sunlight on palm trees and walk around in nothing but a T-shirt and shorts?

And what would Angie Dobbs look like with a real tan, not that lobstery color she sometimes got when she'd been to the tanning parlor in Nome?

Both the Arctic Circle Gun Shoppe and the lumberyard were closed because of the funeral service, and apart from the violet glow from the snake tank filtering through the slats of his blind, his trailer, too, lay dark and silent at the end of the alleyway between them. The Rottweiler in the gun shop barked ferociously as he passed by, and threw itself against the chicken-wire screen in the window.

"Shut the fuck up," Harley said, as he went to the storage shed behind the lumberyard. There was a padlock on the door, but Harley knew that the owner had lost the keys so many times he didn't bother to lock the damn thing anymore. Besides, what was there to steal, apart from the few shovels and picks that were precisely what Harley was after? They probably wouldn't even be missed before he was back from the island with what he hoped would be the jewels in hand. .

The jewels that would buy him his first-class ticket to Miami Beach.

Cracking the metal doors open just enough to slink inside, Harley groped for the string attached to the lightbulb in the ceiling. The whole fixture swayed, throwing shadows over the already gloomy interior. There were piles of rotting boards, a couple of broken-down lathes, sagging sawhorses littered with tools. Toward the back, leaning up against the wall like a bunch of drunks, he saw the shovels and spades and iron pickaxes that they'd need to dig up the graves and crack open the coffins. Just looking at them made his arms ache, and he reminded himself to make sure that Eddie and Russell did most of the hard labor. He was the foreman on this job, and the foreman's job was to oversee things. He could already anticipate the shit he was going to get from the other two.

Skirting a wheelbarrow with a missing wheel, he started to rummage around among the shovels, looking for the ones best suited to the job. He'd need at least one with a broad flat blade in case the snow came down hard, and a couple more with sharper, firmer ends for penetrating the soil. Chisels would be good, too; they could be driven into the ground like stakes and, if placed well enough, Eddie and Russell might be able to remove whole slabs of earth, virtually intact, all at once.

The wind was blowing so hard at the metal doors that one of them banged shut again, and Harley jumped at the sound. The hanging light fixture swung from the ceiling like a pendulum, and Harley wished the damn thing had a higher-wattage bulb in it. Everything in the room cast a weird shadow around the corrugated metal walls, and for one split second Harley thought he caught a glimpse of something moving behind him, as if it had just entered the shed.

Could the damn dog have been let loose? He stood stock-still, waiting, but he didn't see anything skulking along the ground, among the planks and chain saws. And if he listened carefully, as he was doing now, over the sound of the wind he could hear the Rottweiler howling in the gun shop next door, right where she belonged.

But howling like she was freaking out over something.

Harley didn't understand the point of dogs. As far as he was concerned, they were just failed wolves—and you could shoot the whole lot of them, for all he cared.

He went back to picking his tools—he didn't want to spend all day in here, since what he was doing might, technically, be called stealing if the owner caught him at it—but stopped when he thought he heard something moving again, on just the other side of a tall stack of boards.

"Hey," he said. "Somebody in here?"

But there was no reply.

"McDaniel?" he said, thinking it might be the owner of the lumberyard trying to catch him red-handed. "That you? It's Harley."

Still no answer, but definitely the sound of a footfall.

"I just needed to borrow a shovel to clear the ice off my trailer hitch. Hope that's okay." But knowing the reputation the Vane boys had around town, he added, "I was gonna put it right back as soon as I was done." And for once, Christ, it was almost the truth.

With a spade still in his hands, he crept gingerly to the end of the pile, expecting maybe to see McDaniel, or even that Inuit kid who worked as his assistant, but what he saw instead, going in and out of the light, was more like some scrawny scarecrow. At first he even thought it might be a mannequin.

But then it blinked.

"Who the fuck are you?" he said, but even as he asked, he recognized him.

The wet brown hair, hanging down onto the gray tunic with the banded collar. The long black sealskin coat. The big dark eyes, the petrified skin, the yellow teeth protruding from the drawn lips.

It was the body from the coffin he'd found in the nets.

And as he looked on in horror, the creature extended his hand, as if expecting to be given something.

"What do you want?" Harley said, backing up but clutching the spade for dear life. "Get the fuck out of here!"

The young man opened his mouth—and Harley could swear that, even from ten feet away, he got a gust of the foulest air he had ever smelled—and said something in what sounded like Russian. But Russian spoken as if by someone still in the act of drowning, the words gurgling and slurred.

Harley lifted the spade and cocked it back over one shoulder, like a baseball bat.

"Don't come any closer!"

He could hear the Rottweiler next door going crazier than ever, and for once he did wish the damn dog had gotten loose.

The man repeated whatever he'd said, and even lifted a hand—the fingers were nothing but stark white bones, with long, curling nails—and touched an area of his chest.

Right about where the emerald cross had hung.

Jesus Christ. If Harley had had it on him, he'd have thrown the damn thing right back at him.

"I don't have it!" he shouted. And then, as if it would make any sense, "Charlie's got it!"

But the man didn't look like he understood a word of English, and when he took a step forward, Harley found himself backed up against the rear wall of the shed. He brandished the spade, but the man took no apparent notice. He came closer and Harley swung the spade at him, catching him on the shoulder and flinging him like a bundle of sticks and rags into a pile of loose timbers and shavings.

Screaming, Harley leapt over the spot where he had been standing, and with the spade still clutched in his hand, ran toward the door, knocking the wheelbarrow over on its side, then out into the alleyway. The Rottweiler was going crazy, barking in a frenzy and foaming at the window. Looking over his shoulder, Harley suddenly collided with something, or someone, and went sprawling on the ground.

Standing above him, looking pissed and confused, was McDaniel.

"What the hell are you up to, Harley?" His eyes flicked to the spade. "You planning to shovel my driveway?"

"I just needed to borrow this," Harley said, still trying to catch his breath and keeping an eye on the open doors to the shed. Was the damn thing going to come out after him?

"Borrow it?" McDaniel said. "Yeah, right."

He stomped into the shed before Harley could stop him, and after a minute or so, Harley saw the light go out and McDaniel came out again, none the worse for wear.

"You need to borrow some tools," he said, "all you have to do is ask."

"Got it," Harley said, standing on his own two feet now. But what had happened to that corpse in the sealskin coat? Had McDaniel missed it somehow? Or was it just . . . gone?

"That was a pretty good speech you made in the church."

Was it ever there in the first place? Harley wondered if he was losing it.

"Now don't go fucking things up by stealing stuff again."

Harley nodded, and shuffled off toward his trailer, leaving the spade propped by the steps. His hands were so cold and unsteady he had trouble getting the key in the lock. And when he did finally turn to close the door behind him, he saw McDaniel still watching him and shaking his head.

Chapter 18

Tonight, Prince Felix Yussoupov thought, I am going to change everything. Not only the way the world regards me, but history itself.

Oh, he was well aware of the figure he cut in cosmopolitan society. For years, he had deliberately gone about shocking everyone he knew—showing up in the finest women's fashions and draped in his mother's jewels, at cafés and restaurants and parties. He had hosted wild parties—orgies, to be frank—at one or another of his family's many palaces in Moscow, St. Petersburg, or the countryside. He had enjoyed the favors of girls and boys alike, actresses and opera singers and dashing young sailors. And to cap it all off, he had married one of the Tsar's own nieces, the Princess Irina, celebrated for her unparalleled beauty. In truth, he thought he was just as good-looking as she was, but she was a very sought-after match, and together he had to admit that they made a perfect pair.

Tonight, however, the princess was safely ensconced hundreds of miles from St. Petersburg, in the grand Yussoupov hunting lodge in the Crimea. He wanted her nowhere near the Moika Palace tonight, on this fateful New Year's Eve. It was enough that she had served as bait for the trap.

Yussoupov had promised Rasputin that if he came to the palace at midnight, there would be a private party at which the monk would be introduced, at long last, to this famous beauty. "The princess has heard so much about you," Yussoupov told him, "she insisted that I arrange for her to meet you in person." The man's rapacity was exceeded only by his vanity. "I have promised her you would be there."

The prince had sent his own motorcar—the black Bentley with the family crest on the doors—to pick up Rasputin and bring him to the palace. Checking his gold pocket watch, he saw that the car should be arriving any minute. From the upper floor, he could hear the gramophone playing "Yankee Doodle Dandy"—a very popular tune among Russian society these days—and the sound of his coconspirators' voices, simulating the merriment of a party in full swing.

Snow was falling on the flagstones of the court outside and sticking to the thin sheet of ice that covered the canal beyond the gates. Downstairs, in the vaulted chambers where the deed was to be done, all was in readiness. The dainty cakes, laced with cyanide, were arrayed on silver salvers. The Madeira, also poisoned, was decanted and waiting only to be drunk. And when Yussoupov saw Dr. Lazovert, disguised as a chauffeur, pilot the car through the iron gates, he stepped outside to greet his guest.

"Welcome!" he shouted, throwing open his arms, as Rasputin disembarked.

"Felix!" Rasputin replied, grasping him in a bear hug.

For the mad monk, he was positively presentable tonight. Yussoupov could tell the man had bathed—the scent of cheap soap clung to his skin—and he was wearing an intricately embroidered silk blouse and black-velvet trousers. Even his leather boots were shined and clean.

But the pectoral cross that usually dangled around his throat, its emeralds reputedly imbued with some mystical powers of enchantment—for how else could a brute like this have risen to such eminence and power?—was nowhere visible. Yussoupov took it as a stroke of luck, like entering the lists against an opponent with a broken lance.

Cocking his head at the noise from the upper windows, Rasputin said, "You've started the merriment without me!"

But the prince was already guiding him into the vestibule and away from the main staircase. Rasputin resisted, and Yussoupov had to whisper, "The princess will join us downstairs, for our own party, later."

"What's wrong with that one?" Rasputin said, with a glint of indignation in his eye.

"It's a rather stuffy affair," Yussoupov said, urging him again toward the stairs to the cellar. "Several of those troublemakers from the Duma are there."

"I'm not afraid of them!" Rasputin said. "They can rail about me all they want! I eat politicians for breakfast."

"But we have something far better waiting for you."

Reluctantly, Rasputin allowed himself to be led down the winding stairs to the vaulted rooms below. A roaring fire had been set in the hearth, and the air had been perfumed with incense. Grand Duke Dmitri, standing nervously by the bar, held up a glass of champagne and echoed the welcome from their host.

Rasputin looked mollified by his presence. He was an interesting mix, this so-called holy man—one moment a man of the people, speaking for the peasants, and the next a craven adventurer, eager to find favor with the nobles whom he pretended to despise. One thing Yussoupov did know was that Rasputin had become a liability to the aristocracy; with the Tsaritsa completely in his thrall, he was able to make or break the fortunes of anyone at court. And he had begun to use that influence, more and more, to meddle in affairs of state— and even to influence the course of the war. With Rasputin trying to second-guess everything from the military's strategy to the Tsar's choice of ministers, it was plain to patriots like Prince Felix and the Grand Duke Dmitri that something had to be done.

And tonight, they would do it. When the news got out, the prince was certain that he would be miraculously transformed in the public mind from notorious, rich wastrel to the Savior of Mother Russia.

"We've made your favorites," Dmitri said, proffering the platter of cakes that Rasputin normally adored, but to his and Felix's consternation, the *starets* declined them. He wandered around the room, passing under the stone arches and admiring the *objets d'art* that filled the glass vitrines. The granite floors were covered with thick Persian carpets and a white bearskin rug, the bear's head still attached and fangs bared.

"Music!" Yussoupov said, clapping his hands, and Dmitri picked up a balalaika and began to strum. Rasputin began to wave his hand in time to the music, then slumped onto a carved divan. On the table beside him, the cakes beckoned, and as Yussoupov pretended not to notice, Rasputin idly picked one up and gobbled it down.

Dr. Lazovert, who had personally ground up the potassium cyanide and sprinkled it into each pastry, had sworn that death would be nearly instantaneous.

Even Dmitri slowed his strumming to watch.

But Rasputin simply grinned, and said, "Again! And play something more cheerful this time!"

The prince looked on in wonder as the monk picked a crumb from his bushy beard and ate it.

Along with a second cake.

Dmitri's fingers fumbled at the strings of the instrument. Yussoupov waited with bated breath.

Rasputin appeared unaffected.

"Perhaps our guest would enjoy some wine," Dmitri said, a telltale quaver in his voice, and Yussoupov, as if waking from a bad dream, quickly went to fetch the decanter. Filling a crystal goblet with Madeira, he held it out to the reclining monk.

"You want me to drink alone?" Rasputin said, taking the glass, and the prince, feigning amusement, returned to the bar and poured himself a generous snifter of brandy, instead.

"To the New Year!" he said, raising his glass.

"To the beautiful Princess Irina!" Rasputin bellowed, as the clock in the corner struck the hour. "Is she ever planning to join us down here?" He downed the glass of Madeira, wiped his mouth with the back of his sleeve, then held out his glass for more. The prince nearly staggered as he fetched the bottle and refilled the glass.

Was it possible, he began to wonder? Could this creature—this filthy monk from the wastelands of Siberia—truly be some sort of prophet? Even without the pectoral cross, was he invulnerable, watched over by some divine Providence, as he had so often and grandly proclaimed?

The Grand Duke Dmitri, pleading a sudden headache, dropped the balalaika on an ottoman and fled up the winding stairs in terror. Rasputin stirred himself on the couch, then abruptly stood. Thank God, Yussoupov thought, the man was at least weaving on his feet. He ambled like a bear toward one of the vitrines, the one that held a rock-crystal crucifix fashioned in sixteenth-century Italy, and studied it through the glass.

Yussoupov was at his wit's end. As a last resort, he had hidden a Browning revolver in an ebony box behind the bar, and with shaking hands he retrieved it now, and stepped behind the monk.

"Feel free to take the crucifix out of the case," he said, but Rasputin seemed content to leave it where it was. Instead, his hands went to his gut and began to massage his belly.

"You might be wise to hold it," the prince said, his tone more determined than before, "and say a prayer." Yussoupov could see Rasputin's face reflected in the glass, just as the monk could see his own.

Rasputin suddenly gagged, and putting out a hand toward the cabinet, said, "You have poisoned me."

Yussoupov did not reply. Instead, he raised the gun, his hand trembling, aimed it squarely at Rasputin's back, and fired once.

For several seconds, Rasputin did not move or even flinch. The prince tried to fire again, but his finger was so slick with sweat it slid off the trigger. Slowly, the monk turned around, his blue eyes now blazing with rage, before he toppled over, falling flat on the bearskin rug.

Yussoupov heard footsteps on the stairs, and when he turned he saw Grand Duke Dmitri, Dr. Lazovert, and another conspirator, Purishkevich, all staring at the gun hanging from his hand, and then at the body lying prostrate on the floor. The monk lay still, his eyes closed, but there was no sign of any blood. Dr. Lazovert cautiously approached, took Rasputin's pulse, and declared him dead.

"Good, then let's wrap him up in something and get him out of here," Purishkevich, the oldest and most levelheaded among them, said, looking all around the vaulted cellars.

How had they not thought through this part of the plan, Yussoupov berated himself.

"Upstairs," Purishkevich declared. "We'll use the blue curtains from the drawing room."

As the others all too eagerly raced back up the stairs, Yussoupov was left alone again with the corpse. He slumped into an armchair, dropping the revolver on the carpet. He had expected to be overcome with emotion, to be brimming with a sense of triumph. But there was none of that. His hands were still shaking, and his ears were ringing from the clamor of the shot.

A spark flew from the hearth, landing only inches from the monk's outstretched boot.

Which twitched.

The prince's breath stopped in his throat, and as he studied the monk's face, he saw first one eye open, then the other. And before he could even jump up from his chair, Rasputin was back on his feet, spittle flying from his snarling lips, his hands tearing at Yussoupov's clothing.

"You murderer!" the monk said, as his fingers clenched around the prince's neck. They were both being dragged to the floor, but the prince was able to break free and run for the stairs, screaming for help.

"Murderer!"

Rasputin was close behind him, scrambling up the winding steps like an animal on all fours. Yussoupov could hear him panting and felt his hands grasping at the hem of his trousers.

"He's alive! He's alive!" he shouted running into the drawing room and slamming the doors closed behind him. Purishkevich and the others, gathering up the torn curtains, looked slack-jawed with disbelief. "He's still alive!" Yussoupov repeated, barring the doors with his back.

"It can't be," Dr. Lazovert said. "He had no pulse."

"You shot him," Dmitri said. "You shot him in the back."

"He's been poisoned ten times over," Lazovert added.

"But he's escaping!" the prince screamed. "Even now!"

"This is impossible," Purishkevich said, dismissively, but at the same time drawing a pistol from beneath his waistcoat. "Get out of the way."

Pushing the prince aside, he strode out into the hallway with the gun drawn. A trail of blood led toward the marble vestibule, and a cold wind was blowing into the palace through the open doors. Yussoupov, cowering behind him, pointed outside and said, "You see? You see?"

Slipping and sliding in the falling snow, the monk was making his way inexorably across the courtyard and toward the main gates, which fronted onto the canal.

"Murderers!" Rasputin was shouting. "The Tsaritsa shall hear of this! You are murderers!"

"Kill him!" Yussoupov was screaming. "Before he gets away!"

But even as Purishkevich stepped forward and fired, Yussoupov jostled his arm and the bullet clanged off the iron gates.

"Shoot him!" Yussoupov cried, and Purishkevich, pushing him away, took aim again.

The shot went wide, as did the next. Rasputin was fiddling with the lock on the gates. To concentrate, Purishkevich bit his own left hand, then fired again, and this time the bullet hit Rasputin in the shoulder. He slumped to one side, and the next shot struck the back of his head.

By the time the conspirators huddled around the fallen body, his blood was seeping out onto the snow, but his eyes were still staring up at the sky and he was grinding his teeth in pain and fury. Was there no killing this man, Yussoupov thought in horror? Would it never end?

Purishkevich, too, swore under his breath, then kicked the monk in the temple, hard. Yussoupov, for want of a better weapon, removed his heavy, hand-tooled leather belt with the silver buckle and lashed at the body until, at last, there was no further sign of life. Dr. Lazovert raised a hand to stop them. "Enough," he said, "it's done."

The Grand Duke Dmitri emerged from the house, dragging the blue curtains, but before they could roll the body up in them, Yussoupov said, "Stop," and kneeling down, he tore open Rasputin's bloody shirt and searched his neck and chest for any sign of the cross.

"What are you doing?" Dmitri asked.

"The emerald cross—I'm looking for it!"

"Good Christ, Felix, aren't you rich enough already?" Dmitri said, shoving him aside. "Have you lost your mind?"

A fair question, Yussoupov thought, as he sat back in the snow, watching as the others finished wrapping the corpse and tying a rope around the whole bundle. It was late on a cold and snowy night, so to Yussoupov's relief, they saw no one, and no one saw them, as they carried the body down an alleyway, under a bridge, and out onto the frozen Neva River; there, they shoved it through a hole in the ice. In the moonlight, it appeared as nothing more than a dark shadow under the water, drifting slowly, silently, downstream. With it went Yussoupov's dreams of glory. Suddenly it had dawned on him—and how could he have been so blind?—that far from being hailed as a savior, he might just as easily be labeled an assassin. It was hard work killing a man—he'd never done it before—and though the Tsar might secretly rejoice at being rid of the madman, the Tsaritsa would be enraged. Why hadn't he thought these things through more clearly?

All he wanted now, with every freezing fiber of his being, was for the body to remain undiscovered beneath the ice until spring . . . or, better yet, doomsday.

Chapter 19

During the funeral service, Slater had received a running commentary, under her breath, from Nika. As one mourner after another took the podium, she told him who it was, how he or she was connected to the *Neptune* tragedy, how long the family had been working in these Alaskan waters. They were a hardy lot, and Slater felt the anguish of their loss. In a place like this, there wasn't much to hold on to, and they had all just suffered a devastating blow.

But of all the people present, he had to admit that the most riveting bunch were the Vanes—Charlie wheeling in like a dignitary waiting for his ovation, attended to by the two whey-faced women in the long dresses. Harley scuffling along behind, like a kid about to perform at a recital for which he hadn't practiced. Even seated in the pews, they seemed to create an air of turbulence around them, and he noticed that after Harley had made his remarks, and the service had concluded, none of the other congregants seemed all that anxious to hang out with them.

"Not the most popular kids at school, are they?" Slater said, as he and Nika made their way next door to the rec center and the refreshments. There was a wide, empty circle around the two women. Slater had never seen a pair of sisters who gave off a more witchy vibe.

"Most folks in Port Orlov know enough not to get mixed up with them."

Already loaded down with donuts and coffee, Eddie and Russell made their way back outside again.

"With some exceptions," she added.

Slater himself was an object of some interest, he could tell. Everyone in town had seen the Sikorsky by now, and although the mayor herself had backed up his story—"it's a routine training mission for the Coast Guard," he had heard her tell three people already—he was sure that there were other rumors circulating, too. It wouldn't be a small town if there weren't.

But as long as the rumors didn't involve the Spanish flu, he was okay with it.

On the way out, he saw a blue van with what looked like a confab going on inside, among the Vane boys and Eddie and Russell. He wondered if he should post a sentry on the chopper that night or risk having its hubcaps stolen. He'd already been stuck in Port Orlov longer than he'd intended, but bad weather in the Midwest had grounded Eva Lantos's plane, and military red tape had tied up some of the equipment scheduled for arrival on the second chopper. Murphy's Law in action. Slater knew that every mission encountered problems like these—especially one like this, organized virtually on the fly—but it didn't make it any easier to take. Patience had never been among his virtues.

When he got back to the community center, where he'd been bunking with Professor Kozak and the two Coast Guard pilots, he went straight to Nika's office, where he'd set up his own little command post on a corner of her desk and the top of her file cabinet. It was the most secure office on the premises, and she'd been very accommodating, but he still felt a bit guilty about usurping so much of her space. She'd even given him the spare key.

"Don't lose it," she said. "The town locksmith is drunk most of the time, and it's not easy to get another one made."

With Nika off making official condolence calls, and Kozak exploring the local terrain, he sat down in Nika's chair—instead of the stool

he'd brought in for himself—and got to work, checking logistics, firing off email queries, figuring out how this assignment could be completed in the shortest amount of time and with the minimum amount
of public scrutiny. The weather reports weren't good—a storm was
brewing—and he wanted to beat it to St. Peter's Island, at least in time
to get a few of the necessary structures set up. He didn't much relish
the idea of erecting lighting poles in the teeth of gale-force winds.

For a couple of hours, he managed to lose himself in his work,
even phoning Sergeant Groves—and plainly waking him up—to go
over the latest alterations to the plan.

"So what's your ETA now?" he asked, and Groves, audibly yawning, said, "We should be able to load everything onto the second
Sikorsky—including the good Dr. Lantos—by Thursday morning."

It was only Tuesday night now, and Slater had to bite his lip in frustration.

"What time do you want to rendezvous on the island?" Groves
asked.

"We're not going to," Slater said, having given it much thought
since his aerial reconnaissance. "The colony's on top of the plateau,
but it's hemmed in by trees and the remaining wooden structures
The graveyard is in an even trickier spot. There's no room for two
helicopters to off-load at the same time."

"How's the beach? We could use that, right?"

Again, Slater had to nix the idea. "The beach can handle no more
than a Zodiac. It's too narrow and sloped, and the only way up to the
plateau, a considerable distance, is a staircase cut into the stone. I
wouldn't try to carry a kitten up those steps, much less a centrifuge."

"So you'll go first?"

"Yes, and you can follow. We'll leave a two-hour window for the
initial cargo deployment, and start at eleven A.M. on Thursday. It
won't be light enough earlier."

They were discussing a myriad of other details—the order in
which the hazard tents would be erected, the grid of the ground
ramps and location of the generator shacks—when Slater picked up
the aroma of stew and heard a furtive knock on the door.

"Come in," he said, holding the phone to his shoulder, and looked up to see Nika holding a Crock-Pot between two pot holders.

"The Yardarm is doing their version of chicken Kiev tonight," she said. "Trust me, you're better off with my home cooking."

Slater was embarrassed to be caught so much in possession of her office and started to rise from her chair.

"Finish your call," she said, "and meet me in the gym."

"Sounds like you've made a friend," Sergeant Groves said with a laugh before they hung up. "Now don't blow it."

Slater straightened up his papers and tried to leave her desk the way he'd found it, then went down the hall to the community center's gymnasium, where Nika had set up a card table underneath the scoreboard with a bottle of wine, the pot of stew, and a couple of place settings. It was about the least picturesque spot Slater could ever have imagined, which was why he found it puzzling that it felt so cozy and romantic. He instinctively tucked his shirt into his pants to straighten it out and ran a hand over his hair. Maybe he did need to get out more, as Sergeant Groves had often kidded him. "You're divorced," Groves had told him the last time they'd had a drink in a D.C. bar. "You're not dead."

"You really didn't have to do this," Slater said, taking a seat on the folding chair across from Nika.

"Inuit hospitality," she said, dishing out the stew. "We'd be disgraced if we didn't do something for a guest who had come so far."

Slater opened the wine bottle and filled their glasses. He raised his glass in a toast to his host, then found himself tongue-tied. "To . . . a successful mission," he said, and Nika smiled. Clinking her glass against his, she said, "To a successful mission."

"And a terrific meal," Slater said, trying to recover. "Smells great." He draped his napkin in his lap. "Thanks so much."

The conversation went in stops and starts. Slater, who could talk about disease vectors until the cows came home, had never been good at this small talk; his wife Martha had always been the one to carry the day. Between bites of the reindeer stew, he asked Nika about her life and her background, and she was happy to oblige. It even turned out that they had some friends in common on the faculty of Berkeley, where she'd received her master's in anthropology before coming back to serve the people of Port Orlov.

"I wanted to preserve and record a way of life—the native traditions and customs," she said, "before they disappeared altogether."

"It can't be easy to keep them going in the age of the Internet and the cell phone and the video game."

"No, it's not," she conceded. "But there's a lot to be said for that ancient culture. It sustained my people through centuries in the harshest climate on earth."

As they talked, Slater discovered that she had an extensive knowledge of, and even deeper reverence for, the spiritual beliefs and legends of the native Alaskans. It was like receiving a free and fascinating tutorial . . . and from a teacher, he had to admit, who was a lot better-looking than anyone he remembered from his own school days. She was dressed in just a pair of jeans and a white cable-knit sweater, with her long black hair swept back on both sides of her head and held by an amber barrette, but she might as well have been dressed to the nines. If it weren't for the scoreboard above the table, which revealed that Port Orlov had lost its last basketball game to a Visiting Team by twelve points, he could have sworn they were in some intimate little bistro in the Lower 48.

He wasn't even aware of when, or how, she had deftly turned the conversation back to him, but he found himself explaining how he'd been drawn into epidemiology, then about what had happened in Afghanistan to derail his Army career.

"And yet they've entrusted you with this very sensitive assignment," she said, refilling his glass. "They must still have a very high opinion of you."

"I work cheap," he said, to deflect the compliment.

But Nika, in her own subtle way, wouldn't let it go, asking question after question about how the mission was going to proceed, in what steps and over what period of time. Normally, Slater would have been much more circumspect about sharing any of this information, but after she had been so open with him, and considering the fact that she had been so cooperative so far, in everything from sharing her office to letting the chopper remain parked in the middle of the town's hockey rink, he would have felt churlish for holding back. It was only when she asked what time they would be leaving for the island that he heard a distant alarm bell. What did she mean by "they"?

"The team," he said, "will be lifting off late Thursday morning."

"Do I need to bring anything in particular along?" she asked innocently, as she produced two cherry tarts from a hamper beneath the table. "Sorry, I should have brought ice cream to top them off."

"No, the *team* has everything it needs," he emphasized.

"Okay, no problem," she said, sticking an upright spoon into his tart for him. "I've got the best sleeping bag in the world and I'm used to bunking down anywhere."

"Where are you talking about?" Slater said, ignoring the spoon and tart.

"On St. Peter's Island," she replied. "You didn't think I was going to let you go without me, did you?"

"Actually," he said, starting to feel played, "I did. This is a highly classified and possibly dangerous mission, and only authorized personnel—all of whom I have carefully handpicked—are going over there."

Nika dabbed at her lips with her napkin, and said, "I had the tarts in a bun warmer. You should eat yours before it gets cold."

"I'm afraid there can be no exceptions."

"I agree," she said. "Authorized personnel only. And as the mayor of Port Orlov, in addition to its duly appointed tribal elder, I have to point out to you that the island is encompassed by the Northwest Territories Native Americans Act of 1986, and as such it is within our rights and prerogatives to decide who and when and how any incursions are made there."

Slater sat so far back in his chair it almost toppled over onto the gym floor.

"Now I'm not saying that official permission has been denied," she said, taking another spoonful of her tart, "but I'm not saying it's been granted yet, either."

She looked up at Slater, her black eyes shining, an inquisitive smile on her lips. "If I do say so myself, this is one hell of a tart."

And Slater, who had been up against some pretty formidable adversaries in his day, could only marvel at her aplomb. He'd never been snookered so smoothly, or so deliciously, in his life. Her veiled threat to delay the mission could be easily overruled by Dr. Levinson at the AFIP, but the paperwork and bureaucracy involved would tie him up on the ground for several days at least.

"Yep," she said, nodding over her dessert, "a little vanilla ice cream and this would have been perfect."

He had just acquired, like it or not, his own Sacajawea.

Chapter 20

"Goddammit," Harley muttered, "watch where you're throwing that rope."

"I didn't see you there," Russell said.

"And keep your voice down!"

"You keep yours down!" Russell shot back.

This expedition, Harley thought, was not getting off to the best start. First, they'd had to jimmy the fuel pump at the dock in order to gas up the boat.

And then, of course, there'd been that little "incident" in McDaniel's storage shed. When Harley had dared to poke his head back inside the next day, all he'd found by the wall was a pile of old rags and some wooden planks. He'd put the whole thing down to a hallucination, brought on by the stress from making that speech in the church, but he still hadn't managed to completely persuade himself. For now, he just put it out of his mind and resolved to say nothing about it to Eddie or Russell. They'd simply chalk it up to his being stoned on something . . . and want their share of whatever he'd been stoned on.

"What are you two making all this racket about?" Eddie said, coming up from the hold. "I thought we were supposed to keep quiet."

It was a freezing night on the docks of Port Orlov, and the chance of anyone else's being out, much less dumb enough to be setting sail, was pretty slight, but Harley had made it clear from the start that they should go about their business in the utmost secrecy. He hadn't even breathed a word of it to Angie, though that might have had more to do with the way she'd exchanged looks with that Coast Guardsman at the Yardarm than it did with his discretion. He was still ticked off and jealous.

"Let's shove off already," Harley said, "before the weather gets here." The next few days—if days were what you could call the murky gray episodes that separated the long stretches of darkness—were supposed to be stormy. But if you waited around for good weather in Alaska, as any local could tell you, you'd be waiting around forever.

The boat, called the *Kodiak,* belonged to Eddie's uncle, who was usually too lazy to take it out. It was nearly thirty years old and it wasn't much to look at, but since it had originally been built as a Navy launch, it had a very stiff hull, and a heavy steel rudder shoe that could withstand any kinds of trouble—rocks, logs, grounding—that the Bering Strait could throw at it. As on most Alaskan fishing ships, the cabin windows were Lexan and mounted to the outside, so that even the worst waves couldn't blow them out. In his cups one night, Eddie's uncle had bragged that it could withstand a complete swamping for twelve hours without sinking. How he would know such a thing had puzzled Harley—had they swamped it to find out?—but he didn't ask then, and he didn't care to find out now.

In the cabin, he let Eddie hang on to the wheel—after all, it was his uncle's boat—while Russell slouched in the corner with a beer.

"Keep it at half throttle till we're well away," Harley said, "then head northwest."

"I know where St. Pete's is," Eddie sneered.

"And you," Harley said to Russell, "get your ass out on deck and look for bergs."

"Why don't you get out there and freeze your own ass off?"

Harley could have removed the gun that was strapped under his anorak and made his point that way, but he didn't want to make things any worse than they were, and he didn't want to resort to any extreme measures until he had to. Russell defiantly took another long slug from the beer can, and it occurred to Harley that having him out on deck as lookout was a bad idea, anyway. He'd probably fall off the boat.

"Fuck it," he said, "I'll do it myself." Addressing Eddie, he said, "Take us around the west cliffs, then to the leeward side for a berth."

"Aye, aye, Captain Bligh."

Harley slipped a pair of binoculars around his neck, put up the hood on his coat, and tightened the Velcro clasps at the sleeves, then stepped out on the slippery, ice-rimed deck. He hadn't been out at sea since the wreck of the *Neptune,* and he found there was a new sense of anxiety in him. It shouldn't have come as a shock. But now, when he looked around him at the rolling black waters, all he could think of was the night he'd been sure he would be swallowed up in them and lost forever. He thought about how close he'd come to winding up as just another one of those names inscribed on the plaque in the Lutheran church. His hands clenched the railings now, the same way they had clenched the top of that coffin. At first, he had kept the lid propped up in his trailer, next to the snake tank, like a trophy. But then it had spooked him, and he had stashed it under the bed.

Which only made things worse.

Finally, in desperation, he'd stuck it in the crawl space under the trailer where there was a bunch of other old timbers. He'd have just heaved the damn thing back into the sea if it weren't for the fact that he was convinced it would be worth something, to someone, some-day. When that Dr. Slater had told him he should return it to the is-land, he'd actually given it some serious thought; the main reason he couldn't do it now was because it might give that asshole some satis-faction if he did.

The moon was out, which was a lucky thing, since the strait was choppy that night and huge chunks of ice were grinding and rolling through the channel. Off in the distance, the two black slabs of Big and Little Diomede lay like watchdogs at the gateway to Siberia. There wasn't another boat in sight, but the sky was speckled with stars as sharp and bright as needles. Looking up, Harley's eyes filled with tears, not because he was overwhelmed with emotion but because the wind was so cold and so relentless. He wiped them away with the back of one glove, but they sprang right back. He made his way to the bow and took hold of the search lamp there. The boat rose and fell on the swells, spray flying up and freezing on his lips and cheeks. He spread his legs on the deck to keep his balance and peered into the blackness, following the beam of the light.

Were there other coffins out there, carrying their awful cargo up and down the waves, bumping up against the ice floes? If there were, he prayed he wouldn't see them. He'd had enough trouble since finding the first one.

"Coming up on the starboard side," Eddie announced over the bullhorn, as if he was some tour guide. "Welcome to St. Peter's Island."

Shit. Harley wanted to brain him for making so much noise. The whole idea had been to stay under the radar. What if the Coast Guard was already lying low in some cove?

He waved up at the wheelhouse, gesturing for Eddie to keep it down, and after a quick scan of the waters ahead, turned off the bow light. They were just beyond the breakers, and if Eddie didn't do something stupid—which was always a possibility—they'd be okay.

The *Kodiak* plowed ahead, while Harley removed the lens cap from the binoculars, and swept them over the island. The beach, as usual, was shrouded in spray and mist, but in the moonlight, he could just make out a ladder of steps, carved into the side of the rugged cliffs and leading all the way up to a jagged promontory. He'd sailed past this island many times in the *Neptune I* and the *Neptune II*, always giving it a wide berth, but tonight their course was taking them closer to the shore than ever before. As the *Kodiak* rounded the island, with no sign of the Coast Guard, the Navy, or one of those damn choppers anywhere in sight, Harley put the bow light on again and caught the great glistening back of a killer whale, just rising from the waves, its blowhole spouting like a geyser. It took several seconds before the whale submerged again—time enough for Harley to reflect on the guts those old Inuit hunters must have had to take on a creature of that size and power in nothing but flimsy kayaks, with a handful of harpoons. He'd have been afraid to take it on with an Uzi. It was hard to believe that the natives he knew now—those guys like fat Geordie Ayakuk who hugged a desk in the community center, or the old rummies that hung around the Yardarm cadging drinks—could possibly be their descendants. Man, what the fuck had happened to them?

A cloud passed before the moon, a sign of the storms that were undoubtedly on their way, and Harley turned the searchlight toward the island, looking for some safe—and secluded—harbor. But even on this side, rocks jutted up from the sea, and white water foamed over the hidden reefs. People who didn't know anything about sailing always thought that the closer you were to shore, the safer you were. But Harley knew that they were dead wrong. The open sea gave you room to maneuver, time to think, and if you'd read your charts right, the chances that there was something deadly lurking right under your hull were pretty slim.

No, the worst disasters happened as you approached the shore, especially if that shore was as dangerous a destination as St. Peter's Island. In addition to the boat Harley had already lost to these waters, he knew of at least a dozen others that had been driven too close to this coastline by snowstorms and rogue waves and overpowering winds; he had seen sudden riptides grip a boat and completely take control of it, dragging it helplessly in whatever direction it wished, before dashing it against a picket of jagged rocks. You could run the engine all you wanted, you could put on every sail you had, but if the Bering Sea wanted a piece of your ass, it was going to get it.

Up in the wheelhouse, he could see Eddie and Russell hunched over the wheel. Each of them was holding a beer can now and laughing uproariously at something. Christ, if only he had anybody he could actually rely on. He'd needed some help on this gig, and in some ways these two were the obvious candidates. Since getting out of the Spring Creek penitentiary, Russell had been working part-time for the refinery—and was always short of beer money—and Eddie lived off the dough every resident got each year from the Permanent Fund, courtesy of the big oil companies that operated in Alaska. When needed, he supplemented his income with plumbing or selling pot.

More to the point, neither of them would be missed for a few days.

But the *Kodiak* was getting perilously close to shore now, and Harley figured he could no longer leave Eddie at the wheel—not if he wanted to keep the boat in one piece.

Sweeping the searchlight back and forth across the cliffs, he saw flocks of kittiwakes startled into flight, and steep, impregnable walls slick with ice. A ripple of white foam indicated an underwater reef off the port side. The boat was halfway around the island from the Russian colony, and there was no sign of another beach. An inlet or cove was the best he could hope for; they'd have to drop anchor and use the *Kodiak*'s skiff to go ashore.

Fixing the searchlight in place, he went back up to the bridge, and the minute he came through the door, the wind howling at his back, Eddie and Russell, looking vaguely guilty, stopped laughing.

"What was so funny?"

"Nothing," Eddie said.

Harley figured that the joke had been at his expense. Eddie stifled another laugh, and now Harley knew for sure—and he saw red.

"Lighten up," Russell said, a bit blearily. "Have a beer." He held out a can and Harley smacked it out of his hand so hard that the can hit the binnacle and cracked the anemometer screen.

"Fuck," Eddie shouted. "My uncle's going to see that!"

Russell's shoulders hunched, and his fists clenched. Eddie saw it, too, and leapt between them, his arms outstretched.

"Hey, guys, chill out. Come on now, come on. We're all friends here."

"Are we?" Harley said, glaring first at one, then the other. "Because if we're such good friends, we're gonna have to get something straight. This is my gig, and I don't want a couple of drunken stoners fucking it up."

The beer can was rolling around the floor of the wheelhouse, spraying foam through a dent. The wheel, unattended, was turning slowly.

"Who said I'm drunk?" Russell challenged him, weaving on his feet.

Harley smiled, acting like it was all okay now, then spun around, throwing out one leg in a classic martial-arts move that caught Russell behind his knees and dumped his ass on the floor. He landed with a thump that jolted the whole cabin, then he lay there, propped up against the chart table, stunned.

"What the fuck?" Eddie said. "You didn't have to do that."

"And you," Harley said, "get out on deck and keep watch." Harley moved to take control of the wheel, but Eddie grabbed it again, refusing to budge.

"It's my uncle's boat."

Harley shoved him, and Eddie stumbled into Russell, who was just getting to his feet. They both went down, and Harley whipped around, the gun out of his belt now. Eddie put out both of his hands, and said, "Whoa there, pardner! Put that away before somebody gets hurt."

Harley waited a few seconds, just to make sure Russell wasn't planning on anything further.

Russell opened his own hands, as if to show he had no weapon and no bad intentions. "Jesus, Harley. Get a grip."

Harley was just putting the gun back in his belt when the boat lurched, and they heard a grinding noise like a tin can scraping on cement. Harley turned and saw that the loose wheel had spun again, and through the window of the bridge he saw that the bow was pointing straight toward the cliffs, no more than forty yards away. But the boat wasn't moving, and unless he was sorely mistaken, they had just run aground on one of the many reefs he might have seen coming if he hadn't been so distracted.

"Goddamn!" Eddie shouted, leaping to his feet and going for the throttle. Before Harley could stop him, he had thrown the boat into reverse, and the grinding had come again, even louder this time . . . but the *Kodiak* still didn't move.

"Goddamn, goddamn, goddamn!" Eddie hollered, stamping his

feet as he went in circles around the cramped space in the bridge. The boat was jammed on a reef, teetering this way and that like a car perched atop a snowbank. "You *are* bad luck!" he shouted, pointing a finger at Harley. "You are such bad luck, man!"

Even Harley was temporarily at a loss. *Was* he bad luck?

Eddie was just about to try the throttle again when Harley stopped him. "You'll rip its guts out," he said.

"What else can we do?"

"We can wait," Harley said. "Maybe the tide will give us a boost. Russell, go below and see if we're taking on water."

For once, Russell took an order and stumbled down to the hold.

Eddie, fuming, glared at Harley, who turned around and stared at the small portion of the island illuminated by the bow light. At water level, he saw a bunch of tide pools, frothing white, then disappearing, and above them a jumble of rocks, piled halfway up the side of the cliff. That much was a lucky break. The rocks looked climbable, and the remaining slope was pockmarked with caves and crevices and ledges.

"They told me not to do this," Eddie muttered, shaking his head. "They told me not to go to sea with a Vane."

"Who told you what? You were supposed to keep your mouth shut about this. Who did you tell?"

"Nobody," Eddie said, retreating. "I didn't tell anybody. It's just something everybody says, down at the docks."

Harley couldn't be too surprised. His family had lost two boats already, Charlie was in a wheelchair, and for all he knew they'd just beached a third.

Russell, panting, appeared in the hatchway. "It's not too bad. The hull's holding."

"For how long?" Eddie said in a panic.

"Your uncle always said she could be swamped for twelve hours without sinking," Harley said.

"Swamped? Didn't you hear what Russell just said? She's holding. Man, don't put your family curse on it. Let's just get out of here."

"That's exactly what we're *not* going to do," Harley said. "We're going to drop anchor, with enough slack to let the boat drift off the rocks with the next tide."

"And do what until then?" Eddie shot back. "Sit here and wait?"

"No. We're going onto the island, and get started. How else are you gonna buy your uncle a new anemometer?" Zipping up his coat, Harley said, "Get your gear together, both of you. I'll get the skiff ready."

Out on deck, he walked the length of the ship but didn't see much damage except to the paint. Provided she didn't spring a leak, she would stay where she was until the currents, and some clever engine maneuvers, freed her again. He dropped anchor and watched as the chain played out for no more than a few seconds. Stepping to the bow, he maneuvered the light around, picking out the best route through the rocks and tide pools. It wasn't going to be easy to get the skiff through unscathed, but he could do it, even with the deadweight of Russell and Eddie on board. It was only as he flicked off the search-light, in order to see the wet walls of the cliff without the reflection glaring off them, that he glimpsed on the ridgeline what looked like a yellow light, gently swinging. He blinked, thinking it was just an after-effect of the bright bow light going off, like a strobe, but when he looked again, the yellow glow, more like a lantern suspended in mid-air, was still there.

Chapter 21

On the morning that Rasputin's body was to be buried, Anastasia and the other members of the royal family bundled into two long black touring cars and drove from St. Petersburg to the imperial park at Tsarskoe Selo. There, a grave had been dug near the site where a church was later to be erected in his honor.

Anastasia had never seen her mother so bereaved. At the news of Father Grigori's murder, she had utterly broken down, fearing that her son Alexei had lost his most potent protector. And when she learned that the deed had been done by Prince Yussoupov and, worse yet, Grand Duke Dmitri, a Romanov relation, she had almost lost her wits altogether. Anastasia and her three older sisters had taken turns watching over their mother.

Looking out the window now, Ana saw endless, snow-covered fields, lined by white birches and punctuated, like print on a white page, by scribbles of crows. It was a beautiful morning, with a sun so bright and a sky so blue Fabergé himself might have enameled the scene. Icicles hanging from the eaves of the occasional farmhouse glistened like diamonds. Under her own blouse, Ana wore the emerald cross the monk had given her at the Christmas ball. That was the last time she had seen him alive, and she had not taken off the cross ever since.

The body itself had not remained hidden for long. In their haste, the conspirators had left one of Rasputin's boots lying out on the ice of the frozen Neva. The corpse had floated not far off, and when another hole was cut through the ice to retrieve it, the *starets* was found to have been alive even after being submerged in the river. One of his arms had wriggled free of the ropes and was frozen stiff as if raised in a benediction, and his lungs were filled with water. For all the poison in his bloodstream, the bullets in his body, and the bruises from the beating, the monk had died in the end by drowning.

Once the cars had entered the park, and the Cossack guards had closed the gates and resumed their endless patrols again, Anastasia saw that wooden walkways had been built across a frozen field. The cars stopped, and Tsar Nicholas himself stepped out of the first one, his wife leaning heavily on the arm of her close friend, Madame Vyrubova. The Tsaritsa Alexandra was dressed entirely in black, as were they all, but carried in her arms a bouquet of white roses plucked that morning from the greenhouse at the Winter Palace.

In the distance, a motor van was parked by an open grave, its engine still running, a plume of gray smoke rising from its exhaust. As Anastasia drew closer, picking her way carefully over the freshly placed boards, she saw the foot of a coffin—a simple one, made of white oak—resting in the back of the van. Her mother went straight to it and asked one of the attendants to open it.

Looking uncertain, the attendant glanced at the Tsar, who nodded.

The lid was lifted, and though Ana was standing far back with her sisters, she caught a glimpse of the holy man's black beard, stiffly brushed . . . and a ragged hole in his head, above his left eye, as if someone had drilled his skull with an augur. His broad hands, once so full of power and expression, were folded meekly against the shoulders of his black cassock.

All in all, it was the most shocking sight Ana had ever seen . . . but she did not quail, even as her sister Tatiana let out a whimper and

Olga consoled her. In Ana's head, all she could hear were the words Rasputin had spoken to her in the chapel.

"If any relation to your family takes my life, then woe to the dynasty. The Russian people will rise against you with murder in their hearts."

And not only had Grand Duke Dmitri participated in the murder, he had bragged about it the next day.

"The blood of your family is poisoned," the monk had said. *"But this curse you carry in your veins will be your own salvation one day. A plague shall overwhelm the world, but you shall be proof against it."*

Ana still had no idea what these last words betokened. But she wore the emerald cross he had given her, with its secret inscription on the back, nonetheless.

Her mother handed the white roses to her friend and placed two objects on Rasputin's breast. One was an icon that everyone in the imperial family had inscribed, and the other was a letter that she had dictated to Anastasia because her own hand was too unsteady. "My dear martyr," it had read, "give me thy blessing that it may follow me always on the sad and dreary path I have yet to follow here below. And remember us from on high in your holy prayers." Ana had held the letter for her mother to sign. Lifting herself from the divan, where the pain from her sciatica had once again relegated her, her mother had written "Alexandra" with her usual flourish, before pressing the page first to her heart, then to her lips.

Now, the letter, too, was lying on Father Grigori's breast. The attendants closed and sealed the coffin, and it was lowered into the grave. A chaplain read the funeral service, but Ana was listening only to the sound of the winter wind as it rustled through the creaky scaffolding of the church being built close by. She looked at her family, standing silent and still in their black coats and boots and hats, all in a row, and it was as if she were looking at a photograph. A grim photograph that made her think of the monk's dire prophecy again.

"Here," Madame Vyrubova said, softly, "take this." She handed Ana some of the white roses. And then, after her mother and father and sisters had cast their own into the open grave, Ana dropped hers, too, watching the petals flutter like snowflakes onto the lid of the coffin.

"*I am no longer among the living,*" Rasputin had said on that Christmas night.

But even now, even here, some part of Anastasia did not believe it.

Chapter 22

Lying in his sleeping bag on the floor of the cave, Harley checked the time on his cell phone. The phone reception was for shit—what would you expect from a cave on an island in the middle of nowhere?—but the clock told him it was 8 A.M.

And that meant it was high time to get this damn show on the road.

After they'd run the *Kodiak* aground the night before, Harley and his two next-to-useless assistants had off-loaded their supplies onto the skiff and laboriously toted them up the side of the sloping cliff and into the first cave that looked relatively safe and dry. They had left an LED light burning atop a crate all night, and looking around now, Harley saw the ration boxes and knapsacks stacked against the craggy stone walls, along with the shovels, spades, and, leave it to Russell, three cases of beer. Judging from the sound of his snoring, Russell was still sleeping off the cold ones he'd already drunk. Harley crawled out of his sleeping bag, kicked Eddie to wake him up, then, bending to keep from banging his head on the low ceiling, went to the mouth of the cave; they'd stretched a tarp between two crates to keep out the wind. Batting the tarp aside, he looked out on the cold, dark morning and the seawater frothing in the tide pools at the foot of the cliff. The boat was still marooned on the rocks, advertising their presence on the island, but at least it was stranded as far from the old Russian colony as it could get. Harley would have liked to find a hideout farther from the boat, just in case the Coast Guard ever came along and spotted it, but he knew that if he'd asked Eddie and Russell to hump the supplies any deeper into the woods, he'd have had a mutiny on his hands.

"What the hell time is it?" Eddie said, burrowing deeper into his bag to escape the cold blast from the entrance.

"Time to get up and get going."

"Take Russell."

But Harley had already decided to let Russell sleep it off. After the brawl that had erupted on the boat, he was wary of having the two of them along—especially on this first reconnaissance mission. He didn't know exactly what was out there, and a loose cannon like Russell could wind up proving a liability. Plus, he wanted to cover some serious ground.

After they'd both eaten some canned Army surplus meals that Harley had picked up at the Arctic Circle Gun Shoppe, they stepped out onto the rocky ledge. Harley had strapped a twelve-gauge shotgun on his back and wedged a can of bear mace—made from concentrated red chili peppers—in his pocket. Over one shoulder he carried a spade; Eddie had a pickaxe. As they marched off, he had an unfortunate image of the seven dwarfs heading off into the woods.

Fifty feet in, and it started to feel even more like that damn fairy tale. The island itself was small, but forbidding. Densely forested with spruce and hemlock and alder, the ground was rocky and uneven and lightly dusted with snow, with a lot more to come if the weather reports were true. The prickly spines of devil's club bushes snatched at their sleeves, and one of them even pulled Eddie's stocking cap off his head. He had to stop and snatch it back, then, out of sheer annoyance, he broke the twig off and stomped on it.

"You sure it's dead?" Harley said.

"Fuck you," Eddie replied. "You have any idea where you're going, by the way, or are we just out for a hike?"

It wasn't a bad question. Harley had only the vaguest sense of where the colony lay ahead, and he figured the graveyard had to be part of it. "If we keep to a fairly straight course, we're bound to hit it," Harley said, turning around and cutting through some brush. He purposely made plenty of noise as he went since bears were partial to thickets like these, and a startled grizzly was a pissed grizzly. At this time of year, it was unlikely he'd stumble across any of them foraging for food—normally they'd be hibernating in their dens, or, if they were really lucky, the hollow core of a big old cottonwood tree—but it was better to be noisy than sorry, he figured.

Wolves, however, were another matter. Wolves were always on the move, year-round, scavenging dead carcasses, and hunting fresh prey—young caribou or unwary moose. Only on rare occasions had they been known to hunt man, and the one thing Harley had been taught was that you never ran from them. If confronted, you stood your ground, shouted, threw rocks, anything. Running was an invitation to be chased by the whole pack, though who knew how the black ones that inhabited this island—known to be a peculiar lot—would behave. There were all kinds of tales about them. Sailors told stories about seeing them lined up on the cliffs at night, looking across the strait toward Siberia, their muzzles raised, howling in unison. And a couple of hunters from Saskatchewan who had set out to bag a few never showed up again. Their kayak washed up a few weeks later, holding a bloodstained pair of gloves and a wooden paddle that looked like it had been nearly gnawed in half.

At the time, even though the two hunters were presumed dead, there had been some talk of mounting a rescue mission. But nobody had wanted to volunteer, and Nika, the newly elected mayor, had seemed perfectly okay to let things stand. It was almost like she was on the side of the damn wolves.

For another hour or so, they plowed through the forest, the evergreens towering high overhead, and just as Harley was beginning to fear he'd gone off course, he spied a clearing through the trees—and just beyond it, the timbered wall of a stockade. A wall that had fallen into considerable disrepair, its logs listing to one side or the other like misaligned teeth. To Harley's relief, there was even a ragged gap large enough to offer easy entry to the colony grounds.

"Well, I'll be damned," Eddie said, coming as close to a compliment as Harley was ever likely to get.

And given the ghoulish nature of the work they were planning, Harley wondered for a moment if it wasn't true.

"Is that their church?" Eddie said, and Harley, too, lifted his eyes to the crumbling onion dome that rose on the other side of the wall.

"Guess so," he said. "And just as long as they're not holding any services, it's fine with me."

The truth was—and despite the jokes—the whole place was still giving Harley a very uneasy feeling, not that he would ever confess anything like that to Eddie. For years, he had heard stories about the old Russian colony, and that was all before he'd been washed up on the beach that night and nearly lost his left foot to that leaping wolf . . . or glimpsed a flash of that yellow lantern sailors used to talk about spotting. But he had never imagined himself standing in the dark, frigid morning air, with a spade in his hand, about to enter the abandoned colony itself.

"Come on, man," Eddie said, shouldering past him with his pickaxe cradled like a musket against his shoulder. "Let's get this over with."

Harley let Eddie slither through the opening in the wall first, then followed. They were at the back of the church, its wooden walls stripped bare of almost all their white paint by the years of wind and rain and snow. Angling around one side, he came across a window with only a splinter or two of glass jutting up from its frame; a lone shutter banged back and forth. As the church was raised on rotted pilings, and tilting a bit at that, Harley had to stand on his tiptoes to peer inside. Taking out the flashlight, he played its beam around the front of the nave and saw a faded mural painted on the opposite wall. From what he could see in the gloom, it had once been a picture of the Virgin Mary with a halo over her head. But what thrilled him was the touch or two of gold paint that was still left on the picture; those old

Russkies loved their gold almost as much as they loved their Madonna. He hoped they'd buried some of that, too.

"What do you see?" Eddie said. "Let's go inside and check it out."

But Harley didn't want to get sidetracked, especially as all he could make out besides the painted icon was a great big pile of junk—old milking pails, blacksmith tools, broken furniture—piled up against a carved screen. It looked like the place had been pretty thoroughly scavenged, and trashed, by somebody in the past hundred years.

"On the way back," he said, just to shut him up. "Let's find the cemetery first."

As they passed the front steps of the church, with one door sagging and ajar, Eddie cast a longing look back but followed Harley past an old well and into the open area of the colony. They were surrounded on all sides by crumbling old cabins and open stalls. In one of them, Harley saw a rusted anvil, in another a pair of iron-hooped kegs. Plainly, it had once been a working village, with maybe forty or fifty people living in it. But all that concerned Harley was where these people went when they died. There was no sign of a graveyard anywhere, not even on the other side of the church. Weren't folks supposed to be buried in the churchyard in the old days?

At the far end of the stockade he saw what had to have been the main gate to the colony—some weathered beams, off-balance like the totem pole in town, still framed the entrance—and after switching the shovel to his other shoulder, Harley set off for it. Outside, a path led away from the colony, across some cleared land, and straight into a dense grove of trees.

"Not another fucking forest," Eddie complained.

"This one's got a trail," Harley said, striding ahead, and it did. Although it was narrow and winding, the path seemed to be leading him back toward the rim of the island. Gradually, it descended, and to Harley's relief yet again, he saw a gateway ahead, like the colony gates only much smaller. And the posts, he noted as he got closer, were elaborately carved with something in Russian. It looked like the same word or two, chiseled into the wood over and over and over again.

Even Eddie paused to study the writing. "You think it says, 'Welcome to the buried treasure'?" he said.

And Harley could only wonder. Just beyond the posts lay the colony graveyard, no more than an acre, but littered with stone markers and wooden crosses tilting this way and that in the frozen ground. It was starting to get lighter out, the sun fighting its way through a scrim of hazy clouds, and in the faint daylight Harley could also see that many of the headstones had their own curious inscription down toward their base. It looked like a little crescent, but he was damned if he knew what that meant either. Did headstone makers sign their work? Shit, he thought, dropping the end of his spade between his feet, where was he supposed to start?

Eddie was wandering around among the graves, taking an occasional swipe at one of the wooden crosses with the end of his pickaxe, and Harley—who was by no means a religious man—still thought it was wrong and shouted, "Stop it, you dumb fuck."

The gravity of what they were about to do struck him now like never before, and he cursed his brother Charlie, and he cursed himself for always playing the fool. How the hell did he get here?

Eddie stopped to take a piss, the urine splashing on the unyielding ground, and when he finished up and turned around, he said, "So, where do you want to start? I'm freezing my ass off already."

And all Harley could think of was starting where it had all begun. With mechanical footsteps, he walked toward the rim of the graveyard, a precipice overlooking the Bering Strait. A coffin had fallen into the sea, and in only a minute or two he had found the spot from which it must have fallen.

At the very edge of the cliff, a hunk of dirt and rock had eroded away, leaving a scar in the earth. Harley took care not to step too close.

"That where you think it came from?" Eddie said, with a snort.

And Harley said, "Yes." He stared at the jagged earth, and it was as if he was looking at a vanished grave . . . and worse. He could picture the gaunt man in the sealskin coat as he lay in the coffin aboard the *Neptune II*. Or as he appeared in the storage shed behind the gun shop.

Looking for his emerald cross.

"I say we pick the one with the biggest headstone," Eddie said, surveying the graveyard. "The richer the dead guy was, the better the chances he got buried with some good stuff on him."

With no better plan in mind, Harley had to concede it wasn't the worst logic.

Eddie walked off a few yards, stopping beside a truncated stone angel, and said, "This one's good as any." And then, slipping the backpack off and tossing it to one side, he lifted the pickaxe and swung it over his head.

The iron barely grazed the soil before rebounding hard, and Eddie dropped the shaft and danced backward, swearing and shaking his hands.

Harley laughed, and Eddie said, "You try it then."

"Let's do this right," Harley said, taking off his own pack, loaded with the steel climbing spikes and chisel. "If we loosen the soil first, we may get something done before dark."

For the next hour or two, they bent their heads over the grave, alternately driving spikes into the ground, chopping at the surrounding dirt, scraping it away with the end of the spade. It was slow and backbreaking work, and Harley felt the futility of it with every breath. They should have brought dynamite and simply blown the place to pieces before that Slater guy showed up. His only hope lay in the fact that the Russian gravediggers must have had the same problems he was having; the graves they dug must have been as shallow as they could make them.

After taking a break to open some more tins of food—Eddie got Spam, and he made Harley trade it to him for his own can of corned beef hash—they got back to work. Eddie took a turn chopping and mincing at the dirt with the end of the spade, and when he caught what looked like the dull patina of buried wood, he got down on his knees and brushed the soil away with the ends of his sweaty gloves.

"That's a coffin," he exulted. "We did it, man!"

Harley told him to step back, then, lifting the pickaxe, he brought it down with a crash. There was the sharp crack of the blade cutting into wood.

Eddie was pumping his arms in anticipation of the treasure chest he thought they were about to uncover.

Harley wanted to tell him to cool it, but his own blood was up, too. If something did turn up in the casket, he'd have something to throw in Charlie's face. *Who's the fuckup now?*

He raised the pickaxe again, its dull iron blade framed against a sky of the same color, and even as he ripped it down into the coffin, something on the far horizon caught his eye.

The pick, as a result, missed its mark, and landed with a bone-aching thud in the frozen soil to one side.

"Watch what you're doing," Eddie said. "You gotta hit the spot that's clear already."

But Harley was watching that speck on the horizon again. It was just a black dot, but it was coming in their direction.

Eddie was using the spade to make a greater target on the top of the coffin. And when Harley didn't lift the pick for the next blow, he said, "You want me to do it?" He reached for the pick. "Give it to me, ya pussy."

Harley let him, not taking his eyes off the approaching speck. Which was now distinctly coming into view—it was a helicopter, un-doubtedly the one from the hockey rink in Port Orlov—and it was coming right at them.

"Duck!" Harley said, and Eddie looked at him in confusion.

"From what?"

"From that!" he said, pointing at the oncoming chopper.

Now they could hear the racket of its engines and its rotating blades on the ocean wind.

Harley flattened himself against a wooden cross and Eddie hud-dled at the foot of the broken angel, his arms folded over his head. Unless the chopper stopped to hover above the cemetery, it would pass over them so fast they wouldn't be seen . . . though their spade and pickaxe lay in plain sight on the snow. Damn. Harley reached out one arm and grabbed the spade and dragged it under him.

There was a rush of wind and noise as the chopper swooped low overhead, zooming straight over the graveyard and the trees and aiming for the colony grounds. Once it was safely past, Harley leapt to his feet and watched as it did indeed slow down and make a circular pass over the spot where the stockade walls enclosed the old settlement. Red and white running lights adorned its fuselage, blinking on and off, as the chopper, built like some huge green praying mantis, seemed to suspend itself in midair, before descending below the tree line, and out of Harley's view.

"Fuck me, man," Eddie said. "They're here already?"

He was right about that, Harley thought. They were well and truly fucked if these guys were here for anything more than a quick stopover, or, as those douche-bag pilots had claimed, a "routine training mission."

His eyes went back to the splintered coffin in the partially exposed grave. And so did Eddie's.

"No way I'm letting those assholes get what we dug up," Eddie said, rising from the foot of the tombstone.

And neither was Harley, though he knew there wasn't much time. Brushing the dirt and ice from his gloves, he raised the pick and taking a deep breath first, swung it high above his head, then brought it down one more time with a satisfying thwack.

Chapter 23

Dr. Slater, ever the hospitable team leader, had offered the virologist, Dr. Lantos, who had arrived in Port Orlov just a few hours earlier, a window seat on the Sikorsky Skycrane, but she had demurred.

"I'm not a fan of flying," she said, "and looking out the window of a helicopter is about the last thing I want to do."

Even now, as the chopper flew toward the forbidding cliffs of St. Peter's Island, she was sitting very still in the seat facing him, her eyes closed behind her thick glasses and her hands clutched tightly in her lap. Professor Kozak, whose ample bulk was strapped into the seat at Slater's side, was craning his neck for a better view out of his own window.

"We're coming up on the cemetery," he said over the headphones, and as they whooshed over it, he pressed his forehead against the Plexiglas for a better view.

Slater took a look, too, but they were over it so fast it was all he could do to catch a glimpse of the spot where the cliff had given way.

"You see that?" Kozak said, and Slater asked him what.

"Something moved."

"What do you mean?"

"Might have been a wolf down in the graveyard."

"There are wolves?" Dr. Lantos, said, her eyes still closed.

"A few," Slater replied. "But Nika tells me that if we leave them alone, they'll leave us alone." He had assigned Nika to the second chopper, which would follow in a couple of hours, so she could help guide Sergeant Groves and his crew. She'd looked at him a little suspiciously, afraid that this might be some ruse to keep her off the island and out of harm's way, after all, but he had laughed and said, "You know, you should really work in Washington."

"Why?"

"You've got all the natural instincts."

Frowning, she said, "I'll take that as a compliment, for now."

The helicopter started to slow down, banking to one side, and Slater saw Dr. Lantos swallow hard. For all her fearsome reputation in the lab and in academic circles, where her work was always ahead of the curve and so meticulous as to be indisputable, she was plainly as unhappy in the air as she had claimed. He wondered how she'd made it on the five separate flights that had been necessary just to get her all this way from M.I.T.

"We're over the landing zone," the pilot's voice crackled on the headphones. And then, as a gag, he added, "Please make sure your tray tables are completely secured, and your seats are in the upright position." As if these hard seats could be made to budge an inch.

Wobbling back and forth, the Sikorsky slowly settled itself on the ground, its tires giving the craft a jounce as they made contact with the ground. Dr. Lantos let out a long breath, and for the first time since boarding, unclasped her hands and let her shoulders fall.

When she opened her eyes, Dr. Slater said, sympathetically, "Maybe we can get the Coast Guard to ferry you back when we're done here."

"I get seasick, too."

As the rotors wound down with a sigh, Professor Kozak unlatched the cabin door, threw it open, and clambered down. Lantos followed him, a trifle unsteadily, and Slater brought up the rear.

One of the pilots was already on the ground, heading for the cargo hold. And though Slater was eager to oversee the unloading of the lab gear—with the rest of the heavy equipment coming on the second chopper—he had to stop and simply look around. He had not actually set foot on the island, much less inside the colony, until this second, and whenever he arrived at the site of any epidemiological expedition, he immediately needed to get the lay of the land. From the first fly-over three days before, he knew the general layout of the settlement, but it was only when he walked away from the helicopter now and did a 360 that he had a true sense of it.

And it felt like he'd stepped inside a ghostly fort.

Despite all the gaps in the timbers, the stockade wall was still formidable, and the abandoned buildings—with their empty windows and gaping doors—seemed eerily tenanted, anyway. He knew there was no one inside the structures, but that didn't stop him from feeling as if he was being observed. A bucket swung from a rusty chain above an old well, and he marveled that the chain was still intact at all. At the other end of the compound, and tilted slightly on its raised pilings, stood a wooden church with its distinctively orthodox onion dome. He could imagine the hard and uncompromising lives of the Russians who had carved this place out of such an unwelcoming wilderness, making a home for themselves in this most inhospitable and inaccessible spot. A place where they considered themselves impregnable and unreachable . . . until the Spanish flu had found them.

Again, Slater wondered how. What sly mechanism had the virus used to journey across the frozen waters of the Bering Sea, up onto this isolated rock, and in through the wooden gates that stood behind him?

"The ramp's down," the pilot said. "Should we start unloading?"

Slater said yes, and turned back to supervise it. Kozak was smoking a cigar, the pungent aroma wafting in the wind, and Dr. Lantos was bundled up in her coat, the hood raised over her nimbus of frizzy salt-and-pepper hair, stamping her feet on the frozen ground to keep the circulation going. Glancing up at the murky gray sky, Slater reminded himself that he had a window of only a few hours in which to get some tents and other protective structures set up. The alternative—bunking down in the rotted cabins or the leaning church—would not, he suspected, go over very well.

By the time the second Sikorsky flew to the island with Nika and Sergeant Groves aboard, piles of equipment had been off-loaded into the central area of the compound, and temporary landing lights had been arranged in a wide circle. The lights were more than a precaution; although it was only midafternoon, the dark was falling fast.

The sergeant and his crew had arrived that morning, and Nika had been able to bring Groves up to speed. He was a powerful figure, with a thick neck and an intense expression, but she immediately took to his no-nonsense attitude and the quickness with which he grasped everything she had to say, from the topography of the island to the sensitivity of the local Inuit population about what was going to go on there, on ground still considered theirs. She also had the feeling that he would do anything for Dr. Slater; apparently, they'd been through some very tight spots together, and the bond between them was strong.

The moment their chopper landed on the spot now vacated by the first one, Sergeant Groves leapt from the cabin and began directing the crew members on the unloading and disposition of the remaining materiel. He and Slater exchanged a look or two, a few words, and the rest of their communications seemed to be done telepathically, working together seamlessly to get the first things done first, and as rapidly as possible. A generator shed was erected, and thick coils of wire were run across the ground along grid lines that they must have worked out beforehand. A mess tent was set up, and Dr. Lantos was quick to go inside and open her laptop computer on top of a rations crate. In just an hour or two, electric lights were up and running, a lavatory was discreetly but conveniently placed in the shelter of a stockade wall, and flags had been stuck in the ground where the prefab labs and residential tents would be constructed the next day. Nika, impressed by the military precision and speed, did her best just to stay out of the way.

Not that she didn't feel she had her own duties to perform. Dr. Slater might have thought that she had been using her status as the tribal elder simply to secure herself a berth on the island, but he was wrong. She took her duties seriously. She was an anthropologist by training—a scientist—but she was also imbued with a powerful spiritual urge, one that connected her not only to the Inuit people but to the worldview that they maintained. She was not someone to discount the legends and practices of her people, or to deny the possibility of things simply because our ordinary senses could not see or hear or smell them. So long as 90 percent of the universe was composed of something routinely called "dark matter," who was she to set any limits on what might, or might not, be true?

The night had truly fallen now, and while the others gathered in the mess tent—its green walls glowing like a firefly in summer—Nika pulled her collar up around her face and walked into the blackness of the compound. She listened to the wind, hoping to hear the voices of the souls who had once lived—and died—here. She peered into the cabins and open stalls, trying to imagine the settlers' faces peering out. And all the while, she was trying, in her own way, to communicate with them. To reassure them that she, and the others with her, had come not to pillage or intrude, but to accomplish something of great magnitude . . . something that might help keep others from succumbing to the same terrible fate that they had.

Despite whatever benign intentions she was trying to telegraph, however, she was getting no such messages in return. Just a howling, empty void.

Stopping in front of the church, which sloped ever so gently to one side, she felt that she had come, not surprisingly, to the fulcrum of the colony. The one place where the power—and the essence—of the sect had been most concentrated. And even as she heard Sergeant Groves bellowing out into the darkness that it was dinnertime—"and we close the kitchen at eight!"—she dropped her backpack and sleeping bag on the church steps. Precisely because it gave her the willies, and because it had been the one place she could be assured that all the souls here had regularly gathered, she knew that this was where she would need to bunk down later that night.

Chapter 24

Rasputin had been right.

But Anastasia had to struggle to remember his very words.

He had predicted that if a member of the aristocracy, or more specifically her family, were responsible for his murder, it would signal the end of the Romanov dynasty. Pamphlets secretly published by his irate followers proclaimed that the streets would run with blood, brother would turn against brother, and no one in her family would be safe.

And lo and behold, so far it was all coming to pass.

This day—August 13, 1917—was to be the last one the Romanovs spent at their beloved Tsarskoe Selo. The country had been torn apart by war, then by revolution in the streets. Ana could hardly keep straight all the different factions fighting for power—Reds, Whites, Mensheviks, Bolsheviks, the supporters of President Kerensky and his provisional government. All she knew was that her father had been forced to abdicate the throne, and that ever since then, she and her family had become virtual prisoners, kept under close supervision and constant guard.

And not by the Cossacks who had been their loyal defenders, or the four proud Ethiopians who had stood sentry at their doors.

No, now they were guarded by insolent soldiers and common workers, wearing red armbands and surly expressions. Men who had refused even to carry their trunks and suitcases to the train station, from which they were to depart that evening. Count Benckendorff had had to give them each three rubles to do it.

The night before, Ana had been awakened from her sleep by the sound of gunfire, but when she ran out onto the balcony in her night-gown, the soldiers had looked up and hooted, and an officer had lifted the head of one of the tame deer that they had been rounding up and shooting for sport. Her spaniel, Jemmy, barked furiously through the balustrade, and that only made the soldiers, if you could even dignify them with the term, laugh harder.

Now, that same officer was milling about the grand entry hall, poking his nose into their suitcases. Even the count could do nothing to stop him. Her mother and father were reduced to standing meekly to one side as the contingent in charge debated how and when to move their prisoners to the train station. Apparently, there was some question about their safety once outside the gates of the imperial park. It was hard for Ana to believe it was any worse out there than it had been in here.

"Just do as they say," her father had told her, and it made her both angry and sad to see him—once the Tsar of All the Russias—so dimin-ished. "Kerensky himself has guaranteed that he will find a way to get us out of the country."

How could he do that, she wondered, if he could not figure out a way to get them from the palace to the train depot?

It was nearly dawn when the orders were finally given to convey the exhausted royal family, and a handful of their faithful retainers, to the station. A troop of cavalry accompanied them. The train, dis-guised with a sign and flags proclaiming it to be on a Red Cross mis-sion, was stuck on a siding where there was no platform. With as little courtesy as possible, the soldiers hoisted the Tsaritsa and the other women up into the cars. Ana hated having their hands on her, and brushed her skirts madly as soon as she was out of sight inside the cabin.

And so began their long journey eastward, into the wide and empty spaces of Siberia. The train itself was comfortable and well provisioned, and enough of the family's household members were accompanying them—such as her father's valet, her mother's maid Anna Demidova, the French tutor Pierre Gilliard, and best of all the cook—that the trip occasionally took on the aspect of an outing to the royal estates in the Crimea, or some other country retreat. Every evening at six o'clock, the train stopped so that Jemmy and her father's dog, too, could be walked. Ana couldn't wait for these little breaks, to feel the solid soil under her feet instead of the constant rumble of the train tracks. And she found a beauty in the green marsh grasses and endless vistas of the steppes. If a grove of white birch trees happened to present itself, she and her sisters sometimes played hide-and-seek, a child's game that took them back to happier days. Her mother, laid up by her sciatica, would watch them from the train window, and Alexei, if he was feeling well enough, would stroll along the side of the tracks with his father.

Once, when Ana had strayed too far from the train while picking cornflowers, a young soldier, thin as a rail and with a struggling brown moustache, had warned her back. Anastasia, gesturing out at the vast wilderness, said, "You think I would make a run for it? Where do you think I would go?"

The soldier, who seemed flustered to be speaking to a grand duchess at all—even a deposed one—said, "I don't know. But please don't try." His tone was less admonitory than it was pleading. He was doing his duty, that she could see, but he wasn't entirely at ease with it. She smiled at him—he couldn't be more than a year or two older than she was, nineteen or twenty at the most—and he held his rifle as if it were a hoe, something she suspected he was much more familiar with.

"Sergei!" another of the soldiers hollered from atop a nearby hill. "Get that limping bitch back here!"

Sergei blushed deeply; some of the soldiers enjoyed delivering insults to their royal prisoners. Ana, who had grown accustomed if not inured to it, glanced at the bouquet of bright blue cornflowers in her hand and said, "I have enough."

When she dropped one on her return to the waiting train, Sergei picked it up and, bobbing his head as if in a furtive bow, tried to give it back to her.

"You keep it," she said, and if she thought he had blushed before, it was nothing compared to the crimson flush that filled his young face now. He looked so much like a tomato she laughed and said, "Don't let the others see that you have it, Sergei. They'll call it imperial property and take it away."

He stuck it into the pocket of his frayed military tunic as if it were made of gold.

After that, Ana got used to Sergei's guarding her. Whenever she stepped off the train with her spaniel, Jemmy, she expected to see him trailing her at a distance, and the other soldiers, too, seemed to regard her as his charge. Her sisters kidded her that she had found a suitor. Usually, the train would not stop anywhere near a station or a town; Ana didn't know if it was because the Red Guards thought the local people would attack the imperial family, or try to liberate them. On one day, a village was in sight—a prosperous-looking one, judging from the flower-filled window boxes, the green fields, and busy barnyards—but it was safely removed on the other side of the river. Ana noticed that Sergei was gazing at it longingly, his rifle drooping even lower than usual.

"What's the name of that village?" she asked, and at first he was so lost in thought he didn't answer.

When she repeated the question, he said, "That is my home." And then he turned toward her and said, "It's called Pokrovskoe."

Now Anastasia looked at it, too, with special attention. Pokrovskoe. She had heard Rasputin speak of it often. It was his own hometown. And he had predicted that the Romanovs would see it one day.

Could he have imagined it would be under circumstances like these?

She did not need to ask the next question before Sergei said, "Father Grigori lived in the house you see with two stories."

It was unmistakable, looming over all the other cottages in the town the way Rasputin himself had always dominated whatever company he was in. Anastasia wondered who lived in it now—she had heard rumors of a wife and young son. But then there had been so many rumors, most of them scurrilous, that neither she, nor the Tsaritsa, to whom they were often whispered, knew what to believe. She was eager to alert her mother, who was still on the train resting her bad back, where they were; she would want to know.

Coming closer than he ever had before, but keeping an eye out lest the other guards grow suspicious, Sergei said, "There are those who still communicate with the *starets*."

"What do you mean, communicate with him? Father Grigori is dead. He is buried in the imperial park."

Sergei's eyes earnestly bore into hers.

"I put a white rose on his coffin myself," Ana said. Her fingers, without meaning to, went to her chest and touched the cross beneath her blouse.

"There are those who keep the fire alight," Sergei said, just before the whistle on the locomotive screeched. Jemmy barked back at it.

"All aboard," an officer hollered from on top of the royal train car, "and now!" The whistle went off again, and there was an impatient chuffing sound from the engine.

Sergei ostentatiously lifted his rifle barrel and nudged his prisoner in the direction of the train. Anastasia walked back toward the tracks, Jemmy trotting at her heels. Her sisters were already mounting the stairs, followed by her father in his customary khaki tunic and forage cap. He was holding Alexei, identically dressed, by the hand. The engineer was waving a flag.

Anastasia turned around to say something to Sergei, but he was sauntering back to the troop car with a pair of the other guards and pretended not to notice.

Moments later, the train resumed its journey, and as Ana watched from the window, the flowers and fields and whitewashed barns of Pokrovskoe slid from view. She had forgotten to ask which house had been Sergei's, and deeply regretted that now.

Chapter 25

"*Kushtaka,*" Nika said, and Slater had to ask her to repeat it, partly to catch this new word again, and partly because he simply liked to hear her say it.

The lights in the mess tent were wavering, as the wind, only partially blocked by the old stockade, battered the triple-reinforced nylon walls with a dull roar. The temporary electrical grid Sergeant Groves had slapped together was still holding, but the lamps, strung up on wires, were swaying above their makeshift dinner table. Tomorrow, Slater thought, they'd have to get the backup generator online, too—just in case.

"*Kushtaka,*" Nika said. "The otter-men. If you were an unhappy soul, still nursing some grievance on earth, you were condemned to linger here, unable to ascend the staircase of the aurora borealis into heaven. Or maybe you just drowned, and your body could not be recovered and properly disposed of—either way, your spirit could become a changeling, half-human and half-otter."

"Why otter?" Dr. Eva Lantos asked, as she dunked her herbal tea bag one more time.

"Because the otter lived between the sea and the land, and now your spirit lived between life and death."

"We have many such legends in Russia, too," Professor Kozak said, mopping up the last remnants of his stew with a crust of bread. "I grew up with such stories."

"Most cultures do have something similar," Nika agreed. "The *kushtaka,* for instance, were sometimes said to take on the form of a beautiful woman, or someone you loved, in order to lure you into deep water or the depths of a forest. If you got lost, you could wind up becoming a changeling yourself."

"So if I see Angelina Jolie in the woods," Kozak said, "and she is calling to me, 'Vassily! Vassily! I must have you!' I should not go to her."

"You might at least want to think it over," Nika said with a smile.

Kozak shrugged. "Still, I would go."

Slater leaned back against a crate and surveyed his team like a proud father observing his brood. In only a matter of hours on the island, they had begun to come together nicely as a team. Professor Kozak was an industrious bear, quickly unpacking his ground-penetrating radar equipment and itching to get started the next day. Dr. Lantos had checked all the crates of lab equipment and supplies, and advised Slater on where they should set up the autopsy tent. Sergeant Groves was off on rounds right now, securing the premises (from force of habit, since the island held no hostiles) and getting to know the Coast Guardsmen who had been left to complete the construction of the prefabs, lighting poles, and ramps the next day.

If the weather allowed, that was. A storm was heading their way, and already its winds were scouring the colony like a steel brush. Slater prayed they wouldn't get a heavy snowfall, which would mean just that much more digging to get to the graves.

And then there was Nika, whose presence here he had so opposed at first, and who was rather like a spirit herself—a friendly, woodland sprite, filled with native tales and history and lore. Slater found himself immersed not only in her words, but in the light that seemed to be captured in her jet-black hair and eyes. Her tawny skin had taken on a positively golden cast in the glow of the lamps, and he noticed that she frequently touched a little ivory figurine, no bigger than a jump drive, hanging outside her blue-and-gold Berkeley sweatshirt.

He was grateful when the professor, perhaps noting it too, asked, "Is that a figure of a little *kushtaka* around your neck?"

"No," Nika said, holding it out on its thin chain so that they all could see it better. "That would be bad luck. This is a good-luck charm. We call them *bilikins.*"

Slater leaned closer, his coffee mug still in his hand. Now he could see that it was an owl, expertly carved with its wings furled and its eyes wide open.

"The owl represents the perfect guide because he can see even in the dark of night. The leader of the hunt traditionally wore it."

"Walrus tusk?" Kozak said, turning it over in his stubby fingers.

"Maybe," Nika said. "But my grandmother gave it to me, and her grandmother gave it to her, and if the story is true, it's made from the tusk of a woolly mammoth. They're frozen in the soil all around here, and every once in a while one turns up."

What else, Slater couldn't help but think, was he going to find in the frozen soil of St. Peter's Island? A perfectly preserved specimen, its viral load stored within the flesh like a ticking bomb, or a decaying corpse, whose deadly contaminant had been leeched away by decades of slow exposure and erosion?

"Yes," Kozak said, "the topography and geology of Alaska is like Siberia, and is well suited to this sort of preservation." Now that he knew its provenance, he looked even more impressed by the humble *bilikin.*

An especially strong gust of wind battered the tent, and the lights flickered again. Slater reached into his shirt pocket and removed several plastic packets, each one containing a dozen blue capsules and a dozen white.

"I think brandy is more usual after dinner, yes?" Kozak said, examining his packet.

"I'm afraid it wouldn't mix well with these," Slater said.

Dr. Lantos had opened her packet, and said, "Prophylactic measures?"

"Yes. The blue one's a standard anti-influenza drug; you'll need to take it every day for the next six days, whether we're still working here or not. The white one is a neuraminidase inhibitor that's shown both preventative and therapeutic results in trials done at the AFIP."

"I never heard of these trials," Lantos said, examining the white capsule skeptically.

"The results haven't been made public yet. And tomorrow," he said, with a grin, "may be the best field test we've ever run."

"So we are the guinea pigs?" Kozak said.

Slater nodded and washed one of each of the pills down with the last of his coffee. Kozak and Lantos did the same, but Nika sat silently, waiting.

"Where's mine?"

Swallowing, Slater said, "You won't need them."

"Why not?"

"Because you're not coming into contact with any of the bodies."

"Who said so?"

"The exhumations are a very dangerous and very grim spectacle. There's no need to subject yourself to any of that."

But Nika dug in her heels. "Do we really need to go through this again? As the tribal rep, and a trained anthropologist, I insist on being there." She held out her palm, flat.

Slater glanced at Lantos and the professor, and they both looked at him as if to say, "Not my call."

Slater dug into his shirt pocket, removed the packet he was planning to give Groves when he got back from his rounds, and plopped it in Nika's hand, instead; he'd make up another one later for the sergeant. She smiled in victory and held the little plastic baggie up like a trophy, and the others laughed. Slater had to smile, too; no wonder she'd become mayor.

"Now they might make you drowsy," he advised, "so take them just before you go to bed."

"And where would that be?" Dr. Lantos said, glancing around the mess tent, one of the few structures erected that day.

"I'm afraid this will have to double as the barracks for tonight."

"Then I've got dibs on this juicy spot under the table," she said, tapping her foot on the insulated rubber flooring.

"And I will put my sleeping bag on top of that fat pile of cushions," Kozak said, gesturing at the stack of mats that would be laid down to make a path to the graveyard the next day.

"Nika," Slater said, "I was thinking that you could—"

"I already know where I'm sleeping tonight," she said.

"You do?"

"I do."

As they trudged across the colony grounds, covered with crates and bundles of supplies unloaded from the Sikorskys, Slater continued to argue with her, but Nika would have none of it. She felt it was her duty to make this gesture of atonement to the spirits who had once inhabited this place. There was no explaining such a "metaphysical" view, however, to a man as empirically oriented as Frank Slater. She recognized that it was his job as an epidemiologist to look at things as squarely and objectively as possible, and to keep all other considerations out of the equation.

It was *her* job, as she saw it, to remain open and attuned to it all— the seen and the unseen, the facts and the faith. She had grown up among the legends and the folklore of her people. Her first memories were of fantastic natural phenomena—the swirling lights of the aurora borealis, the barking of a chorus of seals draped like mermaids on the ice floes, the sun that set for months at a time. You could not grow up on the coast of Alaska, one shallow breath below the Arctic Circle, and not feel both your remoteness from the rest of the world and your oneness with the vast and timeless elements—the impenetrable mountain ranges, the impassable seas—that surrounded you. Instilled within her was a sense of wonder—wonder at humanity's place in the great scheme of things—and an innate respect for any people's attempt to create a belief system able to encompass it all.

When they arrived at the church steps, she expected Slater to stop, like a boy dropping off his date at her home, but he started up the stairs instead.

"Wait," she said, and he turned to look down at her. One of the two doors had fallen off its hinges and left a narrow opening.

"Don't go in," she said.

"Why not? The whole place is tilting already—let's see if it's safe."

"I'll be careful," she said. What she didn't say was that she didn't want his presence to disturb the vibe inside, whatever it might be—and she knew that if she so much as hinted at that, he'd think she'd completely lost her mind. She was surprised herself at how much she already valued his good opinion of her; it wasn't something she'd experienced in a long time. The dating pool in Port Orlov was meager, to put it kindly.

"I'll be fine," she said, grabbing up her bedroll and backpack and sidling past him.

He looked unpersuaded.

"Here," she said, taking the *bilikin* from around her neck and dropping it down over his head. "Now you can keep an eye on things even in the dark of night."

"You're going to need it more than I do," he said, glancing toward the church doors.

"It's the leader of the hunt who's supposed to wear it."

For that split second it took her to put the necklace on him, their faces had been very close, and she had felt his warm breath on her cheek. She had seen the stubble on his chin, and a faint scar along his jawline. Where, she wondered, had he come by that? And why did she have such an urge to run her finger gently along its length?

"See you in the morning," she said, to break the mood. "Put me down for French toast."

But he still appeared dubious as she slipped between the doors, then flattened herself for a moment against the back of one, with her eyes closed. It was only when she heard his footsteps descend the stairs outside that she opened them again, to a scene of such desolation that she was sorely temped to change her plans.

Chapter 26

By the time Harley and Eddie had found their way back to the cave again, stumbling through the forest with their flashlights and their tools, night had fallen, and the wind had been blowing in their faces the whole time. Even with the black wool balaclava pulled all the way down over his head, Harley's face stung like it been slapped a thousand times.

Eddie, similarly attired, had done nothing but bitch all the way back.

Especially because their haul had been so disappointing.

The moment they staggered into the cave—about the tenth one they'd tried—Russell had been up on his feet and shouting, "What the fuck? You left me here?"

Harley, trying to get the tarp back in place, had told him to shut up, but Russell was just getting going.

"Where the fuck have you been? I wake up, and I'm ready to go, and you two assholes are nowhere around! Where did you go? Why didn't you wake me?"

"Because you got so damn drunk last night," Harley said, gesturing at a few of the beer cans glittering in the glow of the Coleman lamp, "we didn't have time for you to sober up."

"You didn't have time, or you didn't want to share whatever you got? You went digging, right?" His eyes went to the shovel and pickaxe they had dropped by the mouth of the cave. "What'd you find? You holding out on me already?"

"Yeah," Eddie said, slumping in a weary heap against the wall. "We're holding out on you."

Harley tossed his backpack down, reached inside it and threw a string of crystal rosary beads on the ground. "That's what we found."

Russell picked it up, looked at the beads—apparently even he could tell they were pretty worthless—and tossed them away. "What else?"

"What else what?" Eddie said. "It took us hours just to dig up that piece of shit."

"I don't believe you," Russell said, grabbing Harley's backpack and shaking it out. A cascade of PowerBars, Tic Tacs, Chapstick, Trojans, and the like spilled out.

Harley felt his temper start to rise—this day had been bad enough already—and he was about to demand that Russell put it all back in the bag when he stopped himself. He could tell that Russell was on the verge of losing it altogether, and maybe a little drunk even now. He also knew what was really wigging him out—and it wasn't the idea that he'd been cheated. It was having to spend the day alone, cooped up in this cave, wondering what was going on and whether or not he and Eddie were even planning to come back at all. Russell would never admit it—Harley knew that damn well—but he was having a panic attack.

After two years at Spring Creek—and several stays in solitary confinement there—Russell had lost his talent for solitude, or confinement.

"So what's the plan then?" Russell said, looming over him but still having to stoop beneath the low roof of the cave. "Do we leave?"

"On what?" Eddie said. "Last I checked, the *Kodiak*'s on the rocks."

"The skiff then."

"In these seas?" Eddie sneered.

"Well what then? Are we gonna dig again tomorrow?"

That was the million-dollar question that Harley had been puzzling over all the way back. As he and Eddie had skirted the colony on their return, he had seen the propeller blades of the Sikorsky rising behind the stockade wall, and he had glimpsed the stark white light of electric bulbs. That guy Slater and his Coast Guard crew were settling in . . . but for what? If they moved into the graveyard, all he'd be able to do was wait them out.

Or, and this had occurred to him halfway back, he could wait to see if they unearthed anything of value, then steal it from them once they had. It wasn't as if the Coast Guard thought there was anyone else on the island. Maybe, as a result, they wouldn't take the normal security precautions. You never could tell.

"What are we eating?" Eddie said, rummaging around in the supplies. "Let's make something good and hot."

"Sure," Harley said, "and while we're at it, why don't we hang out a sign that says we're here? Why don't we make a big fire, and some smoke, and maybe even attract some animals to the smell?"

Eddie, stymied, rubbed his mittened hands together and waited.

Harley crawled over to the box of canned rations, and tossed them each a couple. The ones he grabbed for himself said BEEF STROGANOFF.

Grumbling, the other two settled into their corners and dug in.

Harley was hungry, too, and after everything he'd been through, even the shit in the can tasted great. That must be how the Army got away with it. Drop a guy into some desert foxhole, and he'll eat anything, and be grateful for it.

The rosary was lying over by the wall, and Harley couldn't help but relive the disappointment he'd felt when they'd finally busted into the coffin. Eddie had been afraid to reach in, so it had fallen to Harley again to take the damn thing out. He'd tried not to look at the face of the corpse this time; the last thing he needed was to be haunted by yet another figment of his imagination, like that guy in the sealskin coat. He'd felt around on the upper body and the face and the neck, checking the fingers too for rings, but this was the only thing he could locate or pry loose. Even the string of beads hadn't come easy; it was as if the corpse was fighting to hang on to it.

When they were done, Harley had shoved the shards of the coffin back into the grave, then covered up the hole with dirt and snow again. He hoped it would snow some more during the night to further conceal his tracks.

Russell belched and popped the top on another beer. Harley was starting to think that the three cases might not last long enough, after all.

Of course it was an open question how long Russell himself would last. The guy was like a ticking bomb ever since he'd come back from the penitentiary, and Harley just wanted to make sure that he was well out of range of the explosion when it happened.

Chapter 27

Standing with her back to the door, Nika fished out her flashlight and played the beam around the interior of the abandoned church. The place was so dark that the light could only penetrate a few small feet of the space at a time. Making things worse, everything was at a slight angle, so that she felt as if she were on a boat listing to one side at sea.

Testing the floor carefully, she advanced a few feet toward some wooden pews. Between them, there was a narrow stretch where the boards weren't too badly warped and the pews might afford some protection from drafts. For a second, she reconsidered going back to the mess tent, but the thought of giving up on her mission, not to mention listening to Kozak snore all night (and there was no way he wasn't a snorer) stiffened her resolve. She took off her boots and wrapped her fur coat around them to make a pillow, then unrolled her sleeping bag and slithered down into it.

Even for someone long accustomed to acting as the mayor, tribal elder, Zamboni driver, and general factotum for a whole town, it had been a particularly hard day, and although she couldn't have predicted that she'd be sleeping in the ruins of an old Orthodox church that night, it wasn't the first time she'd wound up bunking down under strange conditions. As an anthropologist specializing in the native peoples of the Arctic climes, she had slept in igloos she'd carved herself, in shelters made from walrus gut and caribou hides, in long-abandoned iron mines that had once been blasted from the frozen soil. This was hardly the worst spot she'd ever been in.

But it might have been the eeriest. In fact, she still had that uneasy sensation she'd had ever since setting foot on the island. At first, she'd attributed it to the awkwardness of the situation between Dr. Slater and herself; he'd resisted her coming along, but now that she was there, he seemed to feel that he had some special duty to watch over her. The last thing she'd wanted was to add to his burden—the expedition alone was plenty of responsibility for one man—but she also had to admit that a part of her rather liked it. She was so used to taking care of things herself, whether it was a fishing dispute down at the dock or a municipal shortfall, that she'd forgotten what it was like to have someone else looking out for her. She'd been a lone wolf so long, it was nice to come across another of the breed.

No, her discomfort was from something else, something that clung to the island itself, like kelp to a rock. Nika had always been attuned to such things—her grandmother, who had raised her, had said she'd make a good shaman. Supposedly, her father had had such talents, but Nika hardly knew him, as he had gone missing when she was an infant, and her mother, working the late shift at the oil refinery, had been run off the road by a drunk driver and killed on the spot. For this part of Alaska, the story was not that unusual, and Nika had been determined to change her part in it before it was too late.

Instead of sticking around town and getting pregnant at seventeen by some fisherman, she'd hit the books, hard, and won a scholarship to the University of Alaska at Fairbanks; after that, she'd entered the doctoral program at Berkeley. Her old boyfriend Ben had been planning for the two of them to move to Florida, where he'd just received a job offer—tenure track yet—at the University of Miami. She'd even flown there with him for a week to look around at the campus and check out some apartments, but every palm tree was like a needle in her heart. And for someone who'd seen seals skinned and elk field-dressed, it was alarming how grossed out she'd been by the sight of palmetto bugs scurrying across a kitchen counter.

To Ben's surprise, if not her own, Nika had returned to the place she'd been determined to escape. Now that she'd made her point and earned her degrees, she decided to come back to Port Orlov, where she could do more for her people than write ethnographic mono-graphs published in scholarly journals that no one would ever read. She could so something concrete. Maybe it was what priests meant when they talked about their calling.

Down toward the nave of the church, she heard a faint rustling sound, and she held her breath. Rats. That would be all she needed. Her hand slipped out of her sleeping bag and made sure her flashlight was within easy reach.

Slater, she thought, showed that same missionary zeal. Although she'd never have admitted it, she'd done a thorough Internet search on him and what she'd read had been very impressive—impeccable academic credentials, an illustrious Army career in the Medical Corps, a number of published papers on epidemiological issues, all of them based on firsthand reports from war zones and trouble spots. But this man who had once been an Army major was now a civilian again, and reading between the lines on the Web, where she could almost see the fingertips of government censors, it looked to her like something had abruptly gone awry. Had he been drummed out of the service? What could he have possibly done? In her estimation, Slater seemed like ef-ficiency incarnate, a model of rectitude, the oldest Boy Scout she'd ever known . . . but with a world-weary edge to him. And something else, too—a pallor to his skin, a glassy sheen in his eye now and then. It occurred to her that he might have been sick lately. Maybe he still was. But with what?

The sound came again, but this time it was more like little feet pat-tering across the wood, then something being shifted. Dragged. She wanted to reach down and unzip her bag, but she was afraid the noise would give her away. Damn, why hadn't she inspected the place more thoroughly before bedding down? Or better yet, just slept in the mess tent?

She started to work her way out of the bag without unzipping it. She had just cleared her shoulders when the dragging sound came again—closer, louder. And this time she could tell there was a live creature of some kind, warm and breathing softly, inching nearer. She didn't know whether to lie as still and silent as possible, or struggle to free herself from the bag. She craned her head backwards, so she could see into the aisle, and as she did, something slid into view. It was on the ground and only a foot or two from her face. In the moonlight, she could just make out that it was a head, turned toward her. The eyes were wide open, and so was the mouth.

She screamed and turned on the flashlight.

The old man—in an orange life jacket—was staring at her . . . but just beyond him a pair of fierce yellow eyes glittered like coals in the dark.

The wolf, dragging the corpse by its ravaged arm, stood its ground, not budging an inch.

Nika shrieked at it and waved the flashlight wildly.

The wolf lowered its head, growling. No wolf worth its salt ever released a hunk of meat without a greater threat than this.

She swatted at it with the flashlight, and the wolf ducked, still clenching its prize.

She shrieked again, and a few seconds later there was a clamor at the doors, the sound of running boots and men shouting.

The wolf jerked its head, ripping a hunk of frozen flesh from the old man's arm, then lunged back into the darkest recesses of the church.

"Nika! Where are you?"

It was Slater.

Flashlight beams were crisscrossing the air above her.

"Here," she managed to cry out, kicking her legs free of the sleeping bag.

"Where?"

The boots came closer as she scrambled out from between the pews.

"Watch out—there's a wolf in here!"

"Where?" This was the sergeant's voice now.

"It just ran into the back!"

Slater threw a protective arm, tight as a hoop of steel, around her shoulders, then he said, "Jesus Christ," as he took in the corpse on the floor.

"Get out!" Sergeant Groves was shouting. "Get out now! I'll take care of the wolf."

But Slater wasn't going anywhere. He pointed his own flashlight toward the far end of the church. There was a wooden screen, a few feet high and still adorned with scraps of paint, standing behind a jumble of broken boards and furniture.

Among the debris, a black shadow stirred.

"I see it!" Groves said, and she heard his pistol cock.

"Don't shoot it!" Nika shouted.

But the sergeant snorted in derision, and the gun went off with a deafening blast. A corner of an old chair flew apart in a spray of splinters, and the shadow leapt behind a pew.

"Let it go!" Nika said. "If we leave, it will go on its own!" She pulled on the sleeve of Slater's shirt.

Just then, there was a blur of motion as the creature vaulted out of its cover and, to their astonishment, came racing straight toward them.

Groves fired again, the bullet hitting an andiron with a clang, and before he could get off another shot, the wolf, like a gust of wind, went hurtling right past them all, head down, eyes fixed on the open doors. Nika felt its fur bristle against her leg as it charged down the aisle.

The sergeant whirled around, but Slater warned him not to shoot. And then it was gone, into the night.

"Was there just one?" Groves asked her urgently.

"Yes," she said, "that's all I saw."

The sergeant's eyes now fell on the corpse, and after taking a deep breath, he looked more puzzled than appalled. "Who the hell is this?"

"One of the lost crewmen," Slater said, kneeling down, and examining the life jacket in the flashlight beam. In white letters, it read NEPTUNE II.

"Wait—I recognize him now," Nika said. "It's Richter. Down at the docks, where he worked, they always called him Old Man Richter." She became aware that there were several other members of the expedition now, clustered on the steps of the church and peering in through the open doors.

"I guess Harley Vane wasn't the only survivor of the shipwreck, after all," Slater said.

"But how the hell did this old guy get up here to the colony?" Groves, holstering his gun, wondered aloud.

"When they have no choice," Nika said, solemnly, "people can do extraordinary things." And St. Peter's Island was plainly the place to do them. No wonder she'd had the heebie-jeebies since getting there. The island had a bad rep, and it was living up to it in spades.

Chapter 28

Slater awoke in the dark, with no idea of the time. He glanced at the fluorescent numerals on his watch, and saw that it was not even 6 A.M. yet. The sun wouldn't rise, if that's what you could call it, for hours yet.

All around him he was aware of the others, still asleep—Dr. Lantos on the insulated rubber flooring under the table, Kozak snoring on a pile of the ground mats, and Nika—safely removed from the old church—curled like a cat into her sleeping bag between some unpacked crates. The thought of what might have happened to her earlier that night, alone with the wolf and its frozen carrion, made him shudder. He had never lost a man—or woman—on a mission before, and he was not about to start now.

Especially with someone like Nika.

Rising quietly, he went to the flap of the tent and poked his head outside. The air was so cold that just drawing a breath felt as if he'd swallowed a bucket of ice, and the colony grounds were dusted with a fresh coat of snow—not as deep as he'd dreaded but enough to prove a nuisance with their dig. The Sikorsky was parked a hundred meters away, with Sergeant Groves and his Coast Guard crew bunked down inside. Like the Greeks hidden away in the Trojan horse, Slater thought.

As he watched, the hatchway slid open, and Groves, his parka flapping open and his boots unlaced, stepped out onto the snow with his flashlight on. Slater raised a hand, but Groves didn't see him as he made his way to the latrines. There was an immense amount of work to do that day, but Slater knew that if anybody could get it all organized and done, it would be the sergeant.

When he ducked his head back inside, he saw that Dr. Lantos was stirring. "Who let the draft in?" she said, fumbling for her glasses, and even the professor had quit snoring and was stretching his burly arms. All he could see of Nika was the top of her head, burrowing deeper into her bag for a few extra minutes of slumber.

The day was officially under way.

Over the next few hours, Groves and his crew got a hot breakfast going in the mess tent and unloaded the remainder of the supplies in the chopper, while Dr. Lantos and the professor checked over their equipment inventories and made sure everything was accounted for and in order. As soon as the sky showed a glimmer of light, and Slater could see that the crewmen, under the guidance of the pilot, Rudy, were erecting the other prefab structures according to the plans he had drawn up, he left them to it and rounded up his own team for the trip to the cemetery. Dr. Lantos wanted to stay behind for now and personally oversee the construction and placement of the autopsy tent, but the others were raring to go. Kozak, both gloves fastened on the handlebars of his ground-penetrating radar unit, looked like he was about to mow a lawn.

"You sure you don't want to wait until we've seen what kind of access we have to the cemetery?" Slater asked, but Kozak patted the bright red handles of the GPR like it was a trusted dog and said, "It has gone everywhere. And until we do the ground study, what else can you do, anyway?"

Slater had to agree. Digging up graves under any circumstances was a harrowing business, rife with potential problems. But digging up graves containing the hundred-year-old remains of victims of the Spanish flu—remains that might have deteriorated, in coffins that might have disintegrated, in graves that might even have shifted their location underground due to geothermal changes—was a task requiring the utmost care and professional expertise.

Not to mention sensitivity. It was no surprise to Slater that he saw Nika lacing up her boots and slipping on her glove liners.

"I don't suppose I could persuade you to stay out of harm's way today?" Slater said.

"Thanks, but after last night," she said, "I think I've already had my baptism by fire."

Sergeant Groves, with a bundle of wire flags under his arm, smiled and shook his head at his boss, as if to say, *You were dreaming if you thought she wasn't coming.* And though Slater knew he was right, he had had to give it a try. In addition to all the other considerations, exhumations were often dangerous affairs, and the first thing any team leader tried to do was limit the personnel present.

The second thing was to avoid wasting time on battles with headstrong opponents who were bound and determined to pursue their own agenda no matter what.

The sky was a sullen gray when the team finally passed under the main gates of the colony and started down the cleared slope that led to the grove of trees. Slater spotted a narrow break in the woods that suggested a trail had once begun here, and without a word Sergeant Groves wired a red flag to the nearest bough. As they forced their way through the thick trees and dense underbrush, brambles pulling at the sleeves of their coats and low-hanging branches dropping their load of fresh snow on top of their hoods and hats, Groves continued to place an occasional marker along the way.

"We'll need all of this cut away on both sides," Slater said, over his shoulder, and Groves replied, "I can get a team with power saws down here later this afternoon. You want ramping, too?"

"Yes, wherever the ground is particularly uneven."

"Yes, please, I will need that," the professor said, as he struggled with Nika's help to steer the wheels of his GPR around an especially gnarly root formation.

Slater, seeing the difficulty he was having, resisted saying I told you so. He understood the professor's impatience to get started; it was a

failing, or virtue, in his own nature, too. But years of running epidemiological missions had taught him to rein in his impulses by making
a careful plan and following it to the letter.

"What do you want to do about lighting?" Groves asked.

"A halogen stanchion every twenty feet or so, maybe three hundred watts each."

"I was afraid you'd say that."

Slater knew that it would mean running a lot of cables and power
from the generators in the colony all the way through the forest, but
they were going to have to do that, anyway, to power up the dressing
and decontamination chamber.

When they did emerge from the trees again, Slater stopped at a
pair of weathered gateposts, with something—some word or two—
whittled into the wood.

Nika immediately removed a glove and reverently ran one finger
over the faint writing. "It's Russian."

And when Kozak stepped forward and leaned close enough to see,
he said, "It's the same thing, over and over again."

"What?" Groves asked.

"It says, 'Forgive me, forgive me.'"

"I wonder why," Nika said, softly.

But Slater, surveying the graveyard that extended all the way to the
cliffside, wondered who had scrawled it there. Had it been the founder
of the sect, who had brought his flock to ruin in such a bleak and unforgiving spot? Had it been the last surviving member of the colony?

Or could it have been the carrier himself, aware of the calamity he
had brought upon his fellows?

The chances of their ever finding out were slim, nor could he allow
himself to become distracted by such questions. Right now, looking
out across the desolate cemetery, with its tilting crosses and broken
tombstones, he was assessing the lay of the land. Glancing to his left,
he saw a cleared spot covered only by a soft white duvet of snow.

"We'll build the biohazard prefab there," he told Groves, who was
already sticking more of his wire flags into the ground to demarcate
its boundaries. He'd erected such structures before and knew that he

needed a space about eight feet square. These chambers were always a tight squeeze, but the bigger they got, the more chances there were for a sprung seam or a loose flap compromising the whole thing.

Kozak was already trundling his GPR, on its four hard rubber wheels, between the gateposts and onto the grounds of the grave-yard. Parking it beside a rotted tree stump, he pounded his boots on the soil, almost as if he were starting some dance, then knelt, pulling off his gloves, and rubbed the snow and frost away from a patch of earth. He sifted a few grains between his thick fingers, then pressed his cheek against the ground as if he were listening for a heartbeat. Slater and Nika exchanged an amused look, but Slater knew that there had to be a good reason for everything he was doing. Kozak was the best at what he did and he could read the earth like nobody else. Slap-ping the ground several times, then brushing the dirt from his palms and pants, he declared, "The first foot or two is permafrost, but we can cut through. Three or four feet down, there is bedrock."

For Slater, that was good news. The graves would have had to be shallow ones.

"But I will need to do a thorough GPR survey of the whole area."

"There won't be time," Slater said, thinking of his timetable, and of the winter storms bearing down from Siberia any day now. "Start over by the precipice, where the erosion's already started. I need to know that the ground we'll be working on tomorrow is stable."

At the edge of the graveyard, there was a gouge in the earth, where the overhanging rock and soil had dropped off into the Bering Sea like a broken diving board. As Slater approached the spot, he felt Kozak grab his sleeve and say, "Wait."

Pushing the GPR like a stroller, Kozak moved slowly past him, all the while intently studying the computer monitor that was mounted between the two red handles. Nika, at his elbow, looked entranced by the shadowy black-and-white imagery appearing on the screen, and Kozak was only too happy to explain what the images, and the accom-panying numbers scrolling down both sides of the monitor, conveyed.

"The transducer," he said, pointing to one of the twin black anten-nae mounted on the lower part of the carriage, "is sending pulses of energy into the ground. These pulses, they penetrate materials with different electrical conduction properties and make a kind of reflection, here," he said, tapping the interface screen. "It is something called dielectric permittivity. And the data, it is all stored in the computer."

"What's the data telling you right now?" Slater asked as they approached the graves closest to the edge of the precipice.

Kozak paused before answering. "I will need to analyze it later. But there is something strange. Either the monitor is malfunctioning, or the ground has fracture lines that are not geological in origin."

"Oh, you mean from when the graves were dug?" the sergeant surmised.

"Something more than that," Kozak said, still looking a bit puzzled. He pushed the GPR carriage over the plot closest to the area were the cliff had given way, then moved it back and forth slowly, from the top of the grave to its foot. Slater craned his neck to look at the monitor himself, and it vaguely reminded him of looking at a sonogram. What he saw there was a fuzzy image of a long rectangle, with something sharper and harder depicted in the middle of the space. But when Kozak rolled the GPR back again one more time, Slater could see that the edges of the image grew wider and more irregular. Blurred. He could guess what that meant, but he waited for Kozak to say it.

"Frost heaval."

"The coffins have been shifting in the ground?"

Kozak nodded. "The closer to the cliff they are, the more movement there has been."

Movement meant damage, and damage meant any number of things might have transpired in the Alaskan soil, from leakage to contamination to—and this he could only hope for—disintegration and harmless dissipation.

"What are the ground temps?" Slater asked, and Kozak punched a few buttons on the computer, bringing up a separate graph on the screen. "At a depth of one meter or so, where most of the coffins are, it's between minus four and minus ten degrees Celsius."

"Is that good or bad?" Nika asked.

"At the AFIP," Slater replied, "we keep our specimens, for safety's sake, at minus seventy Celsius."

But this then would have to be the grave with which their project began. It was closest to ground zero, as it were, and as a result the condition of the cadaver in the casket lost at sea would be most closely replicated in this one. In any epidemiological mission, it was critical to work from the most hazardous location first, then proceed outward from there to see where, and how far, some contagion or contaminant might have spread. Slater motioned to Groves and told him the excavation work should begin right here, and Groves twisted a wire pennant around the top of the cross at the top of the grave, then stuck another into the snow at the foot of the grave.

"And make sure you keep the soil as intact as possible, so that we can lay it back neatly over the grave when we're done."

Groves made a note of it, as Nika nodded approvingly.

"We want to leave no sign of any desecration behind us when we're done."

"And the sooner you all go," Kozak piped up, waving his hands, "the easier it will be for me to finish my own work here. So, scat— I must make my grid now, and you are all in the way."

Slater knew what it was like to have a bunch of onlookers hanging around when you wanted to concentrate on a serious task at hand, so he ushered Nika and the sergeant back toward the gateposts as Kozak focused on his GPR. If this first exhumation was going to go off without a hitch tomorrow, there were things he needed to do back at the colony today. Kozak was barely aware of their leaving. And though he jiggled the monitor to see if he could remove the squiggly lines that were spoiling the topographic map, they kept coming right back, as did the occasional impression of a hard, probably metallic, object as he rolled the GPR chassis over each individual gravesite. A strong blast of cold wind swept in from the sea, bending the boughs of the dark trees that bordered the barren graveyard, and he pressed the earflaps of his hat closer against his head. It was the same kind of hat he'd worn as a boy, growing up in the Soviet Union. And now, on this strange island, he was revisited by that same crushing sadness that he remembered enveloping him even back then.

That was one reason he had just shooed them all away. When this depression fell, he needed to be alone with it . . . and it fell upon him often in climes like these. He was carried back in time, to a throng of mourners, gathered at an impressive state funeral in Moscow, when he was just a boy. Wrapped in their heavy black coats and fur hats, they had stood impassively as the wind had battered their faces and brought tears to their eyes. Of course, given the reputation for steely rectitude of the dignitary whose funeral it was—a man whom everyone feared and no one much liked—a sharp wind was the only way any of them would have been inclined to shed a tear.

As young Vassily had looked on, the Russian Orthodox priest, in his long black cassock and purple chimney-pot hat—the *kamilavka*—had overseen the *perebor,* or tolling of the bells. First, a small bell had been struck once, and then, in succession, slightly larger bells were rung, each one symbolizing the progress of the soul from cradle to grave   or so his mother had leaned down to whisper in his ear. At the end, all the bells were struck together, signifying the end of earthly existence. The coffin, sealed with four nails in memory of the four nails that had crucified Christ, was lowered into the grave, with the head facing east to await the Resurrection. The priest poured the ashes from a censer into the open pit, and after each of the stony-faced mourners had tossed in a shovelful of dirt and drifted off down the snowy pathways of the cemetery, Vassily had found himself alone there, with only his widowed mother. He had leaned back against her and she had folded her arms over him as they watched the gravediggers, impatient to finish the job, emerge from the cover of the trees to fill up the rest of his father's grave.

Chapter 29

"So, where did you say you got this?" Voynovich asked, while leaning back on his stool. He'd gotten even fatter, if that was possible, since Charlie Vane had last come into the Gold Mine to fence some other items.

"I already told you," Charlie said. "It was a gift from God."

"Yeah, right. I've heard your show. You and God are good buds now."

Charlie knew that nobody believed that his conversion to Christ was the real thing, but so what? There would always be unbelievers and naysayers. Jesus himself had to deal with Doubting Thomas. But he'd driven here, all the way to Nome, because Voynovich was the only person he could think of who could give him a decent appraisal of the emerald cross—and tell him what the damn writing said on the other side.

Voynovich studied the cross under his loupe one more time. "I can't be completely sure until I take them out," he said, "but these stones could just be glass."

"They're emeralds," Charlie said, "so don't give me any of your bullshit." Just because he was a man of God now, it didn't mean he'd become a sucker. "And the cross is silver."

"Yeah, I'll give you that much."

It was only four in the afternoon, but it was dark out, and in defer-ence to the delicacy of their negotiations, Voynovich had lowered the front blinds of the pawnshop and flipped the sign to CLOSED. The place hadn't changed much over the years—the same old moose head hung on the wall, the dusty cabinets displayed a seemingly unchanged array of Inuit scrimshaw, old mining tools, and "rare" coins in sealed plastic sleeves. The fluorescent lights still sputtered and fizzed.

"It's definitely an old piece," Voynovich conceded.

"How old?"

"Best guess? Judging from the condition, at least a hundred years. Of course, if I knew more about how and where you found it—it's why I asked—I'd probably be able to tell you a whole lot more." He shrugged his shoulders under his baggy corduroy shirt and shook a fresh cigarette out of the packet lying on the counter.

"How about the writing on the back?" Charlie asked, shifting in his wheelchair. He was still sore from his long drive from Port Orlov. "What's it say?"

Voynovich turned it over and tried peering at it through the bot-tom of his gold bifocals, then gave up. "Gotta get the magnifying glass out of the back," he said, sliding off the stool, and heading for the rear of the shop. A trail of smoke wafted into the air behind him.

The trouble with dealing with crooks, Charlie reflected, was that they never stopped being crooks. Not emeralds? What a load. Voy-novich was probably hoping to buy the thing outright from him for a couple of hundred bucks, act like he was doing Charlie a favor the whole time, then turn around and sell it for thousands through his own guys down in Tacoma. Well, Charlie hadn't come all this way for a couple hundred bucks, and he sure didn't want to have to tell Rebekah that that was all he got. While she was supposed to be the subservient wife—that's what the Bible decreed—she had a tongue on her that could cut like a knife.

Right now, she was out shopping with her sister. The town of Nome was small—only around ten thousand people lived in the area—but compared to Port Orlov, it was the big city. The streets were lined with bars and bingo parlors and tourist traps selling native handicrafts and souvenirs. Most of the buildings were two stories high, made of weathered wood and brick, and clung close to the wet streets, lending the place the feel of an Old West mining camp.

Voynovich lumbered back to his stool, parked his cigarette on the foil ashtray, and held the magnifying glass over the back of the cross. "My Russian's not what it used to be," he said, "and some of this is pretty far gone. From all the dents and scorch marks, it looks like some moron used the thing for target practice."

"Just tell me what the hell it says."

The pawnbroker leaned over to inspect it more closely. "It looks like it says, 'To my . . . little one. No one can break the chains of holy love that bind us. Your loving father, Grigori.'"

Voynovich studied it for another few seconds, then sat back.

"That's it?" Charlie asked.

"That's it."

Charlie didn't know what exactly he'd been expecting, but this wasn't it. A gift from a doting dad? Nothing there sounded like a clue to some vast buried treasure trove.

"If you want me to hang on to it and see what else I can find out, no problem," Voynovich said, a little too readily for Charlie's comfort. "I've got a big data base for Russian stuff and a few people I could talk to."

"No."

"Fine," Voynovich said. "Then if you just want to sell it, we can go ahead and do that, instead. It's probably worth more in one piece, but we can see what they think down in Tacoma. Maybe breaking it up is the way to go . . . especially if those are emeralds." He started to pick the cross up off the counter, but Charlie reached up and grabbed his wrist—he hated how the damn wheelchair kept him lower than most people—and stopped him.

"I'm hanging on to it," he said, and Voynovich looked confused.

"I thought you wanted to make some money."

"And I will." He wrapped the cross back up in the soft old rag he'd brought it in, then stuffed it into the inside pocket of his coat.

"If you want some kind of an advance," the pawnbroker said, his eyes avidly following the cross into Charlie's pocket, "I could do that. What do you say to two hundred bucks now and—"

But Charlie was already pushing his wheelchair away from the counter.

"Okay, five hundred up front, against whatever we get, plus the usual split."

Charlie was at the door, but to his humiliation, it was the kind you had to pull inwards, and he had to wait there for Voynovich to come over and hold it open while he maneuvered his chair over the threshold.

"Make it a grand," Charlie heard over his shoulder as he wheeled away. "An even grand." But now, with the bid rising so fast, he knew that the thing must really be worth something, after all. Quite a bit, in fact, unless he missed his guess.

The sidewalk, like every concrete surface in Alaska, was pitted and uneven, and it was murder getting the chair down the street. But Charlie knew where he'd find Bathsheba. The Book Nook sold used paperbacks, and she'd be in there stocking up on romance novels.

Somebody leaving the store held the door open for him, and a little bell tinkled overhead. Bathsheba, no surprise, had her nose buried in some piece of trash that she hastily tried to hide when he wheeled up beside her.

"Where's your sister?"

"Just up the street, buying yarn."

"We're going."

"You're done already? Rebekah said we could eat someplace in town."

"Rebekah said wrong."

"But there's that place, the Nugget—"

"I said, we're going."

He whirled the chair around, and Bathsheba put the book back on the shelf and leapt to get the door open for him. Once Rebekah had been retrieved from the yarn shop, the sisters helped Charlie up into the driver's seat of the van, and he pulled out onto the slushy street using the hand controls.

"Look," Rebekah said, as Charlie drove by without even slowing down, "that's the burled arch." She was hoping to distract her disappointed sister.

"The what?" Bathsheba said, taking the bait and turning in the backseat to glance at the split spruce log raised atop two columns.

"That's the place where the Iditarod race ends every year."

"What's that?"

"Remember, I told you about it last time."

"Tell me again."

How in God's name did Rebekah put up with it, Charlie wondered? Always having to explain everything to her sister, even when she'd already explained it a dozen times before? They'd come to him as a package deal—wife and sister, indivisible—and since he'd needed a lot of help around the house, he thought why not. Still, there were times, like right now, when he wondered if he hadn't acted rashly.

Then he chastised himself for the uncharitable thought. Man, staying right with Jesus was a full-time job.

"It's in honor of something that happened many years ago," Rebekah said, with the patience she showed to no one but her sister. "There was an epidemic of a disease, typhoid I think—"

"Diphtheria," Charlie corrected her.

"Okay. Diphtheria. And the children of Nome—the native children—had no immunity to it."

"It was in 1925," Charlie said, unable to restrain himself. "And it used to be called 'The Great Race of Mercy.'"

Rebekah waited a second, scowling, then went on. "The only medicine for it—"

"The serum."

"Was in Anchorage." She lay in wait for another correction, and when it didn't come, she continued. "So teams of dogsleds had to be organized in relays, and the serum was carried hundreds and hundreds of miles, through terrible storms and ice and snow, to get to the children of Nome before the disease did."

"And did it?"

"It did—in only five or six days. And there was a famous dog who was the first one to run right up this street, pulling the sled across the finish line."

"Balto," Charlie said, "his name was Balto. But the real hero was a different dog, one named Togo. Togo and his musher were the ones who took the serum through the hardest and the longest part of the route." There wasn't a kid in Alaska who didn't know the story behind the present-day Iditarod, named after the trail so much of it took place on. But it had always bugged Charlie that the credit didn't go where it really belonged. Once, many years ago, before the Merchant Marine had drummed him out, he'd had a shore leave in New York City and seen a statue there, in Central Park, of Balto. He'd wanted to scrawl Togo on it instead.

"Can we watch the race sometime?" Bathsheba asked.

Rebekah looked over at Charlie. "When is it, anyway?"

"March," he said. "I'll be sure to get us front-row seats." He wondered why it still bothered him, about Togo. Maybe, he thought, it was because he hated stories where the ones who should be recognized for their greatness were somehow overlooked, and somebody else was able to swoop in at the end and get all the glory.

At the corner of Main Street, they passed the famous signpost with a dozen different placards showing the distances from there to everywhere else. Los Angeles was 2,871 miles away, the Arctic Circle a mere 141 miles. A couple of tourists were posing for pictures underneath it. Bathsheba craned her neck to get a better look.

"Get me Harley on the horn," he said, as the van pulled out of the town proper. The lights of Nome hadn't been much, but the night enveloped them the moment they left. Rebekah called up his brother on the car's speakerphone, and Charlie heard the ring tone just before he got a burst of static, followed by dead air. Same as he'd been getting for the past couple of days.

"Goddammit!" he said, slapping his palm against the steering wheel.

"It's an island in the middle of nowhere," Rebekah said, hanging up. "I don't know why you ever expected to get any reception."

"I'm hungry," Bathsheba said from the backseat.

"We should have eaten in town," Rebekah said to Charlie. "Now you'll have to pull over at that roadhouse we passed on the Sound."

Charlie was about to protest, but he realized that he was hungry, too—it was just in his nature to be contrary—and it was going to be a long drive back. The road between Nome and Port Orlov, if that's what you could call it, ranged from asphalt to gravel to hardpan— a compacted layer of dirt just beneath the topsoil—and most of it could be bumpy and rutted and washed out even in summer.

And this was sure as hell not summer.

In the snowy wastes around them, it was hard to see much, but mired in the moonlit fields there were old, abandoned gold dredges squatting like mastodons. Occasionally, you could come across one of these that was still in operation—growling like thunder as it devoured rocks and brush and muck in a never-ending quest for the gold that might be mixed up in it. Even more eerily, railroad engines were stranded in the frozen tundra—left to rust on sunken tracks that had lost their purpose the moment the gold ran out. Their smokestacks, red with age, were the tallest things in the treeless fields.

"There it is," Rebekah said, pointing to the parking-lot lights of the roadhouse—a prefab structure on pylons—perched beside the Nome seawall. The granite wall, erected in the early fifties by the Army Corps of Engineers, was over three thousand feet long and sixty-five feet wide at the base, and it stood above what had once been known as Gold Beach, a place where the prospectors and miners of 1899 had discovered an almost miraculous supply of gold literally lying on the sands, just waiting to be collected.

"You coming in?" Rebekah asked, but they both knew Charlie wouldn't want to have to climb in and out of the van again. Pulling up onto the gravel, he parked and said, "Bring me a sandwich and get the thermos filled with tea. Peppermint if they've got it. And don't take forever."

The sisters got out of the car, buried under their long coats, and scurried up the ramp. Since he'd had no luck reaching Harley's cell phone, he tried calling Eddie's number, then Russell's, but they weren't working, either. What was happening on St. Peter's Island? Had they found a safe harbor for the *Kodiak,* and a secluded cave to hide out in? More important, had they started digging and found anything yet? Charlie had high hopes, but not a lot of confidence; he hadn't exactly dispatched the A-Team and he knew it.

Waves were crashing on the breakwater out beyond the road-house. After the gold had been discovered on the beach—in such quantities that 2 million dollars' worth was gathered in the summer of 1899 alone—steamships from San Francisco and Seattle had carried so many eager prospectors to Nome that a tent city had soon stretched thirty miles along the shore, all the way to Cape Rodney. Charlie had seen pictures of it hanging on the walls of the Nugget Inn in town. Mile after mile of canvas and stretched hides, shacks and lean-tos, all packed with desperate men and women struggling to make their fortunes. He felt the weight of the cross in his pocket and wondered how much had really changed since then? Alaska was still the Wild West in many ways—probably the last of it that was left—where loners and free spirits, people down on their luck or looking to find it in the first place, could come and make a fresh start.

While he waited in the warm car, he kneaded the tops of his dead legs. He couldn't feel anything below the groin, but he knew that it was a good idea to keep the circulation going and the muscles from atrophying. Everything happened for a reason, that's what he'd had to keep telling himself every day since the accident, and if this was God's way of bringing him back into the fold, then so be it.

The sisters, coming out of the roadhouse, with their white faces and wisps of black hair blowing free from the buns at the back of their heads, reminded him of a couple of strutting crows. Bathsheba was carrying the thermos and Rebekah had the sandwich in a paper bag. Salmon salad on whole wheat toast, as it turned out. At least she got that sort of thing right. He ate it while playing a CD of a biblical sermon—sometimes he got ideas for his own broadcasts this way—and then backed the car out of the lot.

They could have spent the night in Nome, but Charlie hated to waste money, and besides, he liked to be back in his own place, with the ramps and everything else he needed to be comfortable. Not to mention the fact that the chances of hearing any news out of nearby St. Pete's were going to be better there than in distant Nome. This first part of the road was blissfully asphalt, with a white line down the center and shoulders on either side, but he knew the rest of the way back wasn't going to be that smooth. At least the van was equipped for it, with two spare cans of gas (a necessity when traveling in the wilderness regions of Alaska), plastic headlight covers to ward off the flying gravel, and, in case he collided with anything big, a wire mesh screen in front to protect the radiator and the paint job. If you hit a moose head-on, it could be curtains for more than the moose.

He hadn't gone twenty miles before he glanced in the rearview mirror and saw that Bathsheba had slumped over in the backseat, fast asleep. Rebekah noticed it, too, and in a low voice, said, "So, how much did you get from Voynovich?"

"Nothing."

"What are you talking about?" She glanced into the backseat again to make sure her sister was out. Some things they kept from her, for fear she could blurt out a piece of news she wasn't supposed to know.

"I hung on to it," he said, patting his breast pocket.

Rebekah folded her arms across her breast and, barely containing herself, said, "You want to tell me why?"

"Because he offered me a grand up front."

Now she really looked puzzled.

"And if it was worth that much to him just to keep me from walking out of the store with it, it must be worth a helluva lot more. If Harley and his idiot friends manage to find any more stuff like it on the island, I'm going to go on down to Tacoma and fence it all myself."

In a mollified tone, she asked, "Did he at least tell you what it said on the back?"

"Yeah, but it's just an endearment. Nothing that says Romanov about it." Or at least so far as he knew. When he got home, and wasn't online ministering to Vane's Holy Writ flock, he planned to be doing whatever research he could. Dollars to donuts, Voynovich was already doing exactly the same thing.

He drove on into the night, sipping the tea, and watching as, first, the center white line disappeared, then as the breakdown lane evaporated; the road became a narrow, serpentine trail, wending its way through snowy hills and along frozen streambeds. There were old wooden bridges, reinforced and supported on cement blocks, stretching across frozen gullies, and highway signs warning of wildlife crossings. Moose, bear, elk, caribou, fox, Dall sheep. At the right times of year, if you had a mind to, you could survive off the roadkill alone in these parts.

Rebekah, too, soon fell asleep, her head leaning against her doorjamb, and Charlie tried to stay awake by paying attention to the biblical sermon on the CD. The preacher was an old man called the Right Reverend Abercrombie, and he spoke in a lulling, monotonous tone.

"And when we read, in Exodus 7–12, about the ten plagues that descended upon the Egyptians, what are we to make of them?" the reverend said. "What was God's purpose?"

To kick Egyptian ass, Charlie thought, *and to kick it hard.*

"The purpose of the Lord was twofold," the reverend continued. "Of course he wanted to persuade the Pharaoh to free the Israelites. But he also had a second reason—and that was to show just how strong the God of Israel was in comparison to the gods of Egypt. It was a point he wanted to make not only to the Egyptians, but to the Israelites themselves."

While the Reverend Abercrombie went through his analysis of the ten plagues, one by one, and expounded on what each of them meant, Charlie kept his eyes peeled for trouble up ahead, looking out for the little red flags that were commonly posted along the roadside wherever there were loose gravel breaks, or where the pavement had cracked from frost heaval.

"'If you do not let my people go,'" Abercrombie recited from the Old Testament, "'I will send swarms of flies on you and your officials, on your people and into your houses.'"

What had always troubled Charlie about the ten plagues was that Yahweh seemed so willing to go another round all the time, whether it was with flies, or gnats, or frogs, or pestilence. For the Lord God

Almighty, He didn't know how to lower the boom, once and for all. No wonder Pharaoh kept agreeing to set the Israelites free before going back on his word every time.

An oil tanker, horn blaring as it came round a bend, barreled past him in the opposite direction, the wind from its passage buffeting the van.

But both of the sisters slept on.

"Then the Lord said to Moses, 'Stretch out your hand toward the sky so that darkness will spread over Egypt—darkness that can be felt,'" the reverend quoted.

Darkness that can be felt. The first time Charlie had read that, he remembered thinking that it was as if the book were describing Alaska. The darkness in the woods at night, or on a lonely road, when a storm was concealing the moon and stars, could be as thick and palpable as a beaver pelt. He had known men to die, frozen to death, on their own land, unable to see or find their way to their houses. And soon, as winter continued to descend, the night would fasten its grip even more tightly, extinguishing the sun altogether.

In his headlights, the only signs of human activity he could see, for mile after mile after mile, were the junk heaps abandoned on the sides of the road. Broken-down old trucks half-buried in the snow, motorcycle frames riddled with bullet holes, a decrepit Winnebago resting on its axles. In Alaska, it was easy to abandon things, but nothing went unscavenged. All of these wrecks had been carefully stripped of any useful parts, like an animal stripped of its fur, its meat, its antlers.

As he approached the wide turn that he knew led to the Heron River Bridge, the road began to washboard, huge ripples in the asphalt making the van buck and swerve. Miraculously, Rebekah only moved her head away from the door and let her chin slump in the other direction, while Bathsheba slept on in the backseat. Behind her, in the rear of the van, he could hear the gas sloshing in the cans.

The ground gradually rose through snow-covered hills, with battered and dented signs along the road warning of oncoming traffic, avalanche dangers, animal crossings, possible strong wind conditions, icy road hazards, you name it. Using the hand levers, Charlie slowed down. Fortunately, he had no one behind him, and nothing, so far, approaching from the other direction. The bridge—a two-lane, steel span—was one of the biggest in the region, even though the Heron River itself didn't amount to much. It lay far below, at the bottom of a granite canyon, and half the time it was frozen solid. At other times, however, when the snowpack melted in the spring, or the rains came, it could become a raging torrent overnight.

Charlie shifted in his seat, and as he switched gears, the silver cross nudged him again in the ribs. It was kind of uncomfortable keeping it there. With Bathsheba asleep anyway, he saw no harm in taking it out and laying it flat, still concealed in the rag, on the console beside the thermos. The road had turned to compacted gravel here to offer better traction, and as he steered past a pair of icy boulders, each one slick with ice and the size of a house, he slowed down again.

"And when the tenth and final plague came, the Lord said, 'About midnight I will go throughout Egypt. Every firstborn son in Egypt will die, from the firstborn son of Pharaoh, who sits on the throne, to the firstborn son of the slave girl, who is at her hand mill . . .'"

There was the sound of something stirring in the back of the van, and then he heard the leather of the backseat creaking. Damn, why couldn't Bathsheba have stayed asleep for just another couple of hours? He did not need to deal with her blather.

"'. . . and all the firstborn of the cattle as well. There will be loud wailing throughout Egypt—worse than ever has been or ever will be again.'"

Rebekah was still snoring, but her sister must be awake.

"Exodus, 11, 4–6."

As the tires rumbled onto the corrugated lanes of the steel bridge, Charlie caught, out of the corner of one eye, a hand reaching over and into the front seat. At first, he figured she was reaching for the thermos, but then he thought, Bathsheba hates peppermint tea.

"Even so, the Lord had provided for his chosen people," Abercrombie commented, "instructing them to mark their doorposts with the blood of the lamb."

Maybe she thought it was root beer, her favorite.

"It's peppermint tea," he said. "You won't like it."

Taking his eye off the slippery road for an instant, he saw that her wrist was surprisingly bony and white, even for Bathsheba, and something wet and stringy touched his cheek. Christ, why hadn't she dried her hair before she got back in the car?

And then she really pissed him off. She went right past the thermos and reached for the rag holding the cross.

"Leave that alone," he barked, reluctant to take a hand off the wheel on the icy bridge.

But she went ahead anyway and picked it up.

Shit. He took one hand off the wheel and grabbed her wrist—it was cold and slick as an icicle—but when he glanced up at the rearview mirror, he saw not Bathsheba's sullen features, but two hollow eye sockets, sunken in the long face of a dead man in a black sealskin coat.

When he turned his head, a thatch of matted dark hair, knotted and rank as seaweed, swept his face. He'd have screamed, but he was struck dumb. The car swerved, scraping the guardrail so hard a shower of blue sparks erupted.

"What?" Rebekah said, startled awake. "What's happening?"

Charlie dropped hold of the bony wrist and wrestled with the wheel. The tires skidded on a thin coat of ice.

Bathsheba was sitting bolt upright, muttering "The Lord is my shepherd, I shall not want . . ."

The car banged the rails again, the hatchback springing open and the alarm bell dinging.

An oncoming truck pumped its horn, switching its headlight beams to bright and sweeping the interior of the van.

"What's going on?" Bathsheba said. Icy cold air was flooding the car from the open hatch.

"And the Lord said to the Israelites, 'I will not suffer the destroyer to come into your houses . . .'"

"Watch it!" Rebekah shouted, as he barely managed to get control before they veered into the other lane.

In the rearview mirror, the dead man was gone, as if extinguished by the gush of light and air. All Charlie saw was Bathsheba, and through the gaping hatch the empty roadway disappearing behind him.

The truck rattled by, its driver thrusting his middle finger out the window at Charlie.

"Did you fall asleep?" Rebekah accused him. The cross, free of its rag, was lying on the floor of the van.

"Ew," Bathsheba said, squirming in her seat.

"And the angel of death spared them, as the Lord had promised."

"Double ew," Bathsheba said again. "It stinks back here."

"What are you talking about?" Rebekah snapped, turning around. "And close that hatch before we lose half the gear!"

The van eased off the other end of the Heron River Bridge, and Charlie, steering it onto the shoulder, took his first full breath in what felt like forever. His hands were shaking, and he was still too scared even to turn in his seat.

"And it's all wet back here," Bathsheba complained, settling back into her own seat after securing the hatch.

Rebekah took a look around the rear, and said, "You should have stomped the snow off your boots before you got back in the van."

"I did," Bathsheba insisted.

"Then what did you step in?" she said, rolling down her window. "It does smell like something died back there."

"Forget about the smell," Charlie muttered to Rebekah. Gesturing at the cross on the floor, he said, "Pick that up."

She did, wrapping it back in the rag.

"Put it in the glove compartment."

She stuck it in the compartment and slammed the little door shut. "And you," she said, glaring at him, "watch your damn driving from now on."

" 'And it came to pass that the Lord did bring the children of Israel out of the land of Egypt . . .' "

Charlie flicked off the CD and punched the radio dial to a country-western station.

"I was listening to that," Rebekah complained.

"You were sleeping," he said, as Garth Brooks came on, mournfully wailing about lightning strikes and rolling thunder. "Listen to this instead."

With his eyes fastened on the road, his hands clenching the wheel, and his heartbeat gradually returning to normal, he steered the van out into the darkness of the surrounding land—*darkness that could be felt*—and pondered the cross they had looted from a Russian grave.

Was the apparition he had just seen in the backseat its rightful owner?

A wolf—a big dark one—was momentarily caught in the headlights, loping along the side of the road, as if keeping pace with the van. But then, with a turn of its head and a silver flash of its eyes, it vanished into the night.

Chapter 30

By the time Slater had reached the bottom of the stone steps leading to the beach, he could hardly believe it.

It had been hard enough coming down them, in the light of day, but to think that Old Man Richter had managed to climb *up* them after being shipwrecked was almost beyond comprehension.

"That guy we found in the church must have been one tough old bird," Rudy, the Coast Guard ensign, said.

"The toughest there ever was."

In some places, the steps were no more than a few inches wide, and they zigged and zagged down the cliff face from the colony grounds high above them. Up top, Slater could hear the sounds of Sergeant Groves's work crew preparing for the exhumations—buzz saws cutting a clear path to the cemetery, jackhammers loosening soil, hammers clanging on metal stanchions as the lighting poles and lab tents were erected. Even now, at high noon, the sun was struggling to make itself felt through the low-hanging clouds, and a hundred yards offshore the bracelet of mist that clung to St. Peter's Island obscured the Bering Strait beyond.

"Just in case," Rudy was saying as he walked a few yards down the rocky beach, "this RHI is going to be left right here."

A bright yellow boat—called a Rigid Hull Inflatable—was sitting just above the high-tide line, tied to a boulder and raised on makeshift davits fashioned from driftwood. A black, waterproof tarp was stretched tight over its interior.

"Chances are," Rudy said, "it will never be needed, but if air transport is unavailable or for some reason temporarily impractical, this will provide a means to get off the island and back to Port Orlov."

"I take it you'll be here to do the navigating," Slater said.

"Yes, I'm staying when the Sikorsky goes, but the boat pretty much sails itself. Port Orlov's just about three miles due east."

The chopper was leaving that night, in less than two hours, carrying the rest of the Coast Guard personnel—along with a body bag containing the remains of Richter. Nika had contacted Geordie to take custody of the corpse and keep it under wraps in the community center's garage until she could get back and arrange for a proper burial.

Slater looked forward to limiting the complement on the island. When dealing with an epidemiological event like this, the fewer people present, the smaller the risk of anything from misinformation to contagion escaping into the greater pool. As it was, there were far too many questions from the Coast Guardsmen, and even though they had been warned that anything they had seen or done on the island was considered highly classified, Slater knew from experience that no secret shared by more than three people ever stayed secret for long. He slapped a hand on the side of the boat, like patting a trusty steed, all the while hoping he would never need to take it out on the open sea. If everything went as planned, the exhumation and autopsy work would be done in roughly seventy-two hours, and the chopper would be back to retrieve Slater's team and their core samples before the weather turned any worse than it already was.

Even for Alaska, there was a bone-chilling snap in the air, courtesy of a Siberian low that had been moving slowly, but inexorably, in the direction of St. Peter's Island. Snowfall so far had been slight, just a couple of inches, but even that much precipitation meant time and effort would be expended to clear it away. The most important thing

THE ROMANOV CROSS   239

for Slater right now was to get into that cemetery and start the dig. He had spent several hours going over all the topographical data with Professor Kozak, and he had chosen the grave closest to the edge of the cliff to begin his work. Not only was it the one most in danger of falling victim to the same erosion that had released the first coffin, it was also the one that might have been exposed to the greatest variations in soil and air temperature, and from the frost heaval that they could cause.

As soon as he returned to the colony grounds, Slater made the equivalent of hospital rounds, inspecting the various labs and facilities, which had been erected in record time. Green neoprene tents, connected by hard rubber matting that provided pathways among them, glowed from within like lightbulbs. Ropes had been strung up alongside all the paths so that, in the event of a sudden whiteout, anyone caught outside could still hang on and grope his or her way to safety. In addition to the mess tent, there were several bivouacs now— one reserved for Dr. Lantos and Nika, who had definitely renounced her notion of sleeping in the old church—and over by the main gates a combination laboratory and autopsy tent. A metal ramp with rails on both sides had been erected to its entrance, where a big orange triangle announced that it was a Biohazard Level-3 Facility, open to authorized personnel only. The tent was shrouded in heavy-duty, double-plastic sheaths, stuck together with Velcro-type adhesive strips; in this climate, zippers tended to freeze and get stuck.

Parting the curtains, Slater stepped inside the laboratory area of the tent. Dr. Lantos was under a table, straightening out a tangle of cords that looked like a pile of snakes. For a second, Slater was taken back to the rice paddy in Afghanistan . . . and the viper lashing out at the little girl. Warm air was blowing in through the vents, but the ambient temperature was still no better than fifty-seven or fifty-eight degrees Fahrenheit.

Crawling back out, feetfirst, Dr. Lantos looked up and saw him. Pushing her glasses back onto the bridge of her nose and glancing at her wristwatch, she said, "Don't tell me you're ready to go."

"Not until you say the lab is done."

Sitting back on her heels, she said, "It may not look like much, but I do think it's fully operational. Want the thirty-second tour?"

"Absolutely."

The truth was, the relatively warm air was feeling really good, and he didn't mind lingering a bit. The new antiviral regimen was playing havoc with his usual malarial meds, and more than once that morning he'd felt a sudden shiver descend his spine. If anyone else under his command had reported similar problems, Slater would have promptly removed that person from active duty and ordered rest and maybe even a medical evaluation. But if he took himself out of the picture, if he admitted what was going on to anyone else on the team, the whole mission would grind to an immediate halt. Even more to the point, if, God forbid, word of the delay got back to Dr. Levinson at the AFIP, he'd instantly be replaced, recalled . . . and relegated to a desk job in D.C. forever after.

And that was not a risk he was prepared to take.

"This is our living room," Dr. Lantos joked, waving her arm around the long, narrow space, illuminated by a row of light fixtures attached to a single aluminum beam that ran the length of the room. Counters had been set up on either side, topped with electron microscopes, racks of test tubes, vials, flasks, beakers, rubber gloves, and antiseptic dispensers. Underneath them there were cabinets and bins with neatly labeled and color-coded drawers.

"You have all the power you need?" Slater asked, and Lantos nodded vigorously, which only served to call his attention to the pencil, and the pen, she had stuck in the frizzy mop of her gray hair. He had the fleeting impression that if he looked hard enough in there, he could find anything from grocery lists to ticket stubs. It was one of the things that had always endeared her to him.

At the rear of the tent, a second chamber—a chamber within a chamber, as it were—had been erected behind its own clear plastic curtains; parting them, he was met by a blast of much colder air. A freezer, about half the size of a normal refrigerator, squatted on the triple-insulated rubber mat that comprised the floor. Standing in the center of the space was a long, stainless-steel autopsy table, and beside it a wheeled cart that held an array of vessels and receptacles for the organs and tissue samples they would be removing from the corpses they exhumed. Slater expected to take samples from no less than three or four, drawn from all quarters of the cemetery, before he was done. After inspecting the air vents, which were serviced by a separate filtration unit outside, Slater was satisfied that the place was indeed ready to go.

"Grab your hat," he said. "It's showtime."

With Dr. Lantos in tow, Slater rounded up Professor Kozak, who was buried in his geological studies, and told them to wait for him by the main gates. Then, with some reluctance, he went to fetch Nika. He wished it could be avoided, he did not want her anywhere near the site and exposed to any of the myriad dangers it might present, but he also knew she'd be livid if he tried to leave her out.

Not to mention the fact that as the duly appointed tribal representative and mayor of the closest town, she could shut him down if she really wanted to.

Poking his head into the flap of her tent, he found her typing furiously on her laptop. She was compiling field notes, he knew, for an anthropological report she hoped to write, and Slater had not yet found the heart to tell her that none of what was happening on St. Peter's Island was likely to see the light of day, much less in some academic journal. The only official report that would ever be written would be his own, and if experience was any indication, it would be restricted to a very small cadre of AFIP scientists and directors to review.

"The digging is done?" she said expectantly.

"It should be by the time we get there and suit up."

Twirling around on her camp stool, she grabbed a worn and faded leather jerkin that was lying on her cot and slipped it over her head. It had a long fringe that hung below her waist, and red and black stitches depicting bears and eagles and otters all over it.

"When I said suit up, I meant a hazmat suit."

"That's fine," she said, winding her long black hair into a glossy ponytail and flipping it over the collar of the jerkin. "But as the tribal rep, I've got to wear the sacred garment." Pulling on a parka over ev-erything else, she added, "And I'll need a minute to say some words over any grave you open."

"But they'll be Russian graves, not Inuit," Slater said, and Nika just shrugged as she slipped past him and onto the rubber-matted pathway outside. Her boots squelched in the icy slush.

"It's our land, our rules," she said with a smile. "The home-field advantage." Slater wasn't sure what advantage it might confer, but he did know that from here on in the rules would be his own. At the colony gates, he and Nika hooked up with Lantos and the professor, and the four of them, bundled up in coats and hats and gloves against the chill ocean wind, trooped down the pathway toward the trees. Sergeant Groves and his crew had cleared a trail through the woods, but the brush had already begun to impinge again; snow-laden branches drooped down overhead and sharp twigs plucked at the puffy sleeves of his down-filled parka. It was a far cry from his usual postings, where the worst impediments were sunstroke and scorpion bites.

Even though it was technically early afternoon, the sun was so dim that the light stanchions, positioned every few yards along the path-way, were all switched on, providing an eerie glow. As Slater ap-proached the cemetery gateposts, scrawled with their anonymous plea to "Forgive me," he glanced over toward the promontory where he could see Groves and a Coast Guardsman, cloaked in their own hazmat suits, repositioning a jackhammer to loosen whatever frozen soil still remained at the parameters previously demarcated by Kozak. The strips of wet sod that had already been removed had been laid, according to Slater's instructions, neatly to one side on top of a canvas ground cover. When the exhumation was finished, the grave was to be returned to a state as close to its previous condition as possible—and the canvas cover incinerated.

Meanwhile, the dressing tent had been set up just to the left of the entrance, and as Groves let loose with one more loud volley from the jackhammer, Slater guided his team into the chamber. The aluminum floor rumbled from the weight of their boots. A rack had been set up, and an assortment of white Tyvek hazmat coveralls and thermal jumpsuits were hanging from the hooks, with visored helmets on a shelf just above them and a row of white boot covers lined up below.

Although he knew that Lantos and Kozak would be familiar with the routine, he advised everyone to doff their overcoats, put on a jumpsuit over the rest, then zip themselves into one of the white coveralls.

As he expected, Kozak was already huffing and puffing to get himself into everything, and Lantos was helping Nika to get properly attired; the leather jerkin wasn't making it any easier, especially as Slater pointed out that it had to go inside, rather than outside, the hazmat gear.

"Otherwise, it'll have to be disposed of afterward," he said.

"No way," Nika said, struggling to get the zipper all the way up and over it. "This has been in my tribe for at least two hundred years."

Once she was in, Lantos pulled on her own outfit, and Slater, similarly encased in his jumpsuit, made sure that the elastic bands at Nika's wrist and ankles were tightly drawn. Then he helped her on with her white booties. Plucking at her sleeve, Nika said, "I think I prefer natural fabrics. What's this made of, anyway?"

"High-density polyethylene," Slater replied, "and it's virtually indestructible. But it'll protect you from any bloodborne pathogens, or dry particles as small as half a micron."

"But aren't we going to cook inside them?"

"Not as much as you would think," Lantos interjected. "Even though they keep out water and other liquid molecules, they'll still allow heat and sweat vapors to escape. Which isn't to say," she added, passing her the headgear that Nika studied skeptically, "you're going to be comfortable out there."

"Okay, helmets, too, now," Slater said, and they all took one last breath of unimpeded air before putting on the visored hoods, the bottoms of which hung down onto their shoulders. With all four of them in the tent at once, and bundled up like sausages, it was getting hard to budge without bumping into each other. Lantos tucked a surgical kit under her arm, and with Slater holding the tent flaps, they exited with a certain amount of nervous laughter, looking like a bunch of beekeepers heading out to work in the apiary.

But the mood changed the moment they got outside and the first blast of wind rippled the jumpsuits. As they trudged through the cemetery in single file, with Kozak carefully leading the way along the path he had already marked with little flags and Slater bringing up the rear, the full import of what they were about to do was brought home. Sergeant Groves and the Coast Guardsman were waiting by the gravesite, standing next to a high-intensity lamp they had set up. Slater relieved them of their duty now that the exhumation work was about to begin. They'd been working for hours and deserved a break. Groves saluted by touching two fingers to the little plastic visor of his helmet, and, toting his jackhammer, headed back to the dressing shed.

The tombstone, adorned with two doors carved into its upper corners, had been laid to one side, incongruously enough next to a stretcher. And even though the name on the marker had long since been worn away, Slater could see that at its very bottom, where the frozen earth had afforded it some protection from the elements, something like a crescent had been carved.

"What's that mean?" he said, pointing it out to the professor. "I've seen it on the posts to the cemetery and on some of the other headstones."

"Some people say it is the symbol of Islam, and it is always at the bottom to show the victory of Christ over the unbelievers."

"It sounds like you don't agree with them."

"I don't. I believe it is meant to be an anchor. In the Russian faith, that is the symbol of the hope for salvation. The hope that the church provides." He scratched at the side of his helmet, as if it were his head. "The two doors, though, those are unusual."

While salvation, Slater thought, might be uncertain, in this particular case, resurrection—at least in the corporeal sense—was painfully imminent. Looking into the open grave, he could see, beneath the thin scrim of dirt and gravel, the pale gleam of wood bleached white by its decades in the soil. He could even detect a couple of deep cracks in the lid of the coffin.

"Just as I predicted," Kozak put in, "the frost heaval has done some damage to the casket."

Lantos and Nika were standing on the other side of the grave, Lantos surveying the site with a professional eye, and Nika, her head tilted down, apparently reciting some native prayer or blessing. Although Slater wondered what she made of the grim spectacle on display, in deference to her work he nudged Kozak and they both kept silent for the next minute or two. All he could hear from under her helmet was a murmured chant, but he detected a slight rocking on her heels, as if she were moving to some ancient rhythm only she could discern. He became conscious of the *bilikin* that he was wearing under his shirt, and for some reason he wished that she knew he had it on.

When she had finished, Slater glanced over at Lantos, got a nod in return, then, like a diver going over the side, he slipped down into the grave itself. It would not have been easy under any circumstances, but the bulky clothing made him uncharacteristically clumsy. With an arm that wasn't as steady as he would have liked—*damn those drugs*—he balanced himself on the rectangular coffin, then crouched to peek through the largest crack. His visor, though it was clean as a whistle, presented yet one more obstacle.

"Vassily," he said, "could you move the lamp to the left? My own shadow's getting in the way."

Kozak repositioned the light, and said, in a voice muffled by his hood, "Better?"

"We'll see," Slater replied, before bending down to peer through the crack again.

He was greeted by the sight of someone staring back at him.

A blue eye, like a clouded marble, gazed upward from under a film of ice, and he reared back in surprise.

"What is it?" Nika said with concern.

"Yes," Kozak said, "what's wrong?"

"Nothing," Slater said. "I was just startled. I thought I was at the foot of the coffin."

"You're not?" Kozak said.

"No. The head's at this end."

"So it's facing west?"

"Yes. What's the difference?"

"That would mean he had been a deacon, or maybe a priest."

"I don't follow," Nika said.

"Unlike his parishioners," Kozak explained, "a church leader is buried facing his congregation."

"Whichever way he's facing," Dr. Lantos said, handing Slater a hammer with a clawed end, "you're going to need this. Try not to leave splinters."

Slater didn't look back through the crack but applied himself to removing the rusty nails from the four corners of the box. They crumbled at the first touch of the hammer. Leaning to one side in the narrow grave, he pried up the lid, which rose halfway before splitting down the middle.

"So much for splinters," Lantos said, as Slater passed up one half of the lid to her, and Kozak reached down to collect the other.

With the lid cleared away, the corpse was on full display, and Slater had nowhere to stand but a very narrow trough along one side. Kozak's surmise, however, was right—the man was dressed in a long black cassock that glistened like ebony beneath a sheen of ice; the sleeves were rolled back to reveal a hint of scarlet lining. His hands were clenched tight, and in one he held a tightly rolled piece of paper. In the other, he clutched a copper icon, the size and shape of an index card, with its picture side down. Slater glanced up at the professor for any further elaboration.

"The paper is the prayer of absolution," Kozak volunteered. "Traditionally, it was placed in the corpse's hand after it had been read aloud by a priest. As for the icon, that must be what showed up on the GPR. I kept getting hits of metal or hard mineral deposits."

Slater looked back at the body, whose face was as arresting in death as it must have been in life. He had hypnotic blue-gray eyes, even now, and blond hair—nearly white—that must have once hung down to his shoulders. His face was clean-shaven, and his mouth had fallen open, as if he were just about to speak; his lips were flecked with dark splotches of blood. His expression was one of surprise.

"I would say, from his youth and the fact that he has no beard," Kozak said, "he was a deacon."

"Deacon or priest or whatever," Lantos said, "I think if you can cut away some of that fabric before taking the samples, we'd be better off. The drill could get snagged."

Slater knew she was right, but it was as if her voice were coming from a mile away. It was more than the muffling of the helmets. He was struggling to maintain his composure and presence of mind, a problem that someone in his line of work should long ago have conquered. He put it down to the effect of all the antiviral drugs he'd been taking, but whatever the cause, he knew that now was no time to lose control.

"You're right," he said. "Give me the surgical scissors."

Anticipating him perfectly, she had them ready. But to put them to use, he would first have to get into the correct position, and there was only one way to do that. Straddling the corpse, he slowly sat down on it, like a rider in a saddle. He could hear the crackling of the ice that coated the body, and it reminded him of the sound of stepping out on a frozen pond. The corpse itself was as stiff and hard as an iron anvil. With the butt end of the scissors, he chipped at the ice on the deacon's chest until a spot a few inches around had been cleared. Shards of ice had flown up into the corpse's face, and he brushed them away with his gloved fingertips.

"I don't think he'll mind," Lantos said.

Turning the scissors, he carefully nudged the tip beneath the black cloth, just enough to separate it from the frozen flesh, then snipped until he could pull a piece of the fabric free. He handed it up to Lantos for safekeeping, then, on the opposite side of the breastbone, he did the same. The exposed skin was the color of old ivory, but with a fine sheen, as if Vaseline had been spread on it.

"The cadaver mat," Lantos said, before he could ask for it.

She handed him a green-rubber sheath the size of a bath towel, which had short vertical and horizontal incisions in it. He draped it across the upper torso, then poked a finger through one hole to loosen it up. In autopsy work like this, the cadaver mat was used not only as a sign of respect but to keep airborne particles to a minimum.

"Okay," he said, "I can start taking the samples now."

Lantos, like a nurse in an ER, slapped into his hand a small, low-speed aerosol drill the size of a screwdriver. After making sure that he had located the spot directly above the left lung, he braced himself with one hand, while with the other he pressed the tip of the drill through the hole. With a soft whirring sound, the blade bored into the corpse, then suctioned up a minuscule sliver of lung tissue, which Lantos immediately placed in a vial already marked for that purpose.

Slater was vaguely aware of a commotion up above. "What is it?" he said, trying to maintain his focus.

"It's nothing," Lantos said. "Keep going."

"It's Nika," Kozak said. "She's not feeling very well."

Slater looked up but saw no sign of her.

Kozak simply said, "Go on," and weakly waved one hand.

Slater nodded—this was grisly work, he recognized that, and nothing could really prepare you for it—but the sooner he collected the *in situ* specimens, the sooner they could all leave the graveyard . . . and that meant the deacon, too. Once these utterly uncompromised specimens had been taken, the whole body would be hoisted out of the shattered coffin and taken back to the autopsy chamber in the colony, there to be thawed out and more thoroughly dissected. He was counting on Kozak to carry the other end of the stretcher.

"Heart next," Lantos asked, "or brain?"

Somewhere in the woods a wolf howled.

"Trachea," Slater said, and the next time he handed the specimen up to Dr. Lantos, he noticed that Kozak, too, was missing from the lip of the grave. He didn't have to say a word before Lantos chuckled and said, "Yep, one more down. Looks like it's just us chickens from now on."

Chapter 31

Apart from a sliver of one small pane, all the windows in the big, brick house had been whitewashed. That way, none of the Romanov prisoners could see outside or be seen in turn by anyone passing by.

Not that the peasants or shopkeepers in the tiny, Siberian backwater of Ekaterinburg would even have dared to look toward the house. Any suspicion that you were a Tsarist sympathizer, and your life wasn't worth a ruble.

The Bolsheviks had evicted the rightful owner—a merchant named Ipatiev—and installed Anastasia and her family, along with a few of their remaining servants and friends, in five rooms on the upper story. The ground floor was reserved for the commissars, most of whom had been angry, disgruntled workers at the local Zlokazovsky and Syseretsky factories before the revolution. A five-foot-tall fence had been built around the perimeter of the house and its interior courtyard, and it was constantly patrolled.

But Anastasia knew when it was time for Sergei to make his rounds, and she always stationed herself at that small slice of window—left clear so that the Romanovs could consult a thermometer attached to the wall outside—when he was due. Even then, she was afraid to wave, and he was afraid to do anything more than cast a furtive glance in her direction. If they were caught, the rest of the window would be promptly whitewashed, and Sergei would be shot as a possible accomplice to the imperial family.

"So, is he there?" her sister Tatiana whispered as she bent her head over her sewing. She was opening a hem in a dress and secreting there a handful of the diamonds the Romanovs had so far successfully smuggled on their long odyssey. They were sewn into every garment, under every button, into the brim of every cap and the stays of every corset.

"Not yet," Anastasia said, "but sometimes he is delayed if the other guard wants to stop and have a smoke with him."

Smiling ruefully, Tatiana shook her head and said, "You know, don't you, that you were supposed to marry a German prince and cement the alliance? Not fall for some revolutionary guard."

"And so were you," Anastasia replied.

"No, I was destined for the Bulgarian."

"I thought Maria was to marry the Bulgarian."

"Maria was going to marry an Austrian duke. I forget which one."

How far they had come from all that, Anastasia thought. Royal weddings, international alliances, princes and palaces and languorous vacations at Livadia, their seaside retreat in the Crimea. Now, here they were, the whole family, confined to a few hot and stuffy rooms, with no locks on the doors and guards who enjoyed nothing more than barging in at any moment to catch them unawares. As a precaution, Olga was keeping watch in the next room; at least the soldiers' boots made a lot of noise as they came tromping down the wooden hallway.

"There he is," Anastasia murmured, as the gangly Sergei sauntered into view outside. He was holding his rifle over his shoulder, as a sentry was supposed to do, but he looked no more comfortable with it than before. In stolen moments together, Anastasia had learned that he had been the youngest son of a farmer, whose wheat fields adjoined those of Rasputin's family; they had all lived in the village of Pokrovskoe from time immemorial, and though Sergei had been conscripted into the Red Guard, his sympathies lay still with the holy man whose healing powers had once saved him from a deathly illness.

And if Father Grigori was a truc and loyal friend to the Romanovs, then so, too, would Sergei be. He did not trust, or even much like, his comrades in arms; Ana had seen that right off. But it had taken some time before she put her faith in him—and even then it was only over the warnings of her family. Ever since, however, he had proved to be a reliable confidant, and a necessary conduit of news from the outside.

He stopped now, knowing he was in plain view of the unpainted window, and without looking up at all held his cigarette between two fingers upraised in a V.

"He has a message for us!" Anastasia said, seeing the signal.

"Are you sure?" Tatiana said, stopping her stitching so abruptly a loose diamond rolled off her lap.

"Yes, yes!"

For weeks now, there had been rumors of a rescue plan—three hundred officers, loyal to the monarchy, were to ride into the town and liberate the Tsar and his family. From what little the Romanovs knew, civil war had broken out all across Mother Russia, and on many of the long Siberian nights, when the dusk lingered until almost midnight, they could hear the distant rumble of artillery and were left to wonder whose guns they were. Could they be the White army advancing on the Red Guard strongholds, determined to overturn the Revolution and save the captives in the Ipatiev house? Last night the cannons had sounded closer than ever before, and as Anastasia had tossed and turned in her metal cot, she had barely been able to constrain her hopes.

And now Sergei had another message from the outside world, which—if their luck held—he would smuggle in with their daily provisions.

Olga coughed violently in the next room, patting her chest operatically, and Anastasia flew away from the window and Tatiana buried her needlework under her wide skirt, then snatched up the volume of Pushkin by her side.

The new commandant, Yakov Yurovsky, a sinister creature with a thick mane of black hair, a black goatee, and a gratingly insincere manner about him, burst in, apologizing for the intrusion at the same time that his cold gray eyes scanned the room for contraband or mischief of any kind. "I expect you heard the barrage last night."

"We did," the Tsar—now simply referred to as Nicholas—said, as he entered from the adjoining study. He was wearing his customary military tunic—with its epaulettes ripped off by the Red Guards—and a pair of threadbare jodhpurs.

"I trust it did not interfere with your sleep."

Anastasia knew, as did everyone, that his concern was a joke, but it was a joke that they all had to play along with. She could see a faint fire blaze up in her father's eyes, but as usual he suppressed it and simply assured the commandant that they had all slept soundly.

"Further precautions may have to be taken to ensure your safety," Yurovsky said, and seeing the Tsaritsa—called merely Alexandra now— inching into the room with one hand pressed to the small of her aching back, added, "A hot compress, with powdered sage, will do much to alleviate the pain of sciatica." He said it with the same bland authority he always assumed. Anastasia had the impression that he wished to be taken for a physician, though Dr. Botkin had assured her privately that the man was a complete fraud.

"Thank you," Alexandra replied, in the same even tone her husband adopted. "If you would be so kind as to provide some sage, I will try it."

Anastasia knew Yurovsky would never send the sage, and even if he did, her mother would never use it. It was all a grand pantomime in which her whole family, and their ruthless captors, continued to engage. The Bolsheviks pretended to be protecting the imperial family from harm, the Romanovs pretended to believe it, and everyone walked on pins and needles, afraid of provoking the situation into an explosion of some kind.

"How is the boy?" Yurovsky asked. "Walking yet?"

Alexei, bored out of his wits at the confinement, had played a stupid trick, riding his sled down some stairs, and the injuries ever since had laid him up. Dr. Botkin, with limited means at his disposal, did everything he could, but the pain was excruciating, and the former heir to the Russian throne was stuck in his bed, his legs raised, and much of the time delirious from fever.

"No, not yet," Nicholas said. "If he could once again receive the electrical stimulation treatments provided by the doctor in town, it might help."

Yurovsky nodded thoughtfully, and said, "I shall look into that."

Ana knew what that meant. Nothing.

"Will we be receiving some rations today?" Alexandra asked, and to this Yurovsky said, "As soon as the soldiers and my staff are taken care of, I'll see what's left."

Oh, how he must have relished the opportunity to put the Tsaritsa in her place like that. Ana thought she even saw her father's right hand clench into a fist for a second, before he slipped it behind his back. She wished that just once her father would let fly, hang the consequences.

After Yurovsky had completed a brief inspection of the premises—lifting Alexei's blanket to be sure his leg still looked purple and swollen, studying her mother's many icons just so he could sully them with his touch, licentiously fingering her sister's nightgowns neatly folded at the foot of their cots—he strolled out, and everyone at last breathed a temporary sigh of relief.

It was then that Ana shared the news that Sergei had another message for them. Several times over the past few weeks, he had brought messages from an anonymous White officer who was planning a daring rescue mission, and perhaps this would be the one announcing that the attempt was imminent.

An hour or two later, when she heard the cook, Kharitonov, outside in the courtyard, she was able to peer through the window and see that Sergei was indeed carrying brown eggs and black bread, curd tarts and a bottle of fresh milk, in a wicker basket. The food was provided by the sisters in the nearby monastery of Novo-Tikhvin, and without it Ana wondered how her family would have survived at all. Yurovsky let the baskets pass because he first helped himself liberally to every one of them that arrived. (The tarts seldom made it past him.)

With her family's silent encouragement, Ana scurried downstairs to the kitchen, with her dog, Jemmy, panting close behind. How she wished she could move as gracefully as her sisters, or that she wasn't quite so chubby. (Her mother always insisted that she was just short-waisted.) But Sergei didn't seem to mind, and even though Ana knew as well as everyone else that this was just a silly fancy, there was so little happiness in her family's life right now—and so little help available to them from any quarter—that no one saw any reason to interfere. Fate, the Romanovs had learned, could be as bitter as it was unpredictable. Be grateful, her father told her one day when they saw a blue jay preening on a tree branch, for every beautiful thing, no matter how small, that the Lord provided.

When she came in, the cook was exclaiming over the provisions he was laying out on the kitchen table. "Look!" he said to Ana. "Flour! White flour. And raisins." She could see he was already debating how best to use them; Kharitonov was a master at making something from nothing.

But Sergei sidled closer to Anastasia, and in a voice that even she could barely hear, he said, "Be ready."

"For what?" she whispered. The cook was showing off his bounty to her mother's maid, Anna Demidova, who had come in to see what all the commotion was about. Anastasia saw her surreptitiously pop a raisin into her mouth as Jemmy scoured the floor for anything that might have fallen.

"I don't know, but telegrams have been coming and going from Yurovsky's office all morning."

"Are we going to be rescued?"

"And a truck has been hired in the village."

Ana had no idea what to make of that, but she prayed it would have something to do with their liberation. Perhaps the commandant was planning to steal whatever he could from the Ipatiev house—there were still some nice sticks of furniture downstairs—and clear out before the Tsar's loyal troops arrived.

"Thank you," Ana said, "for being our friend," and as she spoke she let the sleeve of her blouse brush up against his arm. Just as she expected, he blushed furiously, and she took a delight in that. She, and her sisters, had all led such a sheltered and protected life in many ways. Oh, at the beginning of this war, and before the Revolution of course, they had been allowed to assist wounded soldiers in the Army hospitals—indeed, their mother had made their duties there compulsory—but of romance Ana had known almost nothing. She had briefly nursed crushes on their music teacher or French tutor or riding instructor, but then, for want of any alternatives, so had her three sisters. Sergei, though just a common boy, was at least all her own.

"It is my honor," he said, "to serve you," but his voice was full of greater meaning than the words alone conveyed.

Before she could answer, another guard, a burly fellow with broken teeth, staggered in, and the maid Demidova made a quick exit. Taking one look at the food, he ripped the loaf of black bread in two and stuffed half of it into his mouth, almost all at once. When the crumbs fell and Jemmy went for them, he kicked the dog to one side with the toe of his muddy boot.

"How dare you!" Ana said, snatching up her dog.

"I'd do the same to you," he said, bits of bread flying from his lips. Glancing at Sergei, he said, "Shouldn't you be out on patrol, comrade?"

Sergei wavered, just as she had seen her father do with the commandant, before deciding that discretion was the better part of valor. Turning on his heel, he picked up the empty basket and went out the kitchen door to the courtyard.

Anastasia glared at the filthy guard, who chewed the bread with his mouth open, but when the cook Kharitonov threw her a warning look, she snuggled Jemmy closer in her arms and went back to the stairs.

"We should have a dance sometime," the guard said, no doubt mocking her gait as she climbed the wooden steps.

Chapter 32

"Just shut up," Harley said, as he crouched in the shadow of the crooked church, "and let me think."

For once, Eddie and Russell did as they were told, but he knew it wouldn't last long.

Looking out over the colony grounds, Harley was amazed at how the place had been transformed in the space of a couple of days. There were half a dozen green tents, some in the traditional peaked style, others more like Quonset huts, but all of them solidly built and interconnected by pathways laid down with rubber matting and lamp poles and guide ropes. Even over the sound of the rising wind, he could hear the hum of generators from an aluminum shed, erected near a lavatory platform raised above a pair of portable holding tanks.

But what he didn't see was any people; in fact, right now, the place looked as abandoned as it had the first time he'd been here. The Coast Guard guys were gone, and so was their chopper. When he'd heard it lift off hours ago, he'd hoped that its departure signaled the end of the expedition to the island; at last, he thought, it would be safe to get back to grave-robbing.

But he'd sure as hell been wrong on that score. Somebody was here, and it looked like they were planning to stay a while. *Damn, damn, damn.*

"I'm freezing my ass off," Russell muttered. "What's the plan?"

Harley was having to recalibrate, and quickly. They were carrying their shovels and pickaxe, along with some steel pitons he hoped to use to loosen up sections of soil this time around. He saw no one patrolling the grounds, but he knew it would be far too dangerous to try to make their way across the open colony. If somebody unexpectedly came out of one of those tents, there'd be nowhere to hide.

Crawling backward, he said, "Let's go straight to the graveyard." There was only another hour or two of weak sunlight left in the day, and he couldn't afford to waste any of it.

Skirting the colony by sticking to the other side of the wooden stockade, he led them through the thickets of spruce and alder and hemlock, batting a course through the snow-laden branches, until to his own surprise he saw that a parallel trail had been neatly cut and laid all the way down from the colony gates to the wooden posts of the cemetery. Lights, too, had been strung up the whole way, and they were switched on even now. Although he couldn't figure out how the government had heard about the emerald cross he'd found, he thought it was pretty clear, from all of this construction, that they had heard about it somehow. His brother Charlie wasn't stupid; it was unlikely he'd spilled the beans to anyone, but Harley had a lot less faith in that greedy bitch his brother had married, or her idiot sister. Bathsheba would tell anyone anything.

And now look what he had to contend with as a result.

"Check this out," Eddie said, holding open the flap to a dressing shed built to the left of the gates. Harley glanced inside and saw a rack of white coveralls and booties and visored headgear, all neatly arranged. Before he could stop him, Russell had slunk inside and put on one of the helmets.

"Take me to your leader," he said, with his arms outstretched, and Harley had to snatch the helmet off him and slap it back on the shelf.

"Get out of here," he ordered, "before I kick your ass all the way back to Port Orlov."

"Yeah," Russell sneered, "you and what army?"

The graveyard, luckily, was as deserted as the colony, and the fresh snow had nicely covered their tracks from the previous grave they'd opened. But now there were tight nylon lines stretched all over the place, with little pennants stuck into the ground here and there, marking the whole graveyard off in some kind of grid. And off at the far end, where the cliff gave way, whole strips of sod had been laid, crisscross, on top of a tarp, along with a fallen marker. As Harley got closer, he could see an open grave yawning.

"Looks like they got the job done better than we did," Eddie said. "Shit, I wonder what they used."

Harley was less interested in how they'd done it, then why. They hadn't just dug up the grave and searched for treasures; they'd taken the whole damn body. As he stood beside the empty plot, he wondered what they wanted with a corpse. Did they think there was something inside it, something they could only extract elsewhere? Maybe after thawing the thing out? All that was left here were the remnants of the wooden coffin, a lot of it cracked and splintered.

"Hey, check it out," said Russell, craning his head over the edge of the cliff and pointing down at the beach below. "It's a boat."

Harley gingerly approached the cliff and saw what he was pointing at—an RHI up on davits. This was the first piece of good news he'd had in days; the *Kodiak* was still stuck on the rocks and taking on water, and he had not known how to break it to his crew that the thing would probably never make it back to shore. Now he had an alternative, courtesy of the United States Coast Guard.

The only problem was, he'd be returning virtually empty-handed if he left now. Those rosary beads couldn't be worth much.

"So," Eddie said, scanning the desolate cemetery, "where do we start?"

Harley wished he knew. He'd picked wrong the last time, guessing that the most impressive headstone would be sitting atop the greatest booty. It was like that stupid game show, *Deal or No Deal*. Who knew where the serious loot was hidden?

"Russell, I'm going to need you to keep watch," he said. "Go down that trail about twenty yards, lie low, and wait there. If you see or hear anyone coming, get back here and warn us."

"Wait a second," Eddie complained. "I did the digging last time. Why don't I get to be the watchman?"

"Just do what I say," Harley said, "both of you."

Russell plainly didn't need to hear another word; the idea of not working was sweet, and he tossed his spade to Eddie and meandered back toward the lighted trailhead. Eddie picked up the spade in the hand that wasn't holding the pick and looked at Harley with a sour expression that said, *You'd better get it right this time.*

Chapter 33

Russell couldn't believe his luck. All the way to the graveyard, he'd been thinking how bad it would suck to have to try to dig up a frozen grave. Just chipping the ice away from some of the intake valves on his oil-company job was a bitch and a half. Waiting until he was safely through the cemetery gates and out of Harley's sight, he reached into the pocket of his parka and pulled out one of the beers he'd been carrying. One thing you could say about Alaska—the whole damn state was a cooler.

He went down the trail, looking for a comfortable perch—which wasn't going to be easy. Everything was covered in snow and ice, and the ground was as solid as a rock. He wished Harley and Eddie a lot of luck, especially after their last dig had turned up nothing but a bunch of crystal beads on a string. As far as he was concerned, this whole trip was going to be a bust, and he'd be lucky to get back to the Yardarm with ten bucks in his pocket.

If he wanted to score Angie Dobbs, he'd need more than that as bait. Christ, it was hilarious that Harley thought it was such a big deal he'd fucked her. Who hadn't?

In the harsh glow of the next light pole, he spotted a glistening stump just off to one side of the trail. It was an old tree trunk, covered in moss and lichen, and though it wasn't exactly a Barcalounger, it was the best prospect he was likely to uncover. Brushing the snow away from the matt of rotting leaves around its base, he picked up a bunch of them in his arms and made as much of a cushion as he could. Then he plopped down on top of the pile before the rising wind could blow them away, pulled the string on his hood to cinch it closer to his face, and waited.

Everybody was always talking about the pure and unstained beauty of Alaska—Russell had seen all the brochures and ads and commercials the state tourist bureau put out—but as far as he could see, it was a load of crap. The place was cold and wet and dark and the rotting leaves he was sitting on stank. He took another slug of the beer. Without alcohol, and pussy, there'd be no reason to go on living.

And pot. He shouldn't forget the value of grade-A weed, which was never more plentiful than when he was behind bars at Spring Creek.

He hadn't been sitting on the stump for very long—the can of beer still had a few drops left in it—when he thought he heard something.

Quickly, he swiped the hood back off his head, and listened hard.

Was that a voice, or just the wind sighing in the boughs?

He stood up, gulped the last of the beer, and tossed the can into the bushes.

Yes, it was. It *was* a voice, talking in some weird accent. Russian. For a second he thought, *It's the ghost of one of those dead settlers. The legends about the island are all true!* Then he got hold of himself, and before he knew it, his feet were carrying him back onto the trail, and through the woods, past the lighting poles, between the carved gate-posts of the graveyard. Harley and Eddie were wandering around like they still hadn't picked a target yet, but he knew he couldn't shout at them. Instead, he ran among the graves, waving his arms like a luna-tic, until they saw him and grabbed up their gear and took off in all directions. Russell tripped over a hole in the ground—shit, was this the grave they'd already opened?—and by the time he got up again they were gone.

He could hear another voice, too, now, carried on the wind and coming up the trail, and he ran helter-skelter out of the graveyard and into the surrounding woods. The branches tore at his sleeves and the thicket was almost impenetrable but he just kept running. The breath was hot in his throat, and he realized, not for the first time, just how out of shape he was. Two years in the penitentiary can do that to you. So it was a miracle when he stumbled into a tiny glade where an ancient hut still stood. All that was left of the place was a few boards holding the walls in place and a door made out of wooden staves, but right now it looked better than the Yardarm to him.

He banged through the brittle door, closed what was left of it behind him, then bent over double, gasping for breath. The beer came up in a rush of hot vomit, splashing onto his boots. The wind rattled the sticks of the door. He saw a table, and an old, empty dynamite crate drawn up to it like a stool. He leaned one hand on the side of the table. An old leather book was on it, with the frozen nub of a candle in a pewter dish. His head was pounding so hard he thought he was going to stroke out on the spot. *Get a grip,* he told himself. *You haven't even done anything wrong yet. It was Harley who broke open the grave. I'm just along for the ride.*

He sat down with a thump on the dynamite box, which groaned but remained intact.

All he'd done, he reminded himself, was trespass—and maybe on government property. What could the penalty be for that, anyway? It couldn't be that bad, and if it weren't for the fact that he was still on parole, it wouldn't have even been worth worrying about. But he *was* on parole, and if he ever had to go back into that cramped cell in Spring Creek—where the walls had pressed in tighter every day—he'd kill himself.

First, however, he'd kill Harley Vane for getting him into this mess.

Chapter 34

"What's that mean again?" Dr. Lantos asked, as she extended the masking tape.

Slater finished writing on the cardboard—"*Hic locus est ubi mors gaudet succurrere vitae*"—before slapping the sign on the outside of the thick plastic walls separating the autopsy chamber from the rest of the lab tent. "It means, 'This is the place where death rejoices to help the living.' At the AFIP, we always kept the sign up to remind us why we were there. To help the living."

"I hope the deacon feels the same way."

"He was a man of God, wasn't he?"

Lantos snorted. "You must have a higher regard for organized religion than I do."

Slater had been brought up without any religion at all. And though he sometimes envied those who were able to find solace in their faith—his ex had still attended church on a regular basis—he was convinced that if the seed of belief weren't planted early, it could never really thrive.

Both he and Dr. Lantos were already garbed from head to toe in hazmat suits, and now that they were ready to enter the autopsy chamber, they put on their face masks with plastic goggles. They took a few extra seconds to adjust them and make sure they felt secure, since once they were inside it couldn't be done again without running the risk of breaking the seal. Satisfied, Slater held open the heavy-duty plastic flaps of the chamber, and in a muffled voice, said, "After you."

Lantos, whose hood was raised an inch or two by the frizz of her hair, ducked inside, and Slater followed, turning to seal the long Velcro strips that held the flaps closed. In here, even the rubber floor had a heavy plastic sheath beneath it; that way, when the work on St. Peter's Island was done, the entire autopsy compartment could be rolled up like an enormous sheet of cellophane and incinerated. To Slater, it felt as if he'd stepped inside a jellyfish, with shimmering translucent walls all around, above, and below him.

The body of the deacon, still in his long black cassock with the red lining, lay on the autopsy table staring at the ceiling.

Lantos, poking at the corpse with one gloved finger, said, "They always take longer to thaw than you expect." It was as if she were talking about a Thanksgiving turkey, and though an ordinary person might have been put off by her tone, Slater recognized it for what it was. This was how medical professionals—epidemiologists included— often spoke to each other. The casual banter was meant to dispel the doubts and fears and just plain moral confusion that confronted anyone about to desecrate and dismember human flesh. Otherwise, it was all too easy to see yourself instead lying on that table, a hunk of mortal ruins swiftly on its way to decay.

"Do you want to wait a while," Lantos asked, "or start removing the clothes?"

Slater squeezed the deacon's shoulder, pressed the abdomen, flexed a booted foot, and said, "We can go ahead. The clothing may be stiffer than the skin."

"Then pail and scalpels it is."

Everything they would need for the autopsy was already in the room, from surgical instruments to disposal bins, and in the small freezer in the corner they had already stored the *in situ* specimens from the graveyard; these would remain the cleanest and purest samples of all, transported back to the AFIP untouched.

"You'll have to be careful with that paper," Lantos said, touching the prayer of absolution that the corpse still held in one hand. "It could disintegrate."

Slater knew she was right, and when he separated the scroll from the dead flesh that held it, he gently laid it aside on one of the metal trays arrayed on the counter behind him. As if it were a living creature, hiding from a predator, the paper curled even more tightly in on itself.

Lantos went about removing the icon clutched in the deacon's other hand, but even that was dicey. "He doesn't seem to want to let go," she said, giving it another tug and finally freeing it. Glancing at it through her goggles, she said, "And now I can see why."

She turned it over for Slater to see. It was a picture of the Virgin and Child, preserved enough to show a faint red in her veil and pale blue in the gown she wore. It was Byzantine in appearance, the two figures lacking all perspective, but on the forehead and shoulders of the Virgin there were three diamonds sparkling in the light of the overhead lamp. "We're rich," Lantos joked as Slater admired the brilliance of the stones.

"Wait'll Kozak sees this," he remarked, placing it beside the paper. "I'm sure he'll be able to tell us all about it."

But Lantos, like a busy tailor, was already snipping away at the black cassock, cutting long strips down the length of the body, then peeling them off like Band-Aids. As each strip was removed, she used the foot pedal to open the refuse bin and drop it in. When the fabric was all gone, she and Slater together pulled the boots off the deacon's feet and dropped them in the bin, too. They landed with a clunk.

The body, completely naked now, lay on the table, its arms still stiffly in place, crossed just below the chest. There were puncture wounds where the aerosol drill had suctioned up the initial specimens, and Slater could not but be reminded of the wounds on the body of Christ, especially as the young deacon was otherwise almost beatific. His long blond locks had thawed sufficiently to brush his shoulders again, and his skin, nearly hairless, was a marmoreal white, like the Pietà. His blue eyes were wide open.

Taking the digital camera from the counter behind him, Slater took several shots of the body, first, full-figure, then close-ups of the face and other areas where the first incisions had been made. Next, he checked the weight as it registered on the table scale, and noted it down by speaking aloud: a voice-activated recorder was running in the room. When he was done, Lantos held up the body block, a wedge of firm foam rubber, and said, "Okay, how about you do the heavy lifting, and I'll put it under?"

As Slater raised the upper half of the body from the table, the deacon's eyes seemed to bore into his own, questioning these terrible liberties being taken with him. Lantos jammed the block under the small of the cadaver's back. When Slater eased the body down again, its head and arms now fell backwards, while its chest was stretched and lifted up for easier dissection. Lantos brushed her hands together, as if to say that's that.

"What's your choice?" she said to Slater. "Y or T or straight down the middle?"

There were several standard methods of opening a corpse, but for Slater's purposes in this instance, he had already decided that the first choice was the best. "We'll do a Y," he said, "so we can get the maximum exposure of the neck and respiratory tract."

Lantos nodded, her mop of frizzy hair looking positively electrified under the high-intensity lamp. Handing Slater the shears, she waited patiently while he made two large and deep incisions starting at the top of each of the deacon's shoulders and running down the front of the chest, all the way to the sternum where they met. Once there, he continued cutting straight down the rest of the body, deviating just enough to the left to pass around the navel, and stopping only when he bumped up to the pubic bone. Because the body had not completely thawed, the skin crackled as the blades did their work.

Slater wished he had remembered to put on some music. It helped with focus.

"Very neatly done," Lantos said, her voice muffled by her face mask.

And it was. Even Slater would concede as much; the firmness of the flesh made the cutting more precise. And though autopsies always involved less blood than might be expected—with no cardiac activity, it was only gravity that affected the pressure and flow—he was still surprised at just how little fluid was present. The blood remaining must have crystallized, he thought, or maybe evaporated . . . but that was before he put the shears away and, with Lantos pulling from the other side, split open the torso like cracking a pumpkin. Then he could see why.

It looked like a blowtorch had been applied to the deacon's entrails. Beneath the rib cage, everything appeared blackened and engorged. It reminded Slater of a fire victim he had autopsied years ago, during a stint in Sierra Leone.

"This was not an easy death," Lantos said, in a more somber tone. "This poor guy died in agony."

Slater had no doubt about that, either. Taking the bone saw, he cut through the ribs on both sides of the chest, then, with Lantos helping, lifted the sternum and the ribs, still attached, free of the cavity, and placed the whole section in a shallow silver tray.

For the benefit of the audio record, he announced what he had just done.

Then he turned around to survey the unobstructed viscera of the young deacon.

It was as if the man had swallowed a ball of hot tar. The protective cells and cilia lining the bronchial tubes had been razed as if by a prairie fire, and the lungs looked like eggplants, bruised a deep and livid purple. The pericardial sac enclosing the heart resembled a sheet of torn, black crepe paper, and the heart itself, visible through the holes, was as gnarled and dark as a hand grenade.

"Major necrotic damage apparent to nearly all major organ systems. Evidence of both viral and bacteriological pathogenesis."

"It looks like a bomb went off inside him," Lantos observed, readying a syringe to draw one of many blood samples to come.

"Not a bomb," Slater said, "but a storm. A cytokine storm." The Spanish flu was a diabolical machine, one that hijacked the victim's own immunological response and turned it against him. Under normal circumstances, the cytokines—soluble, hormonelike proteins—acted as messengers among the cells of the immune system, helping to target microbial infections like viruses, bacteria, parasites, and fungi, and directing the antibodies and killer cells to attack them. But with the Spanish flu, the whole system went into overdrive, the cytokines targeting everything in sight, the antibodies sticking like glue to anything they came into contact with, the killer cells blasting everything in range. It was like a wild shoot 'em up, devastating every cell in the body, compromising every defense mechanism, until the victim ultimately drowned in an overwhelming tide of his own mucus and virus-choked blood.

"And such a young man," Lantos said, slicing through the heart sac with the tip of her scalpel. Speaking up for the recorder, she added, "Drawing blood samples from the pulmonary veins and inferior vena cava, although what's left is barely liquid. Thawing is incomplete. Also checking the pulmonary artery, where," she said, leaning close for a better look, "there appears to have been no clotting."

Youth, Slater reflected, had been a detriment when it came to the Spanish flu; for that matter, so was a healthy constitution. The stronger the subject, the more powerful his or her immunological response would have been to the disease—and the more powerful the response, the more lethal it was, in turn, when the disease sent the protective mechanisms spinning out of control. As a result, the Spanish flu was most devastating to the young, able-bodied soldiers shipping off to France in 1918, then to the young doctors and nurses who came to their aid. The first responders, as it were. Infants and the elderly, the already infirm, were, ironically, less likely to die from the disease than those in the vigorous prime of life.

Slater was inevitably reminded, as he went about his grisly work, of his night in the medical archives, when he had first studied the slides of the Spanish flu taken from the young doughboy. The soldier's body had been ravaged just as this one had been, his agonizing death had been the same as the Russian deacon's. The flu had made no distinctions as it cut its swath through the peoples of the globe.

Gradually, the vials and test tubes and specimen jars began to fill with the samples taken from the lungs and heart, the trachea and spleen, the liver and pancreas and stomach. And when that was done, Lantos reached under the corpse and pulled out the foam block. The body settled back, with an audible expulsion of air, as if relieved.

But only for a minute or two.

As Slater lifted the head, the long blond hair hanging in tendrils over his glove, Lantos put the block under the back of the neck. With his bloody scalpel, Slater made an incision behind one ear, and traced a path over the crown of the head, ending at a point just behind the other ear. Using the hair as a handle, he pulled the scalp away from the skull in two nearly equal flaps, one draping itself over the front of the face, the other hanging down in back. The sound reminded him of the Velcro being ripped apart in the tent flaps.

"You getting tired?" Lantos asked. "We could take a break."

But Slater wanted to press on. His stamina was not what it was, and he feared that he could have a malarial chill at any moment; better to keep at it while his hand was reasonably steady and take a break only if he had to. "I'll take the Stryker saw," he said, and Lantos handed it to him. The air behind his face mask was warm and uncomfortably moist.

As she made sure that the skin and stray hairs stayed clear of the blade, Slater methodically sawed a circular cap, the size of a beret, from the very top of the skull. Once the cut was complete, he put the saw down and jiggled the section he had cut. In a couple of spots, it still held firm to the rest of the head, and he had to go back with his scalpel and pry the connective tissue or bone loose. If he were back in med school, he'd have just earned a C.

Then, as Lantos held a clean basin under the back of the head, he lifted the cap free and she put it out of the way.

The brain was now completely exposed; the *dura mater,* normally white, was the color of strong tea. Slater picked up a pair of forceps, his wet fingers almost letting them slip, as Eva took the lid off a container of formalin—a 15-percent solution of formaldehyde gas in buffered water that would be used to preserve the brain samples long enough to get them back to the labs in Washington—and held it out.

Suddenly, the overhead light waned, then brightened, then waned again.

Slater's gaze met Lantos's.

The light flickered.

It was the generator, he thought. It couldn't be anything else.

The light went out, then on, then out again.

The backup generator was kicking in, sensing a break in the current, and coming online. His eyes flew to the freezer vault on the floor of the chamber—the one containing the first specimens taken in the open grave. But then he noticed Lantos looking through the plastic barriers of the chamber and out at the tent walls, which appeared to be undulating in the wind . . . but undulating *in color*.

What the hell?

The flaps of the main lab area flew open, and through the distortion of the plastic sheathing, Slater could make out a figure—moving small and fast—toward the autopsy chamber. Nika.

"It's okay!" she hollered, even as Slater shouted, "Don't come in here!" The biohazard warning insignia—an orange triangle—should have been enough, but Nika was the kind of woman who might race right through it.

"What's going on?" Slater said.

"It's the northern lights!"

"I mean what's happening to the power!"

"The northern lights!" she repeated, impatiently waiting just outside the chamber. "The aurora borealis! It screws up the electrical fields every time."

The walls of the tent were glowing a faint gold.

"You go," Lantos said, "I'll finish up in here."

"Absolutely not," Slater replied, but Lantos held firm.

"We've done all we can do in one session, anyway," she said.

"We've got the brainpan to excavate."

"It can wait," she replied. "To be honest, Frank, your hand isn't as steady as it needs to be. I was wondering when to tell you. You need to take a rest."

Slater was surprised that she would say so, but he was willing to concede that she might be right. He'd been pushing it, and any minute he might have made a terrible mistake. He'd made the right choice in recruiting her for this mission.

"Thanks," he said. "Point taken."

After warning Nika to wait for him outside the tent, he stripped off the hazmat suit and protective gear, depositing them all in the safety bin. Then, after a quick scrubdown in the lab, he grabbed his coat off the hook by the entrance and joined her in the fresh air.

The sky was still swarming with strange shapes and colors. Taking his hand like an enthusiastic kid at the zoo, Nika tried to drag him down toward the colony gates, but first Slater had to make a detour to the generator shed, the snow and ice crunching under his boots, to make sure the machinery was still functioning. Rudy the Coast Guardsman was already inside, keeping a close watch on the twin turbines and their myriad gauges.

"Has the current been uninterrupted?" Slater asked urgently.

"Except for a couple of hiccups, and for no more than a second or two each time," Rudy replied, "it's been okay."

Slater breathed a sigh of relief even as the cell phone in his pants pocket suddenly rang, buzzed, and by the time he took it out, went dead.

"The aurora gives off a really strong electromagnetic charge," Nika said sympathetically. "You probably just lost your address book and emails."

"Let me know if either one of the generators goes down for more than a minute," Slater said, and Rudy, not taking his eyes off the machinery, signaled that he would.

Stepping out of the shed again, Slater let himself be led down to the cliffs, where Sergeant Groves and Kozak were already occupying ringside seats, gazing out over the black expanse of the Bering Strait. A curtain of shimmering lights—green and yellow, purple and pink—were swirling and curlicuing in the air, hovering maybe sixty or seventy miles above the water and extending high into the sky.

"The solar flares are putting on quite a show for us tonight," Kozak said, acknowledging Slater and Nika by cocking his pipe in their direction. The cherry tobacco perfumed the air.

"Solar?" Groves said. "We haven't seen the sun for more than three hours all week."

"The solar wind takes two days to reach us, and when the flood of electrons and protons hits the upper atmosphere, they collide with the atoms there, and go boom!" He took another puff on his pipe. "This collision gives off radiation in the form of light. Different atoms give off different colors. In Mongolia, I once saw them turn to a scarlet red. But that is very rare."

"Yeah, well, these will do just fine," Groves said, staring up at the pulsating veil of green and yellow bands performing elaborate arabesques in the sky. "You don't catch anything like this in Afghanistan."

Slater, too, was impressed—he'd never seen the aurora borealis—but the sparkling green lights bathing the horizon made him think, oddly enough, of that hellish sight on CNN, on the night the United States had initiated its much-vaunted "shock and awe" attack on Baghdad. He'd known that much of America was sitting in front of its TV sets, filled with that strange, guilty exultation that comes with war and displays of military might; when he was young and unthinking, he'd felt that way himself. But his own heart had sickened at the thought of what he knew was happening there on the ground. He had been dispatched to far too many such places in the aftermath of war, places where nothing remained standing and everything from cholera to typhus ran riot. He was aware of the human toll that was being taken before his very eyes.

"For the Native Americans," Nika said, "the northern lights were considered a ladder to heaven."

"I can see why," Groves readily assented.

"Whenever they saw the lights, they thought they were looking at the spirits of their ancestors dancing and playing games as they ascended to the next world."

"Maybe they had it right," Groves said.

"It certainly beats the funerals in Russia," Kozak said, solemnly. He tamped at his pipe and appeared lost in thought.

While they had all bundled up against the freezing wind, Slater noticed that Nika's coat was loosely drawn around her, and her own long hair was streaming out like a mane. As she stood there beside him on the cliff, looking out toward the dwindling lights above the sea—the bands were swirling together now into a glowing lime-green corona—she looked so much like a natural part of this spectacle that it was no surprise to him she had returned from San Francisco to Alaska, or that she had been made a tribal elder of the Inuit people. He could see her ancestors in her.

He must have been staring because she suddenly turned to look him full in the face, her head cocked to one side. "Your first time?"

"The aurora?" he replied. "Yes."

"I'm glad it was with me," she said, with a wry smile.

And right then, as if the streaming display had been suddenly sucked into a black hole, the lights went out, leaving only the pinpoint pricks of the stars and the cold sea wind snapping at their clothes.

"What just happened?"

"They do that," she said.

Still, Frank and Nika remained where they were, as did Kozak and Groves, all looking out at the ice-choked ocean like concertgoers hoping for an encore. But there was none.

And then, from far off in the woods somewhere, Slater heard a howl.

"Sounds like everyone is disappointed," Groves joked, as the howl of the wolf became a chorus.

Nika shivered, and suddenly drew her coat tighter around her as the mournful choir, lost in the woods surrounding the colony, bayed for the lost lights of Heaven.

Chapter 35

Russell had sat in the hut for hours, nursing the last beer he'd carried in his pocket, and waiting for Harley and Eddie to come and get him. Did they really expect him to find his way back through the woods—much less locate that shitty little cave they'd been hiding out in—all by himself?

He had exhausted the entertainment possibilities of the hut in the first half hour. There were old animal skins—otter, beaver, bear—covering some unfinished headstones, and an assortment of rusty old shovels and axes leaning up against the walls. The leather-bound book on the table was written in Russian, but Russell could tell, from the way that the names and dates seemed to be lined up on most of the pages, that it must have been the sexton's ledger. A record of who was getting buried where, and when. For a while, he tore out one page at a time and tried to keep a fire going with his Bic lighter, but each page simply vanished in a puff of smoke without generating more than a second of heat. He stuck the remainder in his pocket, just in case it might prove to be worth something to some nutcase at one of those antique shops in Nome.

It was only after the last daylight had gone, and the northern lights suddenly appeared in the sky, that he realized he was on his own, that nobody was coming to get him or offer a lick of help. He could slowly freeze to death in this hut, or he could try to make his own way back to the cave. The wind whistled through the spaces between the timbers and rattled the staves of the door so hard they sounded like castanets.

Cursing Harley, cursing Eddie, and cursing his luck, Russell stood up and instantly regretted it. He'd twisted his ankle in that pothole in the graveyard, and although he'd thought the pain would pass, the ankle had continued to swell. Rolling his sock down, he could see that the skin was a deep shade of purple already. The throbbing, too, was getting worse all the time. Slowly, carefully, he hobbled to the door, where he ripped one of the staves loose to make a crutch he could lean on.

He hated to think how much it was going to hurt when he really tried to walk with such a bad sprain.

Outside, the sky was still alight with the shimmering glow of the aurora borealis. He'd seen it a million times in his life, so the effect had definitely worn off, but he hoped that the light at least would stick around. He had a flashlight in his free hand—Harley had made sure they carried the essentials—but even among this dense brush and overhanging trees, the aurora lent enough illumination to help him pick his way through the woods. The snowy branches were tinged with the alternating colors in the sky—green and yellow and a pale dusky rose—that made the whole forest look fake and strange, like a scene from some movie. A movie Russell did *not* want to be in.

A strong wind was blowing, too, with flakes of snow and ice spinning through the air. He had only the most general sense of where he was. He knew the colony was off toward the sea, and the cave was somewhere to the west, but when he had heard the voices approaching and run wildly into the forest, he had lost all sense of direction.

The beers probably hadn't helped on that score, either.

As he hobbled along, the flashlight beam trained at his feet to keep from tripping over any uneven ground, he told himself that if the *Kodiak* hadn't been refloated on the tide by now, he was going to call the mainland, admit that they were stranded on St. Peter's, and somehow get the hell back to Port Orlov. Even if there *were* jewels inside those coffins, this guy Slater, and the Coast Guard, had gotten there first by now, so what was the point of sticking around?

When the northern lights were suddenly extinguished—it always reminded Russell of the way his grandfather would pinch a candle flame between his thumb and forefinger—the forest went almost black all around him. Only the moon and stars offered a little help to navigate by.

Trying to ignore the pain in his ankle, Russell focused on what he'd do once he got back home—he imagined himself hoisting a brew in the Yardarm and maybe shooting some pool—when he heard a bustling in an alder thicket. He stopped, expecting a covey of quail to fly out, or maybe a squirrel to scamper underfoot, but nothing did. He waited silently—if it was a bear, it would want to avoid him as much as he wanted to avoid it—and then he said, with as much bravado as he could muster, "Hey, asshole, I'm coming through." It was always best to give a bear fair warning.

But there was no more noise, and no sign or smell of anything lingering in the brush, so he forged on. Not that he didn't wish he could trade his flashlight for a can of that mace Harley carried. He knew there were wolves on the island, but wolves never attacked humans. They looked for herds of elk, and cut the young, or the feeble, ones from the pack. He kept going, leaning on the stave with one hand and using the other one, clutching the flashlight, to bat low-hanging branches out of his way. He never thought he'd miss driving the propane truck, but right now even that was looking good. He just hoped his boss would let him slide for missing a few days of work; he'd told him he had to visit a sick relative, but if the truth got back to him, or even worse if it got back to Russell's parole officer, it'd mean big trouble.

The rustling came again, and this time out of the corner of his eye he saw a flash of movement behind a moss-covered tree trunk. He rubbed the back of his glove across his eyes to clear his vision—the snow was starting to come down faster now—and swept the flashlight beam across the brush. But everything was suddenly still.

Too still . . . as if the usual woodland creatures had fled, or were lying low.

He felt the hairs on the back of his neck stand up. His feet weren't moving, but he knew it was no time to stand still. Should he retreat to the hut, he wondered, where he could grab one of those old rusty spades and at least have some kind of weapon if he needed it? The stave he was holding wasn't going to be much help.

But when he turned around, he realized that he had no more idea how to get back to the hut than he did to find the cave. The trees were so tightly spaced, the ground so covered with moss and leaves and damp muddy snow, he'd have to be one of the native Inuit to thread his way back. And the prospect of getting marooned in that freezing, spooky shack overnight was way too scary to think about.

He turned back in the direction he'd been going and, as stealthily as possible, hobbled on. Even if he could just keep to a straight line, he figured, he'd eventually hit the cliffs on the other side—the whole friggin' island wasn't that big—and from there he could just hug the cliffs until he spotted the boat down in the cove. It couldn't be that hard, or take that long. He told himself that all he had to do was keep his wits about him, ignore the pain in his ankle, and keep making progress.

And then something skittered across the path ahead of him.

Jesus Christ. He stopped dead, wondering what it had been. It had moved like a shadow, black and fast. He'd heard all the native legends about the otter-men, but who ever believed in shit like that? That old totem pole in town, the one that had fallen halfway over, supposedly told the story. His third-grade teacher had tried to tell the class about it one day, but Russell hadn't paid any attention.

Now, he sort of wished he had.

He debated about whether it was better to keep quiet and get the hell out of there, or make some noise and try to bluster his way through. But that would all depend on what he was up against, and so far he hadn't actually seen anything well enough to know.

A twig snapped behind him, on the other side, and he whipped around. A gust of wind blew the snow off a bough and into his face, but even as he blinked to clear his vision he saw a pair of eyes—yellow and intent—peering out from the brush.

Instinctively, he jabbed the stave at the bushes, but hit nothing. The eyes were gone as suddenly as they had appeared.

But Russell wasn't about to wait around. Clawing his way through the woods as fast as he could, the anguish in his ankle overwhelmed by the adrenaline surging through his veins, he plowed ahead, knocking branches out of his way, clambering over the trunks of dead trees, slipping on wet moss, and once, on a brackish coil of goose droppings. His boots were slick with the shit when his toe caught on something hard, jutting up from the ground, and he was thrown flat, his head colliding with a rotten log. The flashlight went flying from his hand.

He lay there, stunned for an instant, but he could sense that he was still being tracked, that something was still watching him, waiting him out. First, he heard a sound on his right—snow crunching under a foot or paw—then he heard a sound on his left, like panting. There was more than one of them. He felt like he was being studied, like his infirmity had been noted, and now the stalkers were just awaiting the right opportunity to bring him down . . . like a wounded animal separated from the herd.

The way that wolves would do it.

He took a hurried breath and struggled to his feet again, leaning on the stave. The more he gave the impression of weakness and fear, the more he would embolden the attackers. If a bear threatened you, it was best to stand your ground, pump yourself up to look as big as you could manage, and make a lot of racket. But if it was wolves, that was something else. They never tired of the game . . . and to them it *was* a game. They would shift responsibilities, one running the animal down, then resting, while another picked up the chase. They would harry and harass their prey, nipping at its heels, barking in its face, racing in circles so that the creature got dizzy just trying to keep the many wolves in its sights. Russell had once gone hunting with his uncle and watched as a pack of them surrounded a starving coyote that had had the nerve to scavenge one of their kills. They had neatly spaced themselves out to cover any possible escape route, then crept closer, until the coyote, suddenly looking up from its feast, found itself with nowhere to run.

And then the wolves had descended all at once, in a bristling fury of fangs and claws.

Russell was so disoriented—and panicked now—that he hardly knew which way to turn. But he did know that the cave was still far off, while the old Russian colony was close. He could give himself up to the Coast Guard, claim he was just some stupid kayaker that the storm had washed up on the shore. Maybe that guy Dr. Slater could even take a look at his ankle, and better yet, give him something for the pain.

The colony, as best he could make out, was off to his left, in the direction of the strait. Keeping a close eye on the brush, and moving as quickly, but as cautiously, as he could, he cut a trail through the trees. The snow was swirling more thickly than ever. Remembering something his uncle had once told him, he thought of breaking the end of a branch here and there as a way of marking his progress, but he knew it was too dark for him ever to find the broken bits again. It would only be possible the next day . . . and he was beginning to doubt he would live that long.

Something leapt over a fallen trunk on his right, and he caught a glimpse of sleek black fur.

And then, from his other side, he heard a yip.

A short one, a signal to its mate.

Which was responded to with the same sound.

He picked up his pace, his heart pounding in his chest. He clenched the end of the stave, his only weapon. His eyes strained to see ahead, to catch sight of the colony. His breath was coming in bursts, and he told himself to breathe more evenly, more deeply. The essential thing was to keep moving. They would only move in for the kill if they thought he was helpless and had given up . . . or if they had already acquired a taste for human flesh.

Focus, he told himself, forging ahead. *Focus.* And through the trees, down a slope, he saw a spot of something bright green. And glowing.

A tent! One of those colony tents!

It was behind what was left of the stockade wall. Christ, it felt like a hundred years ago that he had first seen this damn place. He swung the stave through the brush, clumsily trudging down the hillside, and then exulting as he shimmied through a gap in the timbers.

He was behind that old church, but when he turned, he saw that the wolves—and there were four of them, not two, all black, and their yellow eyes gleaming—were slinking between the logs, too. Their heads were lowered, their hackles raised, and they showed no signs of quitting their hunt.

He swung the stave in a wide arc, but only one of them backed off. The others stood their ground, snarling now, saliva dripping from their jaws.

"Help!" he shouted, but the wind was roaring in his ears. "Somebody help me!"

He could feel the wolves spreading out around him, cutting off any retreat. He swung the stave again, and this time the alpha wolf, in front of the pack and with a blaze of white on its muzzle, snapped at the end of the stick, nearly managing to yank it from his hands. He could feel the heat of its body; he could smell its rank breath.

Whirling around, he saw a hole in the foundation of the church, not much bigger than a manhole cover, but big enough. He backed up toward it, poking the stave at whichever wolf got closest. When the alpha lunged at it again—and gripped the stick between its teeth—he suddenly let go, turned around, and scrambled into the hole. The wood was jagged, and splinters cut through his gloves, but he was pulling himself in with all his might, wriggling his body in after. He was jackknifed into the gloomy interior when something snagged the bottom of his boot. He pulled the leg harder, praying he had caught his shoe on a shard of wood, but the foot was only jerked back even harder.

And now he could feel the bite, the fangs sinking right through his boot and heavy woolen sock . . . and into his skin.

He pulled again, but to his amazement he felt himself being hauled backwards. His hands scrabbled at the thick wood of the wall, trying to find any purchase, but all he got was a handful of splinters and sawdust. He shook his leg, and kicked his foot out. He heard his pants ripping, and felt his own hot blood soaking through his sock.

He screamed again, his cry echoing in the empty church.

And then there was another set of fangs, fastened like a vise on his other foot.

Like a snake being yanked out of its den, he slithered backward, out of the hole, and flopped onto the ground. Turning over to punch at their snouts, he saw above him a frenzy of yellow eyes, black fur, and open, dripping jaws. He tried to lift his hands to fight back, but the alpha had already nuzzled its head under his chin, seeking, and swiftly finding, his jugular. Its teeth felt as long and fine as knitting needles as they sank into his neck.

Chapter 36

The electric chandelier was ablaze with light, and Jemmy, who usually slept soundly on her feet, was stirring. Anastasia rubbed her eyes and said, "What's going on?"

Her father was standing in the doorway in his nightshirt. "The commandant has asked us to dress and go down to one of the lower rooms."

"Why?" Olga asked from her cot.

"He says that there is some unrest in the town, and it will be safer for us if we are not on the upper story."

All four of the girls hastily exchanged looks, wondering what this really might portend, but Anastasia prayed that it was the first news of their deliverance. Sergei had said telegrams had been flying back and forth from Moscow and that something was afoot. Maybe the White Army was indeed within reach. Even now, the night wind carried the faint rumble of distant guns.

The girls sprang out of bed and had no sooner started dressing than their mother appeared and reminded them to put on their special corsets—the ones with the royal jewels so laboriously sewn into all of the linings.

"We have to be ready for anything," Alexandra said. But there was a note of hope in her voice, too, a note that Ana had not heard for so many months of their captivity. "We might not be coming back to these rooms."

Even though they had spent countless hours working on the corsets, the girls had never actually worn them yet, and Ana found that hers weighed much more than she might ever have imagined. It was hard to get on, and with the emerald cross from Father Grigori hanging around her neck, too, she felt like a walking jewelry box.

Like her sisters, she put on a long dark skirt and a white blouse, and by the time they were out in the hall the family's companions in exile had also assembled there—Dr. Botkin, polishing his gold-rimmed glasses; her father's valet, Trupp; her mother's personal maid, Demidova; Kharitonov the cook. Tatiana asked what time it was, and Dr. Botkin consulted his pocket watch.

"Nearly one o'clock."

Her mother came out next, clutching one of the pillows that also contained a cache of jewels inside it (Demidova had the other), then her father emerged, carrying a sleepy Alexei in his arms. Her father was not a tall man, but he had a broad chest and strong arms, and somehow he always managed to carry his son as effortlessly as if the boy were made of feathers. Ana carried Jemmy, who was strangely, but blissfully, silent for a change.

With Nicholas leading the way, the family trooped down the creaking stairway to the foyer. Yurovsky was waiting at the bottom, stroking his black goatee and wearing a long overcoat far too warm for the July night.

"This way," he said, guiding them out into the courtyard—Ana was so glad of the chance to see the stars and breathe the fresh air, perfumed with lilac and honeysuckle, that she almost cried aloud for joy—then back down a set of stairs that led to the cellar. "You will please wait in here," he said. "It won't be long."

The room was not much bigger than the girls' bedroom upstairs, and the walls were covered with peeling wallpaper in a pattern of yellow stripes. There wasn't a single piece of furniture in the room—Ana wondered if Yurovsky hadn't already started his looting of the place— and a single electric bulb, with no shade, hung from a string, casting a harsh white light around the barren space. Just before the commandant closed the double doors behind him, Alexandra said, "May we not have some chairs?"

Ana knew that her mother's back was very bad, but she also knew that it was Alexei she was most concerned about.

"Of course," Yurovsky said, and closed the doors. Ana assumed that they would never see the chairs, any more than they saw the powdered sage or anything else that the commandant promised, but to her surprise, he kicked the doors open a minute later and dragged in two wooden chairs.

Alexandra sat down on one of them, casually placing the pillow behind the small of her back as if for comfort, while Nicholas sat down on the other with Alexei cradled in his lap.

"The capitalist newspapers have been circulating stories," Yurovsky said. "They claim that you have escaped, or that you are not being kept safe. We need to take a photograph to put an end to these rumors once and for all. You will please arrange yourselves so that you may all be seen."

Having had their portrait taken a thousand times, the royal family obligingly fell into their customary spots, with the parents and Alexei in the middle and the girls spread out on either side.

"Yes, yes," Yurovsky said, directing Dr. Botkin and the others into a single file against the wall behind them. "Exactly. Everyone stay right where you are."

Then, he popped back out the door again. There was nothing to look at and nothing to do. Ana fidgeted in her corset, stifling not only from the weight but the heat of it. Who knew that diamonds and rubies could be so heavy? Olga put a hand on her mother's shoulder, and Alexandra kissed and squeezed it hopefully.

Ana wondered where Sergei was, and if he knew what was going on. There was only one window, crossed with iron bars, opening onto ground level, but it was placed high in the wall and she couldn't see anything outside. How many officers, she wondered, were riding to their rescue even now?

Time seemed to stand still in the airless cellar as they held their positions and waited for the photographer to come in with his tripod and his camera and his black cloth. Jemmy squirmed in her arms, but she didn't want to put him down for fear he'd get into some trouble. The commandant had made plain, on previous occasions, that he had no use for dogs.

When the doors did open again, Yurovsky came in, with his long coat unbuttoned and nearly a dozen guards jostling to join him inside. Reading aloud from a sheet of paper he held high in his hand, Yurovsky announced that "in view of the fact that your relatives and supporters have continued their attacks on Soviet Russia, the Executive Committee of the Urals has decided to execute you."

Ana thought she could not have heard him correctly, and her father, after looking quickly at his family assembled around him, turned back to Yurovsky in disbelief and said, "What? What?"

The commandant quickly repeated the sentence, word for word, then drew from his belt a revolver and shot the former Tsar directly through the forehead. Ana saw her father pitch backwards in the chair, dropping Alexei to the floor. She saw her mother fling up a hand to cross herself, and her sisters shrink back against the wall. She heard Demidova cry out and Botkin protest, then everything became an awful blur.

The Red Guards pulled out their own guns and all Ana remembered was a deafening roar as the shots rang out and the room filled with choking smoke and screams for mercy and the hot splash of blood, blood flying everywhere. Jemmy turned into a limp soaking rag in her arms, and as the bullets clanged and ricocheted off the gems in her corset, Ana toppled over and fell beneath the crush of dead and dying bodies . . . and still the firing continued. The lightbulb in the ceiling exploded, and the last thing she saw, as she clutched at the emerald cross beneath her blouse, was the looming phantom of

Rasputin himself rising before her, as if his black beard and cassock were fashioned from the swirling smoke and gunpowder. In her ear, she heard the deep rumble of his voice whispering, as he once had done at the Christmas ball, "I shall always be watching over you, little one." *Malenkaya.*

Part Three

Chapter 37

Lantos, accustomed to working under optimal conditions at M.I.T., was having to make some adjustments. She wasn't used to her feet sticking to damp rubber mats on the floor, for instance, or to Arctic blasts battering the walls of her lab. Nor was she accustomed to the constant roar of the wind, like a ceaseless pounding surf, or the lamps swaying overhead.

The Tyvek suit and rubber apron she was wearing weren't exactly comfortable, either. With her fingers encased in latex, her mouth and nose covered by a face mask, and her eyes protected by oversized goggles designed to accommodate her glasses, she had to move more slowly, and with greater deliberation, than her nature dictated. But she knew that this mission had to yield some answers, and quickly. What were they dealing with—the dead remnants of an extinct plague, or the dormant, but still viable, vestiges of the greatest killer the world had ever known?

For hours she had done nothing but study the specimens taken from the various organ sites of the young deacon, whose body still lay, like a disassembled engine, in the autopsy chamber at the rear of the lab tent. She didn't like leaving it like that, not only because it presented a hazard but because she always tried to be respectful in her work. As soon as Slater got back from the graveyard, where he and Kozak had gone to figure out which grave to open next, she would enlist his help in putting the body back together.

In order to feel confident in their results, she and Slater had decided that they would need to exhume no less than three more corpses, all from separate and distinct spots in the cemetery. To avoid any risk of cross-contamination or confusion among the specimens taken, they had also determined to work on only one cadaver at a time, reap the harvest they required, then put the dissected remains back in their frozen grave. The simplest lab protocols were always the safest and most elegant, Lantos believed, especially when dealing with what were called "select agents"—the most notorious pathogens like ricin, anthrax, and ebola—and under such tricky conditions as these.

After stretching her muscles and pressing her hands to the small of her back, she debated going over to the mess tent for a quick pick-me-up—some hot oatmeal and a mug of coffee—or to get just one more test under way. The idea of a break was very tempting, but it was such a hassle to suit up, then undress again, that she decided to go forward with just one more bit of business first.

The animal trial.

Lantos had a soft spot for the mice she routinely subjected to these tests. They were far more intelligent and even cunning creatures than they were given credit for. But countless millions of them had been bred and used and destroyed by now for the purposes of medical research and scientific gain; it was their misfortune that they reproduced rapidly and had genetic counterparts, some nearly identical, to 99 percent of human genes. She wished there was some other and better way to glean the information the scientists needed . . . but so far no one had come up with one.

Right now she had three glass containers, each containing six white mice, all ranged on a counter. One tank was the control group—who would remain untouched in any way—another was the tank whose inhabitants would be injected with a common flu virus, and a third was reserved for the mice who would be exposed to the viral strains or material that had been extracted and isolated from the body of the deacon.

Nestled in a corner of the lab tent, an open crate of additional live mice was housed for subsequent tests. She had checked their food and water supplies that morning.

One by one, Lantos reached into the second tank, and with a packet of syringes she found it devilishly hard to manipulate through the gloves, injected each with a dose of the strain most prevalent in the human population at the time she had departed for the island. Lots of people, all over the globe, were going to be sick with it that winter, but no one whose health wasn't otherwise compromised would die from it. The mice scrambled around, trying to avoid her grasp, but lay docile in her hand as she made the injections, marked their backs with a dab of blue ink, and put them back among their comrades.

It was with the third tank that she had to be extraordinarily alert and careful. She had made a serum from the blood drawn from the deacon's frozen veins, spun and purified it, and dubbed it SPI—for St. Peter's Island—#1. There would be several others in the days to come. The serum was contained in an innocuous brown vial with a little orange label, and as she filled a fresh syringe with the concoction, then administered a drop or two to each of the six mice in the third tank, she wondered if she was looking at a harmless soup, or Armageddon in a bottle. Each SPI #1 mouse was marked with a daub of orange stain on its back and tail.

The mysteries of flu were legion. The Spanish flu had been an airborne illness, dispelled and disseminated in the coughs and sneezes of its victims; all of their bodily fluids and secretions, from mucus to saliva, tears to feces to blood, were saturated with the virus, and the next victim had only to breathe in a poisoned vapor, or unwittingly touch a tainted surface before then touching that same hand to his mouth or nose or eyes, for the transmission to be made. The flu was onto another host.

And mutating all the while. Just as Lantos felt a certain sympathy for the mice, she also harbored a grudging, if horrified, admiration for the flu. Almost all researchers eventually did. The virus was a veritable Houdini, armed with a thousand tricks and stunts and contortions that would allow it to move through as large a host population as possible, with the greatest possible ease and speed, and keeping one step ahead of its victims' ability to create antibodies or defense mechanisms to defeat it. Even armed with the latest technology and decades of previous research results, the scientific community—Lantos included—was often astonished at the infinitesimally small changes that could transform a flu from a mild annoyance to a lethal disease of epic proportions. In reconstructions of the 1918 flu, research scientists had concluded that it was the polymerase genes and the HA and NA genes in particular that had made it so virulent. But the sequences of those polymerase proteins were not only present in subsequent human strains, but differed by a mere ten amino acids from some of the most dangerous avian influenza viruses seen in the past few years. The flu could morph, Lantos knew, almost before your eyes, changing its genetic structure to blend in with any crowd, like an immigrant putting on a new suit of clothes to walk the streets unnoticed.

And, to make matters worse, it had learned over the centuries to jump species, too, as fluidly as a trapeze artist. No one knew whether the next pandemic was brewing in a pigpen in Bolivia, or on a poultry farm in Macau.

Once all the mice were treated and marked—their tanks separately ventilated, and placed several feet apart—Lantos stoppered the vial of SPI #1 and took it back, for safekeeping, to the freezer in the autopsy chamber. There, she placed it beside the range of samples taken from the deacon's cadaver, along with the diamond-studded icon and the paper prayer he had held in his rigid hands. Slater had promised Kozak that if the initial lab results on the blood and tissue came back clear, he would allow him to thaw out the paper, unscroll it, and read whatever it said. The professor had looked like a kid who'd been promised a trip to Disneyland.

We are all such strange creatures, Lantos thought, closing the freezer. We have our individual passions and interests, most of them formed in some way in our childhoods, then those same interests become translated in our later lives into careers. Kozak had probably collected rocks and geodes, and wound up a geologist, while she had always been fascinated by the natural world and the myriad forms that life could take. Summers had been spent on the Massachusetts coastline, studying the busy life in the tide pools and clamming with her dad. Where did all this activity come from? How did it all survive? She could see how everything was connected, but what then was her place in it (apart from enjoying, guiltily, the clam chowder)? If there was a natural order—or disorder—who or what was responsible for that? Big questions. She had loved to turn them over and over in her mind, and now, by concentrating on one of the tiniest and yet most indefatigable life-forms on the planet, she got to dedicate her life to the big stuff, after all. If you could figure out the flu, it was like turning the key on a box filled with mysteries.

But a Pandora's box, if you weren't careful.

She closed the freezer, and as she turned to leave the autopsy chamber, she thought she saw a yellow glow, like a lanternlight, hovering near the main entry to the lab tent. And maybe someone's silhouette, too—someone on the short side. But she was peering through several layers of thick plastic sheathing, and it was like looking at something at the bottom of a murky pond. She was reminded of the crabs that would scuttle for cover when she fished her hand into the tide pool.

She parted the curtains of the autopsy chamber and stepped out, face mask and goggles still in place, expecting to see Slater, or maybe even the professor, entering the tent. After so many hours of work, she would be glad of the company.

But she was wrong.

More wrong than she had ever been in her life.

She stopped where she was and stood stock-still, but it wasn't as if she could become invisible. The human silhouette was gone, the tent flaps were open, and a black wolf, with a white blaze on its muzzle, planted its paws on the rubber matting, its back bristling from the wind, its eyes glaring with a strangely human intensity.

Chapter 38

"The lines are still on the screen!" Kozak shouted to Slater from across the graveyard. He was pushing his GPR back and forth like a vacuum cleaner on the snowy ground.

"So it's not a computer malfunction?"

Kozak shook his head, his head down and earmuffs flapping, as he studied the digital monitor mounted between the handlebars. The professor had been puzzled by the fissile lines that kept showing up on the geothermal ground charts and had insisted on coming back out again to see if they would reappear.

And they had.

Now, Slater wondered, would he have an explanation? Looking out across the windswept cemetery, Slater could barely imagine how, or why, anyone would have willingly chosen to settle in such a bleak and inaccessible spot as St. Peter's Island, a place where even the simple act of burial would have required a Herculean effort.

"Of course!" Kozak said to himself, loudly enough that Slater could still hear it across the rows of old graves, while smacking his palm against his forehead.

"Of course what?" Slater said, stepping between the stones and markers.

"These are the kinds of lines and deformations you usually see only in minefields."

"There were no mines here," Slater said, coming to his side.

"But there were explosions," Kozak said, pointing at the crazed web of lines that radiated across his computer grid. "You see where they are?"

"It looks like they're everywhere."

"Everywhere in the graveyard," Kozak said, "but not as you come to the end of the rows. Not as you start to enter the woods."

"Okay," Slater conceded, "I'll buy that."

"The colonists were setting off explosions in the cemetery. They were using dynamite, probably, to break up the tundra and permafrost."

Of course, Slater thought, echoing Kozak. It made perfect sense. Global warming might have loosened the hold of the soil, but it was the bedrock beneath that had been fractured already. No wonder that coffin had fallen into the sea.

But what would it mean in the epidemiological sense? What would it mean for the cadavers of flu victims? Would it have created an aerated or unstable ground environment, and if so, would that have contributed to the decay of the bodies and the dissipation of any viral threat? The state of the deacon's body argued otherwise—he was frozen as solid as an ice cube when he'd been dug up—but he could prove to be an anomaly. The only way to know for sure was to exhume at least two or three more.

And to do it before this storm that was blowing in got any worse.

Slater had pretty much decided on which grave to excavate next. It was a dozen yards or so closer in from the cliffs, and if he followed that one up with the plot at the northwesternmost corner of the lot, he'd have a rough triangle that he could then work either in, or out, from, depending on the results he and Lantos were getting in the lab. By now, he figured, she had created a purified blood sample from the deacon, and might even have begun the live-animal trials. He was eager to find out how she was coming along.

"What do you say we pack it in then?" Slater asked.

But Kozak, rapt in the numbers that were scrolling down one side of his computer screen, simply grunted.

"Vassily?"

"You go; I want to study this more," the professor said. "I will see you in camp."

Slater knew enough not to disturb a fellow scientist when he was absorbed in his work—he himself had been known to fall asleep at his desk after ten or twelve straight hours of crunching data—so he clapped him on the padded shoulder of his parka and picked his way back through the graves. But he must have taken a slightly different route because suddenly his foot plunged through the snow and into a hole in the ground. The sole of his boot thumped on top of a creaking coffin.

How could he—and Kozak—have missed this on their general survey of the graveyard days ago?

Pulling his boot out, he got down on his knees and brushed the snow cover away. About two feet down, he saw a casket lid splintered as if it had been hit by an axe. Through a gaping hole in the wood, he saw the dark shadows of a corpse.

Jesus Christ. When had this happened? In the pale and failing light of the day, he couldn't tell if the damage had been done recently, or if this was just an age-old accident that had been overlooked thus far.

Either way, it had to be contained, and immediately.

"What are you doing?" Kozak called out.

"There's a hole in the ground here," Slater hollered, "and a compromised burial plot."

"That's not possible," the professor said, indignantly, heading in his direction. "I covered all the ground, and if there had been a hole of any kind—"

"It's here," Slater interrupted, "and don't come any closer. We'll have to seal this up right away." He was already reformulating his exhumation schedule; this grave, and its dimly glimpsed occupant, would have to be the next one investigated. Grabbing up several of the pennant flags that marked the grid, he stuck them as firmly as he could in the snowy earth all around the perimeter of the grave. "Don't come any closer than you already have," he warned Kozak again, "and don't let Rudy or Groves get any closer than this, either."

He stood up, and looked all around for any sign of intrusion, but the fresh snow had covered any tracks that might have been there. None of this made any sense. If the hole had been made recently, who could have done it? Why would they have done it?

And could they possibly still be on the island somewhere?

"Keep an eye out," he said ominously to the professor. "We might not be alone here."

Even as the professor looked at him slack-jawed, Slater took off for the colony. He needed to put the word out that the cemetery was now completely off-limits to everyone—though it was Nika he had foremost in his mind. He could not risk her coming out here to perform some native ritual so long as an open grave posed any possible danger.

The matted pathway was slippery with snow and ice, and as he hurried down it he had to regain his balance once or twice by grabbing a light pole and holding on. The daylight was going fast. Running through the gates he heard a scream—unmistakably from Lantos in the lab.

What now?

Barreling up the ramp and into the tent, throwing all caution—and safety protocols—to the wind, he saw a black wolf leaping up at the plastic sheathing of the autopsy chamber. Lantos was inside, brandishing the Stryker saw and screaming for help. The plastic was already shredded in strips, but the wolf had not yet been able to claw its way through.

Slater's eyes searched the lab for any kind of weapon, but all he saw were microscopes and vials and glass tanks of agitated white mice.

The wolf swiped at the plastic again, ripping another strip loose, then yanking at it with its jaws.

"Hey!" Slater shouted, just to grab its attention. "Over here!"

The wolf whipped its head around. There was a bolt of white on its muzzle and plastic hanging from its teeth.

He snatched a specimen scale off the counter and hurled it, missing the target but distracting the beast for a second.

"Come on!" he shouted, treading backwards toward the exit. "Follow me, you bastard!" He grabbed a clipboard and threw that, too, the pages fluttering loose as it flew. "Follow me!"

But the wolf refused to take the bait. Now it seemed to know that he was harmless, and with renewed vigor it turned its head sideways, gathered a hunk of the heavy-duty sheathing in its mouth, and began tearing it away again.

Lantos screamed as a great swath of the shredded curtain fell apart, enough for the wolf to squirm its way into the autopsy chamber.

Lantos swung the saw, but the wolf leapt on her, fangs flashing and claws out, and as Slater ran through the lab he saw her fall under its weight.

He tore through the same opening as the wolf, snatched the biggest scalpel on the instrument tray and slashed at the raised hackles on the animal's back. The first cut was ignored, and so was the second, but on the third the wolf howled, and twisted around in rage.

Slater stepped back, the bloody scalpel slick in his hand, bracing himself against the freezer for the attack. To his astonishment the wolf snarled, but instead of charging at him, it turned away and leapt onto the autopsy table, squarely setting its paws on either side of the deacon's corpse, like a predator defending its kill.

"Run!" Slater said to Lantos, who was lying on the floor in her lab suit and rubber apron. "Can you run?"

Lantos scrambled out of the chamber, her hands cradling her abdomen, while Slater, the breath raw in his throat, covered her retreat.

The wolf bent its head to the ravaged remains on the table and sniffed at them. Its own blood matted its thick black fur, lending it an oily sheen.

Slater inched his way backwards, watching the wolf while clutching the scalpel.

But the creature stood its ground atop the table, not even bothering to look at him as he parted the torn curtains and stepped into the lab proper. Still looking over his shoulder, Slater hurried toward the open flaps that were slapping in the wind. Just before he passed through them, he took one last look at the wolf through the hanging shreds of the autopsy chamber. Lifting its powerful head toward the sky, it howled with a sound as forlorn and grief-stricken as any mourner at a funeral.

He staggered through the tent flaps; they were smeared with blood, as was the railing of the ramp. In the last of the daylight, he could see a trail of crimson spots on the white snow, leading off into the colony grounds. All around the stockade, he could hear the baying of wolves, answering the call.

But he could not see Lantos.

The trail of blood and footprints seemed to go first in one direction, and then in another, as if she were staggering blindly, simply trying to put distance between herself and the lab tent.

"Eva!" he called out, and the only reply he heard was from the wolves. "Eva!"

The tents were glowing green all around him, but the blood led him up toward the old well, where he found a deeper and wetter pool. "Eva!"

She was crumpled in a heap, her arms cradling her stomach, against the stone wall of the well. When he turned her over, he could see that the blood was oozing through a gash in her rubber apron. Her face mask was askew, and as he bent over her, he said, "Can you hear me?"

There was no answer, but he felt for a pulse in her neck and found it. "Just hang in there," he said, "you're going to be all right. I promise you." It was a promise he wasn't at all sure he could keep.

Snow had started to fall in earnest, and it was dark. If he was going to save her life, he would have to perform emergency surgery on her and close that wound, but the lab was now off-limits, as were all the other colony tents. Lantos might have been contaminated, and he needed to keep her in quarantine from now on.

The cockeyed church, with its onion dome, rose before him, and picking her up in his arms, he mounted the old wooden steps, kicked the doors open with one foot, then laid her as gently as he could atop one of the pews.

When she groaned, he was relieved to hear it. "Eva, I'll be right back." He placed her hands, still in their sticky gloves, on her own abdomen. "Keep pressing down. You hear me? Keep it compacted."

She grunted softly, and Slater charged out again. The wolves were howling in the woods—had they picked up the scent of all the blood?—as he yanked the doors firmly closed behind him. The green tents, only fifty yards off, looked a mile away. But he barely stopped to catch his breath before he vaulted down the steps on his way to fetch his surgical supplies.

The mission had just gone completely off the rails, but if he didn't keep his head, it could lead to a disaster of epic proportions.

Chapter 39

"But what about Russell?" Eddie complained. "We gotta keep looking for Russell!"

As far as Harley was concerned, they had looked for Russell long enough. They'd gone all the way back to the graveyard, where they'd hidden behind some trees long enough to see some stocky guy with a little silver beard pushing what looked like a lawn mower around on the snow, then they'd tried to follow their drunken buddy's trail through the woods. The only clue they picked up was his flashlight, still shining under a bunch of bushes. But it didn't look good—why would Russell, dumb as he was, have thrown his flashlight away?

"We can't leave a man behind!" Eddie said, his eyes gleaming in the dusk, and at that Harley had nearly puked. *We can't leave a man behind?* What did Eddie think they were—Marines?

"Forget it," Harley said. "He's either frozen stiff somewhere, or he's holed up in the colony right now, warm as toast and telling some bullshit story about how he got lost kayaking."

And the colony was where Harley was heading. He'd had enough of the graveyard, and more than enough of the fucking woods. If the

Coast Guard guys had dug up something special, he'd find it in the colony by now.

It hadn't been hard to slip through the gap in the stockade wall, and just before the daylight completely vanished, he led Eddie to a secluded spot behind the generator shed. Digging into his backpack, he pulled out a pair of night-vision binoculars and looped the cord around his neck.

"Hey, where'd you get those?" Eddie said enviously as Harley adjusted the scopes.

"Arctic Circle Gun Shoppe."

"What'd they cost?"

"How the hell should I know?" It wasn't as if he'd paid for them. He'd swiped them along with the MREs.

The tents were glowing green, but the ground between them was dark, and it was there that the infrared-sensitive lenses came in handy. Harley could sweep the grounds, and if anybody was moving on the pathways, he'd see the blurry outline of their bodies. The only drawback was the slight high-pitched whine that the binoculars gave off, like a mosquito incessantly buzzing around your ears.

Kind of like Eddie.

"I want to see!" Eddie said, groping for the binoculars. "Let me take a look."

Harley had to swat his hands away, and he could see now that Eddie was flying high. Somewhere along the trail, he must have ingested some uppers. And that was all that Harley needed now— a speed freak as an accomplice.

As he watched, he saw some activity up by the church—that Slater guy was running around in one of those lab suits—and he was bringing up Nika Tincook, the mayor, their arms filled with what looked like sheets and blankets and medical instrument bags. What the fuck was going on? Even over the rising wind, he could hear their voices— they sounded alarmed—but what he didn't hear, or see, was any activity down in that big old tent by the main gates . . . where the flaps were waving wildly and the lights were all on inside.

"Come on," he said to Eddie, "but keep low and keep your mouth shut."

"What are we doing? Are we rescuing Russell?"

Harley didn't bother to reply. Crouching low, he set off across the colony grounds, leaping over the PVC pipes and electrical cables that stretched across the snow and under the braided ropes that marked the paths. At the ramp, he slowed down for a second—was that blood on the railing?—but he couldn't very well stay outside either. He ducked under the flaps and waited for Eddie to follow him in.

"Hey, man, did you see the blood on—"

"Shut up," Harley said, looking around but seeing no one. There were counters on both sides, covered with beakers and vials and microscopes; it reminded him of the chemistry class he'd failed. On a computer screen, he saw what looked like a molecule—or was it an atom?—turning slowly on its axis.

"Check it out," Eddie said, gesturing at three tanks of white mice. "Wouldn't your snake like a taste of these little babies?"

Before Harley could stop him, the idiot had reached inside a container and lifted one out by its tail. Its back was stained with orange ink and it dangled frantically in the air.

"Drop the goddamned mouse," Harley said.

Grinning, Eddie lifted it over his open mouth like he was about to swallow it, and Harley shoved him, hard enough that the mouse slipped free and ran squeaking for cover.

"I am going to kick your ass if you do one more stupid thing," Harley said.

"Big man," Eddie said, but he lowered his eyes and didn't issue any further challenge.

Harley turned back to the room; the only thing worth stealing in here might be the laptops, or maybe the microscopes, and they'd be a bitch to carry back. At the far end of the tent, there were ripped plastic curtains that extended from the floor to the ceiling. It looked like some kind of inner sanctum, but one that had been busted into. That alone was good enough for Harley.

He walked down the center of the room, noting that there was blood here, too, and even more on the strips of plastic. Even Eddie was hanging back.

Harley poked his head into what was left of this chamber, and nearly threw up on the spot.

A dismembered corpse was lying on a stainless-steel table, and there were bowls and basins of blood and organs on surgical carts and counters.

"Jesus Christ Almighty," Eddie said, though he was so revved up he walked in mesmerized. Standing over the body and flipping back the flap of scalp concealing its face, he said, "I wonder who he was."

One of the old Russians, Harley thought, though why they'd do something like this to him now . . .

"Looks like a wolf got at him, too."

"What are you talking about?" Harley said, afraid to look too closely. How was Eddie managing it?

"Paw prints," Eddie said, and now Harley glanced over long enough to see that Eddie was actually right about something. There were bloody paw prints—and pretty fresh-looking ones at that—on the tabletop.

Harley spun his gaze around the tiny chamber, as if a wolf might still be lurking somewhere, but all that caught his attention this time was a fridge with a wheel on it like you'd see on a bank vault.

But given everything else in the room, he wasn't so sure he wanted to open it.

"What's in there?" Eddie said excitedly.

Harley had come this far; there was no point in stopping now. He turned the wheel, there was a hissing sound as the seal was broken, and a bright white light came on inside.

Again, there was an array of flasks and vials, many of them marked with stickers and labels, but there was also the unmistakable sparkle of white diamonds—three of them, embedded in an old brass icon of the Virgin Mary. Eddie saw it, too, and made a grab for it, knocking over half of the bottles and tubes in the fridge, but Harley wedged it into his own breast pocket and said, "We'll fence it in Nome."

"Damn straight we will," Eddie said, "and this, too."

It was an old scrap of paper, rolled up like a scroll, and Eddie snatched it off the shelf and scrabbled it open, the page crackling and breaking in several spots.

It was a few lines long, black ink that had faded to gray, and written in Russian.

"What'd you think it was going to be?" Harley sneered. "A treasure map?"

"Maybe it is, for all you know," Eddie said, stuffing it into the pocket of his parka. Then, to Harley's dismay, he grabbed some of the test tubes and vials and stashed those in his pocket, too.

"That stuff's not worth shit," Harley said. "What are you doing?"

"It might be worth something to somebody," he replied, "and they can pay me to get it back." When he realized his own pocket was full, he crammed a couple more into Harley's pockets, too. "And they can pay you, too!" Harley batted him away again—more and more, he wished he'd checked everyone's backpacks for drugs and booze before they'd left Port Orlov—and closed the freezer door. For good measure, he gave the wheel a spin.

"We've got to get out of here," Harley said, and after Eddie had cast one more look at the mutilated corpse—what was he thinking of stealing now, Harley thought, a kidney?—they stepped out into the lab.

"The laptops?" Eddie said, but Harley shook his head. They were government-issue, and probably traceable; besides, he just wanted to get the hell out of this damn slaughterhouse. They had slunk no more than ten or twenty yards away when he saw a burly black guy, in an Army coat, running toward the lab tent with one of the Coast Guardsmen right behind him. They were carrying rifles and they were loaded for bear . . . or wolf.

Ducking behind the generator shed, Harley threaded his way back through the stockade wall. But even with the aid of the night-vision binoculars, it would be nearly impossible to find his way through the woods at night; the surest route would be to stick to the ridgeline and simply follow it around until he returned to the cove where, if he was lucky, the *Kodiak* might by some miracle be afloat.

The problem was, his pal Eddie was still so stoned he could waltz off the cliff, or wander off into the woods, and for the time being at least, Harley needed him alive; the *Kodiak* needed a deckhand. Taking a nylon cord out of his backpack, he tied a tight loop around Eddie's waist—Eddie laughed and tried to twirl as it was done—and then knotted the other end around the tool belt he was wearing to hold his knife and bear mace. He'd left no more than ten or fifteen feet of rope between them.

With the edge of the forest on one side and the ocean on the other, Harley set off along the cliffs, picking his way over the rocks and brambles with his flashlight beam and occasionally feeling the drag of Eddie as he slowed down or missed a step. It would have been an arduous task on a summer day, but in the dark, with an Arctic wind slicing across the Bering Sea, it was nearly impossible. Once he was well away from the colony, he breathed a little easier and let his flashlight pan out over a wider stretch of ground. The snow was crusting, and his boots crunched with every step he took. But one false move, he knew, and they could both go tumbling off the ridgeline.

With no landmarks to go by, it was impossible to calculate the distance they'd traveled. All he could do was plow ahead and count on spotting the cove where the *Kodiak* was anchored; from there, he could easily find his way back into the cave. But if he missed it, or overshot the mark, both he and Eddie could wind up either lost in the storm, or worse. Already, his feet and hands were starting to lose some sensation from the unrelenting cold. As soon as they got back to the cave, he would light the camp stove and make some hot soup or stew. Nobody was going to be out doing reconnaissance on a night like this.

Several times, Eddie stumbled, and Harley had to stop to let him get back on his feet. The farther they went, the more he thought he was carrying Eddie rather than leading him.

"Wake up!" Harley finally shouted at him. "I'm not gonna keep hauling your ass for you!"

"Fuck you!" Eddie shouted back. "I'm freezing back here."

"Yeah, right," Harley said, "like it's warmer in front."

Harley kept plodding forward, glancing at the ground, then off at

the turbulent black sea crashing below. It was only when he thought
he caught a glimpse of the boat that he deliberately stopped to clear
his vision and make sure. He turned the flashlight in its direction, but
the beam couldn't penetrate that far. Taking out the night-vision binoculars, he tried to draw a bead on it, but there was so much snow
flying in the air now, and so little light, that it was useless.

Still, he thought he could hear the groaning of its hull over the
roar of the surf.

"Almost there," he said to Eddie, whose presence he could sense
right behind him. He left the binoculars looped around his neck.

But Eddie didn't say anything.

"Maybe we'll even find Russell there."

Again, there was no reply, which was odd for such a motormouth
as Eddie.

Turning around, Harley raised the flashlight and saw someone—
but definitely not Eddie—standing right behind him.

It was an old woman, in a long skirt and a kerchief tied around her
head. He lifted the beam to her face and saw two blue eyes, hard as a
husky's, sunken into a leathery face, lined and creased as an antique
map. She was staring, but not at his face; her eyes were trained on the
breast pocket of his coat, where the icon was stashed.

She didn't have to say a word; he knew what she wanted.

And he swung at her with the flashlight.

But somehow missed.

He was grabbing for his knife when Eddie stumbled up, and said,
"Holy Christ."

Harley was weirdly relieved that Eddie could see her, too, but
when he wheeled around, holding the knife out and searching for the
old woman in the snow, he got so tangled up in the rope that it was
Eddie he nearly stabbed.

"Watch the fucking knife!" Eddie shouted, as he backpedaled as
fast as he could go.

Too fast, as it happened.

Harley suddenly felt the rope jerk tight on his tool belt, and a second later, he was staggering toward the cliff. Eddie was screaming,

already sliding backwards down the icy slope. Harley flailed around, trying to grab hold of anything in reach.

"Help me!" Eddie shouted, and Harley managed to snag a low-lying branch heavy with snow. The knife dropped to the ground.

But even as he hung on with one hand, his gloves stripping the snow and then the needles right off of it, the branch slid free, and he crashed to his knees. He heard the crunch of test tubes breaking in his pockets, and a moment later the sharp pain of broken glass cutting into his thigh. He was being dragged off the edge of the cliff, too, by the weight of Eddie on the rope.

"Christ Almighty!" Eddie hollered in terror, his boots scraping the rock for any kind of ledge or crevice.

Harley dug his fingers into the snow and ice, and found a ridge in the earth, a solid bit of frozen tundra, maybe three or four inches deep, and hung on for dear life, but the nylon cord was pulling him down, twisting the belt around his waist like a tourniquet. His underarms were burning from the drag on the sleeves of his coat.

He reached for the buckle on his belt, but it was pulled so tight he couldn't loosen it.

"Pull me up, Vane! Pull me up!"

But he didn't have that kind of purchase, and he knew his own strength was going to give out fast. His collar was choking him, the binoculars were digging into his chest. Clinging to the soil with one hand, he used the other to grope for the knife, lying only inches away, and then wedged its blade under the straining cord.

"I can't hang on here!" Eddie grunted. "The rope's killing me!"

With fumbling fingers, Harley sawed at the cord. It was taut as a piano wire, but he felt a thread start to frazzle. He sawed again, harder.

"Pull!" Eddie huffed, sounding as if the very air was being squeezed from his lungs.

Harley's parka was wrapping itself around him like a python, and in a few seconds he wouldn't even be able to move at all. Awkwardly, he worked the blade back and forth, back and forth.

"Pull!"

And then, just as he thought he would pass out, he heard a sharp twang, like a banjo string breaking, and all the pressure, all the weight on him, instantly stopped. The cord whizzed across the snow, while his fingers still held tight to the ground. And then he heard Eddie's terrified cry, fast diminishing and swallowed in the wind. If there was a splash, it was lost in the storm.

Putting his face down, he felt the cold snow bathing his hot skin, and he simply lay there, breathing slowly, in and out, telling himself, over and over again, that he was still alive, he was still alive.

It was a long while before he had the courage, or the strength, to raise his head, look around, and see that the old woman was gone, too. He was all alone in the dark.

Chapter 40

Improvisation was the name of the game. Any epidemiologist worth his salt knew that you had to be able to turn on a dime when circumstances changed—and in the field, circumstances always did.

In a matter of less than an hour, Slater had managed to get a temporary quarantine tent rigged up inside the nave of the church, with everything from an overhead lamp to a powerful space heater, and he had put the wounded and half-delirious Lantos on a pair of IV drips; one contained a broad spectrum antibiotic to guard against the sepsis that was sure to follow from the slash of the wolf's claw, and the other a concentrated solution of Demerol that had kept her sedated enough to allow him to do what he had to do. What he really needed was an anesthetist, but when he came to the island, he hadn't planned to perform surgery on anyone still alive.

Groves and Rudy had been deployed to seal up the windows of the church to guard against any drafts or exposure, and Nika had been enlisted as head nurse. After her reaction to the work he'd had to do in the graveyard—drilling specimens from the deacon's corpse—he wasn't sure she'd be able to handle it, but to her credit, she hadn't even balked at his request. In fact, she'd looked happy for the chance to redeem herself.

"Just tell me what to do," she said, "and I'll do it."

And so she had. He'd had her suit up in everything from gloves to goggles, and now she was standing on the opposite side of the gurney, behaving as if she'd been in operating rooms all her life. When he'd needed her help to set up the IV lines, she took his instructions perfectly, and her nimble fingers did the job without hesitation. When he asked for an instrument, she instinctively seemed to know which one he meant, and when he needed her to hold a sponge, or even put her finger on a suture while he pulled the thread through the wounded flesh, she didn't blanch—or if she did, he couldn't see it behind her protective gear.

"You're doing a great job," he said, his voice muffled by his own face mask.

"Then why am I sweating so much?"

"We all do. It's why we burn these damn suits afterward." It occurred to him that she'd have made a fine country doctor—and from what he'd gathered in town, Port Orlov needed one.

His fears for Lantos, however, were rapidly mounting. She had been slipping in and out of consciousness, and though he'd tried to knock her out enough to perform the necessary surgery without causing her unbearable pain, it was a fine balance he was trying to achieve. He had to keep her unconscious and immobilized, but without depressing her respiratory function any further than necessary.

The work was more extensive than he had anticipated; the wolf, an expert at gutting its prey with a single swipe of its claws, had wreaked havoc in her abdominal cavity, and in addition to that there was the ever-present, and far worse, threat of a viral component having come into play. The autopsy chamber had been filled with bowls of blood and organs, and Lantos had sustained a large and open wound. The Spanish flu was an airborne disease when transmitted by its living hosts, but it flourished in the blood and bodily fluids of its victims. If any of the samples they had taken were viable, then Lantos could have become directly infected, and even now, as she lay on the table breathing feebly through her own face mask, she could be functioning as a veritable flu factory.

Plainly, the entire situation was becoming untenable. Lantos was going to need to be evacuated to a proper hospital, and soon—and the biological materials left exposed in the lab tent were going to have to be gathered up, with the utmost care, and safely destroyed. In their frozen state, the specimens taken *in situ* from the grave itself had been dangerous enough. But once the body had been thawed for the autopsy and the harvesting of additional tissue, there was no telling what had happened to any virus that might still have been preserved in the flesh and viscera. Most probably, it had been inert, or rendered that way by the thermal change.

But there was always the chance that, for even a short window of time, it had been alive . . . and communicable.

Lantos stirred on the table, and her hands twitched. Slater had been in such a hurry to attend to her injuries that he hadn't had time to arrange for any of the usual restraints. He nodded at Nika, and told her how to increase the Demerol drip. Their work was not yet done . . . even if he was only running on fumes and adrenaline at this point.

In fact, he wasn't sure how much longer he could maintain the intense focus he needed, or keep his hands steady enough to do the delicate repairs Lantos required. As it was, he knew that he was just doing stopgap work—enough to stop the hemorrhaging and hold things in place—until a more skilled surgeon, in a fully equipped operating room, could do it right.

But how long would that be?

He heard the doors of the church creaking open again, then Sergeant Groves's voice just outside the sealed flaps of the tent.

"Sorry to report this," Groves said, "but no luck with the Coast Guard. One chopper's grounded for repair, and the other's already on a rescue mission off Little Diomede."

"So what about sending a boat?" Slater said, his eyes still focused on his patient.

"They say the sea's so rough, they doubt they can get in close enough right now. They've got to wait the storm out."

"Which means how long?" he asked impatiently, pulling another suture through.

Lantos moaned, her head twisting on the table.

After a pause, Groves admitted, "No telling. But Rudy said the forecast's not good."

Even in the tent, Slater could hear the howling of the wind, tearing at the old timbers of the church, and he could only imagine the pounding of the sea on the rocks and shoals surrounding St. Peter's Island. Small wonder the strange Russian sect had chosen to take refuge here; it was one of the most impregnable and unapproachable spots in the world. Of all the hellholes Slater had been to—and he'd been to plenty—this one felt cursed even to him.

"Get back on the radio," he snapped, more irritated and distracted than was wise, "and tell them this can't wait. It's a life-or-death emergency."

"Frank," Nika said.

"Find out who's in charge—go as high up the chain as you can—"

"Frank, the bleeding just got worse—"

"And tell them to call Dr. Levinson at the AFIP if they need to get a top security clearance. I guarantee—"

"Frank!" Nika insisted.

And when he looked at Nika, and saw what she was bowing her head at, he could see that there was an upwelling of blood, as if from a layer of the dermis that had been insufficiently closed, seeping between the sutures. Lantos groaned, and though she should have been rendered unconscious by the drip, her hands swung loose, perhaps in involuntary contractions. Nika grabbed at one of them, and missed, and Slater said, "Let me do it—just stand back."

But Nika fumbled across the table in an attempt to snag the other hand—a breach of protocol that a trained nurse would have known not to do—and before either one of them knew how it had happened, Nika flinched and said, "Ouch," as the tip of the suturing needle pierced the palm of her glove. For a split second that seemed like an eternity, the needle stayed there, before Slater yanked it out, and looked through his visor at Nika. She was studying the tiny puncture in her glove, from which a dot of her own blood was now oozing, and then she looked up at him, her dark eyes full of disbelief . . . and questions.

Exactly as he feared were his own.

Chapter 41

Sergei was pushing a wheelbarrow back toward the Ipatiev house when he heard the sound of gunshots. For days, there had been the rumble of distant artillery, but this was small-arms fire, and much closer to home.

It sounded like a string of firecrackers.

The wheelbarrow was filled with several gas cans. Commandant Yurovsky had sent him into town with orders to siphon the fuel out of every vehicle he could find, and if anybody asked any questions, to refer them to the Kremlin. This was not the sort of duty the Bolsheviks had promised him when they came to his village and dragooned him the previous spring.

The shots were coming one at a time now, and Sergei stopped in the middle of the dark road, fear gripping at his heart. Who was doing all this shooting, in the dead of night, and why?

Pushing the wheelbarrow as fast as he could over the bumps and ruts in the dirt road, he arrived at the sharp-staked palisade surrounding the house, and when the sentry called out who was there, he said, "It's Comrade Sergei Ilyinsky. With the gasoline."

"Bring it around back."

In the courtyard, Sergei found a truck waiting, and the stench of gunpowder in the air . . . and blood. His eyes shot to the iron grille covering the basement window, but it was dark inside and he couldn't see a thing.

Yurovsky, stepping out of the house, saw the gas canisters and said, "That's all?"

"There aren't many tractors in Ekaterinburg," Sergei said, careful to keep any emotion out of his voice.

"Go upstairs and get the sheets and blankets."

Sergei mounted the back steps and found the house in commotion. Other guards were trooping up and down the stairs, their arms filled with linens, their mouths crammed with food, a couple swigging vodka from a jug. By the time he got to the room Anastasia shared with her sisters, the four cots had already been stripped bare. Books and diaries, combs and shoes, were scattered around the floor. Arkady, one of the Latvian guards who had recently been brought to the house, was stripping some curtains from the whitewashed windows.

"What's going on?" Sergei said. "Where are they?"

Arkady looked at him quizzically, and said, "In Hell, if you ask me." Then, tossing the curtains to Sergei, he said, "Take these to the basement."

His arms clutching the curtains, Sergei stumbled down the stairs, his mind refusing to accept the awful reality of what must have just happened, then across the courtyard and down to the cellar. The acrid smell of smoke and death grew stronger with every step he took, and Sergei's heart grew as heavy as a stone. At the bottom, Yurovsky, in his long coat, was holding a lantern and directing the operation.

The floor was so awash in blood that the soldiers trying to roll the bodies up in the sheets and drapery kept slipping and sliding.

"Just get them out of here!" Yurovsky was barking. "The truck's right outside."

Sergei scanned the carnage; he saw Dr. Botkin's gold eyeglasses gleaming on his bloody face, he saw Demidova with a bayonet still stuck in her chest. He saw the Tsar's worn old boots sticking out of a sheet, and his young son Alexei—one side of his face obliterated by a close gunshot to the ear—being wrapped in a tablecloth, like a shroud.

But where was Anastasia?

"Don't just stand there!" Yurovsky said, smacking him on the shoulder. "Get to work."

Sergei stepped into the morass, searching for Ana, and found her beneath the corpse of her sister Tatiana, soaked in blood, her little dog crushed beneath her. Her hair was caked with blood, her clothes were ripped to shreds, her hands were clutching something under her bodice.

Sergei felt the anger and the bile rise in his throat, and if he could have done it, he'd have killed Yurovsky and every other guard in the house on the spot. The House of Special Purpose—that's what the Ipatiev mansion had been officially called, and Sergei had always taken it to mean imprisonment.

Now he knew that it meant murder.

He laid the curtains on the floor—they were the color of cream, and imprinted with little blue seahorses—and gently rolled Ana's body onto them. He looked at her face, smeared with blood and ash and tears, then closed the ends of the curtains over her as if he were wrapping a precious gift.

"Move along," Yurovsky shouted, "all of you!"

Sergei could hear the truck engine idling in the courtyard. The Latvians were throwing the remaining bodies over their shoulders like carpets, and carting them out. Sergei picked up Anastasia in his arms, as if carrying a child to bed, and leaving the cellar he heard Yurovsky joke, "Careful not to wake her."

Sergei was numb with shock and grief, and when the guards told him to toss the body into the back of the truck with all the rest, Sergei simply climbed inside instead, and slumped against the side wall with the body between his knees.

"You always were sweet on that one," a guard cracked. "That's why the commandant sent you into town tonight." He slammed the half panel at the back of the vehicle shut. "Now you can help bury her."

He banged on the side of the truck, and the engine was put into gear. With a jolt, the truck lumbered across the courtyard, out through the palisade, and onto the Koptyaki road. The pile of corpses—Sergei counted ten others in all—gently swayed and rocked, as if it were all a single creature, at every bump and pothole in the road. The Tsar and his valet, the Tsaritsa and her maid, their daughters, the heir to the throne, the cook, the doctor . . . all tangled together in an indiscriminate mound of blood-soaked linens.

Sergei wondered where the truck was headed . . . and what he would do when he got there.

An old car, crammed with shovels, gasoline, and Latvians was jouncing along behind them.

For at least an hour, they forged through the forest on old rutted mining roads. Sergei could hear tree branches on either side scratching at the sides of the truck and the tires squelching in the mud.

And then—unless his mind was playing tricks on him—he heard something else, too.

He bent his head.

It came again.

A moan.

He pulled the cream-colored curtain away.

"Ana," he whispered, "are you alive?"

Her eyes were closed, and her face twitched like someone still caught in a nightmare.

"Ana, be still!"

Her face was wrenched in agony, her lips parted, and she started to cry out.

Sergei pressed his palm to her mouth, and said, "Ana, don't make a sound. Do you hear me? It's Sergei. Don't move."

She tried to scream again, and again he flattened his hand on her lips.

"If they know you're alive, they'll kill us both."

Her eyes opened, filled with panic, and he leaned even closer so that she could see him better. Despite all that had passed between them, in looks and words and flowers, the bounds of propriety had never been crossed. Until this night, Sergei would no sooner have dreamed of holding a grand duchess of Russia than he would have imagined himself becoming the Tsar.

Even as his heart soared—the love of his life was cradled in his arms!—Sergei's mind raced. How had she survived the slaughter? Was the blood covering her body her own—or her sister's?

And how could he ever spirit her away from this caravan of death?

The truck was going up a hill, the gears grinding, when he heard the thundering of hoofbeats and wild shouts coming through the forest. The brakes squealed, and even as the truck stopped, Yurovsky was leaping like a demon from the car behind, cursing and brandishing a long-muzzled Mauser.

Was Anastasia going to be rescued after all? Were these the White cavalry officers, loyal to the Tsar, that Ana and her family had long prayed for? Or could they be renegade Czech soldiers who abhorred the revolutionaries? Sergei didn't care, just so long as there were enough of them to overpower the Red Guards. He'd take his own chances.

"Keep still," he said to Anastasia, smoothing her befouled hair with his hand.

He could hear horses snorting, and the creak of wagon wheels.

"We were promised we'd get them!" someone was shouting. "All of them—alive!"

"Well, you're too late for that now," Yurovsky replied. "But this truck can't make it any farther. We'll need those carts to get the bodies to the Four Brothers."

Sergei knew that the four brothers referred to the stumps of four towering pine trees that had once stood where nothing but coal pits and peat bogs now lay. Was this how Yurovsky had planned to dispose of the bodies? By throwing them down the abandoned coal shafts?

"I promised my men that they'd have some fun with the duchesses," the man complained. "And I planned to have the Tsaritsa myself."

"Shut your trap, Ermakov, and do what I tell you." Yurovsky was struggling to remain in command of the rowdy horsemen; that much Sergei could tell from the strained pitch of his voice. "Unload the bodies, and the first man I see stealing anything, I'll shoot."

What would they steal, Sergei thought? The rings on their fingers?

But even as he heard a few of the men dismounting, and the Latvians clambering out of the car, he knew that this might be his only opportunity to save Ana. As soon as the back panel was dropped flat again, and he saw the faces of the peasants leering in at the bloody cargo, he stood up, teetering a little as if he were drunk, and said, "Take them away, comrades."

A few dirty hands reached in, grabbed the dangling arms and legs of the dead and dragged them out of the truck. Sheets were pulled aside, and one man called out, "I've got a duchess, but I'm damned if I know which one."

There was laughter, topped only when another man shouted, "And I've got the queen bitch herself!"

Picking up the body of Anastasia, and handling it with deliberate carelessness, Sergei stepped over the corpses of the maid and the cook and hopped down onto the ground. The road was illuminated by the headlights of the car, but the forest was thick on both sides, and as the hay carts were brought around back, Sergei carried his bundle past one wagon, and then another, and when a cry went up at the discovery of the Tsar—"Who wants to spit in the face of Nikolashka himself!" Ermakov exulted—Sergei pretended to drunkenly stumble off the rutted path and into a pile of brambles.

But no one called out after him, and no one noticed. Everyone was so intent on defiling the corpse of the Tsar that they didn't see him disappear, and hoisting the girl over his shoulder like a sack of grain—and how many times had he done that very thing in the fields of Pokrovskoe?—he trotted into the dense and pitch-black woods. Ana groaned, and all he could say was, "Hush, Ana, hush." She was heavier than he thought she would be, and her body was harder and stiffer, but in all the hubbub and confusion, the Reds might not even notice that one of the duchesses was missing until they assembled all the bodies at the Four Brothers. By then Sergei planned to be miles away, hidden in the one place he knew would provide a safe refuge for the lone survivor of the imperial family.

Chapter 42

Harley had just spent the worst night of his entire life, and he was not about to go through another one like it. He'd broken into Russell's remaining stores of beer and drifted off into sleep for half an hour here and there, but every time he did, he'd awakened again with a start, expecting to see that old lady from the cliffs, or Eddie, bruised and bloodied, cursing him out for cutting the rope.

Or that mangled guy on the autopsy table in the tent.

As far as he was concerned, St. Peter's Island was even worse than all the stories and legends he'd ever heard about it. It was one big haunted house, fit for nothing but the dead and anyone else who felt ready to join them. He needed to get off of it while there was still time.

If there was still time.

As soon as the storm abated enough to let a little daylight shine, he'd ventured out of the cave to see if the trawler *Kodiak* had been freed by the surging tides.

Freed wasn't the word. Scuttled was more like it. The boat had settled deeper into the cove, and he could see pieces of it drifting away on each icy wave. The groaning he had heard the night before was its hull being scraped on the rocks, its cabin flooding, its masts and doors and gangways being rent by the pounding surf.

As for the skiff—not that he could ever have made it back to Port Orlov in that flimsy thing, anyway—it had been dragged down by the tide and reduced to a pile of splinters and sawdust.

There was really only one option left to him—the RHI that he'd spotted down on the beach below the cemetery, where the Coast Guard must have left it for an emergency evacuation.

Well, if this wasn't an emergency, then what the hell was?

Trekking over that way again was about the last thing in the world he wanted to do—that black dude with the rifle was never far from his thoughts—but he just didn't see any way around it. He also knew that if he debated it much longer, he'd lose the few hours of daylight he had left. Earlier, he had emptied his coat pockets—vials, icon, and all—willy-nilly into his backpack, and now he threw in some Power-Bars, a bottled water, and the handgun Russell had been kind enough to leave behind. He'd have liked to take more, but he wanted to be sure he was traveling light. He wasn't feeling up to par and wouldn't have been surprised if he was running a bit of a fever. By the time he got back to his trailer, he'd probably be sporting a full-blown cold.

Walking back toward the beach and the stone steps leading down to the inflatable boat, he saw that his tracks from the day before had already been obliterated. Alaska had a way of doing that. Every sign of human life was soon wiped away by nature, and the stuff that lasted at all—like the colony—just wound up being a reminder of how empty, short, and hollow life really was. Sometimes, like right now, Harley thought it might have been a good idea to go and live some-place else, after all. He should have done it the day Charlie had moved his two crazy women into the old house.

As he approached the rear of the stockade, Harley could hear the cawing of crows and noticed that a pair of red hawks were circling lazily in the sky. If he could have avoided cutting through the colony again, he would have, but the wind on the cliffs was so strong—and his memories of the specter he'd seen there so fresh—he felt the risks were better just scuttling across the campground and out through the main gates. Despite the bitter cold, he was sweating inside his parka.

There were even more birds circling in the sky above the side of the old church, and a whole flock of them on the ground strutting and pecking around a spot close to a jagged hole in the foundation. A snowdrift had been blown up against one wall, but just as Harley crept past, the birds reluctantly took flight, and he could see that there was something lying there, mostly hidden under the crust of snow. It appeared that other animals had been burrowing into the drift, too, and he could see that the snow had a faintly pinkish cast . . . and that what he'd thought was a twig sticking up was actually the toe of a boot. He moved a little closer, and with the tips of his glove brushed some snow away. He didn't need to see anything more than the torn shreds of a propane company work shirt to know that these were the remains of Russell, and that the local critters had been heartily chowing down.

Just as the crabs had probably made the most of Eddie by now.

It wasn't that he was completely heartless—after all, he'd known these guys a long time—but it couldn't help but occur to him that whatever the diamonds in the icon were worth (and it had to be plenty), he'd now be splitting the money only two ways, instead of four. Charlie would probably claim it was all the hand of God at work.

Staying low to the ground, he hurried past the colony tents, through the main gates, and over to the side of the cliff. The mist that clung to St. Peter's Island was lying a hundred yards offshore, but on the beach below he could still see the yellow RHI, firmly tied and clamped between makeshift davits made out of driftwood logs. It was just about the first piece of luck he'd had since this whole damn nightmare had begun, he thought.

The steps that some crazy Russian must have carved into the cliff a hundred years ago were only a few inches wide at most, and zigged and zagged their way down to the waterline. Even if he hadn't been feeling peaked, the descent would have been a bitch. The wind, skirling off the Bering Strait, forced him to flatten himself against the rock and shimmy his way down, putting out one foot at a time and nudging it around until he had cleared the snow and scree—and sometimes the birds—from the lower perch, then gingerly placing his weight there. More than once, the birds came back, flitting around his head, defending their turf, but he didn't even bother to bat them away. He needed both hands to cling to the slippery rock.

The backpack, even with its contents stripped down, was more of a burden than he expected, and the weight of it kept threatening to throw him off-balance. He tried to control his breathing and not to look down any more than he had to; if he panicked, he was a goner. His arms ached from embracing the rocky walls and his knees started to quiver from the strain, but eventually he could hear the waves sloshing on the sand and pebbles, and he could feel the ocean spray blowing onto his face. When the stone steps gave out, and he felt his boots crunching on the hardscrabble beach, he collapsed in a heap, his head down, his hands splayed on either side.

Never again, he told himself, *never again was he going to get involved in something this stupid.*

Still conserving what little strength was left in his legs, he crawled, breathing heavily, across the gravel and sand. The fog had drifted in, which was going to make it that much harder to steer a course through the rocks and shoals that rimmed the shoreline. But then that figured— this island had been bad luck from start to finish, and he couldn't wait to get off it.

Slapping a hand on the firmly inflated side of the RHI, he hoisted himself up onto his knees, enough to groggily assess the craft. A waterproof and heavy-duty black tarp had been tightly sealed across the interior, but as he fumbled at the snaps and knots that kept it in place, he had the discomfiting feeling that there was something under it. Once or twice, under the rumble of the crashing waves, he thought he heard a furtive noise, the sound of something scuttling for cover. He shook his head, trying to clear his thoughts, and focused on loosening the rest of the stays. Once, he even thought he heard the crunch of a boot on the sand behind him, and whirled around groping for his gun, but all he saw was a rolling column of fog . . . and no one in it.

Eddie was gone, he reminded himself. Splattered on the rocks on the other side of the damn island.

And Russell . . . well, Russell was just that lump under the snow-drift.

He untied the last of the straps holding the tarp down, and yanked it back.

Two startled eyes were staring back at him, and before he could even register his shock, the creature flew past him, a blaze of wet brown fur and black claws.

Harley stumbled backwards, as the otter scampered up the beach, its tail swishing, before abruptly changing course, turning toward the water again and slipping silently into the icy wash.

It was all over in a matter of seconds, but it took Harley a minute or two to calm down again and get back to work.

Damn otter. He vaguely recalled some legend about otters, some native bullshit, but since they were probably bad luck—like everything else out here—he didn't try too hard to remember it. On the Vane's Holy Writ broadcasts, Charlie was always trying to prove how the Inuit stories had something to do with Jesus, but Harley didn't buy it. He thought his brother was just trying to con a few more bucks out of the locals.

With frozen fingers, he freed the clamps holding the boat to the davits, then, tugging the braided rope, dragged it down to the water.

The bright yellow boat bobbed on the surf like a rubber ducky, and it took him three tries before he could hoist himself, boots and pants dripping wet, onto its fixed seat in back, and get the motor running.

Turning the boat parallel to the shore, he took it away from some jagged rocks, and slowly out to sea. He knew that no one in his right mind would be trying this, which was precisely why he'd probably get away with it. The fog was so thick it was like churning through clam chowder, but it would dissipate once he got a little farther from the island. His plan was to run parallel to the cliffs, then due southwest to Port Orlov. But he wasn't so dumb that he'd sail it right into the harbor; no, he was going to put in at the old family wharf a few miles away, then, when everything had blown over, maybe he could strip the boat and sell it for parts.

The spray was blowing into his face and even when he wiped it away with his sleeve, he couldn't see much better—his coat, too, was sopping. And he was starting to feel truly shitty. He coughed, and he didn't like the sound of it. What he needed was a good hot meal at the Yardarm, and Angie Dobbs back in his bed. Yes, a little Angie in the night would cure whatever ailed him.

His progress was slower than he thought it should be, and he gunned the engine higher.

Although the boat was carrying so little weight that it should have been skimming along, the current was either stronger than he estimated, or the prow was weighted down somehow. The wind was howling so loudly in his ears that it seemed like he could hear voices; it would have been okay if it had been Angie telling him how good he was in bed, or Charlie—the old Charlie—telling him how to pull off an easy con.

But it wasn't, and they weren't.

It sounded more like Eddie, asking him why he'd cut the goddamned rope . . . or Russell, screaming as the wild animals had taken him apart.

Fuck Eddie. Fuck Russell. They'd taken their chances. Harley wasn't their keeper.

The boat bucked a wave, and Harley clutched the throttle tight.

Christ Almighty he was cold. He pulled the loose tarp all the way up to his waist.

And in the billowing fog that engulfed the boat, he could swear that for just one instant, he saw them both—his two accomplices—sitting toward the bow, waiting for him to ferry them back home. Deadweight, he thought, as always.

When he blinked, they were gone—Harley knew an hallucination when he was having one, and this damn island seemed to specialize in them.

But when he blinked again—oh, sweet Jesus—there they were again, looking at him like it was all his fault somehow.

Chapter 43

It was the hardest call Slater had ever had to make, but with lives hanging in the balance—Eva's for sure, and possibly Nika's, too—he called Dr. Levinson in D.C. Apparently, he had caught her at a dinner party, and until she had moved into a private study, he could hear the sounds of clinking glasses and cutlery in the background.

As succinctly as he could, he told her what was happening on the island, and with every word he uttered he could imagine the expression of mounting disbelief, and anger, on her face. She had gone to bat for him at the court-martial, she had given him this golden opportunity to redeem himself, and he had blown it sky-high. When she finally spoke, he could hear the steel in her voice.

"So you have not one, but two, compromised team members?" she said. He didn't have the heart to tell her that he might make a third.

"Yes. And I will need them to be evacuated immediately to a mainland hospital, where a strict quarantine can be established."

"Why didn't you call for it already?"

"I did, but we're having a priorities problem. It looks like the Coast Guard may need a kick in the pants from AFIP headquarters, or an assist from the Air National Guard."

"Consider it done."

He thanked her.

"Don't thank me, Frank. You know what this means, don't you?"

He could guess, but she told him, anyway.

"Once we get this straightened out, I'll want you back in Washington for a full debriefing. When we're finished with that, your civilian status with the AFIP will be considered terminated."

The same as his military status had already been withdrawn.

"I understand."

"Do you?" It was the first time real emotion cut through the icy reserve she had maintained so far. "You're the best we had, Frank, and I went out on a limb for you. And now you've cut off the damn limb, too."

When she hung up, he stood there in the communications tent for a few seconds, gathering his thoughts, watching as his entire career went up in smoke, until Sergeant Groves, covered with snow, came through the flaps. Slater quickly slipped his face mask back on, and held up a hand to keep Groves at a distance.

"The lab tent's clear?" Slater said. "No sign of the wolf?"

"Long gone," Groves replied, fitting his own mask back over his mouth and nose. "I left Rudy on watch. But there is something you've got to see."

"Is it about Eva? Is she okay?"

"No change, as far as I know."

"Nika?" He had confined her to her tent until further notice.

"No, it's none of that," Groves said. He beckoned Slater to follow him out of the tent.

Slater, who'd had no more than a couple of hours' sleep, pulled his coat and gloves on over his fresh hazmat suit and followed Groves out into the storm. There was only a feeble light in the sky, and to keep the wind from blowing him off his feet he had to cling to the ropes lining the pathway. Groves plodded across the colony grounds to the church, but detoured at the front steps to go around the side. There, he stopped beside a patch where the snow, much disturbed, had a raspberry tinge. It didn't take long for Slater to make out the mangled remains of a body and the shreds of a blue work uniform . . . or to recognize them as belonging to that guy named Russell, whom he'd first seen at the bar, then at the memorial service at the Lutheran church. He was part of Harley Vane's pack.

"How long do you think he's been here?"

Groves shrugged. "Can't be that long. We'd have seen it on the regular patrols."

Slater wondered if he'd been alone on the island, or if he'd brought Harley. Or the third musketeer, the one named Eddie something. Were the others, in fact, possibly still around?

And if they were, what were they doing here? Had they been responsible for that hole in the cemetery? Why on earth would they have been trying to dig up graves, much less now, with his own contingent there?

"Looks like the wolves got him," Groves said.

"Among other things," Slater replied, solemnly. He wasn't sure what these guys were capable of, but Nika would have a much better idea. For now, it was just another wild card to add to the rapidly accumulating stack. In the snow, he saw a soggy old book, with a torn binding, and picked it up. It looked like a ledger, in Russian.

"Dry this out, then let Kozak take a crack at it."

"Will do. And the body?"

"Bag it, under hazard wraps, and we'll send it back to Port Orlov when the chopper gets here."

"When's that?"

Slater wished he knew. Looking at the sky, he saw nothing but roiling gray clouds, giving way to banks of blacker thunderheads moving in across the strait. Whenever the helicopter arrived, it would be a bad time.

"And don't mention it to anyone else yet," Slater said. Groves nodded. On missions like these, they both knew, information was given out only on a need-to-know basis.

Going into the church, he was surprised not to see Kozak sitting on the stool outside the quarantine tent that had been set up around Lantos; he'd been assigned to guard the premises and listen for any sign that Lantos had become conscious again. The Demerol drip should have kept her quiet and sedated, but you never knew. Slater looked toward the far end of the church, where he could see a flashlight beam moving back and forth across the great heap of broken pews and tangled ironwork.

"You've abandoned your post," he said, as he approached the professor. "In wartime, you could be shot for that."

Kozak was supposed to be wearing a gauze face mask, too, part of the costume Slater required for quarantine duty, but he'd let his dangle down around his neck. Slater gestured for him to raise it again, but before he did, Kozak declared, "Do you know what this is?"

"Looks like a pile of junk to me."

"Look behind the junk," Kozak said, finally lifting the mask back into place over his neatly trimmed silver beard. "The junk has been put here to hide the screen that shielded the altar."

"There's an altar back there?"

"Yes, there has to be, and the screen is called the iconostasis. You will find it in all the Russian Orthodox churches. It protects the holy of holies, the sanctuary. In a big church, like the one I went to in Moscow when I was a boy, there were several doors through the iconostasis. Only certain monks or priests could use each one. There were many rules. But in a smaller church, one like this, there was sometimes just a single door—the door of Saint Stephen, the Protomartyr."

"The what?" Slater had never been one for religion. In his experience, it was just another reason for people to kill each other with conviction and impunity.

"Saint Stephen, the first martyr of the Christian church," Kozak said, with a touch of exasperation. "Have you never sung the song about good king Wencelas, on the feast of Stephen?" Kozak started humming the tune, but Slater was already nodding in recognition and he stopped. "Saint Stephen was put on trial by the Sanhedrin," Kozak said, resuming his explanation, "and then he was stoned to death."

"For what?"

"Preaching that Christ was divine."

There you go again, Slater thought. One more entry for his inventory of religious slaughter.

Lifting his digital camera to take a picture of the jumble, Kozak said, "I am going to write a paper about this church, I think."

"Not while you're supposed to be on duty watching Eva."

"She has been sleeping. I have listened to the monitor," Kozak assured him, before adding gravely, "but she should be in a hospital by now, yes?"

"Yes, and she will be soon. A chopper's on the way."

"Ah, so you got through to someone, after all."

"I had to call the head of the AFIP, in D.C. If she can't get them to jump, no one can."

Kozak slipped the camera back into his pocket. "I suspect she was not happy to hear this news," Kozak sympathized.

"No, she wasn't." Now that Slater was aware of it, he could see that there was indeed some sort of screen erected behind all the camouflage. He could even detect the glint of gold paint on a faded mural.

Kozak nodded, looking down. "The bureaucrats, they never understand. The situation on the ground is never the same as the situation in their plans. They think it should always be easy, the way it looks on paper."

You can say that again, Slater thought. He was trying not to dwell on the fallout from his conversation with Dr. Levinson. The rest of his life loomed before him like a great empty plain, and it was almost a relief when his thoughts were interrupted by the sound of a low, but anguished, murmuring from the quarantine tent.

"Eva's awake again," he said, as her voice crackled over the audio monitor.

"But she sounds like she is in pain."

He could increase the drip, even give her an injection, but there was only so much he could do under these conditions. And as he hurried back to help her, he heard an even worse sound.

A spasm of coughing. Harsh and wet. And flulike.

Chapter 44

The breaker of chains.

When Charlie Vane read those four words on the computer screen, he felt as if he had just broken into the vault at Fort Knox.

The silver cross was sitting on a yellow legal pad, its emeralds glinting in the buttery glow of the banker's lamp. Like a lottery winner who needed to study his lucky ticket one more time, Charlie picked it up and turned it over. The inscription was in Russian, but he had written the translation Voynovich had given him on the pad.

"To my little one. No one can break the chains of divine love that bind us. Your loving father, Grigori."

He had been reading it all wrong. Misinterpreting what it said.

But now he knew better. It was as if, with that one simple phrase, he'd just been given the key to a secret code. Now he knew the story. All his Internet research had finally paid off.

By the year 1901, Nicholas II, the reigning Romanov Tsar, had long been praying for a son. He and his wife, Alexandra, had had three daughters already, and to ensure the survival of his dynasty, Nicholas needed a male heir to be born. But on the night of June 18, the Tsaritsa gave birth to a fourth daughter, and to keep his wife from seeing his disappointment, Nicholas took a long walk to compose himself before going into the royal chamber. On that walk, he must have given himself a stern talking-to, because he resolved to make the best of it and honor the birth of this new daughter by freeing several students who had been imprisoned for rioting in Moscow and St. Petersburg the previous winter.

The name he chose for her was Anastasia, which meant the breaker of chains.

As Charlie studied the cross again, he saw how everything now fell right into place.

"The little one"—*malenkaya*—to whom it was addressed was a commonly used nickname for the mischievous young grand duchess, Anastasia. And the "loving father" was not her dad, but a priest. A father named Grigori.

As in Grigori Rasputin, the self-proclaimed holy man revered by the Romanovs and reviled by the nation.

What Charlie was holding was not only a piece of history, but an object of absolutely unimaginable value. The days of soliciting measly contributions to Vane's Holy Writ website were over forever! He could bring his message—personal liberation through total subjugation, in all things, to the holy will!—to millions of people at once. Not incidentally, he could become even richer and more famous in the process, though that, too, was no doubt part of the heavenly plan for him.

He had barely had time to savor his triumph, and imagine the bidding war that would ensue among the world's wealthiest collectors and museums, when the motion-detector lights went on outside the house, bathing the driveway in their cold white glare. Pushing his wheelchair back on the piled-up rugs, he glanced outside, and while he expected to see a moose ambling by, or maybe a couple of foxes scampering across the snow, he saw his brother Harley, looking like he was on his last legs, staggering toward the front steps.

"Rebekah!" he shouted. "Go open the front door!"

"Why?" she called back from the kitchen. "I'm baking." The smell of charred, sourdough bread had filled the house for hours.

There was a hammering on the front door, and Harley was crying, "Open up! For Christ's sake, open up!"

Charlie was maneuvering his chair toward the front hall when he heard Bathsheba skip down the stairs and eagerly say, "I'll get it! It's Harley." She had a thing for his younger brother; she'd once said that he looked like he could be one of those young vampires in her books.

But when she opened the door, Harley virtually slumped inside, slammed the door closed behind him, and threw the bolt. He leaned back against it, his eyes wild, his brown hair sticking out in icy spikes. His boots were dripping onto the carpets that covered the old, uneven floorboards, and his skin was even whiter than Bathsheba's, which was saying something.

"They won't stop!" he cried. "They won't stop!"

"Who won't stop?" Charlie said, the wheel of his chair snagging on the edge of a rug.

"Eddie and Russell!"

"What are you talking about? Are they here, too?"

"No, man—they're gone!"

Gone? Whatever he really meant by that, Charlie knew that he had some very serious trouble on his hands. Bathsheba shrank back toward the staircase. "Okay, Harley, why don't you just calm down? Come on inside and tell me what's going on. Bathsheba, go and tell your sister to bring us some of her hot tea and that bread she's been burning all afternoon."

It took Harley several seconds to pry himself away from the door, and as Charlie led him back into the meeting room where he worked, he heard the clink of what sounded like glass and metal from the backpack slung over Harley's shoulder. Was that a good sign, he wondered? It had been days since he'd heard any news from St. Peter's Island, and while he was relieved to see that Harley was alive, it was plain as could be that he was off his rocker.

"You're okay now," Charlie said. "You can just sit down and re-lax."

Harley went to the window first and stayed there, staring outside until the motion detectors finally turned off and the driveway went black. He yanked the curtains closed and whirled around in a panic as Rebekah came in carrying the tea and toast. Bathsheba peered in, half-concealed, from the doorway.

"Just put the tray down," Charlie said, "and leave us alone."

Rebekah did as she was told, but let it bang on the desktop and the tea slosh over the rims of the mugs in protest at such brusque treatment.

"That bread's not from any store," she said, as if someone had suggested otherwise, then slammed the pocket doors together behind her as she left.

"Drink this," Charlie said, handing his brother a mug. "Tastes like shit, but it's good for you."

Harley took it, his hands shaking, and slurped some of it down. He let the backpack slip onto the floor, between his feet. Then he wolfed a couple of slabs of the toast down, too, without even bothering to slather on any of the homemade jam. Charlie studied him as if he were one of the crazy people who occasionally showed up—online or in person—at his ministry. They usually claimed that there were voices in their heads, or that they were being followed. One of the local Inuit had shown up, screaming that he was being tracked, and it turned out that he was right—he had escaped from a mental ward all the way over in Dillingham and the social workers were hot on his trail.

Harley looked just as bad, but Charlie just let him sit and sip the home-brewed tea—no complaints out of him this time—until he seemed to calm down. *Just what had happened on that island? And what did he mean when he said that Eddie and Russell were gone?*

"You know, you can take off your coat and stay awhile," Charlie said.

But Harley looked like he was still too cold to take it off, and Charlie knew enough not to rush him. And it was the backpack, anyway—not the coat—that he was dying to get into.

"While you were gone, I took a little trip myself," Charlie said by way of distraction. "To Nome."

Apart from nervously rubbing his thigh, Harley didn't react in any way.

"I went to see that thief Voynovich."

Harley's eyes flicked up from the rim of the mug.

"He told me a few things about the cross. And I've done some digging on my own."

Harley was starting to focus again.

"Seems like it might be worth a helluva lot more than we thought."

Harley snorted, like none of this mattered much anymore, and Charlie took offense.

"In case you care," Charlie said, "it belonged to Anastasia, the youngest daughter of the last Tsar. And it was a gift to her from a guy named Rasputin. I figured all of that out by myself, sitting in this very room." He waited for the news to sink in. "How about that?"

"If you ask me, you should throw the fucking thing in the ocean."

That was not exactly the reaction that Charlie was expecting. A puddle was forming on the rug around his brother's boots, soaking the bottom of the backpack.

"You know what?" he said. "I don't know what you're on, or what the hell happened to you, but I'm already sick of this routine. Are you gonna tell me what's going on? Where are Eddie and Russell?"

Harley, finally, cracked a smile, but it wasn't the kind of smile that would gladden any heart. To Charlie, it made him look as demented as that guy from Dillingham.

"Eddie and Russell are dead."

"Dead?" *Holy Hell, what sort of trouble had these cretins gotten themselves into?*

"Sort of."

"What do you mean, sort of?"

"Eddie fell off a cliff, and Russell got eaten by wolves."

Charlie blew out a breath, then said, "That sounds plenty dead to me."

Harley actually chuckled. "Yeah, but I wouldn't bet on it."

Charlie, not overly endowed with patience to begin with, was now fresh out. For all he knew, Eddie and Russell were down at the Yardarm right now, just as stoned and out of it as his brother was. Who knew what they were ingesting? Eddie's mom was known for cooking up some pretty wicked shit. "Pick up that damn backpack," he said, "and give it to me."

Harley tossed the damp backpack onto Charlie's lap.

As Charlie started to root around inside, Harley said, "I'd be careful if I were you," but it was already too late. Charlie had pierced a finger, and pulling it out, stuck it in his mouth to stanch the bleeding.

"What have you got in here?" Charlie said, turning the satchel over and shaking it out on the rug. A hail of broken tubes and stoppers fell out, some of them bloody or smeared with melting flesh. Charlie recoiled at the mess. "Are you nuts?" He didn't wait for an answer. "Where'd you get all this crap?"

"The colony."

"What for?"

"Just keep shaking."

Charlie shook it again, and this time the icon fell right into his lap. The Virgin Mary, the infant Jesus . . . adorned with three sparkling diamonds. Charlie's mood changed in an instant. "Holy Mother of God."

"Damn straight."

Charlie angled his chair to catch the light from the desk lamp better, and to see the diamonds shine.

"This is from one of the graves?"

Harley nodded.

"And there's more where this came from?"

"I suppose so."

What kind of answer was that? Charlie was caught between exultation and frustration. Between the emerald cross and this icon, they had struck the mother lode, but how much more had his idiot brother left in the ground? "Then we'll have to go back."

"Not me."

God, give me strength, Charlie thought. *If it weren't for this wheel-*

chair . . . He was searching for the right tack and trying to keep his temper, when Harley bent over double, calmly vomiting the tea and toast onto the carpets.

Oh, Christ, Rebekah was going to have a fit.

But Harley smiled dreamily, unaffected, before toppling out of the chair, unconscious, and into the pool of puke and broken vials.

Chapter 45

The second Slater entered the quarantine tent, he could see that Lantos had gone from stable to critical. Her brow was bathed in sweat, her normally frizzy hair was limp and sticking to her scalp in clumps, her lips were a pale blue. Delirious, she was thrashing around in the improvised restraints that they had finally had time to fashion for her, and muttering about wolves and blood and mice.

"Eva, stop struggling," he said, trying to pin her arms more firmly to the cot. "I want to give you something for the pain."

"Hospital," she said, barely focusing on him. "I need . . . to be . . . hospital."

"I know, and you will be," he said. "We'll have you off the island very soon. I promise." But was it a promise he could keep?

Fumbling though the minimal supplies in the tent, he searched for a fresh syringe and an ampoule of morphine. In battle zones, the medics carried morphine sticks, like corncob holders, that could be jammed right into the skin, and he'd have given anything for one of them right now. But this mission hadn't been designed for that. He wasn't equipped with a field bag. For that matter, he couldn't even find an unused syringe; what he had was still down in the lab tent and autopsy chamber.

He plugged what was left of the Demerol into one of her IV drips, along with the antibiotics that were being introduced through the other, and said, "I'll be right back. You're going to make it. You're going to be fine."

Then, warning Kozak to keep watch but stay clear, he hurried out into the storm. In the wind and blowing snow, the other tents appeared as no more than green blurs, and he feared that the chopper would never even attempt a landing under such conditions. Clutching the guide ropes, he pulled himself across the colony grounds and down toward the main gates, where the lab tent stood. When he got there, he found Rudy, in his protective gear, huddled just inside the flaps, batting himself with his arms to keep warm.

"Gonna be tough on that pilot," Rudy said, indicating the storm. "I don't know how he's gonna be able to make a landing in this."

But Slater had already been considering the only alternative. "I want you to go down to the beach and get the RHI ready. We may have to launch it."

"In this?"

"Just do it."

Then he went into the lab, past the glass tanks teeming with white mice, and straight to the supply cabinet, which, despite the mayhem from the wolf attack, was still sealed and intact. Opening it, he took out several packets and pouches of the retroviral medications and antibiotics, stuffing them in the voluminous pockets of his coat and, when those were full, the hazmat suit he was wearing over it. He also grabbed some swabs, sterile bandages, and clean syringes.

What else? He was trying to think of everything, but his mind kept fleeing back to Nika. If Lantos was reeling from the effects of her physical injuries, then that was one thing. But if she was indeed sick with the flu, it was possible that Nika, too, had been infected by the puncture wound from the needle. With flu, much less a variant strain that had been frozen for over a hundred years, there was no telling how, or to whom, it would be communicable, and under what circumstances. One thing he did know was that Nika had to get off the island as soon as possible. He rued the day he had allowed her to come along on the mission. She had become far too precious to him, and that was a position no epidemiologist should ever find himself in.

The blood-streaked plastic panels of the autopsy chamber dangled like red ribbons at the other end of the lab; the sign declaring that this was the place where the dead rejoiced to help the living lay on the floor, with a bloody paw print on it. Slater could just make out the crimson outlines of the deacon's body on the table inside . . . which reminded him of something Kozak had told him. The deacon's door in the iconostasis was the one that led to the sanctuary, where whatever was most holy was kept. So this man, this desecrated corpse, had been the keeper of the colony's greatest treasures and deepest secrets.

The body should not have been left on display like that. Even for someone of a purely secular temperament like Slater, it was blatantly disrespectful, and from a medical standpoint it was dangerous. Despite the hurry he was in, he took a minute to part the drapes and go inside.

The chamber was in utter disarray, just as he had left it, but something struck him as odd: the organs that had been removed were untouched in their bowls, and the body itself bore no signs of animal savagery. He knew that many carnivores, no matter how opportunistic or hungry, could sense or smell disease in carrion prey, and he wondered if that was what had happened here. Had the wolf detected something sufficiently awry to put it off its feed?

The corpse had been so compromised that no further research work could be done on it anyway, so he picked up the tarp that had been used to transport it from the cemetery and drew it over the body like a sheet. Before covering up the head, though, he noticed that the eyes, to his surprise, had shifted their direction. He remembered them as staring straight ahead, blue-gray marbles fixed in place beneath pale blond brows. But now they were looking to the left, the lashes still damp from thawing.

An effect of the decomposition, no doubt, but unnerving, all the same.

He followed their gaze . . . to the freezer unit in the corner.

Which stood open. And empty.

Slater instantly hunched down, not believing his own eyes, and even ran a hand around the barren shelves where he had deposited the specimens taken *in situ,* in addition to some of the later specimens he and Dr. Lantos had taken during the autopsy.

All he found was a couple of crushed vials, as if someone had been in such a hurry that he had dropped them before absconding with the rest. But who? Russell? What on earth could he have wanted with them?

None of it made the slightest sense.

And then he remembered that Eva—in her shock at the entry of the wolf—had thrown the paper prayer and the diamond-studded icon in the freezer, too. And they were missing, as well.

That much, finally, did make sense.

And when Rudy burst in to say that the RHI was gone, Slater exploded. "What do you mean it's gone? Why wasn't it secured properly?"

"It was," Rudy shot back. "Somebody untied the ropes, and there's footprints in the snow!" Suddenly, everything was coming together like a terrifying thunderclap. Russell wasn't alone—his cronies Harley and Eddie must have been on the island, too.

And even now they were sailing back to Port Orlov . . . with the virus in their pockets.

Chapter 46

Anastasia awoke to the sound of screaming . . . her own.

Everything around her was black and silent and still, as if she'd been muffled in a cloak of the heaviest black mink.

Or buried in a coffin.

She screamed again, every inch of her body aching and sore, but when she threw out her arms, thankfully they did not collide with the boards of a casket and when she sat up nothing obstructed her head.

But where was she?

She heard hurried, furtive footsteps and then the sound of a door opening . . . but from the floor. Light spilled into the room from a kerosene lamp, raised through a trapdoor, and a woman's voice urged her not to scream again.

"You are safe, my child. You are safe."

A woman in a black nun's habit clambered up the last rungs of the ladder and knelt beside the pallet she was lying on. "I'm sorry," she said, "the lamp must have run out of oil." Her face seemed vaguely familiar.

And now Ana could see a rickety table, with an extinguished lantern on it, and a ceramic bowl and pitcher. The ceiling was sharply slanted, and cobwebs hung from the rafters. She was in an attic . . . an attic that smelled of warm bread and yeast and honey.

"You are at the monastery of Novo-Tikhvin. A soldier, Sergei, brought you here."

"When?" Her voice came out as a croak.

"Three days ago."

Three days ago . . . and then it all came back in a flood, the late-night awakening, the innocent march to the cellar, lining up for the photograph to be taken . . . and the guards bursting into the room instead. The reading of the death sentence. Her mind could go no further before she broke down, racked with uncontrollable sobs. The nun, her face framed by the squarish black hat and the black veils that hung down on either side of her cheeks, consoled her as best she could, all the while counseling her to remain quiet.

"My family . . ." Ana finally murmured, "my family?"

But the nun did not reply. She didn't have to. Ana knew. Just as she knew who this nun was now—her name, she recalled, was Leonida. Sister Leonida. It was she who had sometimes brought the fresh provisions to the Ipatiev house.

"The Bolsheviks are looking for you. They know that you escaped. So we have hidden you here, above the bakery."

The monastery was almost as famous for its bread and baked goods as it was for its many good works. In addition to the six churches it housed within its grounds, the monastery was also home to a diocesan school and library, a hospital, an orphanage, and workshops where the sisters—nearly a thousand of them—painted icons and embroidered ecclesiastical garments with silken threads of gold and silver. Their work had long been considered the finest in the Russian Empire.

Sister Leonida said, "You must eat something," and gathering up her skirts, carefully descended the ladder. She left the lantern beside the straw-filled mattress, and by its light Ana removed her blanket and inspected herself. She was dressed in a long white cassock—a *rason*—that the nuns and priests customarily wore under their outer robes; it went all the way to her feet and the sleeves were long and tapered to the wrist. The clothes she had worn that terrible night were gone—what could have been left of them after that fusillade?—but her corset, lined with the royal jewels, was draped across a chair. She wondered if the nuns had discovered its secret cache . . . the cache that only now, she realized, must have saved her life by deflecting the hail of bullets. Her ribs and abdomen were as sore as if she had been pummeled by a hundred fists, and there were fresh bandages on her shoulders and legs. Plucking the *rason* away from her breast, she glimpsed the emerald cross still resting against her bosom. Coarse woolen socks had been pulled on over her feet; she was reminded of Jemmy, her little spaniel, who used to sleep atop her feet at night, and another round of hot tears coursed down her cheeks.

When Sister Leonida returned, she brought a hunk of fresh brown bread and a bowl of hot lamb stew. Ana didn't want it—her throat was so constricted with grief that she could not imagine swallowing—but Leonida urged her to eat. "You owe this to yourself, to your family . . . and to God. He has spared you for a reason."

Had He? Yes, she had been spared, but to what did she truly owe that strange fate? She could recall the prophetic words of the holy man Rasputin . . . and though she wished she could forget it, she saw in her mind's eye his ghostly image arising from the smoke in the cellar that night.

Once she had eaten enough of the stew to satisfy the nun—"I'll leave the bowl here," Leonida said, "and you can finish the rest when I bring you some of the honey cake that's in the oven right now"—Ana asked after Sergei. "Do the Bolsheviks know he was the one who rescued me?"

The sister nodded. "He is in hiding, too. But I will get word to him that you are awake and recovering well."

"Can he come to me here?" Ana wasn't sure if she was asking for some unthinkable favor, or even possibly putting Sergei into some greater danger than he was already in. But she longed to see him.

"Eat," the sister said, "and rest."

Ana did not know how to interpret that reply but was afraid to push any harder. And truth be told, she was already fading back into a lethargy, retreating from everything she had already learned, needing to forget again . . . and to lose herself once more in the soothing abyss of sleep.

Chapter 47

It was with dread in his heart that Slater rushed to Nika's tent. He couldn't very well knock on the flaps, but he shouted above the wind that he was going to come in and that she should don her mask and gear.

What he saw beneath her goggles was a pair of frightened eyes. The bare lightbulb rigged overhead bobbed on its cord in the billowing tent.

"Let me see your hand," he said, and like a dog with a wounded paw she held out her palm. With his own gloves he inspected the spot where the needle had punctured the skin. The mark was still evident, but so far it wasn't inflamed or suspect in any way. A small relief, but not much more than that. The etiology and incubation period of this flu was uncertain, to say the least. "How are you feeling?"

"Scared," she admitted. Her long black hair was tied in two glistening braids that hung down over her shoulders.

"We all are," he said. "But it's going to be okay, trust me."

"How is Eva doing?"

"I've done as much as I can for her here." Indeed, he had just changed her dressings, replaced several broken sutures, and administered stronger sedation. "But she's going to be evacuated by chopper very soon. You're going, too."

"But I'm all right. If you need the space on the helicopter for—"

"I need you to help me track down Harley Vane and Eddie."

"What are you talking about?"

As quickly as he could, he explained what he had learned, including the fact that Russell's frozen corpse had been unearthed outside the church. Nika appeared incredulous.

"He was attacked by the wolves?" she said.

"No room for doubt on that score," Slater said, before going on to explain what he thought the others had been up to on the island.

"Then there's no way of knowing what they might have been exposed to?"

"No," Slater said, "there isn't. And they don't know either."

Nika, fully grasping the gravity of the situation, said, "But can they possibly have made it to shore in that boat? In these seas?"

"For argument's sake, we have to assume that they did."

"I should call the sheriff in town," she said, starting for the SAT phone, but Slater put up a hand to stop her.

"He's already been notified, and he's been told what precautions to take for himself and his men." Slater had also notified the Coast Guard, the National Guard, and the civilian authorities in the state capital of Juneau. What he needed was a tight ring to be formed around the town of Port Orlov, and a wider ring with a ten-mile perimeter to be formed around even that. Northwest Alaska, fortunately, was sparsely populated, and it wasn't exactly crisscrossed with roads and highways; most of the travel was done by boat and air, and Slater had already arranged for the harbor to be blockaded and the commercial aircraft to be grounded. When he'd encountered any resistance, he'd referred the calls to AFIP headquarters in Washington. By now, he figured, Dr. Levinson was probably planning to put him in front of a firing squad when and if he ever got back.

"Frank," Nika said, "what's going to happen to the people in Port Orlov?"

"Nothing," he replied. "We're going to stop this thing in its tracks."

"I just couldn't bear it," she said, still sounding fearful, "if what happened in 1918 happened again . . . and on my watch. I'm the mayor, I'm the tribal elder, I'm the one they trusted. I remember the stories of my people dying in their huts, the dogs feeding on their bodies for weeks."

"That won't happen," he said, holding her hands in his gloves and wishing that he could just strip off all the protective gear—his and hers—and touch her for real.

"My great-grandparents passed down the stories. They were among the few survivors."

"And God bless your ancestors, because that immunity might have been passed down to you, and others. We're going to take every precaution," he said, "just as we have to do, but we *will* contain the threat."

Unable to kiss her, or even touch the skin of her naked hand with his own, he bent his forehead to hers and rested it there. And though he was aware of how odd and even comical this scene would appear to any outside observer—a couple in hazmat suits, communing in a rickety, windblown tent—it was also the most intimate moment he had experienced in years. He closed his eyes—it felt like the first time he'd shut them in ages—and if it were not for the distant clatter of propeller blades, he might have stayed that way forever.

"Frank, do you hear that?"

He did. "Get your things together and be ready to go in five minutes!"

Outside, and wiping away the snow that stuck to his goggles, he looked up to see the blinking red lights of the Coast Guard helicopter as it skimmed over the treetops, then circled the colony grounds. Sergeant Groves lighted a ring of flares to mark the spot, and the chopper slowly descended, wobbling wildly and whipping the snow into a white froth. Slater didn't even wait for its wheels to settle before charging up to the cabin door as it slid open.

"Follow me!" he ordered, and two medics, already swaddled in blue hazmat suits, leapt out into the storm carrying a metal-reinforced stretcher. At the church, Slater kicked the crooked doors ajar and barged inside, the wind blowing a gust of snow like a little tornado all the way down the nave toward the iconostasis.

"In here," Slater said, stopping to rip open the makeshift quarantine tent.

Eva was barely conscious as he removed the IV lines, gave the medics the latest stats on her condition, and helped slide her onto the stretcher.

"Frank," she mumbled, "I'm sorry . . ."

But the rest of her words were lost beneath her mask and in the commotion of her removal.

"You've got nothing to be sorry for," he said, laying a hand on her frail shoulder.

The medics carried her carefully down the slanting steps and across the colony grounds to the landing pad. Slater saw Sergeant Groves and Rudy hauling the body bag with Russell inside it toward the cargo hatch, and as Groves undid the latches, the pilot jumped out of the cockpit to object to this unexpected and additional cargo.

Even over the howling wind, Slater could hear him shouting, "What the hell are you doing? I have no authorization for that!"

And for Slater it was suddenly as if he were back in Afghanistan, with a little girl dying from a viper bite. "I'm authorizing it," he declared, and as the medics clambered aboard with Lantos, Nika appeared, ducking into the cabin like a shot. The pilot, even under his own gauze mask, looked confused about what to do about all this, but Slater set him straight. "And now we need to take off!" At such times, it was hard to remember that he wasn't a major anymore, only a civilian epidemiologist, but he had learned that if he behaved like one, few people were prepared to question his commands. He climbed into the chopper to close any debate.

Seconds later, the props whirring, the helicopter rose into the air, buffeted this way and that as if a giant paw were batting it around; out the Plexiglas window, Slater could see Groves and Rudy, hands raised in farewell, and as he adjusted his shoulder restraints so that they weren't squashing the little ivory *bilikin* into his chest—so where was the luck the damn thing was supposed to bring?—he spotted Kozak skidding into view, with the earmuffs of his fur hat blowing straight out like wings on either side of his head, and holding his thumbs up in encouragement. It was a good team, that much he had done right. Lantos groaned as the chopper dipped, then plowed forward, its nose down, soaring just above the timbers of the stockade and the onion dome of the crooked church.

Chapter 48

Sergei had never had any trouble going to ground. You could not grow up on the steppes of Siberia and not know how to live off the land and stay out of sight; it was bred into the bones of anyone whose ancestors had ever had to flee a Mongol horde, or hide from a rampaging pack of Cossacks.

But these days it was especially tricky. After he had safely delivered Anastasia into the hands of Sister Leonida, he had hovered around the town of Ekaterinburg, where great changes were under way—particularly at the House of Special Purpose. He had watched from the shadows as all signs and vestiges of the royal family were removed and burned in a bonfire in the courtyard. He could see the Red Guards overseeing local workers as they scraped the whitewash from the windows, scrubbed the obscene graffiti from the outhouse, brought in mops and brooms and buckets to clean out the charnel house in the cellar. And he had managed to forage through the trash in town and find a soiled copy of a local broadsheet, the text of which had no doubt been approved, if not written, by Lenin himself. The headline read, DECISION OF THE PRESIDIUM OF THE DIVISIONAL COUNCIL OF DEPUTIES OF WORKMEN, PEASANTS, AND RED GUARDS OF THE URALS, and the article contained the official party declaration: "In view of the

fact that Czechoslovak bands are threatening the Red capital of the
Urals, Ekaterinburg; that the crowned executioner may escape from
the tribunal of the people (a White Guard plot to carry off the whole
imperial family has just been discovered), the Presidium of the Divisional Committee in pursuance of the will of the people has decided
that the ex-Tsar Nicholas Romanov, guilty before the people of innu-
merable bloody crimes, shall be shot.

"The decision was carried into execution on the night of July 16–17.
Romanov's family has been transferred from Ekaterinburg to a place
of greater safety."

A place of greater safety, he scoffed, crumpling the sheet in his
hands. The bottom of a coal pit at a desolate spot called the Four
Brothers.

But the paper was right about one thing—the Czechs and White
Guards were indeed infiltrating, and overrunning, the area. Eight days
after the massacre, Yurovsky and his Latvian comrades had had to
make a run for it, and now that most of them were gone, Sergei had
risked returning to Novo-Tikhvin late that same night.

"She is much better," Sister Leonida said, ushering him through a
back gate, "though, as you would expect, she is sorely troubled."

"Can she be moved?"

"Why move her? She is safe here, lost among the many sisters."

But Sergei knew better than that; he knew that the tides were always turning in war and that Ekaterinburg was destined to fall back
into Red hands eventually. When it did, the monastery itself would
probably be destroyed; Lenin had no love for religion.

Furthermore, for all he knew, Commandant Yurovsky—no fool—
had figured out that he'd been cheated, that the youngest duchess
might still be alive somewhere. No, there was only one place on earth
where she would be truly secure, and Sergei was determined to take
her there.

The nun led him into the bakery, unoccupied now but still warm
and aromatic from the day's baking, and silently pointed to a trapdoor
in the ceiling. Then she discreetly left him to his own devices. Stepping atop a barrel of flour, he pulled the door down cautiously, un-

folded its steps, and after climbing to the top saw Anastasia sitting at a small table in the corner of the attic, writing in a journal by the light of a kerosene lamp. Dressed in a black cassock with elaborate silver embroidery, and humming some melancholy tune under her breath, she didn't hear him, but continued to scrawl across the pages of the notebook, her head down, her light brown curls grazing her shoulders. Despite everything that they had been through together, he was still shy—a rural farm boy, who felt himself nothing but elbows and knees and cowlicks when he was in her company.

But if it ever came to it, he would risk his life again to save her.

"Ana," he said, and her head came up slightly, as if she had heard a ghost in the rafters. "Ana."

And then she turned from the table, her gray eyes, once so filled with mischief and joy, now brimming with an ineffable sadness. She was not yet eighteen, but her expression betrayed the grief and fear of someone who had seen horrors no one should see and lived through nightmares no one should ever have had to endure. Her cheeks, once plump and rosy, were drawn and hollow, and her lips were thin and downcast.

"I prayed you would come back." Even her voice was subdued, burdened.

Sergei closed the trapdoor behind him and went to kneel beside her at the table. She stroked his head as if she were the older woman—and here he was, twenty, just last month—but when he looked up at her, he could see how pleased she was to see him. "I was so afraid I would never be able to thank you."

The back of her hand brushed the side of his face, and his skin tingled at her touch.

"Sister Leonida tells me you are recovering well."

"They have been very good to me here."

On the table he saw that there was a bud vase with several blue cornflowers in it, and he smiled. "Remember the day you gave me one of those?" He did not tell her that he had it still.

Ana smiled, too, and for several minutes they reminisced about only insignificant things—the flowers in the summer fields as the train had made its way into Siberia, the way Jemmy had loved to jump off the caboose and run in circles whenever they had stopped for coal, Dr. Botkin's passion for chess (and how frustrated he was whenever young Alexei had brought him to a draw). Like so many of the Russian peasants, Sergei had been filled with a native reverence for the Tsar and his family—a reverence that the Reds had worked tirelessly to undermine and destroy. The bloody toll of the war had sealed the Bolsheviks' argument.

But once Sergei had been exposed to the family itself, once he had seen the heir to the throne writhing in pain from a minor injury, or the Tsaritsa ceaselessly fretting over him, once he had heard the laughter of the four grand duchesses and watched the melancholy Tsar pace the length of the palisade at the Ipatiev house, he had changed his mind again. Now they were not just iconic figures to him, the bloody puppets that Lenin had made them out to be, but real people . . . people that the *starets* of his village, at one time the most famous man in all of Russia, had befriended.

Was Sergei going to listen to a prophet from his own town—a man of God, touched with holy fire—or Lenin, an exiled politician that the Germans had smuggled back into the country in a secret train, purely to foment rebellion?

"How have you stayed safe?" Anastasia asked, and Sergei told her how and where he had been hiding out in the surrounding countryside. In July, it could be done; later in the year, it would not have been so easy.

"And does the world know . . ." she said, faltering, "about what happened to my family?"

He told her what he'd read in the broadsheet, including its bold lie about the safety of the family, and a flush of fury rose in her cheeks.

"Murderers!" she exclaimed. "And cowards, too—afraid to admit to their crimes!"

Sergei wondered if that was what she had been writing about in her journal.

"I will tell the world! I will shout it from the rooftops, and I will see those murderers hang!"

Sergei was hushing her when he heard what sounded like a broomstick banging on the bottom of the trapdoor. Sister Leonida must have been keeping guard in the kitchen down below.

"Someday," he said, trying to calm her, "you will do that, and I will help you. But that day is still far off. You have enemies, and you have already seen what they can do. Now is not the time for that, Ana."

Breathing hard, she subsided. "What is it the time for then? Hiding in this attic like a little mouse?"

"No, not that, either." This was as good an opportunity as he was likely to get to broach the subject he had been meaning to introduce. "Now is the time to leave, with me, for the place Father Grigori himself prepared as a refuge. It was part of the vision he had before his death."

Ana remembered well many of Rasputin's predictions . . . all of which had so far come true—even, to her sorrow, the most dire.

"It is a colony on an island, and many of the faithful are already there. I remember the day they left Pokrovskoe, led by the Deacon Stefan. You won't be safe until you are out of the country and hidden in a place where no one can find you."

She did not appear persuaded, but she was still listening. "Where is this secret place?"

"A long way east of here, across the steppes."

"And how do you propose we get there?"

Sergei had spent many hours mapping it out in his head, figuring out where they could board, under assumed names, the recently completed Trans-Siberian Railway, and how far they could take it eastward. When it detoured to the south, they would have to disembark and find a way to continue northward. At some point, they would have to find a pilot, with a plane, willing to take them across the Bering Strait. The right price, he had learned, made anything possible, and payment was the one thing he knew would not be an obstacle. Even as he had carried Ana's limp body through the woods, he had glimpsed the cache of precious jewels sewn into her corset. A bauble or two from that tattered lining and he was confident that he could secure whatever transportation they might need. But instead of outlining the plan in any detail for her now—there would be many weeks to do that—he simply gestured at the emerald cross around her neck and said, "I have read the inscription on the back."

Anastasia blushed, as if he'd caught her stepping out of the bath.

"His blessing has protected you so far," Sergei said. "Why would it end now?"

Chapter 49

The police siren was coming closer, and Charlie just had time to close the doors to his meeting room—where Harley was laid out cold on the couch—before a pair of headlights swept his front windows and he heard tires crunching on the ice and gravel.

Rebekah, still mad as a hen about Harley's throwing up on the rug, stormed toward the door, but Charlie wheeled into the foyer, cutting her off and ordering her back into the kitchen. "And tell your sister to stay there, too!"

Rebekah said, "What? I can't answer my own door now?"

"No, and it's not your damn door anyway. It's mine."

There was the sound of boots stamping off snow on the porch.

"Now scat," he whispered, "and not a word to anyone about Harley."

The knocking came a second later—loud and hard—and Charlie heard the sheriff's voice saying, "Open up, Charlie! It's Ray Blaine."

Charlie took his time about undoing the locks, making sure Rebekah was out of sight, before opening the door. The police cruiser was parked in the drive, the crossbar on its roof flashing blue, but more surprising than that was the gauze face mask covering the sheriff's mouth and nose, the rubber gloves on his hands, and the fact that he stepped back a few feet.

"Hey, Ray," Charlie said. "What brings you out on a night like this?"

"You seen Harley?"

"No. Why? Please don't tell me he's gotten into some trouble again," Charlie said, shaking his head like a parent whose child was forever caught pulling pranks.

"How about Eddie Pavlik?"

"Nope, him neither. Say, what's with the mask? You sick, or is it Halloween already?"

"Don't you be lying to me, Charlie," Ray said, craning his neck to get a look inside. "If you see either one of them, you call me, you got that? And if I were you, I wouldn't let 'em get too close."

"What the hell are you talking about?" Charlie said, just as the walkie-talkie went off on the sheriff's belt.

Ray answered the call and, turning a few feet down the porch, said, "Yes, sir, I'm there now." He listened, then said, "We're setting up the roadblocks just as fast as we can."

Roadblocks?

The sheriff shut it off, brushed the snow from his shoulders, and said, "Don't plan on going anywhere tonight."

"Are you telling me I'm under arrest?" Charlie said, feigning more indignation than he felt. "What for?"

"I'm telling you the roads are closed."

And that was all Charlie needed to hear. As soon as the sheriff had climbed back into his patrol car, Charlie did a wheelie and shouted to Rebekah to pack some food and coffee. "And none of that decaf chicory shit! Make it the real stuff we serve on meeting nights."

Then he threw open the pocket doors and hollered at Harley to wake up. "We're leaving!"

Harley mumbled something but didn't move until Charlie poked his arm and repeated himself.

"Man, I was so fast asleep," Harley said. "Why're we leaving?"

"Maybe that's something that *you* can tell *me*, while we drive."

Although Charlie might now be a man of God, he'd been a man of the world for a whole lot longer than that, and at times like this he reverted to form. He knew that if the law came calling, and they were setting up roadblocks and looking high and low for Harley, it must be serious. Even if it was just about those damned jewels— the emerald cross and that icon with the diamonds in it—it was better to get to Voynovich's place on the double, fence them for whatever he could get, then hole up in the ice-fishing cabin for a while . . . or at least until he could figure out just what kind of shit was going down.

Harley was pulling on his wet boots and complaining about some pain in his leg, but Charlie didn't want to hear it.

"Go get in the van," he said, as he stuck the cross and icon in his pockets. In the kitchen, he grabbed the provisions that Rebekah had stuffed in a plastic sack, then wheeled out the back door and onto the ramp to the garage.

Bathsheba, lingering in the doorway, timidly asked if Harley was okay. "He's not in trouble, is he?"

Charlie had to laugh. "When isn't he?" he said, without even looking back.

As he climbed into the driver's seat and adjusted the hand controls, he got a strong whiff of his brother and wished to hell he'd made him shower first. He looked as bad as he smelled—his eyes with a mad gleam, his skin kind of sweaty. Scratching his thigh. What the hell did someone even as dumb as Bathsheba see in him?

Charlie backed the van down the sloping, icy drive, all the while plotting his route. He'd have to avoid the one and only main road that connected Port Orlov to civilization—if you could call Nome civilization—since the sheriff would be patrolling the local stretch, and Charlie didn't know exactly where this checkpoint would be set up. He'd have to get around it, but once he'd managed that, he'd probably have clear sailing the rest of the way.

At the first turn, he steered the old Ford van across a field, through a couple of rusty barbed-wire fences, and onto an old logging road.

The van bounced up and down on the rutted track and Harley said, "Why'd you do that? You're gonna break an axle."

"I'll break it over your head if you don't tell me why you've got every cop in Alaska out looking for you."

"They are?"

"Don't bullshit me, Harley—did you kill Eddie? Or Russell?"

"Of course not, I told you, Eddie fell off a cliff, and Russell—"

"—got eaten by wolves. Yeah, yeah. I know what you told me, but I also know nobody ever went to this much trouble just to catch a thief." Glancing away from the narrow dirt track for a second, he took in Harley's disheveled appearance and said, "What's wrong with you, anyway? Why's the sheriff wearing a mask?"

"What mask?" Harley said, scratching at his thigh again.

"And what the fuck is wrong with your leg?"

"I got cut, on all that crap Eddie stuck in my pocket. A lot of it broke."

Charlie'd been cut, too, when he'd poked around in Harley's backpack. "Show me your leg."

"What?" Harley protested. "I'm not gonna drop my pants for you."

Charlie stuck out one hand and grabbed his brother by the throat. "Show . . . me . . . your . . . leg." Ever since the accident, Charlie's arms had only gotten that much stronger, but he still needed both hands to steer the van and manipulate the levers. He had to let go, as Harley unbuckled the seat belt and worked his jeans down to his knees. Charlie stopped the van, flicked on the cabin light, and saw a small cut, maybe an inch or two long, on Harley's pale skin. It wasn't much in itself, but radiating from the wound were raised, ropy lines, like red licorice strips.

He remembered the sheriff warning him not to let his brother get too close. "How long have those lines been there?"

"I don't know," Harley said, as if they really weren't his problem. "They look longer now." Suddenly doubling over, Harley coughed and a droplet of blood splatted on the dashboard. "Sorry about that," he mumbled, wiping it off with the sleeve of his coat. "I know how you are about this car."

"How long has *that* been happening?"

"Maybe a few hours. I think I got sick sailing that damn boat over here." He pulled his pants back up and buckled the belt. "I oughta get a medal just for being able to do it."

Something was going on here—something bad—but Charlie didn't know what. And sitting in the woods wasn't going to get him anywhere. Harley needed a doctor, and if anybody would know of a doctor who could keep his mouth shut—for the right price—it was Voynovich. Charlie put the van into gear, and jounced along the logging trail, the wind battering the chassis and snow piling up on the windshield, until he reached the top of a barren crest, where he doused his lights and stopped. Down below on the road, he could see a half dozen guys in National Guard fatigues, setting up highway flares and laying a spike strip across the two lanes.

"Is all that for us?" Harley asked, with a hint of pride.

Charlie angled the van down the other side of the hill and bumped along until he was sure he was well past the roadblock. He'd have continued on through the trees and brush, but he knew there was a series of ravines and gullies coming up, and not even a Humvee could have made it much farther. Besides, while he was heading due southeast, the authorities would still be looking for him northwest of his true location.

With both hands furiously working the gears and gas and brake levers, he maneuvered the van down a long, slick gradient, once or twice nearly losing control.

"You want me to drive?" Harley asked.

"Like you'd know how."

"I know how. Who drove you back from Dillingham the time you got so shit-faced you couldn't stand up?"

"In case you forgot, I can't ever stand up."

"Well, if you could have."

Charlie guided the car along a long drainage ditch, then up an embankment and onto the asphalt. For the first time in over an hour, all the tires were on the same level. But considering the fact that an allpoints bulletin was out for Harley, maybe it would be best, he thought, if his brother was just a little less visible to some good citizen with a CB radio.

"Get in the back," he said, "and use the blanket to cover yourself up."

"Nobody's gonna be out in this shit," Harley complained. "I can just duck down if I have to."

"Are you gonna argue every single thing with me?"

Grumbling, Harley crawled over the front seat, his muddy boots kicking Charlie's Bible CDs all over the floor. Rummaging around among the emergency supplies that every driver in Alaska knew to carry—extra gas cans, flares, flashlights, batteries, a spare tire, lug wrench, some beef jerky, bottled water, mosquito repellent, sleeping bag—Harley pulled out a ratty blanket and drew it around his shoulders.

Charlie checked him out in the rearview mirror, huddled behind the driver's seat, and didn't like what he saw. *Was he shivering?*

"Now lie down and try to get some sleep," he said.

For once, Harley did as he was told.

Driving on into the night, Charlie turned the radio to the local weather station and heard that the storm was only going to get worse. Welcome to Alaska. He pushed the accelerator lever forward, locking in the cruise control at a steady forty-five—any faster than that and he'd spin out for sure—and focused on the road. His headlights illuminated only a narrow slice right down the middle, but he could sense, all around him, the low frozen hills pressing in on him—lonely and empty and dark. A darkness, as Exodus and the Reverend Abercrombie had so aptly put it, that could be felt.

Chapter 50

As the helicopter swept in over the harbor of Port Orlov, Slater could see the Coast Guard vessels bobbing offshore, their spotlights sweeping back and forth across the docks, making sure that nothing came in or went out. Not that it was likely on a night like this. The town itself was largely dark, the snowy streets scoured by the punishing wind.

Dr. Lantos was barely clinging to life, her face beneath the oxygen mask a deep purple, and in Slater's mind there could no longer be any question about what was wrong. She had a hacking cough, mounting pulmonary problems, and a high fever.

She had come down with the flu.

Which meant it was possible that Nika, pierced by the needle, might have become infected, too. But it wasn't certain, there were still too many questions. Was it transmissible that way? Had the needle been infected, and more to the point, had it been infected before the puncture wound occurred? Slater clung to the possibility that it had not, even as he tended to Lantos. The last time he had found himself in a position like this, administering to an endangered patient in the bay of a helicopter, the outcome had been bad indeed, but right now, he had to put those fears, and those terrible memories from Afghanistan, aside. This time, he lectured himself, the patient *would* survive; this time she would get the care she needed before it was too late; this time he would get full cooperation instead of delays and impediments.

As the chopper descended, it skimmed the tops of the evergreen trees, and made for the bright white lights of the hockey rink. It had no sooner settled on the center of the ice, its rotors still winding to a halt, than a refueling truck rumbled toward it. The nearest biohazard-containment facility was hundreds of miles away in the state capital. "Eva," Slater said, laying a hand on her shoulder, "I'll see you in Juneau."

But she did not reply, or show any sign of even having heard him.

The bay doors were thrown open by a medical officer in full hazmat ensemble, and Slater leapt out. He held up a hand to help Nika to disembark but she was already jumping out on her own.

She called out "Ray!" to a man wearing a police parka and a sheriff's badge a few yards away, but her face mask made it impossible to be heard. Pulling it away for a second, she called out again, "Ray! Did you find them?"

Standing on the ice with legs spread wide apart to keep his balance, he called back, "Not yet." As instructed, he was wearing his own mask and gloves, too. "I went out to the Vane house, but Charlie said they weren't there."

"We both know that Charlie Vane couldn't tell the truth if he tried."

"I hear ya, Mayor. But I haven't got a warrant to search the place, and nobody's seen Harley, or Eddie for that matter, for the past few days." Gesturing at the oil truck deployed from the company that employed Russell, he said, "And Russell hasn't shown up for his job, either."

"He won't be," Nika said, soberly. "He's dead."

"What did you say?"

She pointed to the cargo bay, where two Coast Guardsmen, also suited up, were removing the body bag.

"He was found on the island. The wolves got him."

The sheriff, even from half a dozen yards away, was plainly pole-axed.

"Keep him on ice, and keep the bag sealed," Slater interjected, before turning back to Nika and saying, in a low voice, "Maybe we should take that drive now."

"Sure," she said, knowing full well what he meant. Taking care not to slip on the ice, and under the puzzled eye of the sheriff and his deputy, Nika led Slater over to the municipal garage at one end of the rink; the last time she'd been in here she'd been parking the Zamboni. Now she went right past it, along with the snowplows and the garbage truck, and stopped beside Port Orlov's one and only all-terrain ambulance.

"Get in," she said, sliding into the driver's seat, as he raced around to the passenger side. "Where to first?"

"Harley's place."

"Buckle up," she replied, rolling down her window and putting the car into gear.

As she pulled out of the garage, the sheriff scooted in front of the headlights, holding up his hands. "Hey, hang on, where you going with that?" he shouted, holding the mask away from his mouth. "Nobody's supposed to be going anywhere tonight—those are orders."

"The mayor is exempt," Nika called out, swerving around him and heading past the corner of the community center. For a second, the deputy held up his shotgun, as if waiting for instructions to shoot, but the sheriff just stood there, hands on his ample hips, unsure whose authority won out in a situation like this.

Front Street was deserted, the few fishing-gear shops and the grocery closed up tight. Even the Yardarm was dark. The old totem pole, teetering to one side, loomed ahead. Slater looked at its grinning otters and snarling wolves with a new understanding. There was nothing like a trip to St. Peter's Island to broaden your horizons.

With a deafening roar, the chopper, fully fueled again, soared over their heads, red lights blinking, as it headed east . . . carrying its precious, and endangered, cargo.

"Will she make it?" Nika asked.

And this time Slater didn't know how to reply; he had thoroughly briefed the chief medical officer on board, and Dr. Levinson had prepared the team in Juneau. But there was no knowing. "I hope so," he finally said.

In the meantime, all he could do was keep a close watch on Nika.

Turning the ambulance into the driveway between a gun shop and a lumberyard, she said, "Harley lives in that trailer out back." A violet glow could be seen between the tangled slats of the window blind. "He's probably feeding his snake."

Climbing out of the ambulance, she bounded up the steps to the door, banged loudly with the flat of her hand, then leaned over toward the window and peered inside. Slater, standing with one foot in the car and the other out, pulled the mask away from his mouth and took this chance to gulp the fresh night air. The thermals and hazmat suit he was wearing were plenty warm for the car—too warm, in fact—but even after a minute or two outside, the Alaskan cold could start to penetrate them. When Nika turned around, she was shaking her head.

"Eddie's place next?" he asked.

"Eddie's mom's a meth head. Nobody hangs out there, not even Eddie."

"And you say that this Charlie Vane is a liar."

"True enough," she said, getting back behind the wheel, "but I never said he was a good one."

Backing up onto the empty street, she took a right at the edge of the lumberyard and headed down a dark, bumpy track no longer lined with any stores or commercial establishments. This one was just a back road dotted with an occasional shack, slapped together out of weathered planks and tar paper, or a mobile home parked up the hillside. Old wooden meat racks leaned between dilapidated sheds and piles of firewood. On the way, Nika elaborated on Charlie and his church of the Holy Writ.

"And you say he's actually got followers?"

Nika shrugged. "Online, I guess you can find all types. Charlie did even better, though. He managed to convince those two women you saw at the memorial service—Rebekah and Bathsheba—to come and run his household for him."

She tapped the brakes as a large, black object lumbered across the road. As the moose languidly turned its head, the headlights made its antlers and eyes shine. For a creature of such size, the legs looked too spindly and the knobby knees downright fragile.

"He needed them," Nika said, picking up speed again once the moose had moseyed down an embankment, "since his accident."

"What exactly happened?"

Nika reiterated enough of the family history—sunken crab boats, a hundred petty-theft charges, the tragic but harebrained attempt to run the rapids at Heron River—to give him a renewed sense of who he might be dealing with. "But he still gets around pretty well—he's got his wheelchair, and a four-wheel-drive van that's been totally retrofitted with hand controls and an eight-cylinder engine. The only thing that surprises me is that he hasn't cracked it up yet."

The ambulance bucked as it hit a series of potholes, and she gripped the wheel with her latex gloves more tightly. "The Vane family," she summed up, "has an uncanny talent for destruction."

Slater, staring off into the inky blackness, wondered just how deep that talent ran. Even if he found Harley, would he be able to reason with him? If he still had the vials from the freezer in the lab, not to mention the scroll and the icon, would Slater be able to explain to him the mortal danger in which he had placed himself as a result? Would he be able to convince him that no further charges would be leveled against him—that his very identity would be concealed—if he would just relinquish this lethal booty? Slater was well aware of the catastrophe this entire mission had become, but if he could simply contain the danger before it went any farther, it might provide a decent grace note to end his public career on. He could still hear his ex-wife's voice in his head, all those times she had tried to talk him into a nice, quiet, suburban practice, treating allergies and scraped knees, but the idea was still anathema. He wanted his work to matter in the world, to feel that he was doing something valuable and needed and worthwhile.

For a long stretch now, there had been no signs of habitation at all, just a lonely road that had gradually wound its way back down toward the jagged coastline. Snow and sleet, blown all the way from Siberia and across the Bering Sea, slashed against the windows. It was hard to imagine the zeal that must have driven that tiny Russian sect, over a hundred years before, to make that same journey across this icy strait and settle on a forbidding bit of foreign land, a place they dared to rename after their patron saint, St. Peter.

Even more astonishing was the fact that their long-forgotten journey, which had ended in their own annihilation, should now pose such a threat to the world beyond this wilderness.

"It's just around the next bend," Nika said, slowing the ambulance. "You can't miss the lighted cross that Charlie stuck up on his roof."

Slater recalled seeing the cross when he had first flown over the town. But as the headlights swept the sparse brush along the ocean-front, his eyes were riveted on a ramshackle wharf, instead. Lashed to a concrete piling, a small vessel bobbed in the icy water.

It was the RHI.

"Harley's here," he declared. "That's the boat from the island!"

Nika nodded and turned the ambulance up a narrow drive, with snowdrifts piled high on either side, stopping beside a flight of sagging stairs. The illuminated cross beamed beside the chimney stack. There were lights on in the house, and a detached garage that looked old enough to have been originally built as a stable.

"Let me do the talking," Nika said. "They may be crazy, but I know how to handle them."

While Nika went up the stairs, Slater took a flashlight from the glove compartment and sidled around to the garage. As he dragged a rotting log over toward a window mounted high on the wall, he heard Nika pounding on the front door of the house. The booties of his hazmat suit were wet, and he had to work hard to maintain his balance while pointing the flashlight beam through the grimy, spider-webbed glass. Inside, he could make out a stack of used tires, a pyramid of rusty paint cans, and a snowmobile.

But there was no sign of a van, retrofitted or otherwise.

"Step on down," he heard from a few feet behind him, "or else," and when he turned his head, he saw Rebekah, in a long, ratty fur coat, aiming a shotgun at him. Judging from the look on her scrawny face, it was not an idle threat.

He stepped off the log, holding his palms out to show he meant no harm.

"We're looking for Harley Vane," he said, his voice muffled by his mask, "that's all."

"I could shoot you dead," she said, "right on this spot, and I'd be within my rights."

"We just need to talk to him," he said, in as reasonable a tone as he could muster.

"Get going," she said, indicating with the end of the gun that he should walk around to the front steps and go on up them. He could feel the rifle trained on him the whole way. In the entry hall, he found Nika with her own hands in the air, and Bathsheba shakily aiming a pistol in her general direction.

"I thought you said they'd listen to you," Slater said, and Nika shrugged.

"They tell me Harley's not here," she said.

"Go on into the meeting room," Rebekah ordered, and then Bathsheba stood to one side. Beyond her, Slater saw a big room with rugs all over the floor and some folding chairs stacked beside a gun cabinet, which was standing wide open.

Once Slater and Nika had complied, the two sisters seemed at a loss as to what to do next. Bathsheba had forgotten even to keep her pistol raised, and Rebekah kept moving the muzzle of her own double-barreled shotgun from one to the other.

"Charlie's not home, either?" Nika asked.

"Go get some rope," Rebekah said to her sister.

"How much?"

"As much as you can find!"

Slater was quickly assessing this place they called the meeting room; to him, it appeared to serve as more of an office. There was a massive old slab of a desk, with papers and printouts spilling out of wire bins, and two, big-screen computer monitors. One was showing the screen saver—a towering cross, with a white wolf at its base, and the title Vane's Holy Writ. But the images on the other one were a lot more intriguing.

When Bathsheba left to get the rope, Slater inched closer and saw an array of Russian icons, most of them featuring the Virgin Mary in a red veil, holding the Christ child in her lap. The headline read: FROM THE COLLECTION OF THE HERMITAGE MUSEUM, ST. PETERSBURG, RUSSIA. One of them was the spitting image of the icon they'd found in the deacon's grave.

If he'd had a shred of doubt about Harley's complicity in the missing icon—or where he had just been—it was gone now.

As was any doubt about the sisters' plans; they were going to hold him hostage there, along with Nika, as long as it took for the Vane boys to complete their getaway in the missing van.

"Where did they go?" he asked, noting, for the first time, a wet spot on the rug and the faint smell of vomit.

Rebekah's grip on the shotgun tightened.

"You need to know some things," he said, sternly. "My name is Dr. Frank Slater, and I am asking you, as a representative of the Armed Forces Institute of Pathology, in Washington, D.C., to put the gun down and answer my questions."

Rebekah was listening, but the gun didn't budge.

"If you don't cooperate—if you don't tell me, right now, where Harley and his brother have gone—you will face local, state, and federal charges. You *will* be brought to trial, I can guarantee you that, and you, and your sister, will both be sentenced to serious prison time." He stared straight back into her pallid face. "This is your last chance to cooperate."

"Town," she finally blurted out. "They went to town."

"That's a lie," Nika said. "We'd have passed them on our way here."

Bathsheba bustled back into the room, trailing a length of rope on the carpet behind her.

"Although they don't know it," Slater said, "Harley and your husband are in great danger."

"No more than you are," she said, twitching the gun. "And what's with those masks and rubber gloves? You look like a pair of burglars to me. That's what I'll say when they ask me why I had to shoot you."

"They have to be heading toward Nome," Nika said to Slater, as if they were alone.

"Then that's where we'll be going," Slater said, ignoring Bathsheba, who stood by, fiddling with the rope, and Rebekah, still clenching the shotgun but plainly wondering what to do next. "Come on."

He calmly, but with cool deliberation, tipped the rifle barrel to one side as Nika scurried out of the room, and then, holding his breath, he followed her out to the ambulance. They both jumped in, and as Nika threw the vehicle into reverse to back down the driveway, she said appreciatively, "Next time somebody needs a hostage negotiator, I'll know who to call."

"Just drive."

But they were no more than halfway down the hill when Bathsheba, waving the rope like a cowboy, ran behind them, pressing her hands to the back bumper.

"Leave Harley alone!" she was shouting. "He didn't do anything!"

Nika hit the brakes, but the ambulance kept skidding down the slope, pushing Bathsheba behind it.

"Leave him alone!"

Nika, swearing, pumped the brakes again, but the driveway was icy and the vehicle fishtailed. There was an alarming thump, and Bathsheba was sent flying into a snowdrift.

"Oh, no!" Nika said, pounding the wheel in frustration and finally bringing the ambulance to a complete halt.

Frank had unbuckled his belt and was reaching for the door handle when Rebekah came flying down the front steps, screaming like a banshee at the sight of her sister in the snowbank. To Slater's shock, she lifted the shotgun and without hesitation fired a round straight at the vehicle.

As the right headlight exploded in a shower of white sparks and shattered glass, Slater reached across the seat and dragged Nika down under him.

The second shot crashed through the windshield and dented the roof above their heads. A hole the size of a fist had been punched through the glass, but the rest of the windshield, crazed with a thousand fissures, held together.

Slater heard the chambering of two new rounds, but he wasn't about to wait for Rebekah to improve her aim. Throwing open the side door, he rolled out onto the snow. A tuft of dirt and ice exploded behind him as he dodged behind a tree. He heard the crunching of the snow under Rebekah's feet as she ran after him, and when he glanced around the trunk, another shotgun blast tore a big chunk of bark loose, throwing chips and splinters into his face.

But that meant both barrels were empty again, and he had a few seconds at most before she could reload.

Wiping his eyes clean, he bolted out from behind the tree. She had just slapped in a fresh round when he leapt for her. But his booties slipped, and all he could do was bat the barrel away in time for the shot to rip through the treetops and send a flock of birds screeching into the night.

She grunted in anger, and he groped for the gun. She tried to swing it away, but he held on, and with a violent wrench managed to yank it out of her hands. With her fingers extended like claws, she let out a bloodcurdling scream and sprang at his face, and he had no choice but to jerk the stock of the rifle up under her chin. Her jaws smacked shut like a bear trap, her eyes rolled back in her head, and she was out cold by the time she hit the ground.

When the din of the rifle blast had at last stopped echoing in his head, Slater heard Nika over by the snowbank, crying for help.

Chapter 51

The lights flickered and dimmed as an Arctic blast pummeled the walls of the mess tent, and for a few seconds Professor Kozak thought his computer was about to crash. But the generators kept humming and, despite the muffled roar of the wind, the structure held firm. He poured himself another shot of vodka.

It was only a few hours since the helicopter had left with Slater and Nika aboard, but already the colony felt increasingly forlorn and abandoned. Dr. Lantos was gone, and though he hoped for a miracle, he did not think that one would be forthcoming. He didn't see how she could have possibly survived her injuries, or the protracted evacuation to Juneau. Besides himself, only Sergeant Groves and Rudy remained, and they were out on patrol, making sure the island had no other intruders, and that nothing further occurred to disturb the eviscerated corpse of the deacon. Presumably, the poor man was still lying on the slab in the autopsy chamber.

The professor did not envy Frank Slater. This was not a mission report he would ever want to write. Whatever *could* go wrong, *had* gone wrong . . . and badly. He could only assume that it spelled the end of Slater's career as a field epidemiologist.

He returned his gaze to the images on his computer, pictures of what the Russian Orthodox church called the Theotokos. All were representations of the Virgin Mary and Child, but in four traditional poses. The Hodigitria, in which the Virgin pointed to the child as a guide to salvation. The Eleusa, in which the child touches his face to his mother's, symbolizing the bond between God and mankind. The Agiosortissa, or Intercessor, in which Mary holds out her hands in supplication to a separate image of Christ. And, finally, the Pana-kranta, depicting Mary on a royal throne, with the Christ child in her lap; according to the Fourth Ecumenical Council, it was in this con-figuration that the two were represented as presiding over the destiny of the world.

Although Frank had given him only the roughest description of the icon they had freed from the deacon's frozen hand—and which had now been stolen by some unknown hand—Kozak was confident that this last design, more regal than the others, was the right one. The red veil over her head was a symbol of her suffering, the blue dress a mark of her bond with humanity. The three diamonds that Slater had mentioned—on the Virgin's forehead and shoulders—were meant to suggest the Holy Trinity.

From the communications desk in the corner, there was a burst of static, and then a ghostly voice from the Coast Guard station in Point Barrow, warning of another storm front swooping down on the Ber-ing Strait. How, and why, Kozak wondered, had these settlers decided to plant their colony in this most unforgiving of places? The wind howled around the tent, and he was reminded of the terrors he had felt as a boy, reading late in his tiny room at the top of the stairs of the summer dacha. Every June his family had left their palatial flat in Moscow—high on Kutuzovsky Prospect—and gone to this wretched house in the middle of nowhere for "the fresh air." As far as Vassily was concerned, the air was plenty fresh in the city libraries. The house had no electricity, and he had had to read his books by the light of a kerosene lantern. He could smell its smudgy odor even now and envi-sion the rough log walls. Every time a branch had brushed against the eaves, or a window frame had whined, he had imagined that a *rusalka* was beckoning to him from the riverbank. Pale maidens, garlanded with flowers, they were said to lure the unsuspecting to their watery lairs and drown them there; the gardener told him that he had once chased a *rusalka* off the end of the dock with his pitchfork. "So don't you worry, young Vassily," he'd said. "They won't be coming around here anymore."

But young Vassily had worried, all the same.

There was a question from the Coast Guard operator in Point Barrow—"Do you read me, St. Peter's Island? Do you read me?"—and Kozak had finally gotten up from his chair and replied.

"Yes, we read you, loud and clear. This is Professor Vassily Kozak, of the Trofimuk United Institute of Geology, Geophysics, and Mineralogy."

There was the crackle of static, then an uncertain, "The what institute? Are you also with the AFIP mission? Under Dr. Frank Slater? Over."

Apparently, word had not yet traveled everywhere that Frank had been officially relieved of his duties.

"I am."

"Okay then. Well, we're clocking winds speed of over one hundred miles per hour and barometric pressure that's dropping like a stone—ninety-eight millibars at last reading. You might want to batten down the hatches real tight, for at least the next twenty-four hours."

"Thank you for that warning," Kozak said, stifling a belch. "I will batten down all hatches. Over."

Then he had shuffled back to his seat, poured another stiff shot of vodka, and riffled through the tattered pages of the book found in that dead boy's pocket. Nika had said his name was Russell.

The book, as Kozak had surmised at first glance, was the sexton's register, a record of the burials in the colony's graveyard. Where Russell had come by it, no one knew, but Kozak had a pretty good idea. Somewhere in the woods, not far from the cemetery, there was probably an old hovel, tumbled down and overgrown by now, where the sexton had kept his tools, his ledgers, and the headstones. Once the storm had passed, he would have to recruit Sergeant Groves and go looking for it.

The bottle of vodka was running low. Fortunately, he had packed several others.

The pages that had been left in the book showed a surprising scrum of entries all dating from the autumn of 1918, along with some notes on the dynamite the colonists had used to blow open graves to a sufficient depth. Eight-inch sticks, made in Delaware by DuPont. Manufactured to kill the Germans on the battlefields of the First World War, the dynamite had instead been used to help bury Russian pacifists thousands of miles from any front. Kozak was pleased to find this proof of his theory. No wonder this cliffside was crumbling faster than even global warming could have predicted.

But it was when he turned to the last few pages of the ledger, written in a more feminine hand, that he put his glass down and sat up straighter in his chair. The ink was considerably faded, and the pages still damp around the edges, but it was clear that the sexton was no longer their author. Had he died? Was this new writer his replacement? Where the book had been a cursory list of names and dates, there were suddenly plaintive appeals, mixed in among the last death entries, and all written in a more formal Russian.

"Forgive me," one anguished note read. *"I have become the curse of all who know me, both at home and here in this awful place."*

Below it, she had dutifully entered another burial entry, this one for a man named Stefan Novyk, *"Deacon of our holy congregation."* So that was his name—it had been obliterated from the headstone, but now the strange motif chiseled into the stone made perfect sense. The two doors in the upper corners had symbolized the deacon's doors . . . leading through the iconostasis to the altar behind. The place where the true treasures of the church were, traditionally, kept secret and protected. *"It was he who saved me from the wolves, and he who gave me shelter. And this is how I have rewarded him."*

The next few lines had become blurred and illegible, but below them, scrawled in what looked like a trembling hand, one last burial was recorded.

"Tonight, the Lord saw fit to return to me the mortal remains of Sergei Ilyinsky, my own poor, sweet, loyal, and much beloved Sergei. His body was

washed up on the shore of this accursed island, and I have buried it myself in the last grave. I can dig no more. Around his neck, I have placed the emerald cross once given to me by the holy man in St. Petersburg. May it guard Sergei on his journey now . . . and may its chains no longer bind me to this earth. I long to be released, but I fear that its blessing has now become my curse."

Kozak sat back in his chair, deeply moved by the anguish and loneliness of this anonymous woman. The rest of the page was empty, and Kozak turned it eagerly to see if there was anything more.

In the center of this last page were the words, "My soul endures here . . . *forever.* Mother of God, deliver me." Just below, there was a signature that made his heart stop. He quickly tossed down a generous shot of vodka. The lights in the tent dimmed and flickered, and he wondered if it might be the aurora borealis, disturbing the magnetic and electrical fields again. But he was in no mood to go outside and see. Not now.

When the lights burned bright again, he read it once more.

But it was still the same.

He drained the rest of the vodka, and as he plopped the empty bottle on the table, the lights again did go out, plunging him into darkness. Alone with his thoughts, and the ancient ledger, he felt the same eerie chill he had felt as a boy when it was the *rusalka* he had imagined coming back from the dead.

Chapter 52

Slater stood up again and surveyed his work. He wasn't proud of what had happened, but he had dealt with its repercussions as best he could.

With Nika's help, he had pried Bathsheba out of the snowbank, and after a quick examination, determined that apart from a few bruises, the worst damage she'd suffered might be a fractured tibia. She could walk, but not well, and she had had to be suspended between Slater's and Nika's shoulders to make it back up into the house. Even then, she seemed to be more worried about Harley than she was about herself.

"It's all Charlie's fault," she said, wincing with the pain. "Charlie gets him into trouble all the time. All Harley needs is somebody to take care of him, somebody that understands him."

Slater and Nika exchanged a look; it sounded like she was describing one of the bad-boy characters from some romance novel. Using the supplies from the ambulance, Slater set her leg, made her comfortable on the sofa, then, because he could not have her warning the brothers that he was in pursuit—or worse yet, wandering off into town—he gave her a healthy shot of a painkiller before she even knew what he was up to. Enough not only to lessen the discomfort, but to leave her in a happy twilight state for several hours.

Rebekah had presented a bigger problem. He had regretted having to hit her so hard with the butt of the rifle, but when someone was trying to kill you, you didn't have much choice. She was still unconscious, which was a good thing in that it allowed him to check her out without having to fend off another attack. Her lip was split, she had cracked a tooth in front, but her airways were clear and her heartbeat was regular. When she woke up, she'd be in a lot of pain—he left a bottle of Vicodin in plain sight, though he had no idea if her religious convictions allowed her to take it—and then, to be on the safe side, he used the rope her sister had brought to tie her to a folding chair.

"Take the cell phones, too," Slater said, and Nika snatched them off the desk. The guns he took himself. "Okay then," he concluded, "we've done what we can here. Let's hit the road."

Outside, the snow was falling so thickly he had to haul the shovel out of the back of the ambulance and do a little digging to provide some traction for the back tires. Nika confessed to feeling a bit unsteady—not surprising after all that had just happened—and Slater took the wheel. Even with only one headlight working, he could see tire tracks leading out of the Vane driveway and off in the only other direction available . . . toward Nome. Under his shirt, he could feel the ivory owl Nika had given him, and if ever he needed its help seeing in the dark, now was that time.

High overhead, but concealed by the storm, he could hear the roar of another helicopter racing toward Port Orlov. Whichever branch of the military or civilian authority had dispatched it, the overall emergency response, he knew, would be growing by the minute. The town of Port Orlov would be under a complete and rigorously enforced quarantine until further notice, and he was lucky to have gotten out when he did. Only he knew the full extent of the deadly cargo Harley and Charlie might be carrying in their pockets—or in their veins—and he was determined to avert any further catastrophe from occurring. As the head of the mission, he was responsible for allowing it to start, and now he was equally determined to be the one to quell it.

For a second, he wondered who would be assigned to replace him.

Whoever it was had undoubtedly already been chosen. There was no time to waste.

"Call the sheriff," he said to Nika as he gripped the wheel with one hand and rummaged around in the console between the two front seats. "Tell him about the women, and tell him not to let anybody in or out of the Vanes' house until a hazmat team gets there. Full precautions have to be taken." Although they had both been as careful as they could be—indeed, he could feel a pool of sweat cooling inside the thermals he wore under the damp hazmat suit—viruses were among the sneakiest things on earth. And this one, though its primary mode of transmission was airborne, thrived in the blood and flesh and bodily fluids of its carriers.

While Nika made the call—and he could tell she was getting static from Sheriff Ray—he found in the console a pair of woolly mittens, assorted loose meds, and a petrified Almond Joy bar. When she got off, she said, "I think we're both going to be under arrest before this is all over."

"Been there, done that," he said, with a half smile. "Here, have some dinner," he said, offering her the candy bar. "You're looking peaked."

"Not hungry."

"Eat it, anyway. You need to keep up your strength." She was slouched low in her seat though maybe it was just to avoid the stiff breeze blowing through the hole that the shotgun shell had left in the windshield.

With the gloves on, she had to fumble at the wrapper, and as she did so, Slater leaned forward in the driver's seat and stuffed a mitten into the hole. He was afraid that if he pushed too hard, the rest of the window, crazed with a thousand fissures, would give way, but for the moment it appeared to be holding.

"How can you see around that?" Nika asked.

"Who said I could?"

So far, he hadn't passed any other cars or trucks, which meant that the roadblock was probably already in place somewhere up ahead. But he feared that if the Vane brothers hadn't been stopped by now, they might have found a way to slip through the net. And the unfolding of that scenario was too dreadful even to contemplate. How wide would the dragnet eventually have to be? And what kind of panic might ensue if they tried to enforce it on a much more extensive scale?

He rubbed the side of one eye, where a splinter from the tree had hit him, and turned up the heat in the ambulance. From the way Nika was hunching her small shoulders, he guessed she was still chilled.

"You should take off your boots," he advised her, "and put your feet on the heat vent. You need to warm up."

Removing her footgear, she propped her stockinged feet up on the dashboard, wiggling her toes. "Frank," she said, somberly, "what happens if we do catch up to them?"

"I reason with them."

"That's it? That's your plan?" She turned her head to stare out the side window. "These are not the kind of guys who listen to reason."

Slater was aware of that, too.

"I hope you have a Plan B," she said.

"I did take the guns from their house."

She didn't seem overly impressed with that plan, either, but Slater hoped it would never come to that. The roadblock was still somewhere up ahead, and he prayed that when he got there he'd see Charlie's van pulled over on the shoulder and the Vane brothers under arrest.

He drove on, the road winding now through rougher terrain. He wondered if Eva Lantos had arrived at the containment unit in Juneau yet . . . and if she was still fighting for her life. It was a miracle that she had survived at all. The wolf attack could easily have killed her, and so could the viral exposure in the demolished lab, but it was a testimony to her stubborn spirit that she had not succumbed to either one. It was her hardheadedness that had convinced him to enlist her for this mission in the first place.

As he came around a bend, he saw the neighboring hills flickering in the rosy glow of highway beacons that had been set up along the road. Bobbing his head to see around the mitten in the windshield and past the network of cracks in the glass, he still caught no glimpse of a van. He had switched his one headlight to bright, and he slowed the ambulance as he saw an Army officer in a combat helmet stepping out of an armored vehicle parked in the center of the pavement. The officer had lifted both of his hands to indicate that they should stop, and if that wasn't clear enough, two National Guardsmen were kneeling on the asphalt, with their rifles pointed at the grille of his car.

"Looks like they mean business," Nika said.

"They should."

Slater stopped the car and waited until the officer approached. A soldier walked to the other side, his rifle slung over one shoulder but a finger on the trigger. Both of them, he was pleased to see, were wearing gauze face masks over their mouths, latex gloves on their hands, and keeping to a safe distance. Though they had probably never imagined that they'd have to observe these protocols, at least they'd been properly trained in them.

"Okay," the officer said, "let's start with who you are." He had lieutenant's bars on his helmet, and the mask billowed out with each word. "ID, please."

Nika passed her driver's license over, and added, "I'm the mayor of Port Orlov."

Reaching out his arm at full length to take and inspect the license, he said, approvingly, "You don't look like any mayor I've ever seen." Wet snow was starting to settle on his helmet.

"Yeah, thanks," she said, with the weary tone of someone who had heard that line one too many times. She took the license back.

The back doors of the ambulance were thrown open, and the soldier nosed around with the muzzle of his rifle.

Slater proffered his laminated, AFIP badge, and when the lieutenant saw the name and picture on it, he did a double take. "You're Dr. Slater? The one running the mission?"

"Yes." For once, inefficiency was his friend; he was still nominally in charge, it appeared.

"Then what the hell are you doing out here, and driving this piece of junk?" He surveyed the broken headlight and windshield. "You hit a moose?"

"No, but we ran into some other trouble." He was not about to elaborate. The back doors were slammed shut again.

"What have you heard about the Vane boys?" Slater asked, taking back his ID. "Has anyone spotted them?"

"Not yet."

"Keep an eye out for a blue Ford van. We have reason to believe they're out in it."

"Nothing like that's come through here. We've stopped one logging truck and one old lady driving a pickup."

"Are you sure that's all?" Nika said, leaning toward the officer. "They must have hit this roadblock by now."

"No, ma'am, they didn't. We've been up and running since 1800 hours."

"Then they must have gotten around it," she muttered to Slater. "Maybe on one of the old logging trails."

Slater didn't doubt her.

"But even if they got around this, they can't get around the Heron River Gorge," she added. "It's long and it's wide, and there's only one bridge across it."

"How far ahead?" he asked her.

"Forty miles, maybe fifty."

"Listen carefully, Lieutenant," Slater said. Between the helmet and the face mask, all he could really see of the young man's face was a pair of bright brown eyes. "I need you to call whoever's in charge, and tell them to set up another roadblock at the Heron River Bridge. Tell them to do it right away, and to keep an eye out for that van."

He put the ambulance into gear, and the lieutenant said, "Hey, wait—where do you think you're going?"

"The bridge. Now clear the road."

The lieutenant looked torn. "My orders are still in effect, and I'm supposed to stop all traffic in both directions."

"And you're doing a fine job," Slater said. "But I'm the one in charge of this operation—you said it yourself—and I'm telling you to move your vehicle."

Just to shut off any further debate, Slater rolled up his window and flicked the switch that activated the siren and flash bar atop the ambulance. The lieutenant hesitated, but when Slater glared at him and pointed his finger at the truck, he waved to his soldiers to move the vehicle out of the way. A couple of others peeled up a spike strip that Slater only now saw had been placed in the roadway just beyond. He was glad that he hadn't run out of patience and simply decided to barrel through the barricade.

The moment the path was clear, he steered the ambulance through the opening and pulled the mitten out of the hole. He needed the windshield wipers more than he needed the windbreak. And once the roadblock was no longer visible even in his rearview mirror, he killed the siren and flashing lights.

"I don't want to give the Vanes any more warning than I have to," he said, speeding up as much as the slippery pavement and damaged car would allow.

"By now, I'm sure they've figured a few things out," Nika said. "They know that somebody must be coming after them, or they wouldn't be off-roading."

True enough, he thought, flexing his fingers on the steering wheel and plowing on through the rising snowstorm. But did they know that the gravest danger of all was riding right along with them in their van?

Chapter 53

Charlie's mind was churning. He hadn't seen a single other vehicle moving on the highway in either direction, but on a night like this, who in his right mind would be out? Only long-haul truckers would brave it, and that was only because they had to. The snow was coming down so fast, the windshield wipers were having trouble handling it, even at their top speed.

Glancing into the rearview mirror, he saw Harley huddled in the backseat, and if he thought he looked sickly before, it was worse now. His forehead was beaded with sweat, his eyes had a weird glaze, and his fingers kept picking at that damn wound on his leg; all Charlie knew was that he must have gotten into some mean shit on that island. Mean shit, which was probably infecting the whole car by now. He'd have to tell Rebekah and Bathsheba to scrub down and sanitize the whole van once he got back to Port Orlov.

With the back of his hand, Charlie checked his own forehead, and he was as cool as a cucumber. Didn't have a cough or anything else, either. At least not so far. But if Harley *did* have something contagious, and he gave it to Charlie, there was going to be hell to pay.

A sign flashed by in the darkness, saying NEXT FOOD AND FUEL— 50 MILES, and Charlie glanced at the gas gauge; he had about half a tank left, but with the extra canisters in the back he could easily make it to Nome without stopping. He didn't want to risk using his credit card at a service station, or showing his face at a diner. One thing he'd learned was, people remembered the guy in the wheelchair, and just in case anyone came along trying to follow his trail, he didn't want to leave any more clues than he had to. Let 'em guess what the Vane boys were up to.

In a weird way, he found it exhilarating to be out on the road like this. It reminded him of his former life, before he'd given himself over to the Lord. When they weren't out crabbing, he and Harley had always been off running some scam, or hijacking somebody's boat, or burglarizing some rich bastard's vacation home. He knew now that what he'd been doing was wrong, that he was breaking the third, or was it the fourth, commandment, the one about not stealing, but he also knew that he'd felt a rush nothing else could come close to. These days, when he was preaching and really getting into it, really feeling the Presence of the Lord, it was sort of like that.

But if he was completely honest with himself, it still wasn't as good as cracking open somebody's wall safe and finding a stack of hundreds inside. Why was that? It was something he would have to take up with Jesus during his next heart-to-heart.

Fumbling inside his coat, he pulled a cigarette and a Bic lighter out of his shirt pocket. With the women gone, he could sneak in a smoke. He inhaled deeply, and dropped the lighter on the passenger seat. Funny, how a cigarette could make your lungs feel bigger even as, in actual fact, it shrunk 'em up.

A gust of wind slapped the side of the van so hard it roused Harley from his stupor. "The icon," he said, in a worried voice, "what did you do with it?"

"It's right here in the glove compartment. Same as the cross."

"I need it."

"What for?" Charlie couldn't tell if his brother was in his right mind or not.

"To save me."

Now he knew. "How's it gonna save you, Harley?"

"It's got the baby Jesus on it. Jesus saved you, right?"

"Yes, He did. But you don't need an old icon for that."

"I do," Harley croaked. "I need something 'cuz I'm gonna die tonight."

Charlie had never heard his brother say anything like that, not ever, and when he looked in the rearview mirror again, he saw that Harley's eyes were burning like black coals and his whole head was shaking.

"Nobody's dying tonight," Charlie said. His mind went back to the night he'd seen—imagined—the hollow-eyed man in the long coat, reaching for the cross from the backseat. He didn't care how much this Russian stuff was worth anymore—he was starting to wish he'd never laid eyes on any of it. "As soon as we get to Nome, we'll take you to a doctor. Get you fixed right up."

The road was veering now, as it began to track along the rim of the Heron River Gorge. Normally, that alone—the site of the accident that had left Charlie a paraplegic for life—was enough to rattle him, even if all this other crap hadn't been going on.

But it *was* going on, which made his apprehension just that much worse.

A sign said the bridge was coming up ahead. Huge, snow-covered hunks of granite, left by ancient glaciers, lined the shoulders like train cars waiting to be hitched.

"There's not enough time," Harley said. "Give me the icon now."

"I can't reach over that far. I'll get it for you once we cross the bridge."

"Too late," Harley said, with chilling certainty. "That'll be too late."

The van rocked and swayed as it hit a stretch of asphalt buckled from frost heave. Every year, the highway department had to come out in the spring and repair the damage done in the winter. Once in their youth, Charlie and Harley had tried to make off with one of their road graders, before realizing that its top speed was about ten miles per hour.

The gorge cut a deep swath through the land for nearly nine miles, and the bridge over it had been built at the narrowest spot available, between two rocky bluffs. He kept a close eye on the road, which was rapidly disappearing under a shifting scrim of snow and ice. Even with four-wheel drive and chains on his tires, he was losing traction now and then. His brother moaned, and when he glanced in the rearview mirror to check on him, what he noticed instead was a tiny pinprick of light, way down the road behind them.

A tiny pinprick that was moving.

"Harley, quit your moaning and turn around!"

"Why?"

"Just tell me what you see down the road!"

The blanket still wrapped around his shoulders, Harley turned and looked.

"Looks like a headlight. Maybe just a motorcycle."

Charlie studied the tiny light, and damn if it didn't look like it was a single headlamp after all. But who'd be trying to navigate these dangerous roads, in the middle of a blizzard, on a motorcycle? That'd be crazy. Cops would be using a heavy-duty cruiser, the National Guard guys would be in a jeep. The only thing he could tell for sure was that it was moving along at a good clip.

"Keep an eye on it," Charlie said, turning off the cruise control and pushing the accelerator lever.

"Shit. What if it's Eddie on a snowmobile?"

He heard the click of a safety being taken off a gun. A Glock 19, from the sound of it. Oh, Christ, Harley was not only nuts . . . but armed?

"Where'd you get that?" Charlie demanded, though it had undoubtedly come from his own gun cabinet. "Put it away. Now."

But Harley was off in his own delusion again. "Fuckin' Eddie," he muttered, staring out the back of the van.

"Eddie's dead. You told me so yourself."

Harley, still staring, clucked his tongue and said, "Eddie never did know when to call it quits. I never should have let him come back with me."

Come back? Charlie thought Eddie had fallen off a cliff on the island.

"Well, this time I'm going to cap his ass for good."

Charlie stopped trying to make sense of Harley's ravings. All he could do was drive . . . and pray he got to Nome before Harley went off in his van like a bomb.

Chapter 54

Stepping into the tavern, Ana was careful to remain behind Sergei. Dressed in rough old clothes, her hair chopped short, and her eyes downcast, she appeared to be the perfect peasant wife, beaten into subservience and silence. After so many weeks on the run, it was an act she was finally growing used to.

Sergei, in a brown-wool tunic buttoned all the way up the side of his neck, and a black sealskin coat, furtively scanned the tavern and its occupants. A couple of dozen men in leather jackets were playing cards and dominoes and swigging from bottles of beer and vodka. A fire was crackling in the immense hearth, and gas lamps burned along the walls. A phonograph on the bar played a scratchy version of the country's newly inaugurated anthem, the *Internationale*; every note of it made Ana want to smash the record.

Sitting alone at a table in the corner, a bald man in a pilot's uniform raised his chin in acknowledgment. Sergei and Ana threaded their way through the cluttered room, drawing a few glances and a couple of coarse remarks about the rubes, before drawing up chairs at the table.

"You are Nevsky?" Sergei asked in a low voice.

The bald man didn't answer but motioned to the innkeeper to bring two more glasses. Above the bar, a placard promoting the Imperial Russian Air Force had been defaced, and written in red paint on the wall beside it was the new name for the Soviet air force—the Workers' and Peasants' Red Air Fleet. The bald man had several bright medals and ribbons pinned to his shirt.

The innkeeper plunked the glasses down on the table, filled them from a brandy decanter, and said, "Your bill is overdue, Nevsky."

"I'll pay it after you've shot down your first enemy fighter," Nevsky said in a hoarse grumble.

The innkeeper grunted in disgust, and went back to the bar.

"And who is this?" Nevsky said, gesturing to Ana.

"My wife."

"I wasn't told there would be two of you," he said, trying to stifle a cough.

"What difference does it make? The airplane can carry one more passenger, can't it?"

Nevsky threw down a shot of the brandy. "Not for the same price it can't."

Ana wasn't surprised. Although she kept her composure and said nothing, this was the same story they had encountered throughout their journey from the monastery at Novo-Tikhvin. They had been forced to bribe everyone, from wagon drivers to lorry loaders to ticket agents on the Trans-Siberian Railway. Everyone in Russia had his hand out, and nothing could be done or had without some special compensation being offered. The entire nation was starved and desperate and teeming with violence, and much as she tried to find some sympathy in her heart for these people—the people her own father and mother, despite what was said about them, had held so dear—she could not. In every soldier and peasant she encountered, she saw nothing but another murderer.

"What is the price then?" Sergei asked.

"Double. What else would it be?" He refilled his glass. "Do you take me for a thief?"

Sergei didn't even have to look at Ana for approval; funds were the one thing they had. "We'll pay it, but only after you take us to the island."

"And only after you show me that you actually have it," Nevsky said, pointedly looking Sergei up and down. The sealskin coat was weathered, his tunic was soiled, his boots were worn. Nevsky appeared dubious.

Sergei turned slightly toward Ana, and she pulled from under her full skirts a drawstring pouch. Sergei took it into his own lap, and with his hands concealed beneath the scarred tabletop removed two white diamonds the size of teardrops. He held them in his palm as Nevsky craned his neck to look under the table and see.

"One of them now," Nevsky said, "as the down payment."

Sergei gave it to him, and after looking around the room to see that no one was watching, Nevsky took a good long look at it and rolled it between his fingers. Satisfied, he wrapped it in his red handkerchief and stuck it in the pocket of his shirt. Then, leaning back in his chair with a skeptical expression, he said, "But where would someone like you have come by something like this?"

It was a question Sergei and Ana had been asked before.

"The Winter Palace," Sergei confided, as if ashamed of his own actions.

"The Tsar's treasures belonged to the people," Nevsky said, feigning indignation and coughing into the back of his hand. "When the Winter Palace was stormed, that loot belonged to the proletariat."

"I am part of the proletariat," Sergei replied, and at this Nevsky laughed.

"An enterprising one, I'll say that for you." Then, leaning close, he explained that Sergei and Ana were to meet him at the airfield as soon as it was light out. "Keep behind the hangars, and for God's sake, don't call any attention to yourselves. Don't bring anything heavier than a handful of straw. The plane won't carry any more weight."

That night, in return for an exorbitant charge to the innkeeper, Sergei and Ana bedded down between the beer barrels in the cellar of the tavern and waited anxiously for the dawn. Ana had never been in an airplane before, and she was quite sure Sergei had never been, either. She didn't ask him because she knew he liked to pretend to be more worldly and experienced than he was, although, in her eyes, he was just a boy—a gangly creature with loose limbs and a cowlick and a long face that reminded her of her favorite pony.

And she loved him.

Not only because he had saved her life—though wouldn't that have been enough?—but because his heart had remained pure and righteous. She loved him for his innocence, for his devotion . . . and because he loved her in turn. Ana had lived a life of extravagant luxury and immense privilege, but she had also been cloistered and cosseted and confined, and it was only in the past year, when all of that had been stripped away, that she felt she had learned so much of what life was really like. Father Grigori had always told her she had a special destiny—the emerald cross beneath her blouse attested to the un-breakable bond between them—but only now did she feel she might be moving toward such a thing, whatever it might turn out to be. And without Sergei, she would never have escaped the makeshift grave-yard at the Four Brothers, where everyone else in her family lay.

It sickened her that the official Soviet press still claimed that only her father had been shot and the rest of the family was safely seques-tered somewhere. Once she made it to freedom, even if that freedom was only an island in the middle of the Bering Sea, she would find a way to expose these butchers for what they were.

It wasn't yet dawn when Sergei nudged her. She doubted that he had been able to sleep any more than she had. They gathered their few things together in a bundle and crept up the stairs from the cellar. The innkeeper in a nightshirt was lighting a fire in the grate and pre-tended not to see them. Outside, the air was frigid, but the sky was lightening enough that she could see there wasn't even a wisp of a cloud in any direction. Surely this would be good weather for the flight to St. Peter's Island. The thought of being in a place, no matter how barren and remote, where she could openly be herself, where she did not have to fear every encounter and dodge every stranger, where she would be embraced by friends and followers of Father Grigori, promised such relief that it eradicated any fear she might have had of boarding the plane.

By the time they got to the hangars, the plane, with a red star freshly painted on its nose, was already on the runway. Nevsky, a leather cap clinging to his bald head and tinted goggles hanging down around his neck, was circling it, checking the tires and the struts and the wings. There were two wings, a wider one above the tiny cabin and a shorter one below, connected by a latticework of wires, and a long tail that reminded her of a dragonfly. It looked to her almost as flimsy as a dragonfly, too, and she could hardly imagine it carrying them for miles over an icy sea. Sergei had stopped where he stood, and was staring at it with slack-jawed wonder and evident dread, when Nevsky noticed them and, taking a quick look around the empty field, waved them over.

"Come on," Ana said, taking Sergei by the arm and drawing him out of the shadows of the hangar. "We have to hurry."

Nevsky was holding open the small door to the cabin, and he frowned when he saw their bundle. "What did I tell you about the weight?" he said, taking the bundle in hand, gauging it, then grudgingly tossing it onto the cabin floor. "Get in!" he ordered, coughing, then spitting a wad of phlegm onto the tarmac.

Bending double, Ana crawled through the dented metal door and sat bolt upright on a padded plank with the bag wedged under her feet; she could barely move since, in order to keep the bundle light, she had worn the corset freighted with jewels under her coat. Sergei, his eyes wide as saucers, got in and sat on a plank opposite. The space was so small, and his legs were so long, their knees touched. Ana gave him an encouraging smile, but he looked like a lamb being led to the slaughter.

Grunting, Nevsky crawled into the cabin, latched the door behind him, and squirmed into a seat at the front of the plane; it was shaped like a bucket and cushioned by a Persian rug folded double. With thick but nimble fingers, he began turning dials and flicking switches and doing all manner of things that Ana could not fathom. What she did understand was the machine gun firmly mounted at his elbow, and aimed through an aperture in the windscreen. The sight of its black barrel and deadly snout reminded her that this plane had been designed for aerial combat, not for ferrying refugees. It was built to dispense death, not life . . . like everything the Bolsheviks put their hand to.

"There are straps," Nevsky said, over his shoulder. "Fasten them under your arms and around your waists."

Ana found the straps hanging like reins in a stable from the sides of the cabin, and did as she was told; the clasp, she could not help but notice, was embossed with a double eagle, the old insignia of the Russian Air Force. Sergei's fingers moved mechanically as he strapped himself in; his eyes were riveted on the floor, which appeared to have been cobbled together with sheets of steel, then sealed with a coat of tar. The whole compartment felt too insubstantial to withstand the rigors of a rough road, much less flight.

But the propellers, a pair on each side, suddenly engaged, and as the sun came fully into the Siberian sky, Nevsky piloted the plane onto the runway, shouting back to them, "Hold on!" But to what, Ana wondered? There was a roar from the engines, and a rumbling from the tires as they bounced across the ground. Sergei's eyes were closed, and he was as rigid as a stick, his head back against the wall of the fuselage. His lips were moving in what was no doubt a prayer. The roar grew louder all the time, and the cabin rocked and creaked and swayed, and at any moment Ana would not have been surprised to see the whole contraption explode. Looking over Nevsky's broad shoulders, she saw the tundra hurtling past, so fast it was only a brownish blur now—how could anything move at such a speed? she thought— and Nevsky pulling back on an oak-handled throttle that reminded her of one of Count Benckendorff's canes. The speed increased, the roar of the motors became deafening, and just when she thought the shuddering plane was sure to fall apart, the nose tilted up ever so slightly, the jouncing abruptly stopped, and to her amazement she saw the ground falling away. The windscreen blazed with shards of orange light, and she wished that she, too, had a pair of the tinted goggles Nevsky was wearing. There was the strangest sensation in her stomach, as if it had just dropped into her shoes, but it wasn't unpleasant; it was like the times Nagorny, Alexei's guardian, had swung her so high on the garden swing that she had stopped at the top, afraid she was about to spill over the bar, before swooping back down instead. In her head, she could hear Alexei begging to be swung that high, too, and his delighted screams when Nagorny complied.

The grief overwhelmed her again, as it often did, like a crashing wave.

But Sergei's eyes were open now. He refused to look out through the window, but gave Anastasia a wan smile. She reached across and squeezed his hand.

"We will be flying northeast," Nevsky shouted, his words carried back to them on a cold draft. "This damn sun will be in our eyes the whole way."

Ana liked it—she liked the hot bright yellow light, she liked the sky around it, a cerulean blue unmarred by a single wisp of cloud, and she liked it when the dark, snow-patched ground dropped away altogether, replaced by the cobalt blue of the Bering Sea. Glaciers sat serenely in the choppy waters, a pod of breaching whales gamboled among the chunks of floating ice. The horizon was a gleaming orange line, pulled tight as a stitch, and somewhere ahead there lay an island that was no longer a part of Russia at all, an island that housed a small colony of believers. A small colony of friends.

She would have liked to talk to Sergei, if only to distract him, but the howling of the wind and the din of the propellers was too great. Instead, she made do with holding his hand and gazing out at the unimaginable spectacle through the cockpit window. What a pity it was tainted by the machine gun, black, gleaming with oil, and brooding like a vulture.

When the plane banked, she was pressed back against the wall—it felt like lying on a slab of ice—and this time the sensation in her stomach was not so easily dismissed. The plane was losing altitude, she could feel it, and for a second she worried that they were going to crash, after all. Glancing out the window, she saw that the world had tilted to an odd angle, and in the distance, she could see two islands, not one, both of them flat and gray and barely rising above the sea. One was much bigger than the other, and she wondered which of them was St. Peter's. Neither looked especially welcoming.

The angle grew even more extreme, and the engines made a louder, grinding sound, as the plane descended even more, soaring across the channel that narrowly separated the islands, and the windscreen filled with the image of the bigger of the two. Gradually, the plane leveled off, and the coastline appeared. Rugged, barren, choked with coveys of squalling birds. Anastasia caught a glimpse of a collection of huts, clustered on the cliffs above an inlet, as the plane dropped onto a cleared field, its tires bouncing up again as they touched the ground. The propellers whirred down, and Nevsky clutched the throttle with both hands, pulling back on it as if he were subduing a stallion. The cabin rattled, the tires squealed, and only the machine gun remained motionless. For several hundred yards, the plane rumbled and rolled along the tundra, before the engines stopped growling and the propellers stopped spinning and everything came to a halt.

Nevsky, pushing the goggles onto the top of his head, turned in his seat and said, "You can unfasten those straps now." Then he coughed into his handkerchief.

Ana and Sergei undid their straps, and with trembling fingers Sergei unlatched the little door. He clambered out onto the ground, then held out a hand to help Ana. When she bent over, the corset nipped at her ribs, and her feet felt so unsteady she nearly toppled over. Sergei propped her up as Nevsky disembarked. Without a word, he went to a tiny, falling-down shed, and came out lugging two gas cans, one in each hand.

Ana, bewildered, looked all around, but apart from the shed, there was no sign of any habitation nearby, or any people. Were those huts the entire colony? Her heart began to sink. And why was there no one there to welcome them?

Nevsky seemed to be studiously avoiding them, and when Sergei ventured a question, he brushed him off and said, "Let me finish with this first," as he poured the second can of gas down the funnel he had inserted in the tank at the rear of the plane. When that was done, he returned to the shed, came out with two more, and poured them in, too. A brisk wind was cutting across the open field, and Ana huddled in the shelter of the fuselage.

Tossing the empty cans to one side and removing the funnel, Nevsky finally turned to them and said, "I'll have that second diamond now."

"Where is everyone?" Sergei said.

"They'll be here. Now, where is it?"

Sergei looked uncertain, but when Ana nodded, he gave it to him. Nevsky tucked it into his pocket, and threw open the little door to the plane. Then he jumped in, threw the latches, and only appeared again through the window of the cockpit. Sliding the window panel open, he spoke across the top of the machine gun as Ana and Sergei gathered below.

"Right now you're on what the Eskimos call Nunarbuk."

"You mean that's their name for St. Peter's Island?" Sergei said.

"St. Peter's Island," Nevsky said, fitting his goggles back into place, and pointing due east, "is over there."

"That's where we paid you to take us!" Ana cried, but Nevsky just shrugged.

"They have no landing strip," he said.

"Then you have to take us back with you!" Sergei demanded, hammering at the side of the plane.

"Watch out," Nevsky said, as he started to close the window. "The propellers can cut you in half like a loaf of bread."

A moment later, Ana heard the engines revving up. The propellers clicked and twitched, then began to turn, and Sergei had to duck back away from the plane. It bumped along the ground in a wide circle, protected by its four whirling blades, before quickly gathering speed and then, as they watched in shock, altitude, too. It was only as it rose high into the sky, shining in the sun and banking slowly toward Siberia, that Ana realized they had even forgotten to retrieve their bundle from under the seat.

Chapter 55

"Is that it?" Slater asked. "Is that the van?"

Nika craned forward in the passenger seat. "I can't tell," she said, peering through the fractured windshield. "The snow's too thick."

On the right side of the road, a yellow sign said, "HERON RIVER BRIDGE AHEAD. PROCEED WITH CAUTION. REDUCE SPEED." It was pocked with bullet holes, and Slater wondered if there was a single sign or mailbox in Alaska that hadn't been used for target practice.

He stepped on the gas, but he felt the tires starting to lose traction on the icy surface and he had to ease off again.

The road was winding its way through a rubble-strewn landscape of stunted trees and immense boulders. Sometimes, the vehicle in front of him would disappear behind the rocks, or be engulfed in a whirling cloud of snow, but each time he caught a glimpse of it, he was able to pick out another detail or two. First, he could see the boxy silhouette of a van. And then he could tell it was some dark color, blue or black.

It had to be Charlie Vane's car.

He knew that he was driving the ambulance far too fast for the road and weather conditions, but he still wasn't closing the distance. Vane had to be doing at least sixty-five or seventy miles per hour. At any moment, he expected to see the van go spinning off the road or crashing into the rocks.

"Do you think they've spotted us?" Nika asked.

"Absolutely." But what would they be able to see? "Should I put on the siren and lights? Maybe convince them it's the police on their tail?"

"They'd only drive faster."

Which was pretty much what Slater had thought, too.

"There's one more bend in the road," Nika advised him, "but it's a wide one, and it runs behind those hills. When you come out on the other side, you'll see the gorge, and the bridge, off in the distance but straight ahead."

What Slater hoped to see was a National Guard barricade, with spotlights and trucks and armed soldiers, but he was afraid it was too much to expect. There probably hadn't been time to set up something so elaborate, and now he was wondering just how far he would have to keep trailing the Vanes. All the way to Nome? He glanced at his dashboard and saw that the gas tank was already three-quarters empty. But it was critical that he stop them before they reached any population center.

The question remained—how?

Snowy hills rose up on all sides, funneling the wind and snow into a dense fog that almost entirely obscured the road. Steel poles, only four or five feet high, with red reflectors on top, were the only way to stay on course, and rusty signs warned of curves, oncoming traffic, animal crossings, avalanches, hazardous ice. The ambulance clung to the road, the windshield wipers beating furiously, the lone headlight shining on the blur of falling snow. A steady stream of freezing air blew into the car through the hole in the windshield, and Slater prayed that the wipers wouldn't catch on one of the cracks and cause the whole window to implode in their faces.

And just when he thought the hills would never come to an end, he emerged onto a broad icy plateau. Even the van must have had to slow down, as the distance between them now was no more than the equivalent of a few city blocks.

Better yet, Slater could see the steel span of the Heron River

Bridge, rising into the darkness . . . with an Alaska Highway Patrol car parked laterally in front of it, its headlights shining and blue roof bar flashing.

It wasn't a whole platoon from the National Guard, but it would do. Or so he thought.

He watched the van begin to slow down, as if Charlie was debating what to do, and Slater used that chance to close some more of the gap.

"Okay, now let's turn on the lights and siren!" Slater said, clutching the wheel with both hands as he suddenly felt the ambulance sliding on a patch of black ice. "Time to let him know he's surrounded."

But just as Nika got everything blaring, and Slater saw the patrolman stepping out of the car, the van shot forward, its back wheels hurling up a shower of snow and sleet as it rocketed toward the bridge.

"What's he doing?" Nika shouted.

But it was clear seconds later, as the van accelerated to top speed and hit the front end of the patrol car, sending it spinning out of the way like a top, sparks flying and metal screeching. The cop jumped out of its path in the nick of time.

Slater, trying to keep control of his own car, tapped his foot on the brakes and steered into the direction of the skid. But the ambulance had gathered its own momentum now.

Up ahead, the van bounded up the corrugated ramp and onto the bridge, bucking like a bronco trying to throw its rider.

In the ambulance, Slater clung to the steering wheel and Nika braced herself against the dashboard as the vehicle did a full, unimpeded circle before finally coming to a stop, its front fender thumping into a mound of snow.

After the initial jolt, Slater looked out his side window again, just in time to see the patrolman kneeling, one arm bracing the other, and firing several rounds at the back of the fleeing vehicle.

At first, the shots appeared to have no effect, but then, after the last one, Slater saw the van suddenly zig and zag on the bridge, cutting from one lane to the other, before banging into a guardrail so hard that two wheels left the pavement, then all four. As it flipped over, tires smoking and glass spraying, it spun, like an upside-down plate, half-way down the deserted bridge.

"You okay?" Slater said to Nika.

"Yep," she said, in a shaky voice, "but I'm not so sure about the ambulance, or the Vanes." She, too, was looking off at the wreckage on the bridge.

He told her to use the radio to call for medical backup. "And stay on the radio until they get here. Keep away from the accident scene."

Then he leapt out of the ambulance, and raced toward the bridge.

"Who are you?" the patrolman hollered, still holding the gun. Slater was relieved to see that the patrolman, too, had a face mask—the word had gone out—but it was dangling down around his neck.

"Stay clear!" Slater shouted, running past the damaged patrol car. "And put your mask on until I tell you otherwise!"

"On whose authority?"

"Mine!" Slater declared. "And that's an order!"

Before the cop could issue another challenge, Slater ran right past him, his eyes fixed on the van . . . and praying that this was as far as both of the Vanes, and the virus, had traveled.

Chapter 56

It was the chimes Charlie noticed first.

He was upside down in the van, his head up against the broken roof light.

The chimes, the ones that went off whenever you hadn't fastened a seat belt, or closed your door properly, were dinging sweetly.

It took him a few seconds to orient himself.

He remembered slowing down for the roadblock, and he also remembered thinking, *What was the point of trying to get past it? They'd have a chopper tracking him down next.* And then, before he knew what was happening, Harley had flipped out in the backseat and started screaming, "Go through it! Go through it!"

But Charlie wasn't going to be that stupid anymore; he'd seen enough trouble in his life, and he was a reformed man now, anyway. He was trying to reason with Harley when his brother, with the blanket still wrapped around his shoulders, lunged over the back of the seat and punched the accelerator lever.

"Go through!"

The van blasted off and Charlie, knocked back as if he were an astronaut, groped in vain for the hand brake as they smashed into the front of the police car, then, instantly picking up speed again, hurtled past.

His fingers were just able to graze the wheel as the van lurched onto the bridge, but Harley was hanging over him, trying to steer. He thought he'd heard a shot—or was it a tire exploding?—and then they were crashing into a metal guardrail, the windows shattering all around. Gas canisters and gear from the back of the van flew in every direction as the wheels hit an ice slick, and the whole car flipped in the air like a pancake on the griddle.

And now all he could hear were the chimes. The inside of the van smelled like gasoline, tinged with the astringent smell of blood. His neck and shoulders aching, he glanced at the front of his coat, where a wet, dark stain was slowly spreading. The punctured airbag was hanging down like an empty saddlebag, and the glove compartment gaped open. Its contents, including the cross and icon, were scattered somewhere in the jumble of pulverized glass and twisted metal.

"Shit."

He heard that. It was Harley's voice. He was alive—but where?

Gradually, other sounds came to him, too. The dripping of gasoline, the creak of mangled steel, the tinkle of falling glass. The world was returning . . . and with it, agonizing pain.

Charlie tried to turn, but the seat belt was coiled like a snake around his waist, and his legs of course were as useless as ever. He tried moving, but only one arm came up from the wreckage. He tried to reach for the buckle on the seat belt, but the bulk of his coat was bunched up and in the way.

"Where are you?" he asked through gritted teeth.

He heard a moan, and something twitched behind his head. He had the impression it was a foot. "Try not to move," he said, mindful of his own paralysis. "They'll get a medic out here." But how long would that take? They were in the middle of nowhere, in a snowstorm.

"I told you," Harley groaned. "I told you I was gonna die tonight."

Charlie had to admit he hadn't been far off. But the good Lord still seemed to have some other plan in mind for them.

And then, under the howling of the wind, there was the sound of running feet. And a guy in some kind of white lab suit was crouching down beside the wreck. He had a gauze mask on, and rubber gloves. How could medics have gotten there this fast, he wondered?

Peering in at Charlie, he quickly assessed the situation, and said, "Can you breathe?"

"Barely," Charlie replied. "The seat belt."

And then the guy's hands were working the buckle, prying it loose. When it popped open, Charlie's belly fell and he felt a rush of cold air entering his lungs. Then his coat was being opened, and the medic took a long look without saying anything. Two of the spokes from the gearshift were sticking out of him like bent twigs.

"Hang in there," he said evenly, "you're gonna be okay."

Christ, that's exactly what they'd said to him after he'd hit those rocks running the Heron River Gorge.

Then he closed the coat again, and moved beyond Charlie's narrow field of vision, to tend to Harley in back.

"Can you move your head and neck?"

Harley groaned again and swore, but the medic was slowly extricating him from the wreckage. "Don't move anything you don't have to," the medic said. "Just let me do it."

Through the empty space where his window had been, Charlie could see his brother's mangled body being pulled from the van and onto the asphalt. Heavy snow was falling, mixing with a widening pool of something wet and viscous. For a second, Charlie thought, *Could that be blood?* But then he realized it wasn't. It was gas.

Harley's groaning was becoming more of a scream. And he was shouting something about Eddie again. "Goddamn it, Eddie, it wasn't my fault!"

And he was struggling with the medic. It seemed like he thought the guy *was* Eddie.

"Calm down," Charlie mumbled to his brother. Funny how his guts were growing colder by the second. "He's not Eddie."

"Fuck you," Harley spat at the medic, his arms flailing under the blanket drenched in blood. And then, in a flash, one of his hands broke free, and it was holding the goddamned Glock semiautomatic.

"I told you to quit it!" Harley shouted. "I *told* you!"

The medic grabbed for his wrist, but not before a sudden spray of shots went wild into the snowy night sky.

The medic twisted the wrist, banging it on the road and trying to free the gun, but Harley managed to pull the trigger one more time. Charlie saw a blazing arc of light, a bright and beautiful orange parabola that nearly blinded him, as the bullets ripped into the overturned van and punched holes in the gas cans. That was when the whole world lifted off, painlessly and effortlessly, with an all-enveloping *whomp,* and Charlie was carried up into the air, as if by the Rapture itself . . . up out of the wreckage, out of his own maimed body, and into a darkness so deep, so dense, and so comforting that he could actually *feel* it . . .

Chapter 57

Nika froze, the radio handset dropping into her lap, as she watched the fireball unfurl and the ruined van shoot up into the air. A moment later, the impact of the blast reached the ambulance, shattering the splintered windshield and raining glass down onto the dashboard.

The boom sounded like a distant thunderclap, and the chassis of the ambulance shimmied.

"What was that?" a static-y voice asked over the radio. "Are you still there?"

Pieces of the van started crashing down on the asphalt, while others flew in flames over the side of the bridge.

"Please reply," the operator insisted. "Are you okay?"

Nika was lifting the mike when something slammed down on the hood of the ambulance, then ricocheted through the gaping hole and onto the seat beside her. She looked down at it—half a leg, in blue jeans, soaked in blood, the foot still attached. And then, in shock, she bolted out of the car.

She was running for the bridge, right past the patrolman who was standing outside his damaged car, mike in hand and the cord stretched to its limit. She heard him saying, "Emergency! Now!" She just kept telling herself, Frank wasn't wearing blue jeans. He was wearing the white lab suit. He could still be all right.

When she got to the ramp of the bridge, she could see bits of burning wreckage still wafting to the bottom of the gorge. The wind reeked of gasoline and carnage. She ran on, toward the cloud of black smoke and destruction, but as she got closer she had to slow down and pick her way, while squinting her eyes against the acrid fumes, through the smoldering debris.

"Frank? Can you hear me? Frank?"

The storm was whipping the smoke and ashes into an evil, dusky brew. As she stopped for a second to clear the tears from her eyes, the cop ran past her, sweeping his flashlight back and forth. Its bright beam picked out hunks of torn metal and wood and fabric . . . and chunks of scorched body parts.

Please, God, she thought. *Please, God, let me find him.*

"Frank!" she called again, the dirty air searing her lungs as she plowed ahead. She remembered the face mask hanging around her neck, and quickly fixed it over her mouth and nose. She was never so glad to have it.

An axle of the van, with two wheels still connected, lay like a barbell in the middle of the roadway.

The side of her foot bumped against something that rolled, like a black bowling ball, down the white line of the bridge. It was only as it rotated that she saw it was a perfectly smooth, perfectly burned, perfectly unrecognizable head.

She stopped in her tracks, afraid to move another step or see another horror. Gusts of wind kept picking over things that had fallen back to earth, blowing them around as if for further inspection, but Nika couldn't bear to look. She lowered her eyes, breathing hard, and saw something shining in the glow of a burning seat cushion. It was a cross, made of silver. With emeralds that sparkled in the light of the fires crackling all around them. What on earth would that be doing here?

"Over here!" the patrolman cried, holding the mask away from his lips.

He was crouched by the railing.

"Over here!"

Nika jumped over a twisted muffler pipe and went to the railing.

A body, nearly ripped in half, was lying with a shredded blanket wrapped around it. Already she could tell it was missing a couple of limbs.

Her heart plummeted like a rock, but then the patrolman, pointing his flashlight, said, "Underneath! Look underneath!"

She brushed the cinders out of her eyes.

And then she saw that someone else lay there, too, shielded by the mangled corpse.

"Help me," the cop said, snapping his mask back into place and starting to disentangle the two.

They allowed what was left of the body on top to slither to one side. Enough of it remained, even now, that she could recognize Harley Vane.

And beneath him lay Frank, his lab suit soiled with blood and ash, the ivory owl on its leather string draped over one shoulder. When she said his name, she saw his eyelids flutter. His mask was gone, and his face was seared and bleeding. But she saw his lips move.

"Lie still," she said, tenderly brushing soot from his cheek. "Don't try to talk."

But he tried to, anyway . . . and she could swear he said "Nika."

Turning to the cop, she said, "Call for a medical evacuation. We need a helicopter as fast as they can get here!"

But he was shaking his head. "I radioed already, and every chopper is on duty enforcing the quarantine. It'll be hours before any help gets here."

Hours was not something Nika had to spare.

"Then I'll need to take your patrol car."

"Have you seen what's left of it? You'll be driving with no hood."

Her brain was racing. Her only option was the ambulance with the missing windshield, the lone headlight, and not enough gas. "Can you drain your gas tank into the ambulance for me?"

"That I can do," he said, plainly relieved that he could finally offer some sort of help, and headed back across the smoldering minefield.

Nika bent low over Frank, trying to assess his injuries, but he was so saturated in blood it was hard to tell. His face was covered with cuts and abrasions, and she carefully raked her fingers through his hair, stiff and matted, in search of any gash or obvious wound. To her relief, she found none. Loosening his hazard suit and trying to peer inside, she could see no open wounds or protruding bones, but internal injuries, even she knew, could be a lot less apparent and much more deadly.

When the patrolman returned with the gurney, they lifted Frank onto it, wheeled him to the back of the ambulance. On the way, Nika's eye was caught again by the silver cross, glinting among the broken glass and metal, so she stuck it in her pocket. She assumed it was a family heirloom that Vane's wife would want back, and it might make a small peace offering after all that had happened. Way too small . . . but still, something.

After they had secured the gurney, the patrolman said, "I still don't know how you're gonna make it, in this weather and this vehicle."

But Nika was already hauling out the medics' gear stashed in back. She slung on a huge red anorak, with white crosses on its sleeves and a voluminous hood. Her face was barely visible under the dirty mask, and even the remainder she covered with a pair of protective snow goggles. Her hands, still in the latex gloves, went into thermally insulated gloves. When she was done, the cop said, "You still in there, Doc?"

Somewhere along the way, maybe because of the white suit and ambulance, he had assumed she was a doctor—and she had been savvy enough not to correct him. She nodded in answer to his question, but even that movement might have been lost in the folds of the hood.

"I'll radio ahead and let 'em know you're coming."

Then she brushed the broken glass away from the driver's seat, removed the severed leg and deposited it on the roadway, and fastened her seat belt. The patrolman, using his flashlight like an airport worker directing a jet onto the right runway, helped guide the ambulance through the carnage and debris on the bridge—little piles were still burning like signal fires—and then waved her on her way. She lifted a hand in salute, and glancing in the rearview mirror, watched as he was swallowed up in the maelstrom of the storm.

Chapter 58

Once the plane was completely out of sight, even the sound of its motor lost in the rustling of the wind along the abandoned airstrip, Anastasia said, "There was a village, on the cliffs. I saw it before we landed."

But Sergei stood where he was, his black sealskin coat billowing out around him, his eyes still fixed on the blue but empty sky.

"Sergei, he's gone. There's nothing we can do about it."

He was still clutching a stone—he had thrown several in impotent fury at the plane—and looked reluctant to give it up.

Ana, deciding to give him time, went to the shed and looked inside. Plainly, it was a depot for the planes, with gas cans and tools and various pieces of machinery lying around, but nothing she could see that would be of any use to them.

"I'm sorry," she heard over her shoulder. "I was a fool."

"We both were," she said, remembering that it was she who had encouraged him to hand over the second diamond. "Anyone who trusts another Russian," she added bitterly, "is a fool."

Taking his hand, she led him across the field, favoring her bad foot, which had accumulated many blisters on their journey, and back toward the cliffs where she had seen the dismal huts. Halfway there, she saw several figures approaching—three men, squat and broad, swathed in fur coats, with their hoods thrown back and something odd about their faces. It was only as they came closer that she saw the men had ivory disks, the size of coins, implanted in their jutting, lower lips. She knew that these must be the Eskimos; with their wide, weather-beaten features, high cheekbones and black eyes, they reminded her of the Mongolian trick riders who had once performed at Tsarskoe Selo for her parents' anniversary.

Ana and Sergei stopped and let the men close the remaining distance. The two younger ones stood back, while the third, with woolly gray eyebrows and leaning on a staff, raised a bare hand and said, "*Da?*" Yes.

Ana did not know what to reply. The man was looking around, as if he, too, was puzzled at the lack of a plane, a pilot, or any explanation for their being there.

"*Da?*" he repeated, and she wasn't sure he understood what he was saying himself.

"My name is Ana," she said, "and this is Sergei."

The old man nodded.

How, she wondered, should she continue? "I'm afraid that we may need your help." Did he understand any other words of Russian?

"We want to go to St. Peter's Island," Sergei spoke up, pointing off to the east. "Saint. Peter's. Island."

"Kanut," he said, lightly touching his fingers to the front of his coat.

Ana, smiling tightly, repeated their own names, and the old man nodded in agreement again. "Do you speak Russian?" she asked.

"*Da.*" Then added, "Some words."

Thank God, she thought. It might be possible to make themselves understood, after all, but before she could begin, he had turned around and was heading back toward the cliffs. She could only assume that they were meant to follow, especially as his two henchmen waited for them to go on before bringing up the rear. Bewildered as she was, she did not feel threatened, as she would have with her own countrymen.

The village, if you could call it that, was not far off. She could hear huskies barking and smell smoke before she saw the huts again; there were no more than ten or fifteen of them, and they were the crudest structures she had ever seen, low piles of stone with skins stretched across the tops to make a roof. Steep trails led down the cliff to a sliver of rocky beach where canoes and kayaks were laid upside down across racks made of whalebone. Raised on its own poles was a wooden lifeboat with the name *Carpathia*, in Russian, still faintly legible on its side. Sergei squeezed her hand and with the other pointed off across the Bering Strait. In the distance, like a black fist rising from the sea, she could just make out a tiny island, oddly surrounded, even on a clear day like this, with a belt of fog.

The old man bent low and lifting a sealskin flap ducked into one of the hovels. Within, Ana was surprised to find the room so warm and spacious. The hard ground was covered with many layers of pelts and furs, haphazardly overlapping each other, and two women, as short and broad as the men, were tending to a primitive hearth with a tin chimney spout in the corner. Ana heard the bubbling of a samovar and smelled the surprising aroma of Indian tea. When one of the women, smiling with worn-down yellowed teeth, brought them the tea, it was in chipped china cups with gold rims and *Carpathia* written on them again. Ana had the strong sense that these things had all been salvaged from a wreck of the same name.

But it was clear to her that Kanut was doing his best to show them the royal treatment. And though no sugar or lemon or milk was on offer, not to mention the traditional tea cakes, beautifully decorated and arrayed, that she had once been so accustomed to, it was the most welcoming and delicious cup of tea she had ever been served. Much as her heart had hardened since Ekaterinburg, she was equally touched by any small display of human kindness.

"How did you learn to speak Russian?" she asked, carefully enunciating each word. Shrugging off his coat, the old man revealed an embroidered, deerskin vest fastened with whalebone buttons, and a little carved figure of a bear hanging down around his neck. She wondered if it was a bear that also adorned the plate in his lip.

"Traders," he said. "I work on ships." He held up an arm, hand clenched as if to hurl a harpoon. "Ten year."

At her side, Sergei radiated impatience, and she put a calming hand on his arm. "Drink the tea," she said gently, "it will refresh you," before thanking their host directly. Despite the strange surroundings, she felt as if she were back in one of the imperial palaces, welcoming a delegation from one of the far-flung outposts of the empire. Her family had once ruled nearly a sixth of the globe, and now she was reduced to the clothes on her back and the treasures in her corset. How thankful she was, yet again, that she had had the foresight to wear it, rather than stuffing it in their stolen bundle.

For several minutes, they haltingly talked about his adventures at sea—he had apparently traveled through most of the Arctic regions, hunting beavers, walruses, seals, whales—but Ana could sense the pressure building in Sergei. He kept crossing and recrossing his legs, clearing his throat, even coughing. Finally, when he could stand it no more, he broke in to say, "Can we hire you, or some of your men, to take us across to the island? We will gladly pay you whatever you want."

Although the old man smiled politely, Ana could tell he was offended at having his colloquy interrupted. He seldom had a new listener, she imagined. But when he shook his head, it was with more than petty annoyance.

"No. Not there," he said.

"Why not?"

"Bad luck," he said, his fingers unconsciously grazing the ivory bear around his neck.

Was it his good-luck charm, Ana wondered? His equivalent of the emerald cross beneath her blouse?

"Is it because the Russian settlers are there?" Sergei pressed on. "I can promise you, they will do you no harm. They are followers of a great man, a holy man, known as Father Grigori."

But the old man was as stolid and impassive as a boulder.

"He was also called Rasputin," Sergei said. "Surely you have heard of him by that name."

"Place for spirits," he said, of the island. "I tell them, do not go there. Place for the dead. Do not go."

Ana had the impression that he was saying it was a holy place for the Eskimos, sacred ground that the colonists had defiled by their very presence. Even that one glimpse of it that she had had confirmed her suspicions. It was a forbidding spot.

But Sergei was not to be dissuaded. For that matter, neither was she. They could hardly return to Russia now, and they had come all this way to find a safe harbor, if only for a year or two, until the world had come to its senses and the Reds had been turned out of power as ruthlessly as they had taken it. No, she was as determined as Sergei to reach their destination, especially now that it was within sight.

"Well, then, if you don't want to go," Sergei said, "what about selling us one of those boats down on the beach? The one from the *Carpathia*?" He held up his cup and pointed at the word on his teacup.

Kanut frowned.

"How much do you want for it?" Sergei went on, glancing at Anastasia. Reaching inside her coat, she drew out the drawstring bag in which they kept their ready bribes, and Sergei opened it, rummaged around inside, and took out a sparkling yellow diamond. He held it out toward the old man. "It's worth a thousand rubles. And what's that wooden boat worth?"

When the old man showed no interest, Sergei took out a sapphire so big and so blue it looked like a blueberry. "Both of them, you can have them both."

But Kanut still didn't budge. Ana didn't know if this was some bargaining tactic, or if he was sincerely uninterested.

Sergei's frustration was growing, but then he seemed to have hit on something. He dug deeper into the pouch and came out with three gold rings that had once belonged to Ana's sisters. Her heart ached at seeing them. But Sergei was right—the moment the gold appeared, Kanut paid attention. He didn't care about gems, but gold was the currency of the world, particularly in these regions where so much of it was mined.

"The rings—pure gold—you can have all three."

Kanut held out his palm, and when Sergei had dropped the rings onto it, he left it there . . . waiting for the diamond and the sapphire to join them. So, Ana thought, he wasn't so impervious to their beauty, and their value, after all. Sergei reluctantly handed over the jewels, too. They had just bought a sailboat for the price of the imperial yacht *Standart*.

The old man pocketed the booty in his vest, and perhaps afraid that these two fools might regret the deal, stood up and said, "You must go soon. The tides." He shouted some instructions to the women, one of whom was just about to serve them some hunks of cured blubber, and motioned for Ana and Sergei to follow him.

Outside, the two men who had been accompanying Kanut were crouching on the tundra, tossing fishtails to the dogs, who were straining at their chains. The old man issued some order in their native tongue, and the men looked puzzled. The old man said something more, and Ana saw one of them, with a gold tooth in the front of his mouth, look at her and laugh. She did not need a translator to grasp the gist of what had been said.

The trail down to the beach was steep, and with her bad foot, it was difficult to maintain her balance. Sergei put an arm around her waist and virtually carried her much of the way. At the bottom, he was winded, and bending over double, dissolved in a fit of coughs.

Under Kanut's close eye, the two men unlashed the sailboat from the whalebone posts, flipped it right-side-up, and slipped its bow into the frigid, slushy water. One of them stepped between the thwarts, and pulling on a coiled rope, raised a limp canvas sail. The other produced a dented canteen—he shook it so that they could hear it was filled—along with a knotted handful of jerky strips and some cured blubber, then tossed them all into the stern of the boat. Enough provisions, Ana surmised, for them to make it to the neighboring island . . . or die lost at sea.

Sergei, looking alarmingly winded and pale, put out a hand and helped Anastasia into the boat, and once she was settled, he took a seat at the stern, taking the tiller in one hand and the rope connected to the sail in the other. Nodding at the two Eskimos, like a hunter telling the beaters to release the hounds, he wound the rope around his wrist as the natives put their shoulders down and pushed the boat away from shore. It bobbed in place at first, before Sergei pulled the sail higher and the wind suddenly caught it and snapped it tight. The boat veered away from the rocky beach, the cold waves lapping hungrily at its sides as Ana clutched an oarlock. Nunarbuk receded quickly, its squat stone huts lost in the gray cliffside, while St. Peter's Island remained a black knob in the midst of the choppy sea. A flock of birds—all dusky hued and crying discordantly—flew around and around their feeble mast, as if issuing a warning of their own.

But Anastasia merely whispered a prayer under her breath and touched her hand to the place on her breast where the emerald cross hung. In what else could she put her faith?

Chapter 59

Alone on the open road, with Frank strapped to the gurney in the ambulance bay behind her, Nika drove on toward Nome, snow blowing straight into the car through the missing windshield. At times it was flying so thick and fast that it totally obscured the lanes, and Nika had to stop the car altogether and wait for things to clear before she could even tell which way the road was going. The highway reflectors winked red when caught in the headlight, but that was about the only help she got.

She knew there wasn't much in the way of human habitation out here, and what there was would be invisible behind the swirling snow. She coughed behind her mask—at least it kept the snow out of her mouth—but she worried that she was starting to feel light-headed. The candy bar she'd eaten earlier might not be enough to sustain her, though the very thought of food made her nauseous, not hungry. She simply had to keep control of her nerves and stay focused, for another few hours. Frank's life depended upon it.

Glancing in back, she saw that he was lying motionless under several blankets and a thermal cover, a stocking cap pulled low over his brow, all the while drifting in and out of consciousness. She was worried about a concussion, or worse, but what did she know? Despite what the patrolman might believe, she was no doctor.

If only Frank were fully conscious and aware, he could have assessed his condition himself.

She turned on the heater, full blast, but with the window gone, most of the hot air dissipated almost immediately; the rest simply melted the snow and ice piling up in the front of the ambulance until she found frigid water sloshing around among the foot pedals. Still, without the heat on, she felt that her hands, even in the gloves, might freeze.

Once the highway turned inland, the evergreens grew thicker, rising on both sides of the highway and affording some modicum of protection from the wind. They also helped her to see where the road was going, and she was able to pick up speed. She was even able to spot the occasional road sign—usually warning of some treacherous stretch ahead—but sometimes telling her how much farther it was to Nome. She'd have enough gas, she could see that, but keeping the ambulance from skidding off into a snowdrift, or colliding with some nocturnal creature out foraging, could prove deadly. She personally knew of three people in Port Orlov who had died from exposure, and one of them was an Inuit—Geordie's great uncle—and he had lived there his entire life. His hungry malamute had wandered into the Yardarm, alone, four days later.

As she huddled over the wheel, pressing on toward Nome on her own desperate mission, she was reminded of the other malamute, the famous Balto, who had carried the lifesaving serum there almost a hundred years before. She thought of the terrible hardships those dogs and mushers had endured, and even as she suffered a bout of coughing herself, she tried to bolster her spirit with their own bravery and commitment. If they could do it on open sleds, across impossible terrain, why should she be questioning her chances? She had a car, albeit a lousy one. She had a heater—even if it was turning everything to porridge—and she had a doctor on board, despite the fact that he was injured and mostly unconscious. She should have had it made.

The pep rally didn't help as much as she hoped it would.

She turned on the radio, and a country-western station kicked in, despite the storm. She didn't really follow that kind of music, so the singer, crooning about a girl who got away, wasn't familiar to her. But it didn't matter. What mattered was the connection to civilization, the voice from the void, the company it provided, as she drove on through the darkness and the freezing cold. It was a mental lifeline, and one she clung to . . . especially as she felt her own energy slipping.

How much time passed by like that, she didn't know. She was so concentrated on following the road, keeping track of those elusive reflectors posted along the sides, that she was becoming snow-blind. And more than once, without knowing it, she must have closed her eyes for a few seconds, because when she looked up again something in her field of vision had changed—a sign was already rushing past her, or the road had started to bend through a grove of trees. She'd hastily wipe the snow from her goggles, pound her arms to get the blood flowing, and tell herself in a loud voice, "Wake up, Nika—wake up!"

The ambulance was so old it had no GPS, and even the odometer was stuck, so it was hard to keep track of how much farther she had to go. She had to rely upon the infrequent signage. But there was no point in worrying about it, she thought, and less point in turning back. "You'll get there when you get there," her grandmother used to say. Back then, she'd thought it was pretty dumb. Right now, it seemed like the height of wisdom.

Taylor Swift—now there was someone she did recognize—came on, singing an old hit she'd written about some guy who'd treated her badly (who was it, Nika tried to recall, the tabloids said there were so many) when she was surprised by a voice from the ambulance bay saying, "Enough . . . enough."

She quickly turned her head to see Frank stirring on the gurney. The covers were still tucked around him, the stocking hat dusted with snow.

"No more . . . country music."

His voice came out like a frog, croaking, but it was music to her ears. He angled his head so that their eyes could meet—deep bruises were already forming all around his sockets, making it look like he'd just been punched—and she fumbled to turn off the radio.

"Are you okay?" she asked, alternating between looking at Frank and watching the road.

"Where are we?"

"On the way to the hospital, in Nome."

He closed his eyes, as if mulling it over.

"Should I pull over? Do you need my help?"

Opening them again, he said, "What happened, at the bridge?"

Unsure where to begin, she started to describe the patrol car's blocking the entrance, but he shook his head slightly and said, "That much I remember. I meant the Vanes."

She swallowed, and said, "The van blew up. It must have been loaded with lots of extra gas. You were thrown clear."

His gaze traveled around the ambulance, snow drifting around the interior like the white flakes in a snow globe. Plainly, he had noted no other passengers, and Nika didn't think she needed to say anything more. He put his head back down, staring at the roof of the cabin, and she studied the road again. In a good sign, the surface seemed smoother and more recently plowed, which meant she was getting closer to the city.

Even with the heat on high, she was shivering in her coat, and had to bend forward over the wheel when another bout of coughing hit her.

"How long has that been going on?" Slater asked, as if suddenly on alert again.

Nika waved it off, loosening her face mask to catch some fresh air; fear was making her hyperventilate. Despite the whirling snow and ice, she could see lights up ahead. Not many, but enough. With both gloves, she gripped the wheel like a captain determined to go down with the ship and steered for the lights.

A roadhouse was dimly discernible on her left, and the sign above the seawall on Gold Beach. She was driving along the Norton Sound, the wind thumping at the sides of the ambulance like paddles. The new hospital wasn't too far off. On a clear night, she might have been able to see it by now; only four stories high, it was nonetheless the tallest structure in town. The mariners, who had once used the church steeples as their beacons, now looked for the lighted antennae atop the hospital.

When she finally entered the concentrated network of streets that comprised downtown Nome, she felt like a marathoner running on shaky legs toward the finish line. As if to bring the point home, she saw off to her left the wooden archway that marked the end of the Iditarod race . . . and then the wooden sign festooned with placards showing the distance to places like Miami and Rio. The streetlamps swayed and bobbed, casting a wild yellow glow on the bingo parlors and bars, but not a soul was out on the windy, snow-choked streets.

At the corner of West Fifth Avenue, she turned too sharply, and the ambulance nearly slid into a hydrant before she could straighten it out again.

Take it easy, she told herself, *you're almost there.*

Just ahead she could see the lighted sign that read NORTON SOUND REGIONAL HEALTHCARE: EMERGENCY ENTRANCE, and blowing the horn the whole way, she piloted the car down the ramp, under the covered portico, and into the heated garage.

Several members of the hospital staff came charging out through the sliding glass doors—all duly warned, and garbed in hazmat suits— and while two of them jumped into the back of the old ambulance and started trundling Frank, still on the gurney, into the receiving area, a third yanked open the driver's side door. Melted snow and slush slopped out, and Nika felt as if she was about to slide out onto the floor, too. A burly male nurse grabbed her, and escorted her inside, a strong arm wrapped around her waist.

"Quarantine," she said, through her mask. "He needs to be quarantined."

"They know," he said, through a plastic face mask of his own. "The Alaska Highway Patrol called ahead."

She was guided onto the nearest chair, but when she glanced down at her mask, she could see that there was a pink stain on the gauze. "Me, too," she said, in a muffled voice.

But she wasn't sure he'd heard her.

When her gloves were taken off to check for frostbite, she saw in the center of her palm, where the needle had pricked her on St. Peter's island, a cluster of tiny red lines, radiating outwards like the rays of the sun in a child's drawing.

"Me, too," she repeated, drawing away from him and doubling over as a fit of coughing overwhelmed her. "Quarantine."

The nurse instinctively jumped back, and when Nika's breath finally returned, she gasped, "Stay away," before sliding down out of the chair, limp as a rag doll, and onto the gleaming linoleum floor.

Chapter 60

"Let me at least take the tiller!" Anastasia had begged Sergei, more than once, but he had refused every time. His teeth were clenched in determination, his eyes were fixed on the distant prospect of St. Peter's Island, but Ana feared for his life. He had guarded her, cared for her, loved her, for thousands of miles, and now, just as they were within sight of their destination, his skin was turning blue, and his cough had become rough and constant and alarming.

It had also become familiar.

Anastasia and her sister Tatiana had come down with the flu themselves the winter before, but bad as it had been, they had weathered it. Thousands of others, she knew, did not. In the military hospitals, where the imperial daughters helped to tend to the soldiers wounded in battle with the Germans, Ana often passed by the influenza wards, where she could hear the retching and hacking, the agonized cries and the deathly gurgles of its victims as they drowned in a tide of their own blood and mucus. Once gone, their bodies were hastily wrapped in their own sheets, and rather than being taken through the hospital corridors again, and risking a further spread of the contagion, they were slipped out a window, down a wooden chute requisitioned from a grain silo, and straight onto the back of a waiting wagon. Huge pits, swimming in quicklime, had been dug on the outskirts of St. Peters-burg, and the dead were deposited there with no observance or cere-mony of any kind. Who would have lingered in such a place to do so?

She should have known when she first heard the pilot Nevsky coughing at the inn. All the way across the continent, she and Sergei had skirted every danger, from random thieves to Bolshevik soldiers, corrupt officials to marauding Cossacks, but this was the one threat that could not be seen coming. And even if they had, what else could they do? There was no other means of getting as far as they had than to bribe a pilot. She wished an ill fate on Nevsky.

"Sergei," she warned, in the tone of a grand duchess who would brook no dissent, "I cannot sail this boat alone. For my sake, if not your own, you must rest, just for a bit."

But he had acted as if he hadn't even heard her; it was possible he had not. It looked as if the teeth were rattling in his skull, and he had collapsed in another paroxysm of coughing. It had all come on so fast she could hardly believe it . . . though she had seen such a phenome-non before. Even in the military wards, it had often been the hardiest and most energetic young men who had fallen the fastest. It was one of the great mysteries of the disease. Dr. Botkin, who had cared for Ana and her sister, had suggested it was this very constitution that contributed to the victims' demise. "Their own strength is their undo-ing," he had said, shaking his head as he read their thermometers and ordered more cold compresses to bring down their fevers. "Be glad that you are frail and pampered princesses," he'd said, and Tatiana had thrown a pillow at him.

Was that truly what had saved them? Or was it, as Rasputin had darkly ordained, that she carried in her blood a proof against the plague, that the deadly blood disease inherited from her mother, and passed on only to the male offspring, offered some immunity from the worst ravages of the Spanish flu? How strange, that her compromised nature might have been her greatest guardian.

She could serve as the messenger of doom, it seemed, but not one of its victims.

A block of ice bumped up against the boat, and a wave of icy blue water crested the starboard side and sloshed into the bottom, washing up and over her boots. She tried to lift her feet above the water, but she could not maintain her balance on the narrow thwart for very long. Both her feet were nearly frozen, but the left one in particular, wearing the boot specially designed to accommodate its deformity, had no feeling left in it at all. She longed to remove the boot and rub the life back into it, ideally before a roaring fire . . . but St. Peter's Island was still far off.

And the closer they got, the less welcoming it appeared.

A gnarled black rock, swathed in mist and surrounded by jagged rocks sticking up out of the water like spikes, it was the least likely place on earth to have earned the name of sanctuary. But that, she knew, was precisely why it had been chosen. The followers of Father Grigori, who believed, as she did, that he was a prophet, had traveled all the way from Pokrovskoe to take refuge here, to build their church and to await the return of their *starets*. For Ana, his bodily return seemed unlikely—she knew all too well the ravages that had been inflicted upon him before his drowning in the Neva River—but she did not doubt the strength of his spirit. She did not doubt the image she had seen, swirling up out of the gun smoke in that cellar in Ekaterinburg, any more than she doubted the emerald cross, imbued with his powers, that she still wore under her coat and corset.

Sergei had taken his hand from the tiller and was pointing, with one shaking finger, ahead at the island. When she reached out and stroked the side of his face, he drew back in horror, afraid of infecting her, and insisted that she look for the fires. "They will light fires."

And then, racked with a cough that drenched his own hand in blood, he had let go of the sail and let go of life. Blessing her, he had rolled over the side of the boat, and into the churning waters of the strait.

The last thing she had seen of him, as she lunged to the stern and his body was engulfed by the waves, was a frozen blue cornflower bobbing between the shards of ice. It was, undoubtedly, the one she had first given him by the train tracks in Siberia.

She'd have given every gem in her corset to reclaim it.

And then she had turned to the task of steering the boat through the blinding fog and the heaving waves, steadfastly looking for the fires that Sergei said they lighted on the cliffs every night. "They are the beacons to guide their prophet, lost and wandering in the dark, to their new home," he had told her. And when she saw them burning like tiny candles at the end of a long and gloomy hallway, her heart had risen in her chest. The boat, as if guided by some miraculous hand, had passed through the rocks and reefs and tide pools, and ground to a halt on a narrow strip of pebbles and sand. When she had sunk to her knees on the beach, soaked to the skin and gasping for breath, she had thanked God for her deliverance. Over the crashing of the surf, she thought she heard the tolling of a church bell.

And in the last light of day—a day that was shorter in this northern part of the world than anywhere else—she had looked up to see her rescuers running down the beach toward her. But the prayer of thanks turned to ashes in her mouth as they closed the distance.

Far from coming to her rescue, these were a pack of black wolves, their eyes shining orange and their white fangs bared. The boat was gone, drifting back out to sea, and even if she had wanted to try to outrun them, there was nowhere to go. Pulling the cross from beneath her clothes, she clutched it tightly, lowered her head in prayer, and prepared to join her massacred family in Heaven. The wolves came on, and at any moment she expected to hear their bloodthirsty panting and feel their sharp teeth at her throat. But just as she braced herself for the attack, she heard a sharp, piercing whistle from the cliffs above, and when she lifted her eyes long enough to look through the veil of her own ice-rimed hair, she saw the wolves drawing up short, nervously pawing the sand, moving in circles around her, whining and barking like dogs at the kitchen door.

What had happened?

The lead wolf, with a white blaze on its muzzle, stepped closer— she could smell his rank breath—and stared at her hands, clutching the emerald cross, with an almost human curiosity.

The whistle came again, and all the wolves turned to look at the cliffside, where a man in a long black cassock was slowly descending an almost invisible flight of stairs. For a second, Anastasia thought, "My God, it *is* Rasputin!" But as he marched across the frozen beach, she saw that it was someone else—tall as Rasputin and as broad in the shoulder, but with a face that was more benign, less worldly, and un-shrouded by a tangled black beard. There was an undeniable ferocity in Father Grigori's features, but none in this priest's. He waved one arm, and the wolves, except for their leader, were swept back like dust before a broom.

"Anastasia," he said, dropping to his knees beside her, "I am Dea-con Stefan."

It was the man Sergei had told her about, the man who had led the pilgrims from his village.

Taking her into his embrace, he said, "We have been waiting a long time for you."

The hot tears suddenly springing from her eyes warmed her face, and when the wolf with the white nose stepped forward to lick them, the deacon did not intervene.

Part Four

Chapter 61

It was a strange situation. That much, Dr. Frank Slater would have been the first to admit.

On the one hand, he was a patient at the Nome Regional Health Center, most of his time spent lying in the cranked-up hospital bed and under observation by closed-circuit camera and through the glass panels of the ICU doors, and on the other hand he was in charge.

The explosion on the bridge had left him with a concussion, two fractured ribs that made him wince with every deep breath he took, and more cuts and bruises than he could count. His malarial meds had had to be airlifted in—normally, there wasn't much call for them in Alaska—but if anything, it was his chronic disease that had helped to save his life. Because of his already compromised immunological response, and the ingestion of his retroviral drugs, any exposure he had undergone to the Spanish flu had been mitigated. His system was already too weakened to mount the kind of stiff resistance that engendered the fatal cytokine storms that had killed so many millions.

It was the first time he'd ever been grateful for that damn mosquito bite.

But even as he was being nursed back to health, he knew that he bore the responsibility for running this quarantine unit. He had im-

provised it himself—first by commandeering the ICU, then by putting
the staff through intensive, on-the-spot training. They were a lot more
accustomed to routine problems like heart attacks and hunting acci-
dents, but even as they were wheeling him in on the gurney, he had
begun to issue instructions on how to deal with a virus as potentially
deadly as this one. He had strictly cordoned off this area of the hospital's top floor, nearly all communication was done through the intercom system, and only a limited number of personnel, always outfitted
in full hazmat gear, were ever allowed in or out. Right now, the unit
had just one other patient—Nikaluk Tincook.

And she had not fared as well as he had. Like Dr. Lantos, she had
been brought in suffering not only from the flu, but from septicemia,
a flood tide of bacteria clogging her bloodstream. The minute Slater
had been told about the red lines on her palm, he had personally
drained and sterilized the wound site, but it was too little, too late.
The flu and the sepsis were like old pals, reunited now and working in
deadly concert, and if he didn't calibrate his responses perfectly, he
could lose her to either one. The fear gnawed at him like a rat.

Dr. Jonah Knudsen, the crusty old coot who normally ran the hospital, had advised that she be sent on to the state-of-the-art facility in
Juneau, where Dr. Lantos was being treated. Standing outside the
door and speaking through the intercom, he had told Slater that Rebekah Vane and her sister Bathsheba had also been sent there.

"Have they presented symptoms of the flu?"

"Rebekah has," he said, "but then she apparently had greater physical contact with Harley Vane and his bodily fluids."

"His bodily fluids?"

"She served him tea and toast, and later, after he'd vomited, she
cleaned up the mess."

Then it made some sense.

"Although her condition is otherwise stable, she does have a fractured jaw and other minor injuries, and just so you know, she has
named you, in addition to the federal government, in a lawsuit for a
host of damages. First and foremost, of course, is the loss of her husband."

Of course, Slater thought. Even as they were fighting to save her life, from an incident that would never have occurred if her family had not gone on an illegal treasure hunt in the first place, she was lying in her bed concocting lawsuits. It was the new American pastime, and it made him, more than ever, want to find a way to get away from everything that it suggested and implied. He simply wanted to practice medicine again, in a place where his talents and his work would be valued and the bureaucracy extended no further than the usual burden of insurance forms. His days as a globe-trotting epidemiologist might be over—Dr. Levinson had made that perfectly clear—but his efforts to save Lantos, and now Nika, had reminded him of the satisfaction to be had from healing just one person. What was that old Hebrew proverb he'd once heard Dr. Levinson herself say—"If you save one life, it's the same as saving the whole world."

Right now the only life he wanted to save, even more than his own, was Nika's.

All day long, her small compact body, sweating through one hospital gown after another, had been racked with coughing fits and spasms. Her long black hair, tied into a tight braid, had lashed the pillows like a whip. Her platelet count plummeted, her blood gases revealed she had entered into metabolic acidosis, her breathing became so faint that a mechanical ventilator had to be wheeled in; her major organs began to shut down like dominoes falling in a row. Lungs, liver, central nervous system; when her kidneys failed, Slater had had to immediately put her on dialysis.

She'd been young and healthy and athletic, and now it was the very strength of her immune system that was threatening to kill her. It was kicking into overdrive . . . and throwing her whole body into shock. Many patients, he knew, never came back from it.

The hospital staff, panicking, looked to him for guidance, and he ordered up a fresh barrage of IV antibiotics—cindamycin and flucytosine this time—along with vasopressors to constrict her blood vessels and treat her hypotension, insulin to stabilize her blood-sugar levels, corticosteroids to counteract the inflammation. The diseases were burning through her like a forest fire, consuming her just as her Inuit ancestors had once been consumed, and he had to find a way to sustain her long enough to let the contagion burn itself out.

"Dr. Slater," one of the nurses said after he had maintained his vigil for hours on end, "why don't you go back to your own room and take a break? We'll alert you if anything changes."

"I'll stay," he said, perched in a fresh lime-green hazard suit on the plastic chair in the corner. Every few hours, the chair, like everything else in this section of the old ICU, was sprayed from top to bottom with a powerful disinfectant.

Surrounded by the machines and screens, tubes and wires and IV trolleys, Nika could barely be seen. But every fluctuation in her respiration or temperature, cardiac rate or cerebral activity, was being tracked and monitored by the array of instruments that had been brought into the room. Slater, exhausted, slumped backward in the chair, and felt the ivory *bilikin* on its leather string swing against his damp skin.

The little owl, with its furled wings. On the island, Professor Kozak had asked about it, and Nika had said it was purportedly from a woolly mammoth.

Impressed, Slater had looked at it even more closely.

"That would make it, perhaps, eleven thousand years old," Kozak had later informed him.

Slater wondered if it had gained some extra charge, some supernatural potency, over all those centuries it had endured. Although he wasn't a believer in such things—how could he be?—right now he was ready to accept any help he could get.

Dr. Knudsen appeared, hovering in a white lab coat, through the glass panel in the door.

That was not the help he had hoped for.

"I'm sorry to disturb you," Knudsen said, sounding not sorry at all as he bent toward the intercom box, "but I thought you should know."

"Know what?" Slater said, already dreading the reply.

"It's about Dr. Eva Lantos. She died one hour ago."

It was like a hammer blow to his already bruised chest.

"For purposes of public safety," Knudsen continued, "the official death certificate entered in Juneau is recording it as simply a lethal bacterial infection. But her body was immediately removed to the AFIP labs in D.C. by Army air transport."

Slater could see that the doctor was holding a clipboard against his chest, and rocking on his heels.

"I'm very sorry," he said.

But Slater didn't think he looked any more regretful than he sounded; he looked like a man who didn't mind telling his privileged guest, the one who had taken over his own ICU, that he wasn't such a hotshot, after all.

It was the first time Slater had lost a colleague on one of his missions; you could not be a field epidemiologist, in the world's most deadly and undeveloped regions, and not be aware of the risks you were taking. It was something that lurked in the back of your mind the whole time.

But Eva Lantos? She'd been holed up in her M.I.T. lab, safe and sound, and he had lured her out. While nothing that happened on the island could have logically been foreseen—it was a place where logic seemed to hold no sway—he blamed himself, all the same. It was a simple, straight line he could draw—if he had not phoned her that afternoon from his office at the institute, she'd be happily teasing out the rat genome in Boston today. Instead, she was dead in an isolation tank at AFIP.

Slater closed his eyes and wished that Knudsen, this angel of death, would leave him be. When he looked again, Knudsen was gone. Thank God for small favors. And then he realized that, through the fabric of his suit, his fingers were clutching the ivory owl.

The monitors kept up a steady beeping, the ventilator whooshed, the machines hummed, and Nika—silent, still, her eyes shut—fought on. He remembered the first time they'd met, when the helicopter had chased the Zamboni she was driving right off the ice rink. They'd gotten off on the wrong foot, especially when he was so slow to realize that she was the mayor of the town—*and* the tribal elder, to boot. He'd had a lot of catching up to do.

But he had quickly come to recognize her virtues, her skills . . . and her beauty. That last item he had tried to overlook—he knew he had serious work to do, and it was no time to become distracted. Slater had always maintained a strictly professional demeanor in the field, and on an expedition of this importance, it was especially critical. He had never intended to feel the way he did now, he had never seen it coming. Like that fantastic display of the aurora borealis they had watched together one night, it had taken him utterly by surprise.

And now . . . what did he do with these feelings? He had never told her how he felt. He had never told her that he had fallen in love with her. But if she died tonight, in this terrible place, away from her home and the people she loved, he did not know how he would bear it.

He had lost all track of time. There was a clock on the wall, but he had no idea if it was 10 A.M. or 10 P.M. There was only one window, down at the end of the hall, and even that one was tinted and permasealed. Meanwhile, the Alaskan daylight was coming later, and growing shorter, all the time. How the Inuit had survived in this intemperate world astonished him still, but they were a hardy lot . . . and that, in the end, was what he was counting on. Nika's ancestors had been among the sturdy few to survive the Spanish flu epidemic of 1918, and perhaps that acquired immunity had been passed down to the young woman fighting for her life now.

He unzipped his suit enough to pull the ivory owl through, and then he snapped the cord. He smoothed a spot on her blanket and laid the *bilikin* down on top of it. He knew that she was in a very dark place, and if the owl could truly prove to be a guide, then now was the time.

Chapter 62

The deacon, not surprisingly, was the first to succumb.

It was he who had first embraced Anastasia on the beach, he who had held her hands—the very hands that had caressed the cheek of the dying Sergei—as he escorted her up the steps chiseled into the cliffs and through the main gates of the colony. The others, maybe three or four dozen in all, were beside themselves with joy when she arrived. She was brought into the church, where a supper had been hastily laid on a table in the nave, and the bell in the church dome was rung over and over. Her safe arrival was considered a harbinger of a bigger, and even better, thing to come. She was the long-anticipated psychopomp, the bird who heralded the return of Rasputin himself.

Anastasia was seated at the head of a long and narrow refectory table, and to her embarrassment an old peasant woman summarily removed the sopping boots from her feet, and soaked her aching, frozen toes in a bucket of warm, salted water. The embarrassment immediately gave way, however, to a tingling sensation, and a not-altogether-pleasant throbbing as the blood once again began to circulate in her feet and ankles. Deacon Stefan offered her a glass of something she imagined to be grog—Nagorny the sailor had described such stuff—as bracing as it was vile. Other women were still bringing hot bread and pots of stew to the table, and Anastasia, though so grief-stricken at the loss of Sergei that she could barely eat, took what she could, and thanked them profusely. All of them—men, women, and a handful of children—stared at her unabashedly, and she could not help but notice how often their eyes went to the emerald cross. Several times she saw the older colonists cross themselves while gazing upon it. They listened, enraptured, as she recounted the journey that she, and the missing Sergei, had undertaken. It was rare enough, Ana surmised, that they saw anyone new here, and rarer still when that newcomer was one of the grand duchesses of the three-hundred-year-old Romanov dynasty.

Here, if nowhere in Russia anymore, that title commanded respect, even reverence.

A cabin was set aside for Ana, but when she saw that it was filled with someone else's personal belongings—a hand-stitched quilt, an icon of St. Peter, pans and kettles on hooks above a potbellied stove, a dress in the armoire—she tried to decline. "I don't want to put anyone out of her home," she said. "I can sleep anywhere—the church would be fine."

But Deacon Stefan had insisted. "The people vied for the opportunity," he said. "Vera would be mortified if you didn't accept her hospitality. She is honored."

And so she had accepted. She did not even remember saying good-night to the deacon. The second she had sat down on the straw-filled mattress, she had been overwhelmed by fatigue and fallen into not so much a sleep as a stupor. She had a vague recollection of the old woman who had bathed her feet coming into the room and removing her other damp clothes. The quilt was thrown over her, tucked tight to her chin, and a bearskin was thrown over that. Ana did not move a muscle; she felt she couldn't even if she tried. For many hours—she never knew exactly—she lay there, half-asleep and half-aware of everything and everyone. Her mind traveled back over the endless journey that had brought her to the island at last, combing over every detail, revisiting every scene, from the attic room at Novo-Tikhvin to the cramped compartment on the Trans-Siberian Railway (where a conductor had become so inordinately curious about Ana that Sergei had made them disembark in the dead of night at the next fueling station).

Sergei. One more name to add to the list of the dead and beloved in her life. The list was already so long, and she was barely eighteen. How long would it become? *Forgive me,* she prayed. *Forgive me for the suffering my family and I have brought upon so many.* She felt herself both blessed—she alone had survived the slaughter in the house with the whitewashed windows—and at the same time accursed. No one else would have to live on, knowing exactly what had happened there, reliving it in dreams . . . and nightmares.

Late the next day, when she arose, the few hours of sunlight had nearly passed. She ventured out of the tiny cabin and into a frostbitten twilight. All around her rose a stockade wall, and within it a small but tidy colony had been erected. Apart from the church, which stood at one end and appeared to serve also as a meeting house and dining hall, there were cabins and livestock pens, vegetable gardens, a blacksmith shop and apothecary, even a common outhouse, with separate doors for men and women. However bleak the surroundings, it was a world unto itself.

A man splitting logs looked up from his chores and touched the brim of his fur cap. Then he returned to his work. A woman in a long peasant skirt, with a woolen shawl drawn over her head and around her shoulders, carried a bushel basket of roots and mushrooms into one of the cabins; a pale and dismal light crept across the threshold before the door was closed again with a creak and a thump. A cold wind whistled between the timbers of the stockade, and Ana was inevitably reminded of the palisade that had been built around the Ipatiev house. Yurovsky had said it was for the protection of the imperial family as they took the air, but no one had been fooled by that. It might just as well have been iron bars.

"So you're awake?" she heard, as Deacon Stefan strode through the main gates; he was carrying a fishing pole over one shoulder and a couple of halibut on a line. "I looked in on you earlier. You were sleeping like a log."

He wasn't wearing his cassock anymore but a thick fur coat that fell to his ankles. Long strands of his hair, so blond as to be almost white, spilled from under his Cossack-style hat. "Are you feeling well?"

"Yes," she said, "I think so." She hadn't even considered the question, there was so much else to absorb and take in.

"The man you mentioned at dinner—Sergei," he said, his blue eyes cast downward, "there has been no sign of him. I have searched the shoreline."

Anastasia nodded.

"But the sea often yields in the end," he said. "We will keep looking."

Ana thanked him, but he brushed it aside.

"We will say a mass for him every day until he has been returned to us."

And then he coughed, just once, into the back of his clenched hand, and Ana felt her spine stiffen.

"You've been out fishing in this cold?" she said. "I hope you haven't caught a chill." She had not mentioned Sergei's illness. She had only said he was thrown from the boat during the crossing.

"It's nothing," he said, but coughing again. "No one ever recommended this place for its weather."

"No, I don't imagine that they do."

"Let me get these fish into a frying pan," he said. "We all eat together in the church, as soon as it is dark."

"What can I do to help?" Anastasia said. Although a grand duchess by birth, she had been brought up to treat the common people with respect and to share their burdens when possible. It was why their father had made them sleep for years in ordinary cots in plainly decorated bedrooms, and their mother had ferried them to the Army hospitals to tend to the wounded. It was a puzzle Anastasia would never solve, how the peasants and workmen and soldiers of Russia had been convinced by a heartless revolutionary named Lenin that her family had not cared for and loved—yes, "loved" was not too strong a word for it—all of them.

Needless to say, she no longer felt that way at all, and she wondered what Father Grigori would say if she were able to tell him so.

"Never fear," the deacon said in answer to her last question. "There's no shortage of things that need to be done in the colony. You'll fit right in, Your Highness."

He threw her a half smile over his shoulder as he marched on with the fish swinging on the line over his shoulder. She tried to return the smile, but her face smarted, and she wasn't sure if it was due to the cutting wind or the fact that she was so unaccustomed to the expression.

Chapter 63

Nika was running, running so hard the blood beat in her ears and muffled all other sounds. Running so hard the breath was raw in her throat and her lungs ached. Running so hard that her legs were starting to wobble and her shoulders to sag.

But she had to keep going, across the frozen hills, through the brush and barren trees, on and on . . . toward a low rise overlooking a tiny village huddled on the shoreline. There, she stopped, doubling over with her hands on her knees to catch her breath.

It was late autumn, and while some of the natives had already erected their igloos, with domed roofs and walls of packed snow, others were still making do with the tents made of caribou skins, stitched together with long ropes of sinew and anchored with bones. She waited, watching, but even from the ceremonial hall—the *qarqui*—at the far end of the village, there was no sign of any human activity. There were no fishermen hauling their kayaks onto the rocky beach, no children playing, no women tending to the huskies. (And where *were* the dogs?) It was an eerie sight, the lonely village, lying under a fresh blanket of snow, with a dense, dark cloud bank advancing across the Bering Sea and swallowing the last pale rays of the sun as it came.

The only sounds were the wind whipping the waves onto the rocks, and the cries of cormorants circling overhead.

How odd, she thought, to hear cormorants. They had gone extinct years ago.

But then, this *was* years ago. Even now, Nika was aware that what she was experiencing was real, but unreal . . . that she was only a dreamer, inhabiting a dream, in which she nevertheless had a crucial role to play. She adjusted the straps of the knapsack digging into her shoulders, careful not to damage the precious ampoules that she knew—simply knew—were nestled inside.

She felt as if she had been traveling for days without stopping, all the while burning with fever, or racked with chills. She felt racked and depleted, and her mouth was filled with the acrid taste of her own blood. Her mukluks were slick with ice, her sealskin coat damp with her own perspiration. But she knew that she had to go down into the village. It was there her work had to be done.

Her boots skidding in the snow, she slid down the hill and approached the outermost of the igloos. The entryway was dug several feet down into the earth, and driftwood had been used to make a crude door. But when she tried to push it open, it stuck. Crouching down, she pushed harder, and something that was leaning against the other side gradually fell to one side, and she was able to peer into the gloom.

The *kudluk,* the lantern that was normally burning bright with seal oil, was extinguished, but the skylight let in enough illumination for her to make out several people scattered around the floor in contorted postures. Their faces were frozen in rictus, and their eyes stared blankly. Splashes of blood spotted the hides and straw that had been laid down on the hard sod. The body that had been slumped behind the door was a young man still in his rawhide coat, the hood raised, his hands clenched around a hunting knife buried to the hilt in his own gut. It appeared that he had chosen to take his own life rather than endure what the others had suffered.

Nika backed out, pulling the door closed behind her. Horrifying as the sight had been, she was not surprised by it; it was as if she had known what to expect behind that door, as if she had remembered it from some deep well of the collective unconscious. And as she stepped away, she felt her foot catch on something under the snow—a chain. She jerked it up, and found it was attached to a stake embedded in the permafrost . . . to which a husky had been tethered. She brushed some of the snow away, and found the dog, dead of exposure, or starvation. It lay there now like a concrete statue, its tongue, lolling from its mouth, as blue as the ice in a crevasse.

Looking around at the neighboring huts and igloos, she saw similar mounds, where other dogs presumably now lay dead and frozen solid.

As she moved among the dwellings, poking her head in one, then another, she saw similar grisly scenes, native people lying dead on blood-soaked sod and animal hides. As she came to the last one before the *qarqui*, she heard sounds from inside, and thought she might at last find some survivors. Throwing back the antelope skins that covered the doorway, she stepped inside and stopped dead as the startled dogs, their jaws and fur matted with blood, looked up from their feast. A couple of them still trailed the leashes and stakes that they had managed to rip from the ground. Mingled among their paws were the ravaged remains of the corpses they had been tearing apart.

A big white dog, its snout dyed pink by now, growled menacingly, warning her away from the banquet.

Slowly, she stepped back and let the antelope skins conceal her from view.

The clouds had filled the sky now, and the last of the daylight disappeared as she hurried to seek refuge in the ceremonial house, the town hall, as it were, of the Inuit people, where the villagers would traditionally come to sing and dance and perform their sacred rituals during the long, dark Arctic winters. It was a big, oval-shaped building, made from chunks of tundra and slabs of driftwood, knitted together with all sorts of skins and pelts, and the moment she ducked her head to enter the passageway that led to the narrow door—fashioned from what had once been the bottom of a kayak—she again heard noises. But not the sound of scavenging dogs this time. When she stood still, she heard a woman's voice—faint and elderly—speaking in her native tongue.

She opened the door, which swung on a hinge made of caribou gut, and saw the old Inuit woman, short and squat, stirring a pot with a long ivory spoon. In the yellow glow of the fire, several children—their black eyes filled with grief—gathered around the old woman like bear cubs keeping close to their mother.

When Nika said, "Thank God some of you are still alive," they all turned and stared at her as if she were a messenger from a foreign planet. Stone benches lined the walls, and the ceiling was hung with antlers and ornamental figures carved from whale baleen and walrus tusks. A totem pole, identical to the one in the center of Port Orlov, stood proud and tall as a mast at the far end of the lodge. Looking at its vivid colors and erect carriage, Nika was reminded of all that it represented, and felt a wave of shame. If she were given the chance, she resolved to do what she should have done long before.

"Nikaluk," the old woman said in a weak but tender voice, "I knew you would come." She had high, Asiatic cheekbones and her few remaining teeth were worn down to yellow nubs. "I knew it."

If only Nika herself had been so sure. The flu had burned through her as it had burned through nearly everyone else, but somehow, she—like the children and the old people, whose frail bodies could not mount such an overwhelming, and self-destructive, resistance—had lived through it. Her chest, which had once felt like it was filled with smoldering coals, was cooler now. Her throat was no longer choked with a rising tide of her own blood. Her eyes, which had burned like shining pebbles on the beach, felt as if they had been bathed in a stream.

The old woman came toward her, the children clinging to her ragged skirts, and said, "You will save us."

"Yes, yes," Nika said, remembering her mission and slinging the knapsack off her shoulders. Quickly kneeling to undo the straps, she dug inside for the ampoules of serum . . . but to her horror they weren't there. She dug deeper, but all she found inside was icicles, clattering like glass. How could she have been so deceived?

She had failed. At this, the most critical time, she had failed her people, and the shame, even greater now than it had been when she first saw the totem pole as it should have been, made her almost unable to look up into the old woman's eyes.

But then she felt a hand on her head, like a benediction, and when she did look up, the old woman said, "You will save us," and pressed something into Nika's palm.

It was small and smooth, a piece of ivory, simply carved. In the flickering firelight, Nika saw that it was an owl, a guardian spirit of the Inuit people. Nika wasn't sure if she should accept it—perhaps it was the only thing of value the old woman possessed—but she knew it would give offense if she tried to refuse it.

The old woman stroked Nika's hair and smiled. A smile that reminded her of her own grandmother. Or, could it be . . . her own great-grandmother?

In that instant, Nika suddenly understood that she had not come to this place to give at all. She had come there to receive.

Bowing her head, she said, "I will try . . . I will try."

But then, as if from the end of a long tunnel, she heard her name. "Nika?"

This was not the old woman's voice anymore, nor did she feel her hand on her hair. A white light suffused the room, a light too bright for her eyes, and a different hand—in a cool glove—was smoothing her brow.

"I will try," she said one last time, before the old woman faded away, along with the children, the campfire, and the ancestral carvings hanging from the beams of the *qarqui*. The last thing to disappear was the grinning otter on the totem pole.

"Nika," she heard again, and cracked her eyes open enough to see Frank, perched beside her bedside, surrounded by blinking screens and softly beeping monitors. "Nika," he said, pulling off his visor and tossing it aside.

His cheeks, she could see, were wet with tears.

"You're all right now," he said, though somehow she knew that already. "You're going to be all right."

He lifted her hand off the blanket and pressed his lips against it, and she could tell that she was holding something tight. When she opened her palm, she saw the ivory *bilikin* that she had once given him. It seemed like ages ago.

But the little owl had done its job, she thought . . . guiding her through the darkness, through the other world that she had just left, and back into the land of the living. She would never forget its help, nor the sacred trust she now knew that it signified.

"I was so afraid," Frank said. "I thought I might have missed my chance."

"Your chance?" Nika said, her throat as dry as parchment. Frank looked haggard and drawn, and it was plain that he hadn't shaved in days.

"To tell you that I love you."

If Nika had not already been lying down, and drained of all energy, she knew she would have reacted quite differently. All she could do now was squeeze his hand with what strength she had, and say, "That's a relief."

Frank, taken aback, straightened up in his chair and laughed. "A relief?"

"I didn't want to be in this thing alone," she said.

Chapter 64

The next morning, the deacon was not awake to ring the church bell. At dinner, he hadn't had much of an appetite for the fish he'd caught, and he'd complained of a headache and chills. When Anastasia was shown to his cabin, she warned the others not to enter and went in by herself.

Although it was well past breakfast time, the sun had not yet risen. By the light of the oil lamp flickering beside his bed, Ana could see that the deacon had contracted the flu. His white-blond hair was damp and stringy, spread across his pillow, and his brow was beaded with sweat. His pale eyes were wandering distractedly around the room, and there were gobbets of dried blood on his blanket. She had seen soldiers like this in the hospital wards . . . and she had heard their bodies, shrouded in sheets, trundling down the grain chute and into the waiting wagons.

Stepping outside, where several of the colonists were waiting apprehensively for word, she called for hot water and broth, extra blankets, firewood, and brandy if they had it. She tried to remember what Dr. Botkin had prescribed and guess what he would have done, but in her heart she knew that it was all in God's hands already. The Spanish flu took whomever it wanted—the strongest, first—and most of the time it took them fast.

For the rest of the day, Anastasia stayed by the deacon's side, administering to him, trying in vain to get him to take some sustenance, mopping his brow and wiping the flecks of blood from his lips after he had been racked by a coughing fit. Occasionally, he muttered the name Father Grigori, and it was clear to Anastasia that he was speaking to him as if he were there. Several times, the conversation seemed so real that Ana turned in her chair, or went to the door and peeked outside, but each time all she saw gathered in the gloom were a handful of colonists, tolling their beads, clutching and kissing holy icons, and murmuring prayers for the deacon's recovery. So many of them focused on the emerald cross she wore around her neck that she eventually grew self-conscious about it, and tucked it away. Whatever powers they thought it possessed were proving useless against the onslaught of the flu.

Once or twice, she heard muffled coughing among them, which only exacerbated the dread in her heart.

By the following dawn, the deacon was dead.

Anastasia cleaned him as best she could, then took his black cassock, with the sleeves lined in scarlet silk, and put it on him. She crossed his hands across his chest, then sat down at the wooden table that served as his desk. On it, there were writing materials, loose pages from his sermons, and an icon of the Virgin Mary, adorned with three white diamonds. Something so valuable could only have come from the hand of Rasputin himself. Using a scrap of paper from one of his sermons, she wrote a prayer for the soul of Deacon Stefan, curled it up, and slipped it into one of his lifeless hands, then, in the other, she placed the icon. He was as ready to meet his Maker as anyone would ever be.

Not for the first time she longed to make that final journey herself . . . to see Sergei, her family, her friends, kindly Dr. Botkin, Nagorny, the maid Demidova. Despite what the Russian Orthodox Church might believe, Anastasia was sure that her dog Jemmy would be waiting for her there, too. In a world so awash in hate, why should love—of any kind—not find a safe haven in the next?

Weary, and famished herself, she blew out the oil lamp, closed the door, and went to the church, in search of company and a communal meal. But unlike before, when dozens of people had drawn up chairs and pews to the sides of the long refectory tables, there were only ten or twelve souls present, and even they shied away when she came through the double doors. Vera fell to her knees in front of the iconostasis screen, crossing herself three times. The man who had been chopping wood bent his head over his soup bowl and barely dared to look up.

A woman laying pewter plates on the table asked, "How is the deacon?"

"The deacon has passed away," Ana replied, and she saw the woman cast a quick look around the room, as if to confirm that everyone had heard. Several people cried out, an old man hurled his pipe at the floor, and there was a general exodus from the church. Some of them nodded solemnly in Ana's direction as they left, their haggard faces filled with fear and incomprehension . . . but all of them, without exception, gave her a wide berth.

Standing alone in the nave, she realized that she had not only come to the ends of the earth, but to the end of everything this life had to offer. Already, she had gone from the herald of the prophet Father Grigori, celebrated and welcomed, to the harbinger of doom. And though she still carried the aura and the emblem of Rasputin himself, she had sown confusion in his flock. They no longer knew what to make of her, or how to interpret the trouble she had brought upon their heads. Had they committed some error, they no doubt wondered, in their way of life? Had they failed in their devotion? And was Anastasia an instrument of divine retribution?

Even if they had summoned the courage to ask, these were questions she could never have answered herself.

What followed over the coming days was as inevitable as it was tragic. One by one, the colonists came down with the flu, and one by one the survivors used dynamite and pickaxes to open shallow graves in the ground and give the dead some semblance of a Christian burial. Ana attended the interments—indeed, the colonists would not have proceeded without her silent presence, such was her prestige as a princess and Rasputin's chosen one—but after a while it became nearly impossible for her to bear. The graveyard was poised on the cliffs above the Bering Sea, and Ana had to fight an overwhelming impulse to hurl herself off the precipice and into the waiting sea below. All that kept her from doing so was an even greater fear—a fear that the power of the emerald cross was so great she might find herself alive even then, tossing and turning beneath the icy waves for eternity.

Among the last to die was the sexton, and Ana took over his job, dutifully recording the names of the deceased and the dates on which they died. Some of them, in their delirium, had wandered off into the woods, never to be seen again, while others perished on the rocks below the colony, their bodies lying crumpled and still until the tide took them out to sea. For the rest, Ana scrounged among the half-completed headstones and coffin lids that the sexton had left, and provided each of them with as much of a proper burial as could still be managed. The sexton—plainly as industrious as he was fatalistic—had also had the foresight to leave a number of empty graves . . . more than enough, as it turned out, to accommodate his fellow colonists.

And then, one day, there was no one left to bury, no one left to mourn. There was no one else at all. She had walked to the edge of the cemetery, clutching the emerald cross when she saw a dark figure lying on the beach below, the tails of a sealskin coat spread like a bat's wings across the pebbles and sand.

She stopped dead, her toes already extending over the precipice, and stared down at it. Could it be? After all this time?

Making her way down to the beach, she approached the body as if it were a trap waiting to spring. She did not believe her own eyes. But as she came closer, she saw that even now, a brown cowlick, frozen stiff, was standing up at the back of his head. She knelt, the freezing sand crackling under her boots, and gently turned the body onto its back. Coated in ice, Sergei looked as if he were made of glass.

"The sea often yields in the end," the deacon had said. And so it had.

In the cemetery, an empty grave remained; it was the one closest to the cliffs, and Anastasia had wondered if anyone would be left to put her in it one day. Now she could use it to embrace the body of her beloved protector, Sergei, instead—which was precisely what she did.

As he lay there now in his open casket, she reached in under her coat. Lifting out the emerald cross, she read one last time the blessing Rasputin had engraved on its silver frame: "No one can break the chains of love that bind us." A play on her name, as the breaker of chains. But she wanted the chains broken now. She wanted whatever force it was that tethered her to this earth to be sundered forever.

She raised Sergei's head and draped the chain around it, the emerald cross resting on his chest. Then she lifted the lid of the coffin—an elaborately carved piece with an image of St. Peter himself on it—and fitted it into place. Something, she thought, had told her to preserve this coffin until now. Then, driving home the traditional four nails, she shoveled as much dirt and snow as she could loosen into the grave. One of the black wolves that haunted the island appeared at the gates to the cemetery, the gates where she had obsessively whittled her pleas for forgiveness, and raising its head, let out a mournful howl. But Ana wasn't afraid. These creatures, she knew, were only souls as lost and bereft as she was . . . sentenced to the same kind of purgatory. They, too, were trapped in a world not of their own making, as unable to transcend it as they were to find peace. From the moment the black wolf had licked the tears from her face on the beach, she had recognized that their fate and hers were conjoined—weren't they all Rasputin's faithful children?—and she had known that they would only end their unhappy journey when hers, too, had come to an end.

Chapter 65

As soon as Slater saw Nika wheeled to the ambulance, protesting all the way—"I can walk, you know! I don't need a wheelchair!"—he was sure she was back to being herself. Hospital protocols, however, dictated that she leave the Nome Regional Health Center in a chair, and prudence dictated that an ambulance convey her all the way back to her home in Port Orlov.

"I'll see you there in no time," Slater said, leaning down for one last kiss, as the orderly pushing the chair politely looked away.

"The work on the totem pole should be done by now," she said.

Indeed, it was almost the first order she had given once the fever had broken and she had become fully conscious again. Although he had never asked, Slater knew that something had happened to her while she hovered in that land between life and death, something that compelled her to restore the totem pole in Port Orlov to its former glory and prominence.

"The unveiling is going to be a pretty big celebration for a town like ours."

"Sounds like a party I can't miss."

"Then don't."

She was allowed to sit up front with the ambulance driver, and once they had pulled away, Slater crossed the snowy parking lot to the waiting Coast Guard helicopter. This time, he was alone in the passenger compartment, and the pilot, starting the engine, ordered him to buckle in immediately. "We're on a very tight schedule," he said, showing him none of the respect that had been shown back in the day when he was Major Frank Slater, or even the Dr. Slater in charge of the St. Peter's Island operation. Now he was just some civilian taking up government resources.

But far from being irritated, Slater felt like a weight had been taken off his shoulders. His life was his own now—and he had made some definite plans for it.

The chopper headed straight for the sea and followed the coastline north. Slater leaned his head back and stared out the window. He was still weak from the ordeal and needed to put on a few more pounds, but he'd come to grips with what had happened and made a kind of peace with himself. Maybe he couldn't save the world anymore; maybe it was better just to save a little piece of it. He couldn't wait for the right time to tell Nika.

In the weak afternoon light, he could see on the horizon the familiar plateaus of Big and Little Diomede, and the icy blue channel between them that marked the meeting point of the United States and Russia. The sky was clear—a pale gray the color of a pigeon's wing—but as they neared the island, he could see that the wind, the never-ending wind, was busy as usual, stirring the fog around its rocky shores.

Hard to believe that such a short time had passed since he had first made this approach. It felt like ages.

As the helicopter came closer, he noted that there were two or three Coast Guard vessels lying offshore, and that the colony itself was far more extensively lighted, fenced, and occupied than when he had left it. To accommodate the chopper, there was even a circular helipad, marked with reflectors, slapped down between the old well in front of the church and the green tents that Slater's own crew had erected.

"Hang on," the pilot announced over the headphones, as the chopper, slowing down to make its landing, was buffeted by the gusts off the Bering Strait and the whole aircraft wobbled. Slater held on to the straps, and no sooner had the wheels touched down and the engines been cut, the rotors spinning to a stop, than he saw Professor Kozak and Sergeant Groves running to open the hatchway door.

"It is so good to see you," Kozak said, slapping him on the back, as Groves clasped his hand in a firm grip.

"A lot's changed around here," Groves added, shepherding them all out from under the chopper's blades.

"I could see that from the air," Slater replied. Indeed, as he looked around now, he could see that several walkways had been laid down, running between extra tents and aluminum Quonset huts. Aerials were poking up everywhere, and an additional battery of generators was humming away under a covered port. Several Coast Guardsmen were scurrying among the various structures.

"How're you feeling?" Groves asked, but before he could even answer, Kozak interjected, "You are well, yes? You must be, or they would not have let you go." The professor looked him up and down, and regardless of what he might have been thinking, said, "Yes, you appear very well."

Slater smiled; Kozak was such a bad liar. He knew that he still looked like he'd just been in a bar brawl. The bruises on his face had faded to a faint blue, but many of the cuts and abrasions had yet to heal completely, and unless he walked carefully, his fractured ribs gave him a jolt.

"And Nika?" Kozak asked. "How is she?"

"On her way back to Port Orlov," Slater replied.

"They are lucky that she is their mayor," Kozak said.

"You can say that again," Groves said, chuckling. "But she'll be governor before you know it. There's no stopping that one."

And then, as if all of their thoughts had pivoted in the same direction like a covey of birds, there was a moment of deep silence.

"Dr. Lantos was a very brave woman," the sergeant finally said, and Kozak, solemnly crossing himself, added, "And a very good scientist."

"None better," Slater agreed. Whatever else had been lifted from his shoulders, the death of Eva Lantos had not; it would always weigh heavy on his conscience.

Off in the direction of the cemetery, there was the rumble of heavy machinery—to Slater it sounded suspiciously like a cement mixer—but before he could ask about it, Rudy, the fresh-faced young ensign, hurried toward them.

"Welcome back, Dr. Slater," he said, saluting quite unnecessarily. "Colonel Waggoner, the acting commander, has ordered that you report to HQ immediately upon arrival."

Ordered. It was funny how little import the word carried for Slater now.

"Better make sure you straighten your tie and shine your shoes," Groves said dryly.

Slater knew that there was no love lost between what was left of his own team and the new regime.

"It's this way," Rudy said, starting in the direction of the largest Quonset hut, where the lab tent—altogether gone now—had once stood. How, Slater wondered, had they disposed of the deacon's remains? To do so safely, a host of critical precautions had to have been taken. But were they?

"Frank," Kozak said, snagging his sleeve, "we must talk. As soon as you have time."

Rudy stopped and called out, "Dr. Slater? I'm afraid it'll be my ass in a sling."

"It's very important," Kozak added, in a low but urgent tone.

Slater figured it probably had something to do with the geological studies he'd been completing, but what could be that pressing? The graveyard, he had been advised, had been cordoned off—for good this time—and the whole island made a secured site. But scientists, he also knew from experience, always assumed their own work to be critical. "First thing," he assured him, before turning to follow his impatient escort.

The headquarters was bustling with activity, and the far end was reserved for Colonel Waggoner's office. He had the square jaw, the square shoulders, and the square head that Slater had encountered all too often in his military career. He was standing up and on the SAT phone when Slater was shown in, and he motioned brusquely at a chair positioned across from his desk.

Shades of being sent to the principal's office, Slater mused.

When Slater had been made to sit there long enough for the point to have been made, Waggoner ended his call and said, in an admonitory tone, "Guess you've noticed that we made a few changes. We run this operation pretty differently now."

"You should have waited," Slater said. "There are safety protocols that need to be observed."

The colonel looked taken aback. "We have an AFIP officer on-site, handpicked by Dr. Levinson in Washington."

"Who?"

"Captain Stanley Jenkins, M.D."

"He's a good choice," Slater said, relieved. He'd never worked with him personally, but he'd read the man's reports from the field and knew he was an up-and-comer. "Do whatever Captain Jenkins tells you to do and you won't go wrong."

Waggoner looked even more put off. "Dr. Jenkins is here in an advisory capacity only, and he takes his orders from me. Maybe you've forgotten how the military branches of our government work since your court-martial, Dr. Slater."

It was a cheap shot, but Slater let it pass.

"As for your associates, Professor Kozak and Sergeant Groves, I have asked them to restrict their movements to the base. Kozak's been completing some ground studies inside the colony walls. I can't say what the hell they'll be good for, but they keep him away from the cemetery and out of my way. As for you, the debriefing will take place at 0900 hours tomorrow morning, so collect any notes or data you might have left lying around here and bring them. Also, make sure you gather up your remaining gear because as soon as we're done, you and your pals will be flown off the island. There will be no further access."

After ordering Slater, in addition, to restrict himself to the common areas within the perimeter of the stockade, he dismissed him with a flick of his wrist. Slater had the impression that the colonel had waited his whole life to sink his teeth into an operation of this importance—though how long the Coast Guard would maintain its sole jurisdiction here was an open question—and he could tell he would brook no interference.

Once outside, Slater blew out a deep breath and rubbed his aching ribs. The seat harness on the chopper had given them a workout. Looking around, he noticed that high-power spotlights had been mounted atop the stockade walls, and given that the sunlight was already fading, they had been switched on. The grounds were bathed in a harsh white light that threw stark shadows in every direction and lent the colony, with its old log cabins and storehouses, an oddly artificial appearance. The crooked church, with its decrepit onion dome, looked like the haunted house from an amusement park. Yellow tape had been stretched across its doors in a big X, along with loops of heavy chain.

But no one, he also noted, was watching him. Ensign Rudy was nowhere to be seen, and a couple of other Coast Guardsmen were busy wheeling a cart of cables from one tent to another. If he was going to make a run at the one place he was most eager to see—the old graveyard—he wasn't likely to get a better shot than this.

With the colonel's order not to leave the colony grounds still ringing in his ears, Slater sauntered toward the main gate, jauntily saluting the Coast Guardsman stationed there, before heading down the ramp that led to the cemetery. He didn't dare look back, but he had no sooner approached the woods than he saw that a wide swath of the trees had been felled and the ramp had been replaced by a gravel driveway fifteen feet wide. He could see the muddy tire treads, and the rumble of machinery got louder all the time.

By the time he got to the spot where the old gateposts had once stood—they, too, were gone—he had noticed the unmistakable smells of powerful disinfectant chemicals and hot tar. Hanging back, he saw the funnel of a cement truck pouring a thick, even coat of concrete over the remaining ground. All the tombstones and crosses had been removed, and half a dozen workers in full hazmat suits, hard hats, and hip waders—a novel combination—were smoothing the surface as it was laid down. The decontamination shack had been left standing, but huge, empty cylinders of malathion, an organophosphate widely used in places like Central America where DDT had lost its sting, were strewn around outside it. Slater didn't have to ask. Rather than running the risk of exposing any more of the bodies, the AFIP must have decided simply to poison the ground, to saturate it with concentrated, industrial-strength chemicals, then seal the graveyard for good measure under a foot of fresh concrete.

It wouldn't last, he thought. The warming climate would eventually shift the earth again, and crack the cement. But that was government for you. Do the temporary fix for now, then form some committees to debate the problem for several years to come.

A curious worker spotted him, and instead of ducking out of sight, Slater waved and shouted, "Good job! Keep it up!" The worker returned to spreading the concrete.

Then Slater turned around and followed the well-lighted drive back to the colony gates. Behind him he felt like an old and terrible giant had been put to bed beneath a new blanket. He prayed it would sleep there soundly forever.

Inside his tent, he found that his cot and personal effects had been left untouched. A vial of his Chloriquine pills was lying beside an empty coffee cup and a report he'd been annotating. Professor Kozak popped in, and perching awkwardly on a campstool, said, "You saw the cemetery?"

Slater nodded while stacking some loose papers. "Did they disinter any of the other bodies first?"

Kozak shook his head. "They took one look and sent in the bulldozers to level the place."

Slater nodded and started gathering up his notebooks.

"How did it go with Waggoner?" Kozak asked.

"Pretty much as expected," Slater replied, stuffing the notebooks into a backpack. "We've got till maybe noon tomorrow before we're exiled for good."

Kozak stroked his short silver beard thoughtfully. "Then there is no choice. It will have to be tonight. At midnight."

"What are you talking about?"

"We've got to get back in the church."

"Why go back?" Slater asked, mystified. "There's nothing inside the place but old broken pews and tables. What's the point?"

Kozak took his iPhone out of his pocket, swiped his finger across it a couple of times, then held it out. Slater saw a photo of an old headstone, with what looked like a pair of doors etched on either side of a Russian name.

"Okay," Slater said. "Nice carving. But what about it?"

"That is the tombstone of the man we dug up," Kozak said. "Stefan Novyk. The deacon."

Slater still didn't understand.

"The two doors are called the deacon's doors. They are the way through the iconostasis."

"You mean that wooden screen, right, the one with all the junk thrown together in front of it?"

"Yes. The altar is behind it."

"I'll take your word for it. But even if you think there's actually something of value back there, do I have to remind you that we're not the raiders of the lost ark?"

"No, we are not," Kozak agreed. "But we are scientists, yes?"

"Yes."

"And historians?"

That one was questionable, but Slater nodded in agreement anyway, just to get him to finish.

"For instance, wouldn't you like to know how the flu got to this place in the middle of nowhere?"

It was a question that had indeed puzzled Slater, but the Spanish flu had been ingenious that way. All it might have taken was a single lost kayaker from the mainland.

Kozak put the phone down, dug deep into the other pocket of his coat, and produced the sexton's ledger. He must have been keeping it under wraps, Slater thought, or the colonel would surely have confiscated it by now. Turning to the last pages, and with his stubby finger underscoring a final section, written in a florid, feminine hand, Kozak translated the words.

"Here it reads, 'Forgive me. I have become the curse of all who know me.'" Kozak looked up. "Do you remember the words carved into the gates of the graveyard, over and over?"

"They said, 'Forgive me,'" Slater replied, and the professor nodded with satisfaction before returning to the book.

"There is also a burial entry. For the deacon. The writer says that he saved her from the wolves and gave her shelter on the island, and this is how she has rewarded him."

"With what? The flu?"

Kozak simply went on. "This last burial entry was for someone named Sergei. He must have been lost at sea, but his body washed up onshore. She writes that she had to bury him herself, with a cross around his neck, because no one else was left to do it."

Slater was moved by this anonymous woman's terrible ordeal, but before Kozak could go on, he said, "This cross—does she say anything more about it?"

The professor scanned the faded ink again and said, "Yes, since you ask—she calls it the emerald cross."

Nika, Slater recalled, had retrieved just such a cross from the wreckage on the bridge. It was found in her pockets when she passed out at the hospital in Nome, and for all he knew, it had been hermetically sealed and sent to the AFIP labs by now along with every other single thing they had been carrying. The widow Vane would no doubt bring suit to get it back.

"By the time she's done with the journal," Kozak continued, "the writer is claiming that her soul is doomed to live on in this awful place forever."

"Who could blame her?" Slater said. "She must have been raving mad by then."

"Exactly," the professor replied, "No one could blame her, especially considering what else she had already endured. This was a girl—a young woman—who had seen Hell itself."

"You know who it is?" Slater said. "She's signed it?"

Kozak, nervously clearing his throat, turned to the last page. "Here, she is begging Heaven to release her from her earthly bonds. And then, below that, she wrote her name." He underlined the signature with his finger again.

Slater waited. "Well?"

"It reads," Kozak, said, stroking his silver beard and holding Slater's gaze, "'Anastasia, Grand Duchess of All the Russias.'"

Chapter 66

Sitting with Kozak and Groves in the mess tent that night, Slater felt like a mutineer. All around them, the Coast Guardsmen and techies who had been brought in to deal with the cleanup of the colony were chowing down, boisterously trading jokes and telling stories, piling their plates high and unwinding from another trying day, while Slater and his own team were huddled over an aluminum table in the corner, partly concealed by stacked crates, and speaking in low tones about things no one would ever believe.

"But I thought all those stories about Anastasia were bull," Groves said, mopping up the sloppy joe gravy with a crust of bread. "She died along with everybody else in her family."

"Not necessarily," Kozak replied. "There were always rumors that one of the sisters had survived."

"How?" Groves asked. "Unless I've got my history wrong, they were executed at close range."

"According to some accounts—and these were given by the assassins themselves—the bullets bounced off the girls' bodies. The killers became frightened, thinking that the young duchesses might be divine, after all. It was only later, when the bodies were stripped at the coal mines and the corsets were taken off them, that the jewels were found in the lining."

"So it was like they had body armor on," Groves said, a little less skeptically now.

"Yes. And there is also a story of a sympathetic guard who helped to smuggle Anastasia to safety."

"That's a lot of speculative leaps you just made," Slater said. Despite what had been written in the sexton's journal, he could not accept it all as readily as Kozak had. Maybe Kozak had misinterpreted something; maybe it was a hoax—or the entry of a woman who had gone justifiably mad. "For one thing, haven't all the bodies been recovered?"

"Not necessarily," the professor declared. "There are still questions. Eleven people were shot in that cellar, but the physical remains of only nine, maybe ten, were ever identified with some degree of certainty. Remember, the bodies had been mutilated, dismembered, burned, and saturated with acid; they had also been moved from one place to another to avoid detection. It was all a great jumble of broken bones and rotting teeth, scattered in several places."

"But what about DNA analysis?" Slater asked.

"By the time the burial sites were revisited in 2008, the decay had been substantial. Also, please remember that six women were killed there, and four of them were sisters, close in age. Even if a bone could be identified as that of a young woman, it was difficult to know whose it was. Was it Anastasia, or simply a piece of Maria or Olga or Tatiana?" Kozak leaned back in his chair, dabbing a napkin at his beard. "No, my friends, it has never been a settled question. It never will be," he said, "unless we settle it."

"And how is breaking into the church tonight going to help settle it?" Groves asked.

"Everything precious that the colony contained would have been kept in its sacristy, the altar room behind the iconostasis. There should be two doors that lead through it, one at either end. The deacon's own records are undoubtedly inside, listing all the members of his congregation. Is there some evidence of Anastasia there? Who knows what we might find?"

"But that's if we could get in," Groves said. "Have you noticed that they've roped the place off, padlocked the doors, and plugged the hole in the side wall? The colonel's even got a sentry doing laps around the place."

Kozak smiled and unfolded a topographical map between their plates. "The beauties of GPR," he said, pointing to a dip in two of the lines.

"What am I looking at?" Groves asked.

"To prepare a foundation for the church and to level the ground, the settlers set off dynamite. The same way they prepared the grave-yard. Then they sank the corner supports, and built the church with a small gap underneath it."

"A crawl space?" Slater said.

"Yes, and the tilting of the church has left it wider right here, under the northern side. It is probably big enough for us to get through. Then we pry a hole up through the floorboards; most of them are rot-ting, anyway."

"Is that a treasure map you've got there?" Slater heard a derisive voice booming from the entryway. Looking up, he saw Colonel Wag-goner and his retinue stomping the snow off their boots and unzip-ping their parkas. Slater's first impulse was to conceal the chart, but that would only call more attention to it. "Better use it fast," Wag-goner said. "Your flight leaves tomorrow, gentlemen, at noon sharp."

One of his lieutenants said something Slater couldn't make out, and Waggoner, laughing, replied, "What more harm could they do?"

Then he marched on toward the table reserved for the commander, with all but one of the others in tow. Slater didn't recognize him, but he wore a captain's uniform under his coat and, after nodding hello to Kozak and Groves, extended his hand.

"It's an honor to meet you, Dr. Slater."

"This is Captain Jenkins," Kozak said.

"AFIP," Jenkins added. "First thing I had to do on this job was read through all your files in D.C. If you don't mind my saying so, you've done some spectacular work."

"Tell that to your boss," Groves said, lifting his chin toward Waggoner's table.

"Jenkins!" the colonel hollered. "No consorting with the enemy!" He laughed, as if it were a joke, but no one was fooled.

"He makes a lot of noise, but don't worry," Jenkins confided. "So far, he's let me run my own show. We used the professor's ground-fracture maps to pump undiluted organophosphates to a depth of two meters."

"What about leeching?" Slater asked.

"Should be minimal, and we're laying concrete on top in the meantime."

"It's going to crack."

"You know that, and I know that, but the oversight committee in Washington wanted concrete, so I'm giving it to them."

Already, Slater could see that Captain Jenkins was better at the politics than he had ever been.

"In January, once the new budget is done," Jenkins continued, "I'll build in the cost of an impermeable seal. We'll lay it down in the spring."

Slater nodded in approval, relieved to see that the job was in such capable hands. What he'd heard about the captain was true.

Once Jenkins had gone to take his seat at the colonel's table, Kozak said, "At least they used my radar maps for something." Then, leaning forward, he said, "So? You heard the colonel. If we do not do it tonight, we will not have another chance."

Groves looked at Slater, appraisingly, while Kozak drummed his fingers on the map.

Colonel Waggoner laughed loudly at something, banging his fist on the table so hard that plates jumped.

"What can they do?" Slater said, pushing his chair back and glancing at his watch. "Court-martial me?"

Chapter 67

The colony was so bright, Anastasia could barely stand it. Even now, long after dark, long after all the day's activity had ceased, the intruders left their lights on—huge glaring lamps brighter than a thousand crystal chandeliers. What were they afraid of? What did they hope to see? Their green tents glowed from within, their engines hummed all night and day, and their airplanes—strangely shaped machines, equipped with propellers spinning on top like pinwheels—came and went, disgorging yet other machines, trucks and tractors, all of them designed, it seemed, to wreak havoc and destruction.

Already, the cemetery was gone. The posts, into which she had carved her plea for forgiveness so many years ago, had been pulled down. The tombstones had been wantonly swept away, the graves themselves paved over, but she knew, as she crossed the smooth hard surface, exactly whose souls lay beneath her boots at each step. Arkady, the blacksmith, was buried here. Ilya, the woodman, was buried there; his wife rested beside him. When she approached the cliffs, she knew that the remains of the Deacon Stefan had lain below. And just beyond it, at the outermost point, the grave of Sergei had once been located.

Now, the spot was just a jagged scar in the earth.

She stood there, looking out to sea, as she had done for time immemorial, wondering if she would ever be able to join the sleeping souls that she had once known. She had buried the emerald cross with her one true love, but its power over her had persisted. The chains that bound her to the earth still held tight, long beyond any mortal span. Although Rasputin had prophesied just such a curse upon her family if they should be responsible for his death, she alone had lived to endure it. Why oh why had the *starets* not foreseen that?

Or had he? That was what she pondered in her darkest moments of all.

There were boats out tonight, bobbing in the Bering Sea. Even they had their lights on, regularly sweeping their beams across the rocky cliffs and shoreline. The feeble glow from her lantern was swallowed in their occasional flood of light. At first, she had thought all these intrusions on the island might signal some end to her eternal purgatory there, but now she was no longer so hopeful. She did not know what, if anything, these events might portend. Perhaps they would prove just a passing phase, a random incursion into her solitude, ending again in her abandonment. It would not be a surprise to her.

Only death could come to her as a surprise now.

As she turned back toward her sanctuary, she could hear the soft footfall of the wolves who were her only companions. As the settlers had died, the wolves had proliferated—one, it appeared, for each dead soul. And over the many decades, their number, she had not failed to notice, had neither increased nor decreased. They could not speak, but in their eyes she could see a preternatural intelligence, a yearning to reach across the silent divide between humans and animals. She knew that they, too, were held captive here, isolated as she was, caught in the same spell. Their allegiance to the fallen *starets* was as unshakeable as their predatory instinct, and the prophet's power, like Circe's over her swine, lingered well beyond his own watery grave.

The leader of the pack, with a white blaze on his muzzle, trotted ahead, as if to assure her safe passage. It was a journey they had made thousands of times before.

Even the church, normally dark, was bathed, like everything else, in the glow of the colony lamps; its ancient and damaged cupola shone like a beacon as she approached. People in the old country had often joked that the tops of Russian Orthodox churches looked like onions, but Father Grigori had explained to her when she was a girl that it was meant to represent something holy.

"The dome is shaped like a candle flame," he had told her, pointing to the top of the imperial chapel at Tsarkoe Selo. "It is meant to light our way to Heaven."

If only she could believe that. If only, Anastasia thought, she could find such a pathway. Oh, how fast she would climb it, bad foot or no.

But as God had not seen fit to show her the way, and eternal damnation awaited those who attempted to thwart His will by their own hand, all she could do was submit herself and pray for deliverance.

For now, she took leave of the wolves and passed through the secret door that led to her private chamber. Bolting the passageway behind her, she settled her aching bones into this last tiny refuge. Resting the lantern beside her hand, she closed her eyes and willed herself back to other times and other places. Sometimes it was the royal retreat in the Crimea, sometimes it was the garden of the Alexander Palace. Always it was with her family. Like a woodland creature hibernating for the winter, she would enter into a suspended state, a dreamlike trance from which she hoped never to awaken.

And yet, fight it as hard as she might, she always did. The next night, or maybe the one after that, she always found herself awake again, walking the cliffs, lantern in hand and heart as heavy as a millstone.

Chapter 68

Poking his head out of his tent, Slater knew there was simply no way to cross the grounds to the church without being spotted. The colonel plainly believed in lots of lights, all the time.

Slipping his field pack onto his back—one thing he'd learned was to keep his basic supplies, from first-aid kit to syringes on him at all times—he checked his watch. It was just before midnight, and after waiting as a lone sentry stomped across the grounds and off toward the main gate, he sauntered out of the tent, walking briskly between the tents and bivouacs and around the old well. It was a clear night, but frigidly cold—when wasn't it?—and made worse by a biting wind. Even beneath all his thermal gear, he had to fight back a shiver.

He gave the church a wide berth, swinging wide and keeping to what cover he could, before doubling back to the northern wall. So far, there was no further sign of the night patrol.

Nor was there any sign of Sergeant Groves or Kozak, either . . . until he heard a low whistle and turned to see them both huddled in the breach of the stockade wall. The professor carried a shovel and Groves had liberated a pickaxe. Waving them over, Slater grabbed the professor by the shoulder and said, "So where's this crawl space?"

Kozak, moving faster than a man of his girth usually moved, scuttled to a spot a few yards away, got down on his knees, peered at the base of the church, pawed at the snowy ground, and whispered, "Under here—it should be right under here."

"It should be, or it is?" Slater said.

"It is! It is!"

Groves didn't need any more instruction than that. He muscled them both aside, and swung the pickaxe at the ground. Fortunately, the dull clang of the blade on the hard ground was muffled by the gusting wind. After several strokes, he paused to let Kozak shovel the loose soil and snow away.

"Yes, yes, it's here!" Kozak said. "A few more strikes!"

Groves wielded the pickaxe while Slater, crouching, kept watch. When he was done, Kozak quickly brushed the debris aside—slivers of timber and sawdust were mixed with the snow and ice—and ran his flashlight beam back and forth. "Frank!" he urged. "Come!"

Slater reached into his field pack and withdrew the scabbard that housed a nine-inch surgical knife; it wasn't often that he had had to use the knife, but once or twice emergency amputations had had to be performed. If its broad blade could saw through bone, he assumed it would do perfectly well with wood.

"Look!" Kozak said, and peering into the hole, Slater could see that the GPR had been right. A veritable tunnel had been dynamited through the earth and it lay there now like an open streambed. The church teetered over it precariously. Still, if the building had managed to remain standing for the past century, what were the chances it would choose tonight to collapse?

Clutching the scabbard between his teeth, Slater shimmied into the hole, flashlight in hand. The passage was wider than he might have expected—good news for Kozak, who was going to have to follow him—but the floor of the church was grazing his head the whole way. The ground was as hard as rock, and his ribs hurt like hell every time he had to pull himself a few feet forward. The air, what there was of it, smelled like the deepest, dankest cellar, and after going only ten or fifteen feet, the tilt of the church made any further progress impossible. Squirming onto his back and aiming the flashlight at the floorboards above his head, Slater found a gap between two of the planks and, removing the knife from its scabbard, wedged the blade into it. As he worked it back and forth, shavings trickled down onto his face, and he had to blow them away. Eventually, a hole opened—a hole big enough for him to put his fingers through. He pulled down, and after several tugs, the wood cracked. He was reminded of the splintering of the coffin lid in the graveyard. He pulled again, but it was hard to get the proper leverage. Taking a breath and turning his face sideways to protect his eyes, he let go of the flashlight and used both hands to pry the board loose. This time it came away, leaving a gap big enough for him to lift his head through like a periscope.

He was in the nave, a few yards in front of the iconostasis.

Ducking again, he squeezed his field pack through the hole and hacked at the neighboring plank until he was able to loosen it enough to push it aside. With considerable effort, he was able to haul himself up into the church, but only barely. Kozak would need more room, and so, before he signaled him to follow, he chopped at a third board until the hole was as wide as a manhole cover. Then, he sat back and took a deep breath, rubbing his rib cage.

From below, he heard Kozak's voice echoing along the tunnel. "Is it clear? Are you in?"

Slater bent to the hole and whistled through the sawdust on his lips. He could hear a muffled huffing and puffing as Kozak, big but strong, hauled himself along the frozen ground. He imagined this must be what a bear sounded like as it prepared its den for a winter's hibernation. When he saw his flashlight beam growing bright, Slater slipped his head down into the hole and saw Kozak's eyeglasses glinting in the darkness. Slater put his hand down, and Kozak grabbed it with his leather glove. Slater pulled, his ribs giving him a jolt, and the professor eventually emerged from the tunnel, scraped, sputtering, and covered with dirt and ice and bits of wood.

"Next time," he said, "a bigger hole, please."

Slater smiled.

But as Kozak, his legs still dangling underground, gazed around the church, illuminated only by the feeble glow of the flashlights and the moonlight filtering in through the cracks in the roof beams and the holes in the dome, he looked like a kid at a carnival. "It's all ours!" he whispered.

"Not for long," Slater replied. "Let's go find that sacristy."

Kozak got to his feet and lumbered across the sloping floor toward the jumble of wreckage concealing the iconostasis screen. "You look at that end, and I'll look at this," Kozak said, stepping close to the pile of broken furniture and twisted andirons.

"And what exactly am I looking for?"

"You are at the south end, so you will be looking for the entrance— a door with a picture of St. Michael, the Defender of the Faith."

"How will I know it's him?"

"He'll probably be carrying a sword. I'll be looking for the exit door, which should show the Archangel Gabriel, the Messenger of God."

"Which one do we want?"

"Whichever one happens to be open."

Slater pressed his face toward the screen, trying to peer through the debris. His flashlight picked up flecks of paint—in red and gold and blue on old whitewashed boards. Here and there, he could even see the outlines of angels and saints and, in one place, what looked like it might have been a painting of Noah's Ark.

"In grand cathedrals," Kozak said, while inspecting his own end, "these screens were ornately decorated and went all the way to the ceiling."

This one went nearly that high, and in its own day Slater imagined that it, too, had been beautiful in its own simple fashion.

"I have found Gabriel," Kozak exulted, "and he is blowing his horn."

"To welcome us in?"

"No, the door is nailed shut and boarded over. Very unusual."

Kozak came down toward Slater's end. "Maybe we will have better luck with St. Michael."

Pulling aside the broken refectory tables and cracked barrels, they scoured the wall with their flashlight beams until Slater could dimly make out the frame of a doorway—narrow and arched at the top, with the barest outline remaining of a golden-haired saint wielding a silver sword. On this door, there was a rusted chain, hanging loose, and no boards secured across it.

No words needed to be exchanged. With each of them taking hold of one end of an upended pew, they inched it away from the iconostasis. Then, Slater cleared away some other debris, like cutting tumbleweed away from a fence, until he could get to the door itself. If there had ever been a handle, it had long since fallen off and was probably rolling around in the darkness beneath their feet.

"Let me," Kozak said, elbowing past him and putting his shoulder against the wood. "If there's a curse, it should fall on me."

He pressed his burly shoulder against the door and Slater heard its antique hinges squeak, but hold.

"Russians do good work," Kozak muttered, putting his head down and pressing harder. After a few seconds, there was a popping sound, as first one hinge, then the other, gave way. The door, its bottom scraping the floor, creaked open.

Kozak stood to one side, and with a sweep of his arm gestured for Slater to enter first. "I do not care what they say in Washington," he declared. "You are still the head of this mission."

Slater appreciated the vote of confidence and slid through the open space, pushing the door wider as he went. Cobwebs clung to his head, and the air inside was as cold and still and stifling as a meat locker. He had the uneasy sense of intruding upon something sacred and long inviolate. He swept his flashlight beam around the room, but the rays seemed to be swallowed up by the inky blackness. Here, there were no holes in the roof or cracks in the timbered walls to let in the moonlight, and even the floor, when he turned the light on it, gave off the dull gleam of tar. This sacristy had been sealed like a tomb.

"I would give a great deal for a lamp right now," Kozak said.

So would Slater. The flashlight only gave him glimpses of what lay all around him—a wooden altar, covered with one red cloth and one white. A few ecclesiastical vessels—chalices and bowls and salvers. Everything thick with dust.

But a candelabra, too—with the nubs of candles still in it.

"Have you got some matches on you?" Slater asked, and Kozak, patting his pipe pocket, said, "Always."

Slater left his flashlight beam trained on the candelabra, and the professor struck one match after another, trying to find and light the wicks. Eventually, out of six or seven candles, he got four of them lighted, providing a flickering but more diffused light to penetrate the room.

The first thing he noticed was a door, no more than four feet tall, cut flush with the logs in the wall and secured by a crossbar. When he pointed it out to Kozak, he said, jokingly, "I wish we'd known about that in advance."

"Huh," Kozak said, running his fingers over his beard. "A bishop's door. You find such a thing in the great churches of places like Moscow—places where a bishop might actually wish to make a miraculous appearance. But I would never have expected to find one here." He rattled the crossbar in its grooves and it moved easily. "And they could hardly have expected a bishop to come to this church."

"What about a grand duchess?" Slater was beginning to believe what Kozak had translated from the sexton's ledger.

But Kozak shook his head. "I don't think even she knew she would end her days here."

"Who was it built for then?"

"If I had to make a guess," the professor said, "I would say it was her protector and confessor. The man these settlers came here to venerate. Rasputin."

Slater glanced again at the rough-hewn door, fitted so skillfully into the wall that it would hardly be noticed if it were not for the bar. They had missed its existence entirely from the outside.

Against the opposite wall, a mirrored cabinet stood open, with two cassocks hanging from its hooks. Kozak reverently stroked the sleeve of the white cassock, saying, "This one was used only for Pascha. Easter." The other was black, with a scarlet lining, and when he brushed it to one side, he reached into the back of the cabinet, felt the rim of a basin—no doubt the sacrarium used to wash the holy linens

after a service—and started to lift it out. There was the sound of pebbles sloshing around in a bowl.

"Frank." Kozak's voice was filled with awe. "Frank."

The professor moved to the altar, holding the bowl in front of him
as carefully as if it were the host itself. When he put it down, Slater
trained his own beam on it, and it was like he was looking at a kalei-
doscope.

The basin itself was made of white porcelain, with a gold rim, but
inside it, as if they were a heap of marbles, lay a dazzling mound of
gems—bright white diamonds, fiery rubies, sapphires as blue as the
crevices in a glacier, emeralds as green as a cat's eyes. There were
rings, too—of gold and silver—and bracelets and broaches—ivory
and onyx—and ropes of pearls, coiled and tangled, that had faded to a
pale yellow. Kozak dipped his hands in, as if he were tossing a salad,
and let the jewels sift back into the bowl between his fingers. They
clinked and clattered as they fell, the sound echoing around the sacristy.

"Talk about a king's ransom," Slater said.

"No," Kozak said. "A Tsar's ransom."

It was more than Slater had ever imagined finding. He had gone
along with the professor's scheme more out of curiosity than
conviction—not to mention the pleasure of defying Colonel Waggoner's orders—and now they had stumbled upon a long-lost and leg-
endary treasure. They had found what remained of the Romanov
jewels.

The candles guttered on the altar, and one threw a spark that
drifted, glowing, toward the back of the room. Slater followed it first
with his eyes, and then, as he thought he discerned something in the
shadows, with the beam of his flashlight.

Kozak was still absorbed in the gems, but Slater took a step or two
toward the rear of the chamber.

A chair—no, it was more like a throne—had been placed in the
darkest recess, atop a sort of dais. It had huge, clawed feet that pro-
truded from under a long, gossamer-thin canopy draped from the

roof. It was so grand that it made its own small enclosure. Had this, too, been designed in anticipation of Rasputin's arrival?

It was only as he got closer that he thought he saw the tip of a small boot poking out from under the cloth. It couldn't be. He took hold of the canopy and lifted it a few inches—enough to see that the boot was heavy and black, laced high and built with a thick heel, as if it had been molded to a deformed foot. Lifting the faded cloth higher, he saw the ragged hem of a long skirt—dark blue wool, homespun.

"Vassily," he said, "come here."

"Can't you see I am busy?" Kozak joked.

"I mean it."

Kozak ambled over, his broad back temporarily obscuring the candlelight, and upon seeing the canopied chair, said, "And that is called a Bishop's Throne. They must have been expecting Rasputin, after all."

Slater directed his gaze to the boot and skirt, and the professor immediately grew still. "My God," he breathed.

Slater drew the canopy to one side, gently, but even so it began to shred and tumble from its hooks, releasing a cloud of dust that made them both turn away, coughing and closing their eyes. When the dust had settled and Slater turned back again, what he saw stunned him. His first thought was of the mummies found in the high Andes.

The old woman in the chair was sitting as erect as a queen, her eyes closed, her long gray hair knotted into a single long plait that hung over one shoulder of her cloak. Under it, she was wearing several layers of clothing—he saw the collar of a worn blouse, a jacket made of some hide, even the bottom of a richly embroidered corset.

But it was her skin that was the most entrancing. Her face looked like an old, withered apple, lined with a thousand creases, and her hands, which lay on the armrests of the chair, were brown with age; her fingers looked as brittle as twigs. One hand cradled the base of an old-fashioned kerosene lantern.

"Do you think . . ." Slater said, but before he could finish, Kozak had said, "Yes. Even the boot confirms it. Anastasia's left foot was malformed."

For at least a minute, they both stood in respectful silence, wrapped in their own thoughts. Slater was already wondering how he would broach these discoveries to the colonel, who had strictly confined him to quarters. Waggoner could rant all he wanted, but confronted with the proof itself—a bowl full of gems and a frozen corpse—he would have no choice but to alert the higher authorities in the Coast Guard, the AFIP, and Lord knows how many other agencies.

"What do we do now?" the professor finally said, and Slater switched himself back into the scientific mode. If it weren't for the astounding, even unbelievable, nature of what they had just discovered, he asked himself, what would he have normally done? Under more logical circumstances, what would the next order of business be?

Evidence, and the systematic gathering of it. On any epidemiological mission, the first objective was to collect all the available data and evidence at the site, and that's what he needed to do here and now—even before notifying the colonel. Once Waggoner was apprised of the situation, Slater was not at all confident that he would be given any further access. In all likelihood, he would be put under guard and whisked off the island as fast as the first chopper could take him—and in handcuffs, if the colonel had his way. No, this, he recognized, might well be his only chance to do any science at all.

Slater took off his field kit and opened it, planning out the task ahead. Unlike all the others on the island, Anastasia plainly had not died of the flu—she was immune, as was he, after weathering the storm at the hospital in Nome. But he did not forget that it was she who had carried it here, nearly a century ago. As a result, it was critical that he still observe the necessary and standard precautions—especially in regard to the bystander Kozak.

Digging out a gauze face mask, he told the professor to put it on and to stand back by the altar.

"Why?" Kozak said. "What are you planning to do?"

Donning another mask himself, Slater said, "Provide your friends at the Trofimuk Institute with a little DNA evidence, if all goes well."

"Yes, thank you," Kozak said, slipping the elastic bands behind his ears. "I think they would rather have that than the royal jewels."

Slater lifted the lantern off the arm of the chair and placed it on the dais beside her boot. Puzzlingly, there was moisture there, and even the hem of her long skirt looked damp; he assumed he must have been dripping melted snow from his coat.

Then he surveyed the corpse, deciding on the best area from which to draw the sample. The hair could provide some DNA, especially if he made sure to capture the follicle, too—the shaft would provide only mitochondrial evidence—but it was terribly degraded and might not do the job. Her bony wrist, on the other hand, lay perfectly exposed, and if he could suction up some petrified skin and blood cells from a vein, he would get the richest and most viable sample possible.

Laying his own flashlight on the opposite arm of the chair, he reminded Kozak to remain at a distance, "But try holding up the candelabra. I need all the light I can get."

Kozak raised the candles, and in their flickering glow, Slater located the vein—a barely perceptible blue line under the mottled brown skin—and took an empty syringe out of his kit. To get a better angle, he turned the hand slightly—it moved more easily than he expected—drew back the plunger, and touched its tip to the skin.

Then he depressed the plunger.

And the hand flinched.

Slater recoiled, leaving the syringe stuck.

Even Kozak must have seen what had just happened. "Mother of God," he intoned.

Slater stepped back, first in astonishment, and then in horror.

The woman's eyes opened—they were a pale gray—and she looked at him as if she were still asleep—asleep and unwilling to wake up. She stirred in the chair, like a dreamer merely turning in bed, and her boot inched the lantern off the dais, where it shattered on the floor. Rivulets of kerosene ran in all directions, soaking the fallen canopy.

"Mother of God," Kozak said again, stumbling backwards, the candelabra shaking in his hand. A lighted candle, toppling from its perch, dropped to the floor.

There was a crackling sound, as the flame caught the kerosene and raced across the floor of the sacristy.

Slater could not believe his own eyes.

The old woman herself looked bewildered, but oddly unafraid. Nor did she move to avoid the erupting flame.

"We have to get out!" Kozak shouted, and Slater could hear him fumbling with the crossbar that secured the bishop's door.

The fire grazed the edge of the canopy, and the dry old fabric went up like a torch. The licking flames snagged the hem of the altar cloths and they, too, ignited, engulfing the sacrarium like a ring of sacred fire. The rubies glowed like coals, the diamonds blazed, the bowl itself blackened and cracked, spilling the gems all over the altar.

"Come on!" Kozak shouted, as Slater heard the crossbar thump onto the floor. The tar was heating up, melting.

But he couldn't leave the old woman—whoever she was—to die here.

"Now!" the professor shouted, throwing open the bishop's door. A gust of icy wind roared into the room, as if it had been eagerly awaiting its chance, and before Slater could make a move, the whole sacristy was suddenly aswirl with fire and ash, smoke and snow. The old woman never budged from the dais, and Slater could swear that she even opened her arms to the maelstrom, as if she were welcoming a long-lost lover. He even thought that he heard her calling out a name— "Sergei!"—again and again.

The kerosene around her feet sent tendrils of flame shooting up her body. As her hair exploded in a crackling corona of fire, Slater felt Kozak's heavy hand on his collar, dragging him out of the church.

Outside, Kozak rolled him onto the ground; he hadn't even noticed that his pants were smoldering and his boots were sticky with hot tar. Groves appeared and patted him down with handfuls of snow, all the while pushing and pulling them both away from the mounting inferno.

"What's going on?" a guard shouted, running toward the billowing smoke. It was Rudy, with a rifle that he quickly turned away when he saw who it was. "What the hell are you doing here?"

Rudy looked into the sacristy, just as Slater did, but it was like looking into the belly of a blast furnace. The flames were white-hot now, hissing and spitting, and they had soared up into the onion dome, its holes and cracks making it glow like the candle flame it was meant to represent. The whole church began to collapse in on itself with a thunderous clatter and crash, throwing sparks and streamers of fire into the night. Carried on the wind, they landed on the wooden cover of the old well, the roof beams of the neighboring cabins, the old blacksmith stall.

Coast Guardsmen and men from the work crews were tumbling out of their Quonset huts, pulling on parkas and boots and gloves, shouting and running helter-skelter across the grounds of the colony.

First one structure caught fire, then another, until it was as if the whole stockade was forming a ring of orange flame. Slater and Kozak and Groves scrambled down the hill toward the main gates, colliding with Colonel Waggoner, his coat open, his boots unclasped, his hair wild. He took them all in for a second, but it was enough for Slater to know that he'd figured out who was responsible. Slater's pants were scorched black and flapping around his legs.

"We've got a hose going, Colonel!" a Coast Guardsman hollered to him, but Waggoner looked around at the looming wall of flame and waved the man toward the gates.

"Just get out! Get out now!" He stumbled up the hill a few yards, but the smoke was getting thicker by the minute. "Evacuate!" he shouted to anyone who could still hear him. "Evacuate the colony!"

With the sergeant plowing a path for them, Slater and Kozak joined the others jostling toward the main gates, and by the time they reached the safety of the cliffs and turned around, breathless, to see, the colony was nothing but an immense bonfire, teased by the treacherous winds off the Bering Sea and filling the sky with a cloud of smoke and cinders. Slater could feel the ash settling on his bare head and shoulders.

The church had long since fallen off its foundation, and there was nothing left of it to be seen. Somewhere under the towering pile of burning debris lay the Romanov jewels—and their last rightful owner . . . the Grand Duchess Anastasia. Of that, Slater was now sure, though no one else but Professor Kozak would ever know, or ever believe, it.

Nor would he ever tell anyone—not even Nika. It was better if the ground was considered barren and sere, better if the last of the Romanovs was allowed to rest in peace, free from ghouls and treasure-hunters like Harley and Charlie Vane. She had waited a very long time for this, and whatever spell had kept her here on this lonely island, long beyond any ordinary human span, Slater hoped that it, too, had been extinguished at last.

Let the bulldozers and the organophosphates, the concrete and the impermeable seal, come, and let the colony be buried forever. Let Anastasia's grave remain unmarked, undisturbed, unknown.

But not unmourned. From all over the island, the wind carried the baleful howl of the black wolves . . . a keening that lasted all through the night.

The fire burned until the next morning, and it was only then—though it was still dark out—that the colonel pulled together an exploratory crew to venture back into the smoky grounds and assess the situation.

When Slater volunteered to lead the team, Waggoner glared at him, and spitting his words out like bullets, said, "I should never have let you back on the island."

And for once, Slater thought he had a point.

Chapter 69

The helicopter didn't even cut its engines. It simply touched its runners to the ice of the hockey rink, and as soon as the hatch was opened, Slater, Kozak, and Sergeant Groves were virtually ejected from the cabin, along with their backpacks and gear. The professor's GPR was rolled out of the cargo bay, and a moment later, the propellers, which had never stopped turning, lifted the craft back into the night sky. Slater watched as it headed back toward the devastation on St. Peter's Island, his heart filled with a sense of deep regret—nothing in his life had ever gone so terribly wrong—mingled with an undeniable relief.

It wasn't his problem anymore.

The debriefing he had been scheduled to undergo that morning had been canceled due to the conflagration, and Colonel Waggoner had asked him only one question.

"Was the fire deliberate, or accidental, Dr. Slater?"

"Accidental," Slater replied. What use was there in denying it?

The colonel, whose hands were full as it was, told him he could keep his notes and records, and file a full report from Port Orlov, "or anywhere else you go. Personally, I don't ever want to lay eyes on you again, and trust me on this, they feel the same way at the AFIP offices in Washington."

Indeed, he'd been right about that. Frank had made one last call to Dr. Levinson, who'd listened coldly as he gave her an edited account of what had happened at the site—omitting any mention of the gems or, God forbid, their owner—and when he'd stopped to take a breath, she had informed him that Rebekah Vane had also succumbed to the Spanish flu, while being treated at the biohazard facility in Juneau.

"I thought she had been stabilized," he mumbled.

"So did I," Dr. Levinson said. "We were both wrong."

He could hear the disappointment, and even dismissal, in her voice.

"Have there been any other breaches," he asked, dreading the answer, "or casualties?"

"Not so far. We think we got there in time and established a suitable quarantine zone." There was a pause on the line. "Needless to say, your report will be classified top secret. You, and the remaining members of your team, are under a strict information embargo."

"Understood."

"Is it, Dr. Slater? Because nothing else on this mission seems to have been."

He took the shot. He deserved it.

"I'll look for your report in one week. And oh," she said, icily, before abruptly hanging up, "don't expect any references."

If it hadn't been so painful, he might have laughed. But given what his plans were now, he doubted that he would need any.

"So what do you say?" Groves asked him. "Should we drop off our stuff at the community center and head into town for some grub?"

Slater nodded and the three of them trooped wearily off the ice.

Inside the center, they found Geordie holding down the fort all by himself.

"Yeah, I figured that chopper might be bringing you guys back," he said. "But if you're looking for the mayor, she's already at the celebration."

"What celebration?" Kozak asked.

Even Slater had forgotten that it was scheduled for tonight.

"The rededication of the totem pole," Geordie said, as if it were world news. "You remember how it was crooked? Some people in town, and some of the stores, have gotten together to have it fixed up again."

"How come you're not there then?" Groves asked, and Geordie glanced at the clock on the wall. "City hall officially remains open until six P.M. I've got almost a half hour to go."

The men shared a chuckle, and Slater said, "I admire your work ethic, but if everybody's at the party, who's gonna call?"

Geordie mulled it over for a second or two, then grabbing his coat from a chair, said, "Come on—you don't want to miss this!"

On the way, they passed the Arctic Circle Gun Shoppe, and stopping for a moment to look down the alley, Slater could see Harley Vane's old trailer. No lavender light was shining through the blinds anymore, and a FOR RENT sign was hanging forlornly from the door handle. What a lot of trouble had come up in his nets that night, Slater thought, and what a lot of lives, including Harley's own, had been lost as a result.

Front Street was lighted up from stem to stern, and the Yardarm was doing a land-office business. Although the totem pole itself was shrouded in a canvas sail prior to its unveiling, it did appear to be standing erect.

"I wish they had let me do a ground study first," Kozak muttered, as Groves peeled off toward the busy bar. "If it is not done properly, it will tilt again."

A flatbed truck was parked between the pole and the harbor docks, and two huge speakers in its bed were blaring the Black-Eyed Peas. Maybe a hundred people were milling around, rubbing their hands together over blazing trash cans, guzzling beer from ice-cold cans or hot cider from steaming mugs, laughing and shouting at each other over the music. A few were dancing to try to keep warm.

Lifting the earmuff on one side of Geordie's hat, Slater leaned close and said, "Where's Nika?" and Geordie turned around, pointing at the harbormaster's shack.

Behind one of its lighted windows, he could see her now, head down, reading something. He approached the shack and stopped just outside. The walls were plastered with charts and flyers, fishing nets and rods hung from the rafters.

Nika was jotting down notes in the margin of a wrinkled sheet of paper and did not see him at the window. For a moment, he simply savored the chance to observe her unnoticed. The last time he had seen her she was being wheeled out to the ambulance for the ride back to Port Orlov, and though she was not as wan as she had been, she still appeared paler than usual. Her black hair had been plaited into two pigtails, and perhaps in honor of the occasion, she had adorned them with tightly tied ribbons and colorful beads. She looked, he thought, as natural, and as naturally beautiful, as one of her ancestors.

And then she looked up, as if sensing he was there. Squinting into the darkness, she raised a hand, and Slater went around to the door.

By the time he got it open, she was already in his arms. He kicked it closed, and they simply stood there, cradling each other in their arms, wordlessly. And if Slater had still had any doubts at all, if he had any lingering reservations about the decision he had already made but not yet shared, they melted away in the heat of their embrace.

Before he could find the right words, Nika, with her face still pressed against his chest, said, "I was working on what to say."

"About the totem pole?"

"I can't forget to mention any of the donors who helped to raise the money or do the work."

It was as if their hearts were so full of more important things, they could only address a more immediate and inconsequential topic.

"I'm sure you'll do fine," he said.

"Public speaking is not my favorite activity."

"You'll be a smash."

He hugged her more tightly in encouragement, then they separated enough that he could look down into the dark pools of her eyes. It was a sight he knew he would never tire of.

"I've been doing some thinking," he said, his voice faltering; already, he regretted that he hadn't come up with some better opening.

"About?"

"About what I'm going to do now that I'm no longer working for the AFIP. I was thinking that—"

There was a banging on the door and a snowball hit the window as a bunch of teenage boys, horsing around outside, hollered, "Get a room, Mayor!" and "So when do we get to see the totem pole?"

Nika, laughing in embarrassment, pulled away. Glancing at her watch, she shouted, "It's not time yet. It's officially scheduled for six P.M."

"Looked like it was the right time to me!" one of them hooted outside the window, as the others, dispersing into the night, guffawed.

Slater tried to regroup, but Nika had returned to the table where she had left her speech and was looking it over one last time. Making one final addition—Growdon's Lumberyard and Mill—she folded the paper into the pocket of her coat. "Oh, I almost forgot I had this on me," she said, pulling out an opaque plastic baggie labeled Nome Regional Health Center. "The orderly gave it to me on the way out."

Slater took the bag and unzipped it.

"I found it on the bridge, and they gave it back to me along with my other personal belongings."

Slater could hardly believe what he was seeing. A Russian Orthodox cross, made of silver, and studded with emeralds.

"It must have been Charlie's, or maybe it belonged to his wife."

Slater knew better.

"But now Charlie's dead," Nika said. "And Harley, too."

Slater knew that a memorial service for the Vane boys was scheduled for the following Sunday, but he wondered just how many mourners would turn up.

"I guess we should just give it to his wife," she concluded.

"Rebekah didn't make it, either," Slater said. "She died from the flu, at the treatment center in Juneau."

Nika hadn't known that, and the news rocked her for a moment. "What's to become of Bathsheba?"

"Last I heard, she was heading back to the cult in New England. Apparently, the lost lamb is still prized there."

Nika nodded, looking relieved. But then, studying the cross again, she said, "So what do we do with this then? It looks awfully valuable."

It was a terrible breach of medical protocols, Slater thought, for the cross to have been returned at all—under normal circumstances, he would have raised hell over it—but in this one instance, it was a godsend. The worst mistake he could make at this point would be to make its existence known, or to release it to anyone else, ever again. Turning it over, he saw that there was an inscription on the back, in Russian of course, and even as he wondered what it said, he slipped the cross into the pocket of his own parka and said, "I'll take care of it."

"Come on, Mayor—we're freezing our asses off out here!" one of the teenagers shouted from the pier.

Nika said, "Maybe we should get this over with."

Slater opened the door, and they walked toward the commotion around the totem pole, which was still veiled in its tattered sail.

Calling out to a couple of the partiers, she asked them to swing their trucks and cars around, and aim their headlights at the pole. Then she climbed up into the back of the flatbed, disconnected the speakers from the long, trailing power cords, and plugged in a microphone instead. The music abruptly stopped, and the crowd grew quiet as the vehicles pointed their lights at the pole. The only sounds were the crackling of the fires in the trash cans and the rustle of the wind, the never-ending wind, blowing off the sea. The night was clear.

Standing in the bed of the truck, mike in hand, Nika welcomed them all, first in English, then in the Inuit's native tongue. There was a lot of happy nodding in the crowd, especially among the older people, at the sound of their own, almost forgotten language being spoken. It wasn't hard for Slater to see how this vibrant young woman could also have become their tribal elder.

"Before I get to the reason we're all here tonight, I want to take this opportunity to answer a few of the important questions that have been coming into the community center all day," she said.

"Yeah, what burned last night?" a kid in a down parka called out. "I heard it was St. Peter's? I can still smell the smoke."

"Yes, there was a fire in the old colony. But I have been informed," she said, nodding toward Slater, who was standing close to the truck, "that it has been entirely contained, and the Coast Guard will be overseeing the island from now on."

"That's still our land," an older Inuit man complained. "It's ours, by treaty."

"They can have it," another one answered him. "The damn place has been cursed for a hundred years."

Nika held up a hand, and said, "It's still ours. But for the time being, it's off-limits."

Slater knew that it would stay that way—strictly off-limits—forever.

"And what was the deal with that quarantine?" a white guy in a Green Bay Packers hat asked. "That's bullshit, the government telling me where I can, and can't, go. I couldn't get to my ice-fishing shack."

There was a lot of muttering and nodding heads, and Slater heard two or three people saying something about conspiracies.

"That was an emergency measure," she said, and here she spoke carefully, following the script that she and Slater had rehearsed in Nome. "I can tell you now that there was the remote chance of a communicable disease reaching Port Orlov, and to be on the safe side we had to cordon off the immediate area. There is no threat now, however. None whatsoever."

"And what really happened to the Vanes?" the Packers fan asked. "Charlie Vane still owes me a hundred bucks for a snowblower."

"As I reported in the community newsletter," Nika patiently explained, "Charlie and Harley Vane died in a car crash on the Heron River Bridge. We're planning to hold a memorial service next Sunday."

"That won't get me my hundred bucks back."

Nika, wisely, let that one pass, and just when Slater thought the whole event was going to devolve into a Tea Party rally, she asked everyone to gather around the foot of the totem pole for the unveiling.

"For too long now," she said, "we have all been living with a disgrace in the center of our town. And as your mayor, I take a lot of the blame for that. This totem pole was built, by some of our Native American ancestors, two hundred years ago, and it was bequeathed to their descendants. It's more than just some stately souvenir. It represents the Inuit people—their history, their legends, their spirits. It was meant to remind us of our heritage, and at the same time to watch over us in the present day."

She allowed her words to sink in before continuing.

"But we have not watched over it. We've allowed the paint to fade. We've let the wood crack. We've let it almost fall over."

The Inuit in the throng looked distinctly uncomfortable at this reminder of their own neglect, and even the nonnatives looked vaguely embarrassed, too.

"It's the symbol of Alaska, and as such it should always stand tall. The way that all Alaskans, whatever their background, and wherever they came from, do."

This was one sentiment that could be counted on to meet with general approval, which it did.

"And that's why we have come together tonight, all the people of Port Orlov, to set things straight—in every way." Referring to the paper in her hand, she read off the list of donors and citizens and businesses that had contributed money, time, and labor to fixing the totem pole. The hardware store had contributed the paint and cement, the Growdon Lumberyard had worked to restore the wood, a local contractor had supervised the construction of the new base. Many others had chipped in five or ten dollars to the cost. And the Yardarm had provided free drinks for the celebration. "But only one beer per customer," Nika warned everyone, with a smile.

There was a smattering of applause when she was done with the list, and as Nika nodded at her nephew Geordie, he stepped forward and took hold of the rope that held the covering in place.

"And so, with no further ado and before we all freeze to death, let's take a look at what we can do when we all pull together. Geordie, let 'er rip."

Geordie gave a sharp tug on the rope, but, anticlimactically, there seemed to be a snag. Changing position and wrapping the rope around his wrist, he tugged again, and this time the old sail neatly unfurled from the top of the pole, rustling and pooling around the base. The freshly painted faces of the otters and bears, foxes and wolves, gleamed in the light of the arc lamps; their teeth were now white and shining, their fur a rich brown or inky black, their eyes a deep, metallic blue.

At first there was an appreciative silence from the crowd, then the Packers fan tossed his hat in the air, and hollered out the state motto, "North to the Future!" Everyone laughed and started to applaud, and even Slater felt himself caught up in the general exultation.

Kozak sidled up to him, his free beer in hand, and said, "I will still do a ground study before I leave. No charge."

Slater nodded in thanks.

"But it is quite beautiful now," the professor acknowledged.

Sergeant Groves, standing a few yards off, gave it two thumbs-up.

Nika put the mike away, ducked down behind the speakers, and plugged in the CD player.

But it wasn't the Black-Eyed Peas she was playing anymore.

Now it was a native song, a rhythmic chant, accompanied by a low, steady drumbeat. A respectful silence fell over the town square, and some of the older Inuit people instinctively lowered their heads. With eyes closed and arms held akimbo, they began to gently sway and stomp their boots in the snow. The area around the base of the totem pole cleared away, as the elders, and a few of the younger Native Americans, too, started to dance in a slow circle around it. The old women moved like hawks soaring on the wind, arms spread wide, while the men lumbered like bears on the ice. Everyone else made way, watching this ancient ritual unfold in the shadow of the pole, feeling the power, the majesty, and the unspoken sadness, of the dance. It was a nearly forgotten vestige of a world long gone, a world that had started to slip away on the very day the first Russian explorers sailed into these waters in the eighteenth century.

Nika, too, was absorbed in the music and the dance, her shoulders undulating as she stood between the speakers, her eyes closed in mystic communion. It was this ineffable connection that had brought her back to Port Orlov, and it was this same connection that would make it impossible for her to leave. She had come back to rescue her people, to save their culture from extinction, and Frank, watching her now, knew that she would never give that up . . . even for him.

Just as he knew it would be wrong of him ever to ask it.

The spell cast by the music was interrupted by a crackling burst of static, and the lights in the storefronts suddenly dimmed, then shut down altogether. The speakers on the flatbed sputtered and fizzled, and the streetlamps along Front Street blinked out one by one.

Slater could guess what was happening.

The dancers, like everyone else, stopped and looked up at the omen revealing itself in the sky. The tribal elders hummed and chanted in place, their upturned faces growing wet with tears.

A gigantic ribbon of green light, smooth and shiny as satin, was slowly unspooling . . . then rippling wider, like a curtain spreading itself open across a blackened stage. It was only the second time Slater had seen the aurora borealis, but he could not have conceived of a more portentous time for it.

Nika, looking delighted, jumped down from the bed of the truck and grabbed his hand.

"Don't tell me you planned this," he said, and she laughed.

"I wish I could take credit," she replied, "but I'm only the mayor, not God."

Most of the crowd stayed right where they were, but some drifted off toward the shoreline to watch the lights over the water.

Nika, like a kid at a carnival, dragged Frank toward the harbormaster's shack, then out onto the pier. At the very end, they stood alone with the sky shimmering above them. Slater wrapped his arms around her, and she leaned back into his embrace. Together, they gazed up at the spectacle unfolding in the night, the green now joined by a flickering orange flame that spiraled like a staircase up into the heavens. Even the air seemed to crackle with the electrical energy.

"The spirits are rising," Nika said, her dark eyes shining in the orange glow.

Across the black waters, Slater could swear that he heard the wolves on St. Peter's Island baying at the sky.

"They're going home."

And he believed it. The lights were like a celestial staircase, and he could envision the old woman—Anastasia, Grand Duchess of All the Russias—climbing the steps at long last.

He could see other things, too. He could see himself remaining in this place, with Nika forever at his side, and running the medical clinic that the town so desperately needed. For too long, he had tried to save the world. Now he would concentrate on saving just this tiny, much-overlooked part of it.

When the lights went out, snuffed like a candle, and Nika turned her head in the darkness, he bent down and kissed her. All the words he'd meant to say evaporated, all his questions were answered. There was no need to speak at all.

And even the wolves, he noted, had gone silent. Apart from the cry of a hawk, soaring overhead but impossible to discern in the night sky, there was nothing but the empty and incessant howling of the wind.

Still holding his hand, Nika started back down the pier, but Slater stopped a few seconds later and said, "I just have one thing to do."

Nika, though curious, stayed where she was as he reached into his pocket for the emerald cross and returned to the end of the dock.

The hawk, still crying, swooped past the dock, some wriggling prey clutched in its talons.

Nika saw him raise his arm, and heard a distant splash, and when he came back to her, she didn't ask him what he'd done. She didn't have to.

The lights in town flickered back on, and arm in arm, they walked toward home together . . . as the hawk settled into its perch atop the Yardarm. There, it went about devouring its hard-won meal—a tiny white mouse, with an orange stain on its back and tail.

Afterword

As some readers may have noticed, certain authorial liberties have been taken with the Alaskan backdrop of this story. For instance, you won't find on any map St. Peter's Island, the town of Port Orlov, or a road leading directly from the northwest coast into the city of Nome. Consider the road my gift to the citizens of Alaska.

And while I'm here, I would like to take a moment to thank my indefatigable editor, Anne Groell, and my faithful agent, Cynthia Manson, for all their help with this book. As any author knows, writing a novel is a long journey, and it's nice to have such wonderful company along the way.

ABOUT THE AUTHOR

ROBERT MASELLO is the author of many previous works of fiction and nonfiction, most recently the novels *Blood and Ice* and *The Medusa Amulet*. A native of Evanston, Illinois, he studied writing under the novelists Robert Stone and Geoffrey Wolff at Princeton, and has since taught and lectured at many leading universities. For six years, he was the visiting lecturer in literature at Claremont McKenna College. He now lives and works in Santa Monica, California.

ABOUT THE TYPE

This book was set in Monotype Dante, a typeface designed by Giovanni Mardersteig (1892–1977). Conceived as a private type for the Officina Bodoni in Verona, Italy, Dante was originally cut only for hand composition by Charles Malin, the famous Parisian punch cutter, between 1946 and 1952. Its first use was in an edition of Boccaccio's *Trattatello in laude di Dante* that appeared in 1954. The Monotype Corporation's version of Dante followed in 1957. Though modeled on the Aldine type used for Pietro Cardinal Bembo's treatise *De Aetna* in 1495, Dante is a thoroughly modern interpretation of that venerable face.